ANN ROYAL NICHOLAS

Muff Stuff By Ann Royal Nicholas

This book is a work of fiction. Names, characters, places and events are products of the author's imagination; historical names and information, should either appear, are used fictitiously. Any resemblance to actual persons, living or dead, locations or events, is strictly coincidental.

Published by Bournos 2019
Los Angeles, CA

Printed in the United States of America

Cover Design by Fred Baxter
Interior format by coversbykaren.com
Edited by Elizabeth Nunes

ISBN No. 978-0-9907080-3-2
www.Bournos.com; BournosMedia@gmail.com

BOURNOS

Muff Stuff is dedicated to the safety of muffs everywhere.

PROLOGUE

OF ALL the ways I might imagine my unfaithful husband meeting his end, it's hard to know which would be most satisfying. Could he just, in a word, *die*? Perhaps succumbing to a simple yet sudden brain hemorrhage, brought on by tortured, too-tardy angst over his extramarital sexcapades . . . On second thought, hemorrhaging involves blood, often shooting through orifices it shouldn't be shot through. The visuals of that scenario—and I *am* a visual person—would forever be etched upon my retinas. Or would it be cerebellum? It's something in the cranium, but I have no idea what part of the brain images get etched on. That's for neurosurgeons and novelists to decide.

"Gwruff, gwruff . . . Gwrrrrruff!"

Barking. That French Bulldog, Flan. Specifically, *our* French Bulldog, Flan. At times like these, when feeling wounded by my philandering spouse, Nate, I refer to Flan as Nate's mother's dog. But he was ours now, adopted when he'd proved unsuitable for her Wilshire Boulevard high-rise because of his need to take walks. Imagine that; a dog that needs to stop sitting on the sofa looking adorable and be taken on walks. Well, there's the problem right there. If you fail to walk your dog outside, he or she will eventually do what nature demands inside your apartment.

Nate's mother, Sophia, bought a lot of stuff, usually online and usually on a whim. She then quickly found what she bought unsuitable and cast it off—mostly to us—with the words, "It was a mistake." In the case of the mail-order dog, she was quite clear: The Aubusson rugs took priority.

Some of what Sophia cast off was useful but most of her purchases, like the set of fake Vuitton luggage, which she insisted was real, were ridiculous. Especially ridiculous was the idea of giving the stuff to us. The luggage was not only ostentatious and ugly, we never went anywhere. My only hope was selling the whole set to someone on Craigslist so I could pay the mortgage; that is, if things between Nate and me didn't get better. Selling it now would only get me into trouble at a time when there might still be some hope of saving the marriage.

When it came to the French Bulldog, whom she'd named "Elton John," Sophia had tired of him after three months. The constant carpet cleaning was exhausting, she said, as if she'd been the one cleaning up after Elton John's messes. So she gave the dog to her grandson, "Natey," a.k.a Nathaniel or Nate Jr., so as not to confuse him with his father. Unlike the luggage, we all loved the adorable fawn-colored beast and willingly accepted him when offered. But the name had to change. All Natey knew of Elton John was the cover of the "Goodbye Yellow Brick Road" CD, and he wasn't impressed. So Elton became Flan, named for Natey's favorite dessert. Whichever name he went by, the dog was insanely cute, especially while sleeping, when his many quirks, barking foremost among them, subsided. His quirk of farting was, however, unaffected once the snoring started. Still, we'd grown to love the little beasty in spite of his issues.

"Flan!" I yelled uselessly as the barking continued.

Off went the kitchen faucet with a forceful turn of the wrist as I finished rinsing the last of the morning dishes and baking utensils required for my most recent attempt at revolutionizing the Santa Monica baked goods market. No amount of mindlessly running water was going to kill Nathaniel Pizzo,

I thought, my mind drifting again. *Unless* . . . No, it would be unwise in drought-stricken California to go over our water allotment, which is what it would take if Nate were to have some sort of accident and drown in our son's kiddie pool. He really was too old for that pool—my husband, not our seven-year-old. Though it was the elder Nate who most enjoyed splashing around in it.

If such an accident were to occur, I'd be the one who had to pay the fine for the overage, post-drowning, which, given what I knew about water-use transgressions, would equal half our mortgage payment—not that we'd made one in the last two months. And foreclosure was inevitable if something didn't change soon.

"Flan, that's enough!"

The barking stopped and seconds later the fawn phantasm bolted past me into the living room where he would no doubt leap onto the couch, muddy paws and all, to resume yapping at some perfectly well-mannered Labradoodle committing the unpardonable sin of being walked in front of our Santa Monica house. The house that we'd loved and had bought out of love when all was bright and promising.

I followed Flan into the living room, a rag and cleaning solution at the ready, and sure enough, he was on the back of the couch, barking at not a Labradoodle, but a Pit Bull—"not the kind of dog you want to mess around with," I said before collapsing next to him.

Money; that was the root of our problems, I thought. Money—or lack of it; along with the resultant feelings of inadequacy. Lack of money was why Nate had the affair—all right, three affairs—in the first place, or so he'd revealed in couples' therapy. And this behavior was prompted, if our therapist is to be believed, by Nate knowing he was about to lose his job. Not that Nate had shared any of this with me before the infidelities started racking up and he announced we should have an open marriage.

It was subject matter we'd gone over and over, never reaching a different outcome. What's the definition of an idiot again?

I suddenly knew how Nate would die. He's walking along, and boom—an errant motorist, driving while texting, jumps the curb and careens into him right in front of Fromin's Deli, killing him instantly. Or something even more dramatic—an asteroid strike. Nate might even choose that particular cause of death: A small bit of outer-spaced carbon-based material—not that this, in and of itself, would be all that revolutionary as everything's carbon-based—comes hurtling toward earth and is broken up mid-hurtle by a projectile launched by the SETI Institute, and then one of the smaller pieces—about the size of a fossilized dog turd—continues on its new trajectory, toward California, Santa Monica, Montana Avenue and then into Nate's skull, smashing his entire frontal, posterior and bilateral cortices while he slurps on a Havana Cappuccino at his favorite table outside Peet's Coffee. He might even be viewed a hero for "taking the turd," after which, Nate Jr.'s first-grade bullies would be impressed enough to include him in all their little reindeer games and Nate Sr. would be famous. Someone might even install a plaque:

> Peet's Coffee wishes to commemorate the table where Nathaniel Pizzo—unfaithful husband and failed architect—regularly consumed enhanced coffee beverages and was struck down by Asteroid Astrid.

No one needs to know it was my fault, that it was me who wished the space debris upon him for repeatedly breaking my heart and turning me into a woman I didn't recognize and never would have become but for his infidelities.

By now you're probably wondering who I am and what, more specifically, my husband did to make me think about his death. I will provide the answers, but first I need you to know that I, Sarah Pizzo nee Myers, am not usually the type of person who considers another person's early demise, least of all a person I married for love and happily ever after. But lately, I've felt that at times like I'm going a little crazy. The next thing you need to know is that I have the correct version of events—about Nate and so many other things that have heretofore been reported, some incorrectly, by two members of *The Muffia*, a group of women you may be familiar with, and whom I count among my friends and will defend with teeth and claws if necessary. But I will also say right off: They are unreliable narrators a lot of the time. They don't lie, exactly, but many of the muffs have been known to—exaggerate? Stretch the truth? Leave things out? Withhold information? Maybe all these things. They don't do it maliciously but—okay I'm guilty of doing all that myself on occasion—I just believe that I will carry on the story of *The Muffia* with more veracity and compassion (when I'm not considering ways to do away with my husband) than either of the two previous narrators, the last of which was my friend and fellow muff, Quinn Cunningham, who works in show business. Enough said.

To repeat: my name is Sarah. And as you've no doubt pieced together, I am a mother, dog owner, and the unhappy wife of a man named Nate Pizzo. But I had a life before any of this. I also represent one ninth of the aforementioned Los Angeles–based women's book club known as *The Muffia*. If you were to read our mission statement, that is if we had a mission statement, you'd find out we get together every couple of months to talk about a book. In reality, books feature very little, what with Mossad agents and bodies in freezers and Eastern European con-women. It's insane, of course, but to hear some of the muffs tell it, you'd think we were involved in international espionage!

Please don't confuse us with the other muffia, a group of online lesbian pornographers because, as far as I know, Jelicka's the only muff who's had a brush with pornography. And "brush" is probably overstating it. She had one exploratory meeting in her quest to become an over-40 porn star before nixing the idea when she realized she'd need thousands of dollars of body contouring to make her feel comfortable being coital on camera.

As for the muffs being lesbians, Rachel, who refers to herself as bi-polyamorous, is the only one who's explored an intimate relationship with a woman and told us about it, though she provided few details. I wondered if being with a woman was easier than being with a man but decided the answer to that question was, not much. So any idea of switching preferences for the sake of making life easier would be a waste of time. And the reality is, I enjoy the smell of a man and a real penis, so I'm shit-outa-luck.

The LA *Muffia* consists of Madelyn, Jelicka, Quinn, Kiki, Lauren, Paige, Rachel, Vicki and me. If this is your first muff adventure, there's a handy reference about us in the back, listing our attributes and idiosyncrasies, likes and dislikes; even the books we've read. But because I don't much enjoy flipping around in books in attempt to keep things straight, here's the abridged version: The muffs have been friends for a very long time, some of us since our late teens. We came together as a group after 9-11, when we all felt vulnerable and in need of our friends, so we started a book club. Books were a good a reason as any to get together, and here we are, still going strong. And that's because *The Muffia* isn't just about the books. Which is good, since I'm not much of a reader, though as someone who worked in the design field for many years, I always appreciate a set of leather-bound volumes, neatly placed on a fine-crafted, built-in bookshelf. Then again, no one reads those books.

Don't misunderstand, I like to read, it's just finding the time. I often wish I could get the stories without having to read them and have even borrowed a few audio books from the library. But hearing actors read, while CDs skipped and scuttled, didn't do it for me, either. These days, I'm rarely in a fixed location alone long enough to listen, including my car. Gone are the days making long-distance, surprise store visits for my job with Williams Sonoma, mired in the LA traffic that would guarantee knocking off several chapters in one day. Perhaps when I'm older, I thought. Then I'll have time to spend leisurely afternoons in a hammock, margarita within reach, and while away the hours engaging with an assortment of classic novels, contemporary romances, memoirs, and cookbooks. But until Nate Jr. was in college and I figured out a way to make a living on my own again, pleasure reading would remain a dream.

If you've been following *The Muffia*, you'll know each of us gets the chance to tell part of our story; that is, each of us narrates a book. Madclyn and Quinn got the first two. And though they may not have been entirely reliable, I acknowledge that they and others might not be totally on board with *my* version of events.

This brings up an interesting point—can any of us ever be completely reliable? We see what happens through our own pair of colored lenses, each of us focusing on what's most important to us. When a group of friends meets someone new, for example, I expect each of these friends to describe this new person differently. One might focus on her hair, others her dress, others what she has to say or how she says it. It's amazing we humans agree on anything, really, given how our brains work.

But in my telling, I'll try to be objective. The idea here is to provide you, the reader, with multiple perspectives on people, places, and things so you can decide for yourself.

One subject that most of the muffs will disagree with me on is sex. Because the first two books were narrated by two unmarried women who apparently don't get enough sex and think about it constantly, you may have the idea that every muff spends her days preparing for her next erotic encounter. Well, let me disavow you of that idea.

Sex is fine. Sex is even fun. But sex is overrated. And if someone asked me whether I'd rather give up sex or baked goods, at this moment in my life, I'd choose sex. Married muffs know that regular congress with a husband is often perfunctory. It's certainly less dramatic than the brand of sex Madelyn and Quinn are having, or claim they're having. And if the sex is truly as dramatic as they say, why all the fuss about vibrators? Aren't they busy enough with the real thing? They both have jobs and obligations, never mind finding time to clean their houses. Seriously—we have had entire book club gatherings where we talk about the newest and best in self-stimulation, while giving very short-shrift to the book that brought us together.

All right, maybe I should give Quinn a bye because before she met and fell in love with Frank "Seal Team Six" Sexton and started bowing out of events to have "sex with Sexton," I don't remember her talking about it as much as Madelyn or Jelicka. And why would she? She was having weekly intercourse with a married man at the Peninsula Hotel and was understandably ashamed. She didn't *want* to talk about it, particularly when I was around, given all the infidelity I was experiencing. In fact, once she confided in us about her affair, I remember her telling us, more than once, that it was over when it wasn't. So how *could* she talk about it after that? Now that Frank is her one and only, and has been for months, I suspect Quinn will eventually stop bragging about their bedroom antics like any normal person in a long-term relationship.

As for Maddie, she wasn't really *bragging* about Udi, her super-hot Israeli lover, so I cut her some slack. She's a mediator, and bragging isn't her style. It was the muffs' fault, drawing the details out of her in search of vicarious thrills. Maddie was just obliging—and, I admit, I asked my share of questions. Udi sounded incredible, actually; lifting her, turning her, making her come twenty times in the course of an hour. So yeah, she can talk about that, I guess. Before Udi showed up, she hadn't had sex in years, so it's possible that anybody would seem great. But twenty orgasms in an hour? And then he went and died on her. Literally ON her. There they were in that glassed-in sunroom in Madelyn's Agoura Hills McMansion, making love on the couch, and *bammo*—coronary. She said she felt it happen. Sort of like some men might collapse after they come. But this time, Udi came, collapsed, and didn't get up. Fortunately, Maddie got out from under him before her daughter came home.

That's all I remember, really because when this was going on, Nate and I were going through a particularly bad period. I wasn't focusing on Madelyn and Udi. But at some point, Jelicka came to believe that Udi hadn't really died. Her proof—? Some scary guys came to retrieve his body. I'll agree, it's odd that scary guys knew where Udi's body was, but apparently he was microchipped—okay, that's also a little odd—and when he didn't move for a couple of hours, they came to investigate. Then Quinn, who even saw Udi dead not long after the coronary, swears she saw him after that walking around an airport in China, or maybe it was India. Doesn't matter—she was in a foreign country checking on one of her famous actor clients who was shooting a commercial. Now both Jelicka and Quinn say Udi is alive and his fake death is part of an international spy plot.

Some people just have too much time on their hands, that's what I think. Or they're watching too many "can't-miss-TV" crime dramas. Jelicka, who's a conspiracy freak anyway, is convinced she knew right away he wasn't dead, how she's absolutely positive he's not dead because she went to Israel for two weeks for her birthright and has inside information on what Israeli spies are like. I mean, I went to Israel, and I don't think this way. The two of them are out of control. You'd think they'd want to help Madelyn get over the guy, but they just keep resurrecting him. Fortunately, I haven't heard much on the topic for a couple of months, not since before Lauren's Alzheimer's benefit where both were well-behaved. Madelyn even had a date, so maybe they've finally decided to let it go.

Now that it's my turn to pick up *The Muffia* story, I confess you're not seeing me at my best. I am at a crisis point and have to make some decisions. One decision I have already made is to become a better person, and that starts with coming clean about what I *am* and am *not*. So here goes: I'm forty years old with one child, one gassy yapper of a dog, and a house about to go into foreclosure. Earlier in my life—how much earlier, I don't remember—people considered me attractive, even very attractive, but getting to that state involved a fairly extensive hair, makeup and workout routine, which these days I don't have a lot of time or energy for. Decision number two: I will get back to a self-care regimen I can stick with! I also have the aforementioned husband, Nate, who was getting unfaithfully laid before he got laid off, which was probably the inciting incident that led to our failed open marriage, which we're now trying to mend through therapy we can't afford.

So there's a lot to deal with, and staying completely, one-hundred-percent positive may not be possible. There are just too many things to worry about. Oh, God, I'll probably lose my house and get divorced. You see? There I go again! Please, Universe, don't make me end up a pissed-off, resentment-filled woman with pucker lines around her mouth. Whoops, too late, they're already there.

And in the interest of coming completely clean, I've strayed some myself, as being in an open marriage suggests. The idea of being free to have sex with whomever either of us wanted to might have sounded appealing, but in practice, it didn't work. Unlike Nate, however, with his multiple trysts, I only strayed from the marriage once. Some muffs—Paige and Lauren for starters—said I'd strayed too far, ending up pregnant and not knowing who the father was, which I agree would have been terrible. The thing is, it's not true. Though I did get pregnant, I knew Nate was the father. I was just so mad at him and the situation he'd put me in that I let the muffs believe the baby was the result of a bout of passion with a guy named Clive.

Why let them believe this? Pride, I suppose. I was either a victim or a willing participant in the open marriage, and admitting I was the victim was too embarrassing. Then when I lost the baby it was devastating and hurt in every conceivable way. Would I have been able to hold on to him or her if our lives weren't such a colossal mess? She probably took a peek at the life she'd be entering and ended things. When all this was happening, I was confiding in an old friend who lives in Chicago, a non-muff who I thought would judge me less. That was several months ago, and I still hadn't told the muffs the truth. But I intended to; it just hadn't happened yet.

Another thing that's clear is that despite everything that's happened and hasn't happened, Nate and I loved each other once, so I hope we can avoid the traps sparring couples get into. No matter what we decide, whether together or apart, we have our sensitive, cerebral son to consider. So we have to find a way to let go of the bitterness and resentment, because the damage done by holding onto those things is obvious—Rachel for example—you can see how rage-filled she is, her protestations to the contrary notwithstanding.

Rachel hasn't narrated a story for *The Muffia* yet, and I dread when she does. I love her for her wit, her bravery, her standing up to "the Man"—but no matter how many Kabbalah bracelets she wears around her wrists, she's still an angry white woman; angry at men and the world. Lucky for her she's a stunner and people put up with her. And lucky for her she's been able to take that anger, harness it, and create a thriving business painting large canvasses featuring men missing vital pieces of their anatomy. The ones with the genitalia missing sold immediately, suggesting she's not alone, there's a large number of angry female art collectors out there, too. Maybe holding on to anger isn't always bad if you find a tribe of people angry about the same things?

At any rate, I'm telling the *Muffia* story now. It's my story. When it's the next muff's turn, she'll tell it differently. What's that old saw? There's your story, my story, and the truth? Well, that's crap. There's your story, my story, his story, her story, and everyone else's story. Truth is something no one knows, like the horizon that never quite arrives. Because on top of all the differing perspectives, there's the fact that we, the tellers of stories, are also changing and shifting as time marches on. Our stories change, too.

The timer went off, and I pulled a batch of muffins from the oven. I was calling them Resist Muffins, which made a kind of sense, as I am undergoing my own personal resistance to the status quo. I wanted a revolution, to become someone better, someone different, someone stronger than the Sarah Pizzo I've been. Baking has always been something I've shown a talent for, so it seemed like a good way to do something positive. My hopes of revolutionizing the baked goods industry was still just a dream. Articulating it was scary. So thus far, I hadn't told anyone except Natey. My Resist Muffins, if successful, would be revolutionary because of the secret ingredients, but also because they contained very little flour and lots and lots of blueberries and raspberries, making them patriotic to boot. But as I considered my most recent effort, I had to admit defeat. The muffins were flat. On the other hand, maybe they weren't muffins; maybe they were scones. Resist scones?

Flan's barks had turned to whimpers and I rejoined him at the window. Stroking his warm, soft body immediately soothed me.

Flan, however, would not be soothed.

He whimpered some more, and I followed his gaze, just in time to see a woman wrapped in a shawl, running after a white van that was screeching around the corner. On the sidewalk, the woman's shawl fell, and she seemed to slump, defeated.

"What's that about?" I said aloud. Flan glanced at me before letting out a final whine. Everyone has troubles, I told him.

CHAPTER 1

THAT SATURDAY, the storms rolled in, bringing with them the rain Southern California desperately needed. They also brought a few things I could have done without.

The rains from the first storm were waning when the second hit: Nate arriving to fetch Nate Jr. for a friend's birthday party. He came in and made a beeline for the kitchen. So much for respecting that he didn't live there anymore.

"Hey, bud, time to go," Nate called up the stairs while he circled my latest baking endeavor cooling on the counter. "These muffiny-sconey things smell really good. Can I have one?" He handed me $200.

"You don't have to pay for it."

"It's for the mortgage," he said, taking a bite.

"The mortgage is two *thousand* dollars, not two hundred."

"I'll get more, don't worry about it." Now he was chewing. "These are pretty good. What are they?"

"Scuffins? Munes? Mones? Part muffin, part scone. Mostly they're butternut squash."

I was taking a break from the patriotic Resist Muffins.

Nate stopped mid-bite and examined it more closely. "Huh." Then he popped the rest in his mouth.

I wanted to believe him—about the mortgage—but my years of knowing him had taught me his well-intentioned promises contained little in the way of follow-through. And now that he'd been laid off, where was he going to get the money? So I'd had to take action without him.

"I sold the vintage coin collection," I said. "No choice."

"Why'd you sell the coins? You could have sold these things," he whined, eyeing the collection of oddly shaped baked goods.

"I'm working on it, but these 'things' aren't ready for market, and it seemed more important to keep the roof over our heads."

Just then Natey called from the top of the stairs.

"Mama?"

"Yes, sweetie?" I said moving to where I could see his worried face.

"Is Cowin Bwagpoo going to Sarah Jane's Maze Pwace Party?"

Nate shot me a piercing glare. "Who's Cowin Bwagpoo?"

"I don't think so," I called up the stairs before facing Nate. "Blackpool," I whispered. "He still has trouble with his "Ls."

"We need to fix that," said Nate, a little too loudly. For someone who'd had his own learning issues, Nate could be incredibly cruel and rude. He started in on another scone, a big chunk of which hit the floor where it lay ignored.

"Don't harp on him, okay? It's getting better."

I reached down to pick up the dropped piece of scone just a second too late. Flan, the canine vacuum, had already Hoovered it.

"Flan, no!" I said, at which point Natey bounded into the kitchen laughing and crumpled to the floor to cuddle his dog.

"He's going to get fat."

"Who cares?" said Nate, holding his arms out. "Hey buddy."

Natey got to his feet to hug his dad but he was looking at me.

"Are you sure Cowin won't be there?"

"Pretty sure," I told him. "Sarah Jane doesn't like Colin, so I don't think she'd invite him."

"I don't want him there," said Natey. "He's a buoy."

"*Bull*-y," said Nate, hitting the double Ls with the force of a pool player busting a rack.

Natey made his most obstinate face. "That's what I said!"

"Ready? Let's go." Nate was halfway to the front door. "We'll work on your Ls on the way to the Maze Place."

"Have fun," I said, glaring at Nate before dropping to my knees in front of Natey. "Don't worry about Colin. He's not going to be there, okay?"

"Okay . . ."

"Let's go," yelled Nate, now out the door and moving toward the car.

I stood and gave Natey a kiss on top of his head, smelling baby shampoo and dog, then watched them drive away.

The next storm hit when I logged on to the computer and was deluged with email from *The Muffia.* There were at least twenty emails already in the thread. This happened whenever our next book club meeting was imminent. No matter how many Google calendars or doodles we set up, hoping to keep organized, people liked disorganized email threads. But responding took time, and no sooner had I responded to one muff, when another muff's email came in responding to something five emails ago. It was a storm, all right—hurricane, tornado, sleet, snow, and rain all at once.

"What's the book again?" wrote Lauren. "I know I should know, but let's just say it's the 21st century's distracted mom's excuse of 'the dog ate my homework,' so somebody tell me!"

"When are we meeting?" wrote a typically over-scheduled Rachel, with whom I'd had more contact since her worst suspicions about Nate had been borne out. In her mind, we were sympatico because we'd both been married to assholes.

From: rachelbakerart@mac.com_
To: The Muffia
Subject: Muff Stuff
Hoping to be there but am going to Chicago then London to meet with a gallerist. It might take longer than expected. Poor me, a London overstay. xo
R

Rachel's art circle was certainly expanding. It appeared the angry women of England want to buy paintings of men without genitals too!

Still scrolling, I saw that Kiki's email was next, and, as host for the next *Muffia* book club, the one that had generated the thread:

From: kookykiki@gmail.com
To: The Muffia
Subject: Muff Stuff
It's book club time again, that special evening when all good muffs gather to discuss a book and kvetch, this time in the sweltering Valley. For those who haven't been paying attention, you should have read ***Where'd You Go, Bernadette?*** I loved the book, particularly how Bernadette called the parents at her daughter's school "gnats." We have gnatty parents at Troy's school too and can you believe he still gets crap for being biracial. If only I had Bernadette's balls. Lauren's out of town but I hope the rest of you can make it. Fly back from London pronto, Rachel. I'll be serving something in the spirit of the Pike Place market. Just bring yourselves and lots of cool drinks. x K

Kiki always serves fish. She'd been pescatarian for years and recently went gluten-free. She'd also given up dairy and something else I couldn't remember.

Ding—

> From: rachelbakerart@mac.com
> To: The Muffia
> Subject: Muff Stuff
> Will bring vegan side dish, that is if I can come. xx
> Rachel

Great, another dietary restriction. I'd forgotten Rachel went vegan.

It was getting to the point where the only thing we could safely serve at book club was wine. This suited most of us, but people had to eat, and with all the exclusions, there was some pretty uninspired eating going on. Fortunately Kiki was host this round, and as the pickiest eater in the group, had the most experience cooking imaginatively with her limited selection of edibles.

The computer dinged again. "What was the name of the female lubricant some of you were recommending?" This question came, uncharacteristically, from Paige, our resident tennis pro and founder, who wasn't one to participate in conversations about vibrators and lubricants. And here she was starting one. Of course this question led to yet another multiple email thread as everyone weighed in on their favorite lubes—those to avoid, those that carried known carcinogens—which was then followed up with gossip about a disgraced former muff's vaginal rejuvenation surgery, which hadn't been as rejuvenating as hoped. No one had seen pictures of said vagina, but everyone had an opinion about it; from Jelicka saying the former muff had "asked for it," to Lauren's "Why not give that money to charity?" I just thought the whole thing sounded painful.

Opening emails on any given morning feels like being downriver in too small a boat that threatens to capsize from the tiniest ripple. *The Muffia* electronic onslaught, though amusing and generally pleasurable, only increased the likelihood of sinking. Ordinarily I'd pour a glass of wine before facing a muff email thread, but given the early hour, I poured a second coffee and considered what pithiness I might contribute. Meanwhile, the onslaught continued:

> From: cunningquinn@Talentpool.com
> To: The Muffia
> Subject: Muff Stuff
> Hi Ladies. All good at work these days. And Frank just gets more and more amazing. I still can't believe I'm with a Law Man! No gnats in my life since the exodus of Titania. Loved book but also read too long ago to remember. Bringing Prosecco and gluten free dessert. Love you Man, Q

Earlier in the year, Quinn was getting sabotaged at work, which could have ended in disaster. It didn't, fortunately. And if it hadn't been for the attempted sabotage, she wouldn't have found her amazing boyfriend. Frank solved the case after Lauren, a.k.a Deep Pockets Muff, had her husband's company loan out the ex-Seal Team member to help Quinn figure out who was trying to take her down. Turns out the saboteur was none other than the wife of Quinn's married ex-lover. Then the whole thing got really nuts when Quinn's co-worker, Titania—whom Quinn originally suspected of being the villain—was revealed not to be the lesbian in love with Quinn's female boss that she pretended to be, but a two-timing bisexual! Quinn even got props and a raise from her boss for exposing the lying opportunist. So, if good things come from bad, I could use some of that.

Ding went the computer and this time, I lowered the volume. I needed no auditory notifications while in the middle of the storm.

> From: vonhooter@gmail.com
> To: The Muffia
> Subject: Muff Stuff
> PS I heard Reese Witherspoon is playing Bernadette in the movie version. That makes three muff books getting turned into Reese movies. She's probably reading them first, otherwise I'd say she should pay us. It's an easy read and you have one more week!
> xP

Ah yes, this was the Paige I knew—Nazi Muff—toned down now, but she used to blow a gasket when someone didn't finish that month's book selection. She'd all but given up on me. Let's be honest, they all call me "Slacker Muff." To my face. They think it's cute and view it as a term of endearment at this point. "Pulling a Sarah" is synonymous with failing to read the book. Once, when I actually finished a book, and Rachel, in a surprise twist, hadn't, Paige dubbed Rachel "the new Sarah."

Being known as the one who doesn't read isn't something I'm proud of, but I have, or *had*, an excuse. I told the muffs I was mildly dyslexic. It's true—I *am* mildly dyslexic. But what I didn't tell them is that I've learned to deal with the dyslexia very well, to the point where I can read, and only about ten percent slower than they do.

Like the father of my miscarried baby, I let them believe something that begged for clarification. In my defense, I tried to bring the topic up a couple of times, but the muffs thought I was being defensive. I remember Jelicka and Vicki taking me aside at different points giving me some version of "It's okay to be dyslexic."

So now I just let them think what they want. It's easier. And no matter what I say about reading or not reading the book, they give me a pass. I suppose the upside is I never read any bad books, not that the muffs read bad books. But I read no books at all, other than the picture books Natey loves so much. Our favorite is *The Only Boy in Ballet Class* and I've read it to him so many times, I know it by heart. "There they were—the boys who play football. And they were doing . . . pliés!" If only. I think football players doing pliés should be mandatory. We should see them do pliés before every NFL game. It might civilize the rough beasts in the audience to see the gentle side of the players.

The downside to my "Slacker Muff" status is I worried about the muffs kicking me out. And with good reason. That's what happened to a short-lived muff known as Kat who was a member before my time. But the way Madelyn tells it, Kat not only didn't read the books, she tried to use book club to "network," which in our group is a very dirty word. Networking is what strivers and ambitious people do at a cocktail party, not what we do in *The Muffia*. But I still worry, and that is why I tend to go overboard with what I bring to eat and what I serve when I'm host. And why I get a little annoyed with the damned food limitations—it limits what I can cook. For this book club date, however, I was ready and planned to make a few of the vegan, gluten-free baked goods I was creating, including the brand new, renamed Muffragette Muffin. So I finally joined the thread, aiming for a quick in and out.

From: Sapizz11@connect.net
To: The Muffia
Subject: Muff Stuff
Can't wait to see everyone. I'll bring something delish and healthy for dessert that you cannot get anywhere else. ~ S xx

> From: MissJelickaG@aol.com
> To: The Muffia
> Subject: Muff Stuff
> Sounds yum, Sarah. Should I work out first so I can eat more? Almost done with the book and, IMO, Bernadette should not have been allowed to have a child. Is Reese W typecasting? Yes, I'm judgmental but will reserve total judgment until end. Bringing salad. X Jel
> PS I'll be a little red b/c of laser lift treatment. Don't want to scare anyone. ☺

Jelicka is the muff who briefly considered a career in elder porn. She's the muff with the smoothest skin, plumpest lips, smoothest bod, and the wherewithal to keep it up. Genetically speaking, she started with a pretty nice package, and the things she's had done have been subtle. And the fact that she hasn't given birth means she hasn't suffered the body stressors of childbearing and nursing, which might make a woman seek plastic surgery. But yeah, she's a fan of plastic and dermatological enhancement technology, just not to the extent she needed to feel good about being naked doing elder porn. Nothing could make me feel good about being naked doing elder porn, though given my financial situation, if somebody offered me hundreds of thousands of dollars, I'd have to consider it.

It's interesting that Jelicka will often pout and tell us her preoccupation with her appearance is all because she doesn't have children to worry about, that she'd take our leaky bladders, stretch marks and saggy skin any day in return for the unconditional love of a child. Paige will usually call her out when she gets like this and tell her to stop whining. Paige starts pouting herself and says, "There's no guarantee of unconditional love." Then we will sigh, even Jelicka, because everyone knows Paige has teenagers who pretend not to know her when they're out in public.

Having answered the call, I got off the thread and closed the computer, sipping the last of my now-cold coffee. Nate shouldn't be upset about the coins. They were mine, inherited from my Grandpa Jack. They weren't Nate's to be possessive of. Had they been gold, I would have tried to sell something else first. I mean, I'm not stupid. I realize gold is a valuable, fixed resource. But we needed the money, and as far as Grandpa Jack's coin collection goes, I researched the values and was able to pocket a tidy $3K, which would cover a month's mortgage, pay off our credit cards, and put food on the table.

How dare he judge when he was contributing nothing. $200 here and there wasn't going to prevent foreclosure. Worse, he had no ideas about getting another job, even temporarily, until "the architecture world realizes how bad it needs" him. Yeah, like that's going to happen. Didn't people adjust to the changing landscape when their chosen career path doesn't work out? Not Nate.

He'd even dropped hints about going away. Away-away: to Tahiti, South America, Antarctica, somewhere where life made fewer demands on him. I took all this to mean I was on my own.

In retrospect, I should have kept my job at Williams Sonoma. I had been happily toiling away for the kitchen and furniture empire in the middle of middle management, under the supervision of my mostly decent boss, Tobias, when Nate and I met. After starting as an in-store chef, I'd worked my way up the corporate ladder into a good gig, with loads of upside that allowed me to travel and didn't require me to be based in pricey San Francisco. I'd given up all of it when Nate Jr. was born. Nate Sr. didn't say I couldn't keep working, but he made it clear he preferred that I stop.

The thing is, before Natey was born, I'd always planned on going back to work when he reached some reasonable age—whatever that was—even if just part time. Having had a career, I couldn't envision myself being only a mom, not that there's anything wrong with that. But as most new moms will tell you, something happens when the baby arrives. Suddenly, you can't imagine being anywhere but with him, and there's no one you'd entrust him to while you go back to work.

All that was, wow, over six years ago. Since then, the job market had changed dramatically, as had required job skills. I might not even be employable anymore. How long was it, I wondered, before what a person did more than half a decade ago became irrelevant?

This was my project for the afternoon: To find out what the job market was demanding and determine if any of my skills were still marketable.

Though I continued to visualize myself as a successful baker, I needed a "right now" kind of job. The strategy of reaching single mom financial security would require a multi-pronged approach. So, the first order of business was to go online and find out who was hiring.

I opened the computer again, logged out of email to avoid the distraction of more muff messages, then logged into the job search engines—Zip Recruiter and LinkedIn, for starters—to find out what types of employees employers were searching for.

After a couple of hours, I was forced to acknowledge that if I was going to be an appealing candidate, I'd have to lie. And even if I were to get someone to hire me, the soonest I'd see a paycheck might be a couple of months from now. I leaned back, considering the options for next month's mortgage.

That's when the last storm of the day hit, with the rain long gone: Where was Flan? He'd uttered nary a whimper in hours, which was so rare as to say it had never happened.

"Flan!" I called. "Flan, come!"

Nothing.

I stood. "Flan—cookie!"

Again—no sound. Usually, when I said "cookie" he came at me so fast I had to jump out of the way or risk a bruised shin.

"Flan, c*ookie*!" I said louder.

My brain focused on the words *Flan Cookie* for a millisecond. Did such a delicious possibility exist?

There was no time then to consider whether flan cookies might be the tentpole of my baked goods empire; I had to find our dog.

CHAPTER 2

BEFORE DASHING out the front door, I took a quick glance in the mirror. Good thing too, I had egg on my face. I often had figurative egg on my face, but this time it was real; the gooey, yellowy-orange kind, and this quarter-inch clump was positioned at one corner of my mouth. How long had it been there? The fact that it was there at all was strange, since I hadn't eaten egg since yesterday. Had Nate noticed and not said anything? Sheesh, I really was losing it. How long had it been since I'd looked in the mirror?

I threw on a jacket over my sweats and Keep Portland Weird T-shirt, and, with the sun breaking through the clouds, went in search of Flan.

People say animals can teach us something about ourselves, that they can make us better members of society. So what was Flan trying to teach me? That I needed to leave him alone because he is an independent spirit? Well that only went so far, or I could be accused of animal abuse. That I needed to be more vigilant? Or was I supposed to learn patience and not worry about him? After what I'd been going through with Nate, I should know patience. If Flan was teaching me anything, it was that I had no business owning a dog—particularly when my life was in such disarray. It would have been better if Sophia had given us a cat who would just cuddle and purr, comforting me through my multiple crises.

"Did you see a dog?" I said, approaching a young woman a half-block away.

She glanced up, seemed to determine I wasn't a threat and then began swiping at her phone. She appeared to be lost, muttering to herself as her gaze drifted between her phone and the houses and apartment buildings on Sixteenth Street.

I suddenly felt hot, really hot. Of course, I'd been running down the sidewalk, which will make a person hot. But Santa Monica isn't supposed to be this hot. I guess the "heat dome" is descending faster than scientists predicted.

"There's a dog," said the young woman, as I slowed in front of her. She pointed to a Shepherd of some sort, trotting along a fence. "Border Collie. Nice breed, but they need a lot of exercise."

"I'm looking for a snarky little French Bulldog. He escaped."

"Maybe it goes with the territory?"

What was she talking about?

She smiled. "French?"

"Ah," I said, puzzled. "So French people escape?"

I'd never understood why so many Americans dislike the French. I can only guess that the famous French arrogance is too much like their own.

She shrugged. "Just making conversation." "Well, thanks anyway," I said, starting off. "Flan," I called. "Flan, come."

"Wait—I'm one-tenth French, and I think the French get a bum rap."

I turned back to face her. She might be one-tenth French, but she was also Asian, or part-Asian—exotic and strikingly pretty with light-brown skin and hair in a high ponytail.

"Sorry about your dog, but could you maybe help me? I'm trying to find 409-A Sixteenth Street. I see 409, but I must have it wrong, because there's no 'A.'"

As she swiped at her phone again, I noticed she was wearing riding britches. Real ones. Not the designer kind that would rip as soon as you spread your legs to sit in a saddle.

She held her phone toward me. "See? There's supposed to be a detached studio apartment for rent."

Fleetingly, I had the idea that I should check out this detached studio for Natey and me. Yes, I should sell the house and we'd live modestly while I got back on my feet, find a job, then seek out investors to start a bakery. A studio would be tight, not that we needed a lot of room. Natey was a *little* boy and . . . I was getting ahead of myself, and I didn't want to deprive this young woman of an affordable rental in Santa Monica. She seemed nice; she rode horses; she knew her dog breeds.

"Sorry," I said, moving off. "I don't know anything about a studio for rent. But if it exists, it's gotta be back there." I pointed. "You've got the right street. Sorry, I have to find my dog."

"Flan," she said.

"Flan, yes. Good luck finding the apartment."

"Good luck finding Flan. I'll keep my eye out for the little guy."

I scooted off again, and again she stopped me. "Wait—if I find him, who should I call? And hey—here's a treat for him." She held up a dog cookie. "I ride at a barn where there's this really screwy Rottweiler. He's behind a gate, but I always give him treats in case he escapes one day. You don't want to be on the wrong side of a Rotty."

Nor, like I'd done, do you want to leave your house in search of your dog without grabbing some treats.

"Thanks," I said walking back to collect the cookie. "He's very food-motivated."

"Aren't they all?" said the pretty girl, handing me a few. "If you want, type your number into my phone in case I find him."

I took the phone from her and entered the phone number.

"Yeah, Rotty the Rottweiler is pretty rotten," she said. His real name is Belvedere."

"What's your name?" I said. "Since we might be neighbors."

"Apryl."

"Hi, I'm Sarah. I live on the next block." I handed the phone back. "For now, at least."

Maybe I shouldn't volunteer information, but the young woman—girl, really—didn't trigger any alarms. On the other hand, she could be a con-artist, skilled at making people feel comfortable, all the while planning to finagle her way into your heart and house so she can steal your silver and identity. But since I'd already sold most of the silver, I had nothing to fear.

"Are you selling?" she asked, with some semblance of shock. "Isn't this one of those neighborhoods you shouldn't sell in? The appreciation's gotta be close to a sure thing."

"Yes, it's completely stupid," I said. "But we might have to. Depends on how the couples' counseling goes."

"Gotcha," said Apryl. "Been there."

"You don't seem old enough to have been married and divorced."

"Asians look young for their age," she said.

If I'd said that, it would probably have been considered culturally insensitive, even though I'd have meant it as a compliment.

"I'm twenty-seven. Yeah, we started early, but no kids."

"Certainly less complicated," I said.

Natey *was* a complication—a joyous, rewarding complication, but still a complication, making the decisions I now faced all the more challenging.

"Have you considered renting out a room in your place? A lot of people are doing that as a way to cover their mortgage. Airbnb, or more long term?" Apryl was still talking. "It can bring in cash, and, well, a room is all I really need," she went on, putting her phone back in her bag and giving me a charming smile.

I'd heard about the sharing economy, of course, but the thought of joining it hadn't crossed my mind.

Was she hustling me? She *was* a con artist.

"I hadn't thought about it," I said. "Give me your number, or some way to reach you. Who knows? I might consider it, but right now, I really have to find my dog."

"Right, sorry, I'm keeping you."

"Not at all." I *was* too nice.

"Here's my card," she said, quickly pulling from her bag a worn piece of cardboard. "Sorry it's a little mangled. My purse is a disaster. Let me know, or if you hear one of your neighbors might want to rent a room. I'm open to almost anything."

Under her name, Apryl Saito, appeared the words 'Equestrian/Riding Instructor,' along with a phone number. "Do you have references?"

"Lots," said Apryl.

"Okay, see ya."

With card and dog biscuits in hand, I pivoted and picked up a jog.

She seemed nice enough. Maybe a roommate was a good idea. And as I moved down the uneven sidewalk, I resolved to check her references. What could it hurt? I'd also consult the muffs. It was time to be honest, and they'd have some good ideas for sure. But at that moment, I had to find Flan.

CHAPTER 3

"IT'S UNACCEPTABLE," Nate said.

"Madelyn's a trained attorney and mediator and she cares about us," I protested. "Why is it unacceptable for us to talk to her?"

The summer afternoon was unusually gloomy. Most days, the gray cleared out by noon, but today's early overcast had lingered. Add to that a grumpy spouse and the portents of a dismal therapy session were in place. We got out of the car and shut the doors harder than necessary.

Lately, Nate seemed to be both trying and not trying to make things better with us. He had come over early to patch the hole in the fence through which Flan had squeezed his body in order to escape. He'd patched up the hole with two-by-fours and heavy-duty nails. Now the rest of the fence would give before the patch, and there would be no more escaping through that particular hole. And, fortunately, a chaotic mass of bougainvillea hid the bad patch job so that if we were forced to sell, the prospective buyers wouldn't see it right away. More gray thoughts.

I found Flan on Eighteenth, a couple of streets away from where I'd met Apryl, the attractive Asian horsewoman. When I finally came upon him, he was on the sidewalk shaking, apoplectic to the point of silence over an aging orange tabby lounging on a chair under a front pergola. The cat was on the other side of an iron fence, but Flan seemed to believe if he stood there long enough the cat would come out from under the pergola and make herself easier for him to bite.

"Sorry buddy. It's not gonna happen." I picked up the squirming mass of dog and headed for home. He didn't need one of Apryl's biscuits. He was getting heavier by the day, thanks to my dropping bits of baked goods on the floor and Natey slipping him food under the table. Like slipping money or drugs surreptitiously, there were bound to be consequences. Clearly, we needed to put the beasty on a diet and exercise plan.

There was no sign of Apryl on our way home as we passed Sixteenth Street, so maybe she found the place. Once back in the house, disaster averted, I called Nate about the hole in the fence.

Now, a couple of days later with the fence repaired, the two of us were arguing in the parking lot outside our therapist's office.

"Madelyn already knows our problems," I said, in the soothing voice Nate prefers from me, even though having to adjust it makes me squirm with annoyance. "That's a good thing. Plus, we'd save time and money. She's like a marriage counselor who knows about legalities. And if we decide to separate, we won't have to go through everything again with someone new. She'd give us a good deal."

At least a free consultation, I thought.

"Is that what you want?" Nate appeared genuinely hurt. "To separate?"

I flashed on our beautiful son, whom I'd dropped off at his friend Chloe's house before this meeting. As he got out of the car, he told me he was going to marry Chloe and that he will love her forever and ever. So I felt a lot of pressure to work things out.

"You know it's not my first choice," I said, meaning it.

"I'm just saying that where we are in this relationship, we don't know what's going to happen. Seeing a mediator means we'll be covering more bases, and we won't have to repeat ourselves if—" I realized baseball was more a metaphor for dating, not divorce.

"If what?"

"It shows we tried," I said.

"How pragmatic," said Nate, getting pissy. "*The Muffia* put you up to this? You're like a coven."

He'd always claimed to like the muffs, but he harbored a certain amount of jealousy that he didn't have a similar pack of men friends.

"I don't think it's a good idea to have a muff mediate anything between us," he went on. "Madelyn is *your* friend. Plus, she's oversexed. You said so yourself."

I *had* said it, but quite a while ago, and I didn't see how it was relevant to the present conversation. I was envious of Madelyn at the time, and deluded enough to think that telling Nate about her wild night with the Mossad agent would spice up our sex life. Given what happened to Madelyn soon after, my envy was short-lived. Anyway, the plan backfired, and Nate only felt inadequate.

"It was just that one guy she was with," I reminded him. "And if you'll remember, he died. Right on top of her. During the act. So be careful what you wish for."

"He died?" Nate said. "No, you didn't tell me that. I think I would have remembered."

I wasn't too sure. My theory is guys don't like to imagine themselves dying while coming, so any discussion of other guys dying while coming gets deleted from their data banks pretty quickly, lest it happen to them.

"Besides," I said. "She's your friend, too. In fact, she kept *your* little secret from me for a good long while."

Several months ago, before the miscarriage, Maddie had been shopping for a dildo in West Hollywood and, after an exhaustive selection process, had finally settled on a vibrator and went next door for an espresso—like she needed more stimulation. Inside the coffee place, she met a tall, handsome guy who'd apparently been watching her while she played with all the dildo options. He told her he admired her grip and the two of them were getting on so well, they decided to extend their impromptu date and move on to the tapas joint down the street. That's where she saw Nate sitting in a Naugahyde booth, kissing and feeling up a big-breasted woman on a weekday afternoon. "Tart" was the term Madelyn used later. She meant the sour taste seeing Nate kiss this woman made on her palate. She also said it put a damper on her date. At any rate, seeing Nate going at it with the woman in the tapas bar was the secret Madelyn kept to herself.

This had happened when Nate and I were in our open marriage—a time when some couples often engage in ménage a trois, quatres, and full-on orgies, as well as finding supplemental sex partners. In theory, it could be fun. But because we were only in it because Nate wanted it, it was decidedly not fun. I was a new mom and too tired for orgies.

There was one especially awkward evening we spent swinging with the Jacksons, which was a personal low-point in my sexual education. That is, nothing happened. Mr. Jackson—Jeff—was not into me at all, nor me him. We couldn't have been into each other less. Meanwhile *Mrs.* Jackson—I've blocked out her first name—couldn't get enough of Nate. Jeff and I had gotten as far as taking our clothes off and giving each other a little fondle before we retired to the den for shots of tequila Viejo and to watch a documentary on the possibility of a *Friends* reunion. *Friends* was a TV show I never watched the first time around, so I could hardly be excited at the thought of a reunion, and it made the documentary extremely confusing. Who were these people? Had I missed something important by not watching? Perhaps not watching *Friends* had contributed to my current problems. Who knew? Another shot of tequila Viejo por favor . . .

"That episode didn't exactly make her my fan." Nate said, still making the case against Madelyn. "Plus, she's *your* friend and that should automatically disqualify her from mediating. That is, *if* we were mediating. There's the whole bias thing, like how politicians have to avoid being seen on their donor's private jets. It's all about the optics; just looks bad."

"That's true, but this isn't presidential politics," I said. "We just want to talk to someone who understands us, who will listen and help us figure out what we want to do and not charge us tons of money."

"Well, I want to work things out," Nate said. "You don't."

"That's not true. I do . . ." Or I thought I did. The latest infidelity sort of broke me. "I don't think I can have what I want. We are different people than we were ten years ago."

"True story there," said Nate, giving me his saddest expression. "Where did we go?"

"How have the two of you been faring?" Lloyd, our therapist, took both of us in with his kind smile and boundless empathy.

Nate and I had settled onto separate ends of the three-sectioned couch, with all sorts of space between us. The couch just made it obvious.

Nate let out a long sigh. "As well as could be expected, I guess."

"And how about you, Sarah?" Lloyd pushed the Kleenex box closer to me, and I hadn't even said anything yet.

Ever since our first session months ago, when I sobbed for a full fifty minutes, Lloyd seemed to expect—nay, hope, for another session involving tears. I haven't been to many therapists, but the ones I've seen generally want to help you cross your perceived vast tundra of pain. Tears are the therapist's clue that there's real "emotion" happening, a physical manifestation of something to attend and move through.

"The same," I said, without tears. "I'm ready for this to become something else."

Lloyd took off his glasses, too small for his handsome black face, and took a cloth to the lenses. "Any idea what that something else might be?"

I glanced at Nate. For almost our whole relationship, I'd handed the power over to him because I'd learned that when I tried to hold onto it, even a tiny bit, he'd retreat and withhold. So I didn't challenge. He was the guy, and it seemed important to him to have the first and last word—even when he was wrong, even if it meant we as a family made a mistake. So what if not challenging him tore small pieces, and gradually large chunks, from my soul?

Before Natey was born, I had a good idea of who I was. I had a job I loved, and I made almost as much money as Nate Sr. Starting out as a freelance chef, I traveled around to various Williams Sonoma stores demonstrating products throughout Southern California. Then I moved on to store design before managing other designers and chefs. I was a mentor. People wanted to know what I thought, and they took my advice. Nate and I met when Williams Sonoma hired his architectural firm to redesign and rebrand the interiors of the California stores. Nate and I were brought together by fate and fell in love. He admired me, told me he loved my quiet power and artistic eye and my way around a kitchen. Over time, that guy disappeared and I had lost the power he said he loved. I know this happens a lot, but I don't know how we continue to fail to learn from it.

"Sarah and I need to be back in our house together again, seeing each other more and sharing parenting duties." Nate was turning on the charm.

Lloyd peered at me over his glasses. He must have sensed this was not an option as far as I was concerned.

"Is this what Sarah wants?"

"Ever since the firm let me go, she's become a different person," Nate said, like it was all my fault. "She's selling stuff—stuff we owned together—and she says she's getting a job. That's not good for our son."

I snorted. "Should I just let everything fall apart?"

"She has to be patient. Junior architects aren't in high demand right now. Blame automation." Nate was talking to Lloyd as a man, not talking to me.

"Why do you insist I am only annoyed because you lost your job?" I said, smarting at the suggestion. "Our problems started long before I even knew you'd lost your job. Maybe even before I gave up my job, which now seems pretty obvious I should not have done.

If you'd told me you were worried about the firm dumping you, I would have been sympathetic. Hell, I *am* sympathetic. What I can't fathom is that instead of telling me, you embarked on a series of affairs, asking me to have an open marriage, and that it was only after I found out about all the infidelities—plural—that you admitted to losing your job. And by that point, we were in this huge financial hole. *This* is what I am having trouble with."

"Lloyd, tell her it's different for guys." Nate had tried this line before. We'd actually had this entire conversation before, but that didn't seem to stop Nate from wanting to have it again.

Lloyd's mouth opened but no words came out. For a second, I thought he might take Nate apart for revealing a secret about the Brotherhood or the Knights Templar or something. Then Lloyd recovered and did his therapist's re-framing routine.

"What Sarah is saying—and correct me if I am wrong, Sarah—is that she was hurt when you initially didn't come to her about losing your position at the firm, which has put both of you in financial jeopardy. And that the women you became involved with could have been avoided if you had talked to her honestly at the time it happened."

God, he had patience. Then again, he'd heard it before.

"Yes, Lloyd, that's exactly what I'm saying. And then some. Why put me—why put us both through all those extra layers of bullshit? We might have been closer than ever had you confided in me."

"But I'm the guy," Nate said. "I'm the provider. I couldn't provide any more and I felt . . ."

I knew this was as close to an apology as I was going to get from him. Part of me wanted to comfort him. But what he'd done had been such a violation of our vows and what people who *say* they love each other should do, that I felt no forgiveness in my heart.

All I felt was unmoored. I needed my muffs and was glad book club was just a few days away.

CHAPTER 4

THE FOLLOWING afternoon, with Flan on the leash, I set out for the local elementary school ten blocks away to pick Natey up from Science Camp.

Since his escape, our expanding French bulldog had been behaving better, other than displaying his annoyance at his reduced food rations, and his seemingly constant presence in the kitchen waiting for falling baked goods.

Though having him under foot was an annoyance, his omnipresence served as a constant reminder to attempt the creation of flan cookies, which thus far, had resulted in two unappetizing batches. One was lacking in flavor and the other had the texture of gravel. So, they were nowhere near ready for market.

I was daydreaming the perfect baked delicacies and people lining up to buy them, when Flan the dog and I turned the final corner to the school, where there's a spot of grass, a bench and a community bulletin board, covered in glass. I stopped to read up on local happenings, while Flan fidgeted at my feet. As I scanned the notices for a town zoning referendum and a neighborhood fundraising effort to plant trees, my eyes settled on a picture of a Boxer dog and underneath the picture was a plea:

Missing: Beloved Pet Boxer " Sasha"

$1000 Reward

Wow, that's a lot of money, I thought. They must really have loved their—

Suddenly, Flan was yanking me away from the bulletin board, pulling so hard I almost lost my balance. Before I knew it, Natey was throwing his arms around him, with the little beasty snuffling and snorting in delight, poking his face into Natey's pockets, searching for treats.

French Bulldogs aren't very big, but they're still bulldogs and can yank, spin, and pull with the best of them. The "bully" breeds, or "buoy" as Natey says, share some other tendencies as well, notably obstinacy and gassiness. Grunts, belches, farts—it can almost become endearing. Owners of such breeds will complain about the behavior, but should their beloved bully die, they will nevertheless often seek to replace him with a farting, belching replica. People like Barbra Streisand have even gone so far as to clone their dogs. Okay, Barbra wasn't cloning her bully, but that's only because she hasn't had one.

The sight of my boy and his dog was so sweet and funny to watch, it took me a few seconds to realize Natey had been sitting by himself. There he was on a bench along a strip of macadam that led to the playground. No wonder Flan pulling on me at that moment seemed wrong. Natey shouldn't have been there.

"Where are the other kids?" I asked, trying not to seem concerned. "And the teachers—where are they?"

"Inside." He was pouting, talking to Flan. "Fanny, Fwanny, foofy . . ."

"Let me see you," I said, squatting down in front of him and pulling Flan around to the other side.

"Honey, you've been crying."

His pout deepened.

"What happened? Come on, I won't tell."

"They broke my 'speriment," he said, trying to get to Flan. "Fwanny, fanny . . ."

"Wait, Flan—stay," I said, holding him back. The dog snorted his displeasure.

"They broke your experiment?"

Natey nodded. He was sniffling but nothing else seemed amiss.

"Why would they do that?"

He shrugged, wiping his nose with the back of his wrist.

My eyes scanned the empty play area, wondering what to do or say next. Not a soul was on the playground.

"Why are you out here all by yourself?"

"I came out the doors."

The "teachers" of this so-called Science Camp were not supposed to let seven-year-olds go outside without an escort. Sheesh, they shouldn't let entire groups of older campers go outside without supervision. My concern quickly turned to fury as I looked around for a place to vent. My eyes once again settled on my son. But whatever my failures as a mother, I know you don't yell at your kid when he's the victim.

At that moment, the doors to the gymnasium opened and a tousled redhead of about twenty stepped out in wedge sneakers and headed toward us. There she was: Emily, the so-called head of Science Camp. She was still in college but should have been well aware of all the horrible things that can happen to an unattended child. I resisted the urge to yell at her.

"There you are, Nathaniel," Emily said, squinting into the sun as she reached us. "Mrs. Pizzo, nice to see you."

"Emily, how did Natey get outside without anyone noticing?"

"Oh, we noticed," she said. "That's why I came out, to bring him back in. No worries."

"No—worries?" I said, moving closer and trying to keep my voice low. "There are plenty of worries. I've been here for at least five minutes, which is long enough for something bad to happen."

"Oh, nothing bad was going to happen. See up there?" Emily pointed at the flagpole.

"The flagpole?"

She smiled. "More specifically, the camera on the flagpole. Security staff has been watching Nathaniel this whole time. We knew he was out here, and the reason I'm out here, in fact, is because one of our security personnel saw you show up with the dog and was concerned you might be, well, unfriendly."

"*Unfriendly*?" I said. "Does this security person not know what parents look like? I've been coming every day for a week."

Emily turned to Natey, making it quite obvious she was giving up on trying to convince me she was in control of the situation. "What's your doggie's name?"

"Fwan," Natey said.

"Oooh, that's a nice name. I like flan."

"Me too. We named him Fwan because my mom makes fwan and it's really, really good."

"Thank you, sweetheart." He was so damned cute. The thought of him in the grips of some horrible, creepy—I stopped myself because down that road was torment.

"I like both flans," Emily said. "The dog *and* the dessert."

"I like both fwans too!" said Natey, beginning to let go of his pout. "My mom is making fwan cookies!"

"Mmmm," cooed Emily. "Those sound yummy."

"Honey, would you hold on to this Flan for a minute," I said, handing the end of the leash to Natey. "Hold on tight. You know how he pulls."

"Can I speak to you a moment?" I said, drawing Emily away. "Leaving aside for a minute the fact that he should not be out here without an adult, what is this about some other kids messing with his experiment?"

"I was going to call you about it later."

"I'm here now."

She seemed to get smaller at that point. Like it was one too many explanations she had to cope with in too short a time frame. “All the kids were working on the slime experiment with the balloon.”

“I’m unfamiliar with that experiment.”

“Everyone was playing well together, but as the slime was finishing and we were ready to do the balloon portion of the activity . . .” She hesitated, choosing her words. “One of the kids accidentally popped Nate’s balloon and spilled his slime.”

I glanced over at Natey, then back to Emily. “Doesn’t sound like an accident,” I said. “Both things together? I could understand just the slime spilling being an accident, but the slime *and* the balloon?”

“Cowin Bwagpoo did it on purpose,” Natey said. Guess we hadn’t moved far enough away.

Emily was shaking her head. “I don’t think—”

“Listen,” I said, “I’m a little disappointed in you, Emily.”

“I’m sorry, Mrs. Pizzo.”

“Sarah.”

“All right, um. Sarah?”

Emily cowered, but I hadn’t asserted my full motherly entitlement. “I would like you to ask Colin Blackpool a few questions. Colin and Nate go to New Roads together—” there was no need to tell Emily we might not have the money to keep Natey at New Roads “—and the boy is trouble. He’s an instigator. Ask around.”

“Yes, I—all right. I’m sorry Mrs.—Sarah, I mean.”

“You may need to take some sort of action. Remove the troublemaker rather than have all the good kids suffer?”

She nodded again.

“Also,” I said luring Emily further from Natey. “And I don’t want to be difficult, but imagine you’re me. You have a kid, and you love him, so you want to do the best you can for him, right?"

She crossed her arms. "Mrs. Pizzo—"

"So you send him to 'Science' Camp to keep his brain occupied and to give yourself a few hours each day to get other things done. But slime? Balloons? Could the kids do something more, I don't know, practical? How 'bout an experiment so they'll understand gravity?"

Emily probably had no control over the curriculum, and I didn't mean it to sound rude, but it seemed what they were doing was less science than goofing off.

"I'll ask my boss. And see if these seven-year-olds can do something more significant."

Was she making a dig? I didn't care.

"Thank you. I'd appreciate that, Emily," I said, taking Flan's leash from Natey who jumped up and kept on jumping.

"Let's go Fanny, Fwanny, Fo-fanny . . ."

At the end of the leash, Flan began jumping and wriggling, too.

"Well, someone's excited," I said, holding on to thirty-five pounds of dog that seemed to want to pull me off my feet. "See you," I said.

Emily waved. "See you tomorrow, Nathaniel."

"Bye Emiwy, see you tomorrow."

I got Flan to settle and took Natey's hand. "All right, guys, let's go home."

CHAPTER 5

WHEN ONE ventures from Santa Monica to the San Fernando Valley, she's usually accompanied by tens of thousands of cars, traveling at a pace only slightly faster than an aging tortoise. She's also faced with a twenty-five-degree increase in temperature. The difference in the heat index between the two micro-climates is palpable, causing a driver to crank up the AC as she crests the hill of the 405 Freeway, on top of which sits the Getty Museum, in all its chunky, imported, Italian-marble glory. The 405—synonymous with Carmaggedon and a never-ending construction of additional lanes, which Angelenos agree never do anything to ease congestion.

Most summer days, when the car thermo-sensor reads seventy-five degrees Fahrenheit at the beach, by the time one gets to Encino where Kiki lives, it reads a screaming, breathtaking one hundred. On this sweltering summer evening, however, as Paige and I made our way to Kiki's and book club, I was breathing easy for the first time in days. Paige was driving, which was almost thrilling—not having to drive myself—particularly along this tedious, torturous strip of the 405. Paige driving wasn't unusual. The muffs make an effort to reduce our carbon footprints by carpooling whenever possible. But tonight, carpooling was mandatory. My credit cards were maxed out and there was no cash to buy gas. Without Paige to drive, I couldn't have made it to book club. I'd left all this out when I asked Paige for a ride, but I added it to the list of things I planned to tell the muffs.

Paige looked great, and she was the happiest I'd seen her, recently remarried and returned from her wedding and honeymoon on North Carolina's Outer Banks. Her glowing complexion, Jelicka swore, was due to some covert plastic surgery. But if Paige had plastic surgery, I couldn't tell. She just appeared more content. And it was nice to listen to her talk about her husband, Richard, and his transformation since the wedding. She guessed he had been feeling more insecure than she realized about their relationship, and now that they were married, he was confident they were a solid couple.

Not so long ago, I'd felt a sort of peculiar rivalry coming from Paige, and I couldn't figure out which one of us was responsible. But if I'm to remain a reliable narrator, I'd have to say we both were. The competition between us, if that's what it was, had to do with cooking. It was like any gathering of the muffs, particularly those where our significant others were present, became an opportunity to show off a fancy dish. But why did we have to compete with each other? Why couldn't we both be good?

The thing I felt she never took into account was that food had been my *career*—I'd been a latter-day Martha Stewart without the financial security. If I hadn't been good at "kitchen and lifestyle," I would have lost my job. Still, I could feel Paige's quiet . . . was it jealousy?

Perhaps I had gloated on occasion—something I'm not proud of—because at the time I believed I was on top of the world. Well, that tide sure had turned. These days, it was Paige who seemed to have it all, and to her credit, kept any gloating well out of view.

"Don't sweat it, ladies," said Kiki as she opened the front door to Paige and me, the two of us melting on the front stoop in the hundred-degree heat.

"You'll be sipping cocktails by the pool in under five minutes," said Kiki, ushering us in and looking cool in a spaghetti-strapped camisole and short shorts. Her body always made me feel guilty and this evening was no exception. I hadn't worked out in weeks.

"I'm counting on it," said Paige, handing Kiki the bottle of dry pink rosé she'd selected for the evening. "It was cold when we left the Weststide but it could use a zap in the freezer."

"I brought dessert and cocktail fixings," I said. "And I guarantee this will not be your mother's sangria!"

"Good. Because I want *my* sangria." Kiki closed the door. "Quinn's going to be late, so let's do this."

We made our way to the kitchen as the cool, conditioned air wafted through the house. I could almost see hundred-dollar bills wafting along with it. Kiki's husband made tons of money as an attorney and could afford to keep the house this chilly, but was it really necessary? *Wonder what their carbon footprint is.*

Madelyn appeared from the hallway, holding an empty wine glass. "I got an email. Where's this 'something we can't get anywhere else'?"

"You'll get it, but you have to wait," I said, giving her a hug before emptying the shopping bag of cocktail fixings. "Right now, I'm mixing up something that's also hard to find. In the meantime, if it's wine you're looking for . . ."A smiling Paige held up her bottle.

"I'll have both," said Madelyn, sitting down to wait on a stool at Kiki's kitchen island, while Kiki poured wine into her glass before Paige could get hers open.

Rachel came in next, embracing us both. "Ladies. So good to see you. *Mmmmm*, cocktails."

We muffs did enjoy our cocktails.

"The Westsiders have arrived!" said Vicki, as she and Jelicka joined us.

I've told you about Jelicka, but Vicki not so much. She's one of the quieter muffs, but also one of the most trustworthy. I'd confided in her about Nate in the past, and she had kept the confidence. She took an orange out of my hand and gave me one of her restorative hugs.

"Sorry we're late, but we have little kids," I reminded the group. "We can't spend the day getting our nails done in anticipation of seeing you all."

"Or Dysport." Rachel directed this comment at Jelicka, who rolled her eyes.

"What the hell is Dysport?" I asked. "Some anti-sports activist group?"

"It's like Botox—face immobilizer, muscle killer. You get it injected into your face. You know . . ." Rachel made a fright face.

"You'll have something done one day, Miss Holier-Than-Thou," said Jelicka. "Besides, it's not scary unless you have them do too much and you end up with frozen face." She started making facial expressions. "I can still smile; I can still squint."

Her expressions only seemed to go about halfway toward what they should have.

"See? I can still raise my eyebrows at you, Sarah Pizzo. Did you read the book?"

"Some of it," I said. "But more importantly, I brought cocktails Bernadette would approve of."

"Way to keep your priorities clear," said Madelyn. "Hurry up with that."

"How do you know what Bernadette would drink if you didn't read the book?" Paige said, sounding hostile all of a sudden. Was she serious? Nobody else was saying anything.

"Umm . . . I asked Rachel?" I put two lemons on the

counter.

"I'm kidding." Paige gave me a gentle punch. "Come on, if I stopped being book club Nazi, you'd all miss it."

She was probably right.

"You're funny, Paige," Madelyn said. "Woman gets married and becomes a comedian."

Kiki examined the cocktail ingredients I'd assembled. "How long does it take to mix up this 'not-my-mother's sangria'?"

"Not long." I said. "Get me your biggest pitcher."

"Absolutely." She dragged a stepstool over to one of the multiple banks of custom cabinets that lined her vast kitchen and pulled open a set of doors, revealing pitchers of all sizes and styles. She chose one—large and made of glass—which, if filled and consumed, would ensure we'd all be sauced.

"Don't worry," I said to Paige, "if you feel like drinking, I'll drive us home."

"Oh, I'm not worried," she said, smiling. "I'm just standing here so I get the first glass."

While I did the mixing, occasionally stopping to scoop up Vicki's fresh guacamole on a farmer's market tortilla strip, we fell into our normal comfortable book club rhythm, chatting about the surface subjects that always paved the way to our book discussion and the deeper roundy-round. One of those subjects was LA geography and the ongoing spat between those who lived on the Westside, the Valleyites, and the muffs who'd chosen to live in Hollywood and communities to the east. There were so many great little neighborhoods spread out over the city of LA, the truth was that every area had its benefits. Take the Valley for example—it was too hot in the summer but always more comfortable and warmer in the winter months, plus it was easier to park; the Westside was usually more comfortable weather-wise, but more expensive, with far fewer parking options. Hollywood and the Eastside had adorable little pockets like Larchmont and Silver Lake that might once have been more affordable, but parking and climate could both be iffy. The reality is, we'd never agree on the best place to live in this vast megalopolis, but despite the conversation having no end, we never seemed to tire of having it.

"I'm lucky to get here at all," Paige was saying. "Not only do I have kids, the new afterschool tennis program I coach is in freaking Mar Vista."

Mar Vistas wasn't freaking, it was just further away from the Valley.

"I get it," Kiki was saying. "Just next time I have to drive to Brentwood, don't get mad when *I'm* late!"

"Come on, Kiki," Vicki said. "At that hour, the traffic is going the other way."

See? We'd never agree.

Soon we were happily ensconced by the pool with the pitcher of sangria, wine, and, having polished off the guacamole, had moved on to onion dip—a muff mainstay—courtesy of Kiki.

"What did everyone think about *Bernadette?*" Kiki asked, depositing a fresh bowl of dip, the first having been consumed in under three minutes.

"The book or the character?" Madelyn asked.

"I've never been to Seattle, so I can't say for sure," said Vicki. "But I'd say she was too smart for the neighborhood."

"Like so many women in so many neighborhoods," Rachel said, shaking her head. "If you're smart, you have to downplay it. Otherwise you upset both the dumb women and all the men. Can't win."

It was bound to happen at some point in the evening. Something would be said to get Rachel going on the battle of the sexes, and here was her entry. I didn't disagree with her, it's just what does one do to fix it?

"I think she was too smart, too," Kiki said, pulling a piece of paper from her copy of *Bernadette.* "But here's something I think is very interesting and worth discussing: The rash of book titles ending with a question mark. I'd like to read off a few and discuss: *When Will There Be Good News? Where Do Babies Come From? Do Androids Dream of Electric Sheep? Are You My Mother? Are You There God? It's Me, Margaret. They Shoot Horses, Don't They? Where's My Cow? Who Moved My Cheese? Why Do Men Have Nipples? Can You Sue Your Parents for Malpractice? What Price Glory? Is Everyone Hanging Out Without Me? Why Be Happy When You Could Be Normal?*

My question is, what is the significance of a title that's a question?" Kiki put the paper down.

"At least with this book, the title has something to do with content," said Vicki. "There *was* a character named Bernadette and she *did* go missing. As opposed to *Who Moved my Cheese?* which was some sort of motivational metaphor using mice with cheese as the MacGuffin."

"A MacMuffin?" said Jelicka snorting.

"Elliptical titles drive me crazy," said Kiki. "Authors should be answering questions, not asking them."

"Agreed," said Paige. "Now, getting back to what we were talking about before. As the mother of two young children and a couple of step-kids, I agree with the people who said Bernadette wasn't much of a mother. And Lauren agrees. I talked to her."

"What—are we voting?" said Rachel. "I vote she's a good mother. So what if she got carried away with the berry bramble."

"Wow, I wish I'd read about Bernadette's berry bramble," I said. "But I abstain. I'd be making my decision based on hearsay, and that's never a good idea. Right Madelyn?"

"Not admissible," said Madelyn, our resident legal authority.

"Bramble, scramble. She loves Bee," Vicki said, also coming to Bernadette's defense. "That's why she did what she did.

She wanted to model confident, assertive behavior for her daughter, and fortunately Bee was smart and recognized that, so she didn't feel abandoned."

"Kind of a reversal from a parent knowing her child is 'different' and making excuses. Here it's the child making excuses for the parent." Madelyn put her unfinished glass of sangria on the table. "I think I've had enough."

Listening to the muffs so invested in the characters from the books always made me wish I'd read them. And yet every time a new book was assigned, I never seemed to get to it. So that night, I let the rest of the discussion wash over me. I sipped my glass of sangria in the fading light, while I planned what I'd say in the roundy-round, that most important part of book club when we put the book to bed and talked about ourselves. In the end, as we lit the outdoor candles for dinner, the muffs agreed Bernadette's motives were pure, and therefore forgivable.

Kiki served a delicious Branzino with grilled vegetables and a gluten-free pasta dish, while Saul and their son, Troy, made the occasional appearance on the patio, helping themselves to food and to catch a bit of girl gossip. Soon we were back around the pool for the roundy. Quinn finally appeared, delayed by an unruly celebrity with drug issues, but that's as far as she'd go. She left it to us to keep guessing who it could be, giving us nothing more. Instead, and as expected, she raved about how great Frank was. It was getting a little nauseating, but that was probably because my own love life was so bleak. She'd recently installed a pole in her apartment so she could pole dance naked for Frank, and it was a visual I had trouble shaking. I much preferred the topic of Quinn's lesbian boss, Jamie, and her former lover and ex-employee, the beautiful and intriguing Tatiana. Apparently, Jamie was in safer territory now, dating the wife of a Hollywood producer.

Madelyn went next. "Nothing new, really. Lila's good. I'm good. I have a date . . ." This was met with excitement and exclamations of "Wow," "Really?" "Do tell," and the like. She hadn't had many dates since the Mossad agent.

"Remember Cullen," she began. "The handsome guy I met after dildo shopping that day when Quinn didn't show up? I know Sarah remembers."

"Oh, yeah," I said.

It was common knowledge that if not for Cullen and the impromptu date at the tapas bar, Madelyn wouldn't have seen Nate with one of his buxom paramours.

Vicki and Rachel both gave me expressions of support.

"Lucky for everyone I couldn't make it," Quinn said. "You never would have met him, and poor Sarah might still be with the quadruple-timing bastard."

"Easy, Quinn," said Rachel. "Sarah's still with him."

Everyone turned to me.

"I'll fill you in during the roundy," I said.

"Wasn't Cullen the guy pushing his mother around in a wheelchair?" Kiki asked. "The day we went to visit Vicki in the hospital? He was gorgeous."

"Gorgeous in a pushing-your-mother-around-in-a-wheelchair kind of way," said Madelyn. "I know men who love their mothers are supposed to make good husbands, but I think there are limits."

Kiki sighed. "You don't need to tell me that. Before Saul's mom passed, we could never go anywhere. Seemed like every holiday—Christian, Jewish, Mayan, didn't matter—we had to stay in LA so Mom wouldn't get lonely."

"Well, Cullen's mom passed a few months ago," Madelyn went on. "So long story less long, he called last week and we're getting together. I always liked him, and, other than the mother fixation, we were a good fit; so, we'll see." She gestured for someone else to begin.

"I have to say," Kiki said, seamlessly taking over. "Saul and I are doing better than ever and not just because we have more time together. Troy's really grown up lately, at school and at home, so there's no friction at the moment." She then gestured toward the house next door. "And the new neighbors are quiet."

There'd been a rather tumultuous time several months ago when some porn producers were operating next door to Kiki. I never saw them, but apparently there were all manner of scantily clad people in the backyard and film crews operating every hour of the day and night. But the muffs helped bust them in spectacular fashion one night after the city failed to act.

Kiki's teen son, Troy, got an eyeful that night, seeing his mom's friends dressed as hookers in order to get inside the house. She'd been concerned about him being too young and sensitive to witness such activity, but we told her he was aware of far more than she gave him credit for. Troy gained a new respect for his mom that night, because she'd taken on the pornographers, and, through that, their relationship had matured. It was like they'd bypassed the whole process of figuring out when to stop talking to your kid like he's a kid and begin talking to him like he's an adult.

Kiki was still working on becoming a nurse practitioner, and it was taking longer than hoped. In the fast-changing world of medical insurance and accountability, new required courses kept getting added to the curriculum. It didn't help that she was only taking a couple of classes a semester so she could continue being a good mom.

Vicki spoke up next. She was still cancer-free after her lumpectomy a couple of years earlier and looked beautiful. And, as sometimes happens after chemo, her hair was fuller and more luxurious than it had ever been. Whenever anyone mentioned it, she'd say, "You too can have hair like this, you just have to have a whole lot of radioactive crap pumped through your body."

She was excited about a new documentary project—her first since her son graduated from college and left the house. He was off to start his life, and she'd gotten hers back. The project was still in the research and planning stages and she was superstitious about jinxing it, so she would tell us nothing except it was "political." As for romance, all she'd say was, "I'm too old for Tinder, but my eyes are open."

Jelicka announced that her real estate license was imminent. Seemed like she said this every book meet, but there was a little matter of passing the real estate exam, which she'd flunked once so far. This time, though, she'd heard from a reliable source—someone with psychic powers—that she was going to nail it.

"So *if*—" she said, turning to me. "No pressure. But *if* you have to sell your house, I am the person to get you top dollar."

Jelicka might not be my first choice in realtors, but she was a dynamo. If she found the buyers and brought her commission down, I'd be willing to consider the arrangement.

"I'll let you know," I said. "Things are still up in the air."

There was a weighty pause, and suddenly I realized everyone was staring at me.

"Yup, it's you, Sarah," said Vicki. "Spill."

So I spilled; everything you know so far, and then some. That I didn't hold out much hope for Nate and me, and that we'd probably have to sell the house if I couldn't find a way to pay for it. I told them I was considering taking on a tenant to help pay the mortgage, and that I wanted my old job back at Williams Sonoma. I told them about my dreams of creating a baked goods empire and, as evidence, brought out the tasty baked experiments they couldn't get anywhere else. The muffs were encouraging, even gushing as friends should, but we all knew the journey from experiment to empire wasn't an easy one. Lastly, I apologized for letting them believe the baby I'd miscarried was the result of a torrid affair, and not Nate's.

"Wow," said Rachel. "That's a huge conceal."

Jelicka smiled knowingly. "Even muffs have their secrets."

"I feel a little hurt," Paige said. "Sorry, but I do."

"It was such an awful time. I wanted to block it out," I said, dabbing at my eyes . "I'm sorry I didn't tell you."

Vicki put her arm around me. "I just hope you were talking to *some*one."

I nodded. "Someone who's known me a very long time. I probably wore her out with all the talking." I scanned their faces and made an effort to smile. "The truth is, I think I was ashamed to tell you."

"*Noooo,* don't say that," said Kiki. "That makes me sad."

Madelyn put her arm around the other side of me and squeezed.

True to form, the muffs understood and accepted all; though they said from now on they'd be monitoring me closely and made me promise that the next time something happened to me, I'd tell them.

As we prepared to leave and gave each other final hugs, Paige consulted her phone, swiping across a few screens to find out who would be the next host.

"I haven't hosted in forever, it's about time," said Jelicka in her usual hyperbolic fashion."I thought I was next," Vicki whined, but Paige's notes on the subject were not to be questioned.

"My goal for our next meeting," Jelicka announced, "is to choose a book that even Sarah will read."

I let out a laugh. "Good luck with that. If you keep it under twenty pages you have a deal."

"One thing's for sure," said Jelicka, picking up her purse.

"I will be a card-carrying realtor by then, so we're drinking champagne—the real stuff, from Champagne."

"Let's keep our priorities clear," said Kiki.

That was something we could all drink to.

CHAPTER 6

AFTER TEN years in Santa Monica, I should be accustomed to the haze that grips my seaside community most summer mornings, that I'd be confident in the knowledge that the "marine layer"—as those averse to the word "fog" call it—would burn off before eleven o'clock exposing bright blue skies.

But the fog of the mind operates differently. It doesn't burn off on schedule, and there's no guarantee you'll ever see your way out of it. There are no fog lights to buy to help you—not that auto engineers have ever been truly successful in building a light that cuts through the stuff.

Lately, even when I think I'm seeing clearly, it doesn't last. The fog returns to mind and sky alike. I pondered this and more while I lay in bed, waiting for Natey to stir, the gray lurking outside the window in the early light.

At this hour, the fog was supposed to be there, but I found myself hoping Natey and Flan would come in and distract me from my thoughts. What I needed was the physical jolt that would shake me from them, the kind that always came from Natey jumping on the bed and the snuggling that always followed. That would do it.

So I listened, hoping for sounds of stirring coming from Natey's room down the hall, but there was only silence, and soon I was back in the fog with my swirling thoughts. And, at that moment, the thought competing hardest for recognition was how I was going to handle my meeting later that day with my former boss, Tobias Miserocchi.

When I called Tobias a week earlier after book club after the muffs encouraged me to, he'd seemed surprised to hear from me. It should not have been an unexpected reaction. Since I'd left the company, my communications with Tobias had been limited to the annual holiday card exchange and occasional messages via LinkedIn. But after the awkward beginning, we were soon chatting about all the people we had in common and catching each other up on our lives.

When the time came to tell him about the real reason for the call, however, I lost my nerve. I knew it was lame, but all that Monster and Hive job board failure had left me feeling insecure. So what I said was I'd like to take him for coffee to discuss a business idea. This was true, after all, given my dreams of becoming a baking maven, and there'd be plenty of time to spring the job question when he was sitting in front of me.

I wriggled my way over to the edge of the king-sized bed, so much easier now that Nate Sr. wasn't in it forming a crater in the center toward which all things rolled. Did I miss his warm body? Yes, I did. Would I take it back? Yes, I would. But there was a big "but" attached to that now. Things needed to change before that happened. In the meantime, I was stressed and horny.

I sat up and watched the swirling mist. It was all going to work out, I told myself. I just needed another way to de-stress. The muffs were always advocating vibrator use, and at Kiki's they told me that, given my current sexless situation, I must use it regularly, even daily. I said I would. But the truth is, I always feel a little silly when I realize I am moving a rubberized vibrating penis in and out of my vagina, wondering if I'll come before the batteries die. I should try again. I'm more desperate now, so perhaps I'll feel differently once I get into it. I just had to find the damned thing.

More swirling thoughts. What I really needed was exercise. But I hate exercise. I could try yoga, which Madelyn swore by. Running is cheaper, but my knees won't take it, though they might tolerate the stairs a couple times a week. "The stairs" are two sets of seemingly endless steps that descend down a Santa Monica cliff to busy Channel Road, and whenever I pass them, scores of people are going up and down and up and down again, nose to tail. People swore by the toning benefits of these steps. Some had even met their future spouses there, sharing joys and misfortunes during rests between ascent and descent. I resolved to try it once for the combined benefits of body-toning and man-gazing. If I didn't like it, no big.

Fortunately, the stress I was under had caused me to lose weight, though I feared this could change at any time. I come from a long line of baked-goods-making-and-consuming Jewish-Italian immigrants and, as a rule, the women in my family are not thin. By age forty, most might be politely described as "well fed."

I was thus far an outlier but needed to remain vigilant. There were days I could feel my metabolism changing, and my body along with it. My breasts seemed lower and fuller, my thighs somehow a different shape, and my upper arms felt like they were swinging in a different direction than the bones. The change I most noticed was a little extra skin—or was it fat—circling my mid-section. I wondered if all this, too, could be genetic.

More swirling. Yes, I decided. Everything that was wrong in my life was the fault of my "people." Oh, how easy it is to blame someone other than ourselves.

As the random thoughts kept coming, I didn't hear Flan come in, but suddenly he was snorting and wriggling and rubbing his head against my leg, pulling me into the present.

"All right, Fwanny, flanny, fanny," I said, getting to my feet. "Let's wake up Natey and get that snuggle."

CHAPTER 7

I WAS SNAPPING Natey into his car seat, preparing to drive to Science Camp, when I noticed a woman across the street going door to door leaving notes, sliding them into mail slots and under doors. She had wild, red hair and flowing Eileen Fischer-esque clothes, and she seemed vaguely familiar in the way neighbors do.

Was she that woman who was always canvassing for political causes? She was out early, I thought; probably to catch people as they left for the day. Or as they're strapping in their kids to take them to Science Camp.

I inserted the last safety clasp into its buckle and stood. Too late; she saw me.

She rushed down the set of overwrought stone steps of a fake Italianate McMansion and headed toward me. As she got closer, I realized perhaps I didn't recognize her, not from the neighborhood, anyway. Maybe I'd seen her at Trader Joe's. Because I did see a lot of people who look like her at Trader Joe's. Was I age and clothes profiling?

As she got closer, I could see her outfit was not Eileen Fischer at all, but a hastily put together outfit consisting of yoga pants, flip-flops, and an incorrectly buttoned billowing paisley cotton blouse that might have belonged to a man. Her red hair was coursed through with strands of gray, which were going every possible direction, and a set of reading glasses hung from a piece of twine around her neck. I determined at that point that she was probably not a political canvasser. Or, if she was, it was only a matter of time before the signature companies replaced her.

"Hi, I live on Thirteenth Street?" she said as a question, her voice filled with panic. "I have a little white Pug, and, and," She was choking up, unable to continue. "She's missing, and no one even answers the door." Now she was flat out crying.

"Mommy?" Natey said, picking up on the alarm.

"It's okay, honey. Let me talk to the lady."

If I passed this woman on the street, I'd probably notice her, though I doubt we'd nod or say hello. But when confronted directly by suffering, the kind she was now displaying, I had the opportunity to become my better self, and to replace my usual dull, insular reaction to the tragedies of the world with compassion. Granted, it's always a choice, but this time, I knew what to do.

"I'm so sorry," I said. "How can I help?"

"I'm Ellen," said the woman, dabbing her eyes. "Ellen Pirosh. I live on Thirteenth. Like I said."

"Hi, Ellen, I'm Sarah. That's my son Natey in the car."

Ellen managed a small wave. "Sorry, I don't want to keep you. I'm a mess." She fumbled for a tissue.

"So your little white dog is missing," I said, hoping to move things along. "Did he escape?"

She shook her head. "*She* is albino. An albino Pug. They're extremely rare." Sniffle, sniffle. "And no, she did not escape."

"They're so crafty," I said. "Our dog was getting out through a hole in the fence." *This isn't about you, Sarah. She wants to talk about her own dog.*

"Pearly Girl was stolen. I'm sure of it," said Ellen, regaining her composure.

My brain flashed on the bulletin board and the missing Boxer. *What had happened to that dog? Had he run away or been stolen?*

"She's albino," Ellen was saying again. "I'm going around the neighborhood to ask if anyone's seen her, or if they've seen anything suspicious, but nobody even opens the door!" She was crying again. "That's what has me even more upset! Who do these people think is knocking on their door? Some political canvasser? I'm just trying to find my Pearlie Girl."

"Just a second." I closed the car door, realizing too late that Natey didn't need to hear about a stolen dog. He was probably already traumatized by the sight of a wild redheaded woman.

"What's that?" said Ellen.

"My son," I whispered. "He's sensitive."

"What kind of society have we become!?" She exclaimed, making a mental leap into subject matter with the potential of trapping me most of the day.

Ugh—I just wanted to offer a little solace to my neighbor about her missing dog, not hear upsetting details about melting icebergs and the gyre of plastic crap swirling in the Pacific Ocean.

"It's true," I said, agreeing with her about our societal and planetary ills, while at the same time deciding that if she launched into politics or climate change, I'd politely tell her I'd keep an eye out for her dog and be on my way. I care about halting climate change and international geopolitics as much as the next single mom, but now was not the time.

"I'd call the authorities," she said, back on track. "But you know how they are. They're going to ask me, 'Have you attempted to locate your animal, Ma'am?' They're going to ask me that because that's the kind of thing they ask. That's why I'm doing this—talking to people, or trying to. I'm attempting to 'locate.' Not that I hold out much hope at this point. Pearly Girl is a rare albino Pug, and someone stole her!"

"Listen," I said, trying to get Ellen to calm down and focus. "I think you should call them—the authorities, I mean.

Maybe other dogs have gone missing. Ask about a Boxer dog named Sasha."

"Sasha?" said Ellen.

Maybe this had been the wrong thing to say. She only looked more upset.

"Mama?" Natey said, pulling my attention.

"Okay, we're going."

I turned back to Ellen. "The way I see it, you can tell the authorities with all honesty that you attempted to find him, I mean her, your dog. I'm a witness. To your attempting, that is."

"You think? I don't know . . . no, you're right. All right, I'll call them. But let me give you my number, and if you see her or hear something, call me. Will you?"

"Of course," I said, watching her scribble her name and number onto her notepad. "It's awful—I mean if she was stolen. But you're certainly doing everything you can."

"She has a microchip in her, so maybe . . ." said Ellen. "I'm trying to stay positive." She tore off the top page and handed it to me. I tucked it into my bag next to the young equestrienne's business card.

"That's what I try to do every day myself," I said, giving her my biggest possible smile under the circumstances. "Think positive thoughts and maybe something good will happen, right?"

"It's not likely," Ellen said, frowning. "But what the hell else can you do?"

And with that she was off down the sidewalk and heading to the next house.

Sure, I thought getting into the car, it was only two dogs that had gone missing. But it crossed my mind that there was something unusual about it.

The meeting with Tobias was not until eleven, so the morning plan was to take Natey to Science Camp and stay to observe the social dynamics. I didn't want to be a helicopter mom, but in light of last week's episode involving the destruction of Natey's slime experiment, I needed to find out just what kind of glorified daycare operation Emily and her co-counselors were running.

Social dynamics were on full display upon our arrival, and as we came through the front door of the gym, I spotted Colin Blackpool acting up in typical form, this time pulling a girl's hair. If I had my campers correct, the little girl in question was Lucinda Rattner, and the counselors, whom one would think would be monitoring the children in their care, were nowhere to be seen. Lucinda's mother, however, was on the other side of the gym, oblivious, laughing and chatting with some other parents. So, with Natey in tow, I headed over to tell her what was happening to her child.

Lucinda's mother was, like the women she was talking to, toned and beautiful, wearing what I'll call expensive Pilates clothes. The kind of outfit you can wear to stretch into strange shapes without perspiring too much, before eating lunch at the Ivy. Expensive gold jewelry dangled from her ears, neck, and wrists, and she had a bag over her shoulder that I happened to know was over five thousand dollars, because Jelicka had one. I found Lucinda's mother intimidating. But at least I wasn't dressed like a schlub.

I put on my best face, telling myself I would one day be able to afford all she had, and more. But instead of this ostentatious display of wealth, I would donate most of my money to worthy causes that advanced the causes of human rights and those that saved us all from our worst impulses. I certainly didn't need to impress people with how expensive my bag was.

"Hi, are you Lucinda's mother? Because—" was all I got out before she wheeled around and finally saw her daughter crying and kicking out as Colin yanked on her hair. A second later, she and the other bejeweled moms sprinted to the other side of the gym, converging on Colin and forcibly yanking him away before he was able to tear Lucinda's lovely blonde tresses from her head. No wonder they all had athletic attire on. You never know when you'll need to be supermom.

Then these same athleisure-clad mommies unleashed a flurry of accusations at the very same Emily whom I had taken to task for her neglect of Natey the week before.

This time, Emily could hardly say, though she did, that "they were monitoring the situation," that "the cameras were catching everything," and "counselors were ready to intervene if things got out of hand."

"Things *are* out of hand," said Lucinda's mother, gold swinging. "And you're doing nothing. My daughter has been traumatized by that brat; that, that . . . future sex predator." I suppose seven-year-old hair pulling could be a gateway offense to sexual predation, but Colin was an equal opportunity bully. This time, he'd messed with the wrong little girl. Lucinda's father was a Hollywood player with power and money, and Lucinda's mother would see to it that it was wielded without hesitation. Emily and Colin were not long for Science Camp.

Generally, I don't like to see people lose their livelihoods, but part of the job description when taking care of children is just that—taking care of the children. So if you can't or won't do that, don't apply for the job in the first place.

Confident that the moms and remaining counselors had things well in hand and that Colin would pose no further trauma to Lucinda, Natey, or any other child that day, I was off to meet my former boss with hopes of a job.

Tobias and I had agreed to meet at Huckleberry, where we could have anything from drip coffee to a truffle grilled

Portobello mushroom on garlic turnip puree. A restaurant-come-gourmet-take-out, Huckleberry also provided me the opportunity to show off samples of my revolutionary baked goods to Tobias and the Huckleberry staff. I'd already slipped my box of samples to a waitress named Kate, whom I'd met on a few previous visits to the restaurant. She'd tasted some earlier efforts and had become a fan, and had even volunteered to pass on any pies, cakes, cookies, muffins, or scones I might devise to Maximo, the manager.

While it was true the restaurant policy was that all baked goods must be produced in-house, I hoped Maximo would stop by our table today after taking a bite of a Revolutionary Berry Blast Scuffin—the name still needed work—and offer me a part-time baking gig. Even if Tobias offered me a job, it couldn't hurt to have him know that Maximo wanted me, too. In fact, when Tobias heard Maximo offer me a job, he would say, "Sarah, everyone knows you can bake rings around Paul Hollywood and all the Great British Bake-off winners, but Williams Sonoma needs you!" Yes, a girl could dream, though her dreams rarely comport with reality. I gazed out the window to wait.

Tobias walked in, handsome as ever, possibly even more handsome in his perfectly fitting suit. Though still thin and elegant, there was something slightly different about his face, and I soon realized the small double chin he'd always complained of was gone. Good for him—if you don't like something, change it. Lucky for him he could afford to.

"Sarah, doll. How goes motherhood?" he said, giving me a double cheek-graze as I stood to greet him.

"Motherhood's good, matrimony not so much. You look exactly the same."

He feigned indignance. "Better, I hope."

I leaned in, whispering. "The glottal is gone?"

"Bingo. Got rid of that gizzard a year and a half ago. So long turkey neck."

I gestured for Tobias to sit.

"I wish I could get rid of this," I said, taking gentle hold of my new muffin top. "But someone has to taste my baking experiments."

I sat back down at the table Kate had secured for us at the window and reached over to adjust the blinds. "Thanks for meeting me."

"Girl, are you getting enough sleep? You are stressing; I can tell."

He was always direct.

"Well, I have a kid, and my marriage is a mess. So yes, I am stressed."

"What's my excuse?" he said scanning the restaurant. "Where's our waitress? Somebody should have been here already."

Great—he was having one of his bad attitude days. I remember those. I'd have to work even harder to stay positive.

"They're just busy," I said, aiming for a cheery tone. "The service is usually pretty good."

"You've been lucky then. I always find myself waiting to be waited on."

"Do you want to go somewhere else?"

"Never mind," he said. "I'm not that hungry. Besides, I'm here for you. So how can I help?" Like I said, he's direct.

"Oh—well, first off," I said, surprised the small talk was already over. "Thanks again. I know how busy you are."

He was watching me closely. Not mean, just assessing.

"I've told you things aren't good with Nate," I went on. "But I have a—" And just as I was about to launch into my prepared pitch, Kate reappeared to take our order.

"There you are," Tobias said.

"I'm sorry. Have you been waiting long?" Kate glanced at me. *Ugh—now I needed to handle both egos.*

"Hi, Kate," I said. "Tobias, this is Kate. She's our overworked waitress, but she's also helping me with one of the things I want to talk to you about today. Kate, Tobias Miserrochi."

Kate appraised my well-appointed companion. "Hello, can I get you two started with some beverages?"

"Lovely to meet you," said Tobias, standing to remove his jacket. "What kind of tea infusions do you have?"

Crossing her arms over her chest, Kate began the recitation. "Raspberry, lemon, ginger, thyme, pomegranate, grenache, pumpkin, coconut . . ."

"*Mmmmm* . . . anything else?"

". . . frangipani, persimmon, mandarin orange, chili pepper . . ."

"Got it. Give me the ginger-pepper-grenache."

"Three teas then?" she asked, throwing me a raised eyebrow.

"Together, please. The prophylactic properties are superb." Tobias reseated himself and turned his attention back to me.

"Well, it's different. I'll give you that," said Kate, barely concealing her amusement.

I shrugged. "Just water for me."

Kate took down the order and handed each of us a menu. "In case you'd like something else. And, oh—" she said, leaning in. "Maximo's about to taste your stuff. I'll get the scoop." She gave me the thumbs up and was gone.

"Scoop on what?" said Tobias.

"I brought over some high concept baked goods for the boss to try. It's my 'long' plan."

"The long plan," repeated Tobias. "Which means there must be a short plan. Let's not pull each other's pajamas—you want a job."

"Am I that obvious?" Clearly, my acting skills needed work.

"Don't worry about it," said Tobias, putting his hand over

mine. "I actually expected you to ask when you hinted at what was going on."

Suddenly his head shot up, his eyes panning the room for Kate. "Damn—I should have asked for breadsticks. Do you see how other people have breadsticks?" He thrust his hand up into the air, way too high. "Why didn't your friend bring us some?"

"I'm sure she will, Tobias, but you're right, I do want to go back to work and was curious about what was going on at the company, you know—if there might be any opportunities there. Obviously, I'm completely willing to start lower than where I finished."

"Well, you'd have to." He brought his hand down. "But, girl, things there have changed, changed, changed. All new people. You wouldn't recognize the place."

"You've been promoted," I said. "Which is great. You must have been involved in a lot of that change."

"Well, you know, time marches on and on and on. One can only do what one can."

It felt like he was leaving something out.

"Change is good though, right?" I said. "I mean, that's what people say. 'Embrace change!' I hope they're right, because that's what I've been telling myself, as things have not gone according to any sort of plan I might have had for my life. But for you—you must have a lot of power now."

"Oh, you'd be surprised how little power I have," he said, pulling his phone from his jacket pocket. I noticed cotton-ball sized circles of perspiration in his armpits.

A server deposited two glasses of water.

"Water but no breadsticks?"

This was addressed to me, because the server was already gone. I'd forgotten how exasperating he could be. "Toby, we'll get the breadsticks. It's busy in here."

His face—and it was not a happy face—snapped around,

his eyes narrowing on me. Was it that I called him Toby?

"I used to call you Toby, and you didn't mind."

"It's fine," he said, softening. "It's just no one's called me that since you left, so it took me a minute. But enough about me; how are you—really?"

Hadn't I told him already? Something was up with him. His tea order alone suggested a fissure somewhere. But I had to press on. I needed his help. The question was, how much of my current situation should I tell him about? I hadn't decided that ahead of time.

If I told him my marriage was over, I might seem more desperate, and desperation is never appealing. On the other hand, telling him might make him want to help me more. It was hard to gauge his state of mind and how best to present my case.

"I'm fine," I said. "I mean, well, you know, being married to Nate has been . . . challenging. I'm trying to figure out if I can stay married after all that's happened."

"After all 'what' that's happened?" He was zeroed in, concerns of missing breadsticks temporarily replaced.

"Ohhh . . . infidelities, broken promises, disappointments," I said. "The usual."

"Oh, honey, I'm sorry," he said, taking my hand again. "Have you tried open marriage? It seems to be very popular. Again. These things are cyclical."

"Tried it. It didn't help," I said, eliciting very little by way of response. "A couple needs to have good communication and lots of love if they're going to make polyamory work."

"Things you were fresh out of, I gather."

"Like they're out of breadsticks."

"The difference," he said pointing his index finger, "is this is a bakery. They shouldn't run out of breadsticks."

"Moving on from marriages and breadsticks," I said. "I'm glad you're doing well, advancing up the ladder and making money and everything, but tell me, I want to know: Do you think the same thing would have happened for me too, if I'd stayed? I mean, we started out as peers, equals really—making almost the same money. Though you're a guy, so you probably made more for doing the same work."

This last bit was only partly in jest. The muffs have had multiple "unequal pay for equal work" conversations over the years and all we do is grumble. Finding out that I, too, was a victim of this state of affairs might annoy me, but I wanted to know what kind of money I passed up by leaving the company.

"If you want my help, telling me that because I'm a guy I got paid more than I deserved is *not* the way to do it," he said. "I'm not just a 'guy.'"

I knew what he meant.

"Doesn't matter," I said. "It's the penis club. Gay or straight, and no matter the color, men have penises and, generally speaking, penises make more money than vaginas."

"Really," he said.

"I would have put on one of the muff's strap-ons if I thought I'd get into the club."

"Whose strap-on?"

"A friend's; a member of *The Muffia*. A few of them have strap-ons."

"The *Mafia*? You lie like that about the Mafia, you can forget about getting a job. You're likely to end up dead."

I held up a finger. "Hold on a sec."

A different server approached with Tobias's tea, and we waited until he'd arranged the assortment of sweeteners before continuing.

"It's my book club," I clarified once the server had gone.

"Honey, I guarantee nobody in the Mafia is much of a reader."

"Are you sure? Seems a bit of a generalization. Besides it's *Muffia.* M-u-f-f. It's an all-women's book club, so obviously we have them—muffs, that is. And, as a rule, muffs like sex toys, strap-ons included."

"As well they should." He winked.

"Not me so much," I said. "Never mind."

"No wonder your sex life went on the skids."

"Because I'm not into sex toys? Listen, forget I even brought it up. I wanted to take you for coffee because I need your advice: If Williams Sonoma won't rehire me, what would you advise if I want to stay in the field of cooking, kitchenware, design and all that?"

He sat back in his chair. "First thing is to get more specific. 'All that' is not going to cut it. People now are into very specific designing of very specific things—fork prongs for example. That's how specialized. Middle fork prong design is one big area of concentration. So you need to know what you want to do."

"Spoon or knife design, then. I'd rather not focus on one of several prongs. I'd feel competition from the other prong designers."

"This isn't a joke, Sarah," he said wearily. "How do you think we got the Spork?"

"I'm speaking to you as a friend, Tobias. We used to be friends, remember?"

He dropped his head, his expression suddenly changed. "I know; I'm sorry. And I'm sorry I can't help you."

He brought his hand up to his face, and I swore he might cry.

"Tobias?"

Then his spine shot up straight and he was back from the brink. "I was 'let go,'" he said, with no small amount of defiance. "A few days ago. An insipid consultant and former butter plate imagineer with delusions of whole store design came in and made a pitch for consolidation. After all the time I've spent getting the best people and increasing shareholder value, this is the thanks I get! Of course, he's sleeping with the CFO, so who cares about talent and experience?"

"I'm so sorry, Tobias."

"So be it," he sighed. "If you want to know the truth, I wasn't happy in corporate. It just wasn't me so in the long run; maybe they did me a favor."

"Still, it must be a shock."

"The scariest thing is, I just bought a condo, and I've never been what you'd call a saver. So if I don't rent it out, I can't possibly make the mortgage."

"That is scary."

"The good news is I have an interested party if I decide to go through with it."

"But where will you go?" I asked him.

"Oh, I don't know. Stay with a friend for a while, or do Airbnb." He gave me a wan smile. "Or you could rent me a room. Still in that cute Santa Monica house?"

I nodded. But, whoa—this meeting sure hadn't gone the way I'd expected. Tobias was in as big a pickle as I was.

"Renting me a room might defray some of your costs while we both find jobs. Dare I say, 'win-win'?"

I wondered—could I rent rooms to both Tobias and Apryl? If I did, I'd be able to pay my own mortgage. But was the house big enough?

"It might just work," I said, returning his gaze. "Right now we should probably leave. Neither one of us has any business spending money on lunch out."

"No, I've got this," he said. It was the first genuine smile since he sat down. "They haven't closed my gold card, so we are going to sit here, eat overpriced salads, drink antioxidant tea, and figure this out."

He thrust his hand in the air again, and called out, "Waitress!"

CHAPTER 8

"WELL—?" said Rachel, later that evening. I had just put her on speaker so I could pour myself a glass of red wine, the size of which was perfectly acceptable to drink alone. "What happened with your old boss?"

Her voice bounced off the metal pots and pans hanging from the two pot racks in the kitchen. I turned down the volume.

Natey was tucked into bed and the house was otherwise quiet, save for an occasional grunt from Flan, snoozing on his doggie bed nearby.

I took a sip of wine. "I'd be lying if I said it went the way I hoped."

Rachel was a funny one. From the time Nate and I were doomed to failure, she'd made more of an effort to be friends. I didn't question it, really, but just figured she thought now that we were both single, we had more in common.

But Rachel being single, and for so long, was odd in and of itself. She was smart, attractive, and successful, and yet she'd never had, for as long as I'd known her, a significant other, of any sex, for longer than a couple of months. Despite her obvious talent with a paintbrush and the fact that her art shows sold out, Rachel always struck me as a little sad. Other muffs called her brave and "nasty" in the best sense of that word. And she was all that. But to me, she often seemed angry and lost.

I'd never bought into the idea that in order to be a

successful artist one needs to cultivate angst and torment, that unless one is in pain, she can't create true art. To the extent there's any truth to this, Rachel was successful, as far as selling paintings was concerned. She made you feel she was filled with angst, and, whether related or not, she had regular showings in LA, NY, and now London, and her paintings had been purchased by people on every continent.

But whereas Rachel cultivated a certain disturbed quality, it was the subject matter of her paintings that was truly disturbing. Almost every new series she painted was about men missing something—most often a piece of their anatomy. There were whole art shows consisting of paintings featuring men missing faces or penises. But she's also painted them missing hearts, minds, and souls, though she told us the physical representation of a soul still eluded her.

It was as if, with her work, she was saying she'd never met a man who didn't have something missing. I could relate, to a point. Nate had been missing the vital "honesty" gene and the less vital "help-wife-in-kitchen" gene. But with Rachel's paintings, there was a disconnect. The muffs had tried to talk to her about it over the years, suggesting that we're all missing something—that none of us is perfect. But she maintained that we were missing the point and didn't elaborate on just what the point was. I wondered what Lloyd, our couples' shrink, would make of Rachel, and whether he'd agree with my guess that in reality, she was painting herself.

I gulped down more wine. It was not without flaws, but what did I expect for $4.99?

"What a drag," said Rachel. "What happened? Sorry I didn't call earlier. I was out helping my neighbor look for his missing dog."

"Really?" This got my attention. Of course Rachel lived in Hollywood, miles away, but I'd never heard of three dogs going missing in such a short time span. It's probably not surprising that three dogs in LA had gone missing. But what *was* surprising was I knew about it. Until the Boxer, I don't think I'd ever heard of a single one.

"What?" said Rachel.

"It's just I've heard of a few missing dogs lately," I said. "So sad."

"Tell me about it," said Rachel. "My neighbor's almost suicidal. The dog was some sort of expensive spaniel and he was her therapy dog."

We both sighed, agreeing how awful it was before Rachel broke the spell. "Back to your lunch. What happened?"

"Well, for starters," I said, guiltily pouring more wine into the glass, "Tobias just got canned himself, so he was hardly in a position to offer me a job. Beyond that, he told me Williams Sonoma recently acquired another similar company, so they're busy putting America second and 'letting people go,' as they like to say. The jobs they couldn't transfer to India, like all the minimum wage, in-store salespeople, were folded into each other and now everyone who remains is expected to work harder for less money. There's one job for what used to be four, except for fork prong, designers apparently. The point is my job no longer exists and it makes me glad I was already gone."

"Sorry I asked," said Rachel.

"On the plus side, the owner of Huckleberry likes my Revolutionary scone-muffin things and he said he'll consider me for a staff baking job as soon as someone leaves, whenever that is. I also have two prospective tenants, one of whom is that very same former colleague."

"You'd think he'd have some sort of nest egg with that salary he was getting."

"Right?! Turns out he's in deep on an expensive condo and is looking to rent while he leases out the condo and searches for another job."

"Who's the other prospect?"

"That girl I met. Did I not tell you all about her at Kiki's?" I said, digging in my handbag. *No, I don't think I did.* "She's an equestrian—trains horses, or people; maybe both."

"I've always thought that's a weird way to make a living," said Rachel. "Where'd you meet her?"

I pulled out a granola bar wrapper, followed by a crumpled paper with the phone number of Ellen Pirosh, the owner of the albino Pug, then finally Apryl Saito's business card.

"You're considering opening your home to a woman you met on the street?"

Rachel's sense of alarm seemed misplaced.

"It's not like that," I said. "She was very approachable and completely normal. Her card says she's a riding teacher and equestrian. She didn't say if she has her own horse, but horses are expensive. Maybe it's like it is with writers, actors, and other artists, you know? It's virtually impossible to make a living at it, so everyone teaches."

"I don't."

"Which is good, because you'd just scare your students," I teased. "It's no secret most artists have to support themselves with a day job. Anyway, her name's Apryl, and she seems really nice. And it's not like she doesn't have references. She texted me about fifteen of them. And get this—she's only twenty-seven and already divorced."

Rachel let out a grunt of sorts. "I wish I could say that was surprising, but I swear these days some girls just want to have big weddings right out of college so they can be divorcees before they're twenty-five."

"What a waste of money."

"Yeah, I read it somewhere, so no guarantee of its veracity," she said. "But if her references are good, she'd probably be a better roommate than your former colleague. It would be depressing having a guy around, constantly moaning about how he lost his job."

"He *is* kind of a whiner," I agreed, recorking the wine bottle and sticking it in the fridge.

"Just make sure you call her references. You can't be too careful. Crazy people out there."

"Crazy people everywhere. Thanks for calling, Rachel. It's sweet of you to worry."

"Thanks, but we both know I'm not sweet."

"No? Calling to find out how it went with Tobias was kind of sweet."

"We both know my brand is bitch."

"I regret to inform you that I don't think you *are* a bitch, regardless of the branding you're trying to achieve."

"Then I better watch myself. I don't want it to get out that I'm secretly nice. People might get confused about my mission statement," she said with a laugh. "Hey, did Jelicka pick a book yet?"

"Not that I've heard. But you know me and reading. It's probably in an email I haven't read yet." I swore this would be my last sip of wine for the evening.

She laughed. "You're too much."

"At least I'm predictable," I said. "There's no confusion over *my* brand."

"Haha. Why not turn over all your leaves at once? Go single, read a complete book, become a landlord, create a baking empire . . ."

"Sounds great," I said. "But if and when I actually have a baking empire, then I'll definitely be too busy to read."

"Sarah, the whole point of being successful is you can hire people to do the stuff you don't want to do. When you have money, you'll have plenty of time to do all the other things you never had the luxury of doing before."

That did sound good. Though still improbable. I like to

work and can't imagine stopping just to read a book.

"I wish she'd hurry up and pick something," Rachel was saying with a sort of longing. "I need to distract myself from what passes for news these days; not to mention my new painting series."

"What's the matter—painters block?"

"It's hard when you don't want to repeat yourself and the world seems to be falling apart."

"Hard, yes. But it's also a great source of inspirational material isn't it?" I said. "I mean, think about 'Presidents without Brains,' 'People without Leaders.' What's the next series called?"

"I haven't decided. It will be a continuation of people missing things, but I can't force it." She sighed. "Maybe I'll go to Book Soup and get started on some escapist beach-read-mystery-erotic-thriller until Jelicka picks something."

"I'm surprised she has time to think about books at all," I said. "What with her real estate exam and the fact she's re-reopened the investigation into Madelyn's dead Mossad agent."

"Oh my God," Rachel said, letting out a snort. "Udi. Just let the guy die already. Or admit defeat, quit real estate and become a private investigator. That's what she really wants to be, a PI."

"I think it's more of a hobby," I said. "Avocation not vocation."

But Rachel was on a roll. "She's full bore now. Did you hear? She's saying the note Quinn found in her carry-on in Japan wasn't translated correctly. Apparently—surprise, surprise—the two weeks she spent in Israel did not teach her everything she needed to know about Hebrew and the lives of Israelis abroad!"

"Well, duh," I said. "And Lauren said Quinn told her it was tucked into a bunch of travel brochures, so anyone could have written it. Some Israeli traveler wrote himself a note, tucked it into a brochure and forgot about it. Then, when he left the country, he was a responsible person and put the brochures back in the rack for another traveler to use. For all we know, it was a grocery list."

"Or hit list."

"Rachel, you're not helping."

"I'm agreeing with you! Seriously, what's the upside of investigating this? If Udi's alive and not contacting Madelyn—who believed he was the love of her life—that's not good for Madelyn. If he's dead and he really was a Mossad agent who died under suspicious circumstances, then Jelicka actually uncovering a secret operation could get us all killed. And if Udi really had a heart attack and died, then the whole pack of them have spent way too much time trying to disprove something that you and I both know was the case from the beginning."

"Jelicka has conspiracy brain disorder, and there's no cure," I said. "So much for her real estate career being a game changer. Did you hear her at Kiki's? She's going to get her Israeli friends at Peet's Coffee to send their translations of the note to a secret email address. If she's right that Udi was a Mossad agent, then the Mossad can monitor online conversations, and the 'secret email address' isn't going to fool anybody."

"*Now* who's thinking like a spy?"

I let out a laugh. "No more than you."

"The difference is," she said. "I could quit anytime. Like I said, I just need distractions."

"Go find one then. A healthy one. And thanks for calling, Rachel. I should check out those references before it gets too late."

"I'm here if you need me. Stay strong Sarah."

The phone went dead.

Stay strong? That would suggest I already *am* strong. But the only time I feel fierce is when I'm defending Natey. Short of quitting life, there was nothing to do but keep putting the one proverbial foot in front of the other.

If by tomorrow evening, no one could make me believe Apryl was a lying, thieving drug dealer and kidnapper, I'd be offering our guest bedroom to the young equestrian divorcee.

I held up my wine glass and examined the last of the swirling red liquid against the light. Then I poured it down the drain.

CHAPTER 9

HERE'S the thing about phone notifications: They're helpful when there's an emergency, but there's no easy way to screen them other than to turn off most people on your contacts list. You get a tone or tingle for everything from an Amber Alert to a ten percent discount code for sexy lingerie at a store you went to once and never will again.

But as unnecessary notifications go, Jelicka's "Good morning, wenches!" made me smile. Though I was hardly a wench as most might envision one, it was another gray Santa Monica morning, and I'd been lying in bed, once again worrying about the uncontrollable. Any opportunity to think about something else was welcome.

Wenches are bawdy. Wenches are sexy and irreverent. Once upon a time I might have pulled it off. Maybe all I needed was to cinch up a corset that would serve up my boobs on a platter and I'd feel like a sassy bar maid. It was a matter of attitude. So the next time that lingerie store pinged me, I resolved to check out what they had in the way of discount wench attire. Fake it 'til you make it, right?

Jelicka's group text was about possible dates for book club, along with a couple of choices for *The Muffia*'s next read. Apparently both possibilities were New York Times bestsellers, and, true to form, I only vaguely recognized the titles. Jelicka threatened that if we didn't respond with our book choice by tomorrow, she'd choose for us. Rachel and Paige might bristle at this direction, but I preferred it. I count on the muffs to tell me what books to read and which to avoid, so I appreciate when a hostess just picks. I don't really care about what makes a book *Muffia*-worthy. Over time, I have been able to sample their breadth of reading choices and found that they are all worthy. One thing they do agree on is what a *Muffia* book club choice is *not.*

Take *Fifty Shades of Gray.* A few muffs read it outside of book club and said don't bother, but I thought they had to be wrong—a hundred and thirty million people bought that book. It was turned into a major movie franchise with what's-her-name and what's-his-face, and even became a book club book in a terrible movie called *Book Club.*

So when Nate gave me *Fifty Shades,* (after his first infidelity, I later realized, probably in hopes of jumpstarting our sex life) I cracked it open and looked forward to telling the muffs just how wrong they were. But that thought was short-lived, since I couldn't get past the set up. Where did Christian get all his money—twenty-two and a billionaire from his own efforts? The guy never worked. He may have dressed better than Steve Jobs or Bill Gates, but those guys were busy changing the world. They didn't have time to dress up like Christian Gray and act like a demented playboy with a hardware habit and too much time on his hands.

And Anastasia? If she'd said, "Oh, my!" one more time . . . I wanted to jump into the book and hand her a thesaurus. And remember, I'm not a reader. Nor am I a wordsmith. But even *I* could find alternatives to "Oh, my!"

And though I might empathize with Anastasia wanting to help sad, lost (let's be real—richest, handsomest), Christian get over his issues, the smart-women-trying-to-rescue-damaged-men trope is played out. Anyone who's been to an Al-Anon meeting knows you can't rescue people, though no amount of saying so keeps people from trying. Maybe that's why so many people liked the book—they identify with Anastasia's hoping against hope, and the idea that if she could only save rich, handsome Christian from himself, she'd be set for life. Just as readers would like to be.

It's noble in a way, I guess. The trying. Hell, I'm guilty of it myself, hoping Nate would reform after I accepted yet another apology for his faithlessness. But I'm already married to the guy. But I digress; the point is, the muffs were right about *Fifty Shades*—not worth the paper or electronic page it's printed on. I texted back that whatever Jelicka chose was fine.

"Mom—" Natey called from his room down the hall. "Can we go to the beach today?"

Sprawled on my back, facing the ceiling, I saw the day unfolding on that expanse of white—fog burning off, sand, and the rhythmic sounds of the waves. The day needed filling, and I couldn't think of anything I'd rather do then hang with my boy on the beach.

"Sure, babe," I said. "We could take the bike, if you want." That way I'd get some needed exercise.

"Yay!"

His footfalls on the landing came shortly after, as he raced toward my room, followed by a leap onto the bed. "Yay, yay, yay, yay!"

"Hey, watch out. My legs are under there. *Ow*!" All this jumping threatened my ability to pedal.

He collapsed onto the bed and snuggled up next to me, as I realized that Flan was snuffling and snorting bedside, paws up, requesting a lift.

"Can Fwan come on the bed?"

"I can't cuddle you if Fwan's on the bed," I said, squeezing Natey's sides. It was game I loved, going for the giggle as he squirmed to escape.

"Mama—" *giggle, giggle* "—no tickwing!" Flan snorted louder. He made some feeble attempts to get on the bed, but it was too high for him to jump.

Natey was laughing so hard it hurt *me. Giggle, giggle; snort, snort.*

Then I suddenly stopped and pulled back to see his face. In this moment, I felt such overwhelming love, and the fear of losing it was devastating. "We're good, aren't we buddy?"

I wanted to take the words back as soon as I'd said them. He stopped giggling and stared. Sure, he knew Mom and Dad weren't getting along, but he didn't need to know how worried I was about it, nor about how worried I was that the rift was affecting him.

Flan started whimpering at precisely the wrong time. "Go lie down," I ordered. "Go." The dog did not obey. "You're impossible."

I picked up Natey's hand. "You miss your dad. I know," I said. "But he's still around, and he always will be. Plus, we have fun, you and me, right?"

He nodded. I wasn't convinced he agreed with me. But then he beamed. "And you made Cowin Bwagpool go away. That was awesome."

"It wasn't only me," I said, glad he refused to be pulled into my dark mood. "Colin was a bully. Other people wanted him to go away, too."

"But why is he so mean?" Now Natey's expression did grow pensive.

I considered the question from my boy's point of view, and then from my own. Sadly, I don't think bullies ever truly grow up. They just learn to bully in a more acceptable form—they're aggressive in business dealings—some to the point or being charged with embezzlement or fraud—or become mob bosses. They use their power to make unwanted sexual advances.

But the question of why some people treat others so badly is one we don't have definitive answers for. Adults often come up with multilayered responses to the question, including that the bully or perpetrator was the victim of poverty, divorced parents, being abused, or all of the above. There's also been studies saying bullying is genetic. I certainly didn't have the answer.

"Maybe Colin is unhappy, so he wants other people to be unhappy too," I said.

He considered this then nodded.

"Hey," I said, realizing. "You just said 'pool.' You said the 'L,' do you realize that?"

"Pool," Natey said again. "It's because it's at the end I can say it."

"But that's incredible, Natey! Can you say 'tool'?"

"Tool." He smiled.

"Yes! Can you say 'call'?"

"Call." His smile got bigger. Mine did, too.

"Awesome sauce. How about 'balance?'"

"Bbawance."

"That was a trick question," I said, still smiling. "Honey, this is huge! Soon those middle L's will be like the ones at the ends of words, and like every other letter in the alphabet."

I kicked off the covers. "Okay, let's go to the beach."

"Yay!" said Natey, leaping off the bed ahead of me. "I get my trunks."

"Breakfast first, and it's *I'll* get my trunks."

"I'll," he said, hitting the Ls hard.

Flan jumped up to join us and together we padded our way out of the bedroom and into the day. There was still the matter of sharing the news that we were about to have a roommate. But that could wait. Today I hoped would hold no more drama than sandcastles and ice cream sandwiches.

CHAPTER 10

"YOUR HOUSE is so pretty," Apryl said, stepping into the entryway, luggage in tow. "I am going to love living here, I just know it. And I will be a model tenant, you'll see."

That was the idea. And to ensure things went in that direction, I'd taken the precaution of putting anything of real or sentimental value—great granny's silver terrine, my engagement ring, a selection of diamond trinkets—safely away in a locked closet. Though Apryl came with great references, there was no reason to offer temptation.

The young woman stood in the entryway, having deposited her two large suitcases and a smaller duffle onto the floor. What might have been a laptop case still hung from her shoulder, making her appear more official than a mere rider of horses. And she probably was more; I hadn't probed.

While Apryl took in the living room and flea market art, Natey held tight to my leg, peering around me to assess the girl.

"And you must be Nate," said Apryl, spotting him.

I felt him pull back to a place that to him must have felt "out of sight," given the wideness of my hips.

"He's just a little shy, is all," I said. "We've mostly just had family stay."

"It's fine," said Apryl. "I'm used to it. I work with all kinds of kids teaching riding." She tried to make eye contact with Natey, but I felt him shift behind my other hip. "Don't worry,

Nathaniel. This is your house. You're the boss. But maybe you can help me figure out how stuff works?"

When I told Natey we were getting a new roommate, it sent him into a minor panic. "Will she be in my room?" he'd asked me. The drama could have been avoided had I used the word *house*mate. After all, housemate was the right word, and if I'd used it from the get-go, the conversation would have gone very differently. I was reminded again how kids keep adults honest if we let them.

"Don't worry," I'd told him, squatting down to be at eye level. "She won't be in your room. She'll be in the room where Grandpa used to stay."

"Will she want to pway in my bathtub?"

Pway, play, pray . . . in Natey's mind, there wasn't much of a difference.

"When Apryl is here, you can use my bathtub, how's that?"

He liked that idea just fine. My bathroom held all sorts of mysteries a seven-year-old found fascinating. Too many. It was Natey who'd finally located my vibrator, saying, "It yooks yike Daddy's wee-wee." He was holding the vibrator, which he'd switched on and was watching it swirl.

"I'll take that," I said, wondering where he'd pulled it from. "It shouldn't be in the bathroom. It belongs in the, um . . ."

"In the where?" He was all innocence, waiting for my answer.

"In the . . . garage," I said. "You use it to, ah—get started—I mean, start the car."

"How does it work?" He looked puzzled, as well he should.

"Yup," I said. "Sure does. It'll start 'er right up."

It *was* a valid description of what a vibrator could do. At least that was one sales pitch I'd heard—start 'er up *and* finish. Though I can't say the purple prober had done so for me. My answer seemed to satisfy him, because without a hitch, he moved on. "How do you train a horse, Mama?" he asked.

"We'll ask Apryl when she gets here, but I bet it's hard. Some horses can buck and run really fast."

"Horses don't have to say 'Ewh.'"

Huh? Oh right, he means L.

"No, they're lucky," I said. "They don't have to talk at all. On the other hand, people climb on top of them and make them do things they might not want to do, like prance and jump. So would you rather be a horse, or try to say 'L'?"

"Mmmm . . ."

He was at an age when prancing and jumping seemed more fun than work. Anyone doing still doing aerobics at age thirty knows it's hard.

"I know which I'd choose," I said.

"I want to say my letters," he said finally. "Is Aprewh yike Aprehw the month?"

"She spells it differently, but you say it exactly the same. Hey, what happened to your perfect Ls at the ends of words?"

"Oh yeah," he said. "Apryl."

"There ya go."

Natey sat on the bathtub rug and arranged his features into an expression resembling The Thinker's. "It's okay," he said finally. "She can come."

But that was last week. Hiding behind my legs now was a step backward.

Then Flan appeared from the backyard to welcome her. When she came to see the house and what would be her room, she'd fussed over him a lot. Now the little beastie was back for more.

She sat down on the floor, rubbing Flan's wriggling belly and cooing to him. She had his number, that's for sure.

Natey took all this in, and I could feel him relax. Slowly, he moved from behind me to my side, then inched forward. "That's Fwan," he said. "He's our dog."

"Yes he is," agreed Apryl, moving her hands over the Frenchie's favorite spots. "He's your very funny dog." She scratched behind Flan's neck. "You just want lots of love, don't you, you funny, funny dog?"

Flan grunted and Natey moved a little closer to the action.

"Do you want to rub him too, Natey? Hey—do you want me to call you 'Natey' or 'Nathaniel'?"

He moved even closer and joined Apryl on the floor. "I yike Nathaniew, but I have troubew with my ewhs."

"Nathaniel it is then," Apryl said, ignoring the L issue entirely. He shifted her hands on Flan's belly so that Natey had a place for his.

"I love flan," said Apryl. "Flan is your dog, but it's also that yummy custard, right?"

"And cookies," Natey quickly corrected.

Confusion clouded Apryl's face.

"I'm trying to create a flan cookie," I explained. "It's still a work in progress."

"It's a secret," Natey said.

Apryl smiled. "Well, I can keep a secret, don't worry. I'm a very good secret keeper."

"Natey, do you want to bring Apryl to her room? Maybe she can tell you how she trains horses."

He leapt to his feet, offering Apryl his hand.

Wow, there I was getting another lesson from my child—how quickly things can turn around when you're open to change.

As Natey began leading Apryl down the hall to the guest room, I made out the beginnings of her horse story:

"When I was a little girl, my father liked to go to the

racetrack, and he used to bring me with him . . ."

There had been something about the way Apryl said she could keep a secret that struck me as significant, but it would be weeks until I knew what it was.

CHAPTER 11

ANOTHER ATTEMPT at a flan cookie recipe was on its way into the oven when I heard an inconvenient knock on the front door. Inconvenient because when creating anything new in the kitchen, it's never wise to step away; especially if you're the easily distracted type like I am.

Step away from one task and an easily distracted mom sees a hundred more that need doing: Laundry, changing light bulbs, cleaning up your dog's destruction, Swiffering stairs; even just taking a shower. The list of chores is endless. And though we know we shouldn't allow ourselves to be distracted when doing something as important as creating a baking empire, my mother told me to answer the door when someone knocks, because there's always the possibility that there's something great on the other side. But because there could also be a couple of well-dressed cult members, one has to open doors carefully.

There's no peephole on our front door, and that's because I saw *Hard Target* as a kid and never got over it. In that film, a character goes to the peephole to see who's outside and—well, let's just say the bad guy who knocked puts his shotgun to the peephole and blows a hole through the head of the guy inside, using one of his pretty blue eyes as the entry point.

My technique is a lot safer. I go to the bay window in the living room and crane my neck around the curtains to see who's on the stoop.

As I craned my neck, I could make out the wild red hair

of the woman who'd accosted us while I was getting Natey in the car for Science Camp. What was her name—Aileen? She'd been looking for her dog, that much I remembered.

"Good morning," I said quickly, moving to the foyer and pulling the door open.

"Oh, hi," she said. "Nice to see you again. I was just going around the neighborhood one more time, trying not to give up hope."

"You haven't found your dog, then?" Stupid thing to say. It was obvious. The poor woman was exhausted. "Would you like to come in for a minute . . .?"

"Ellen, Ellen Pirosh."

"That's right, Ellen. She's a Pug—your dog, I mean."

Ellen nodded, shuffling some papers in her hand. "Albino Pug, yes."

She stepped into the foyer just as Flan came racing in from the backyard through the hall, leaping onto the couch and assuming his favorite position: Paws on the back of the couch and barking, this time at a Schnauzer named Schnickers innocently strolling by with his owner on the far sidewalk.

"Flan, cut it out," I said, without much conviction. "You've seen Schnickers a hundred times."

"You found *your* dog," said Ellen, her voice filled with longing.

"Yes, we were lucky. He was a few blocks away, hoping a cat would fall out of a tree."

"Well," she said, sniffling and close to tears. "You better keep an eye on him. French Bulldogs are valuable to dognappers too, just like Pearlie Girl is, or was. They go for lots of money in Colombia."

"Is that true?"

I suspected that if a dognapper knew about Flan's peculiarities, he or she would pass him over as a resale prospect. People who are guilty of receiving stolen goods often are quite discerning, and a farting Frenchie is no one's idea of the perfect dog.

"Excuse me a second," I said, ducking into the bathroom and quickly returning with a box of tissues, which I placed within her reach.

"Oh, yes. Colombia's just one of the hotspots," Ellen went on, dabbing her eyes. "Miami, London . . . I've been doing a lot of research, and it's become a worldwide epidemic." She sighed. "I can only comfort myself knowing if Pearlie went to Colombia, they don't eat dogs there."

"That is a relief."

"But this time—" said Ellen with a quick change in demeanor. "*This* time, I'm going around to tell people that Pearl is not the only dog that's gone missing."

I'll admit that originally I thought Ellen was just being dramatic. She just *looked* dramatic. But now I flashed on the picture of the Boxer dog on the community bulletin board, and remembered Rachel's neighbor's dog—*what kind of dog was that?* Could there really be a band of dognappers? Not that that should be surprising. Some people will take pretty much anything if they think they can get away with it.

How many dog are there?

"A Bichon Frise from Bay Street, a Maltese on Magdelena, and a Norfolk Terrier on Tenth. Anybody with a purebred under forty pounds, watch your dog! Hell, not just the under forties; they're all vulnerable. People have to train their dogs to kill."

"I don't know about that," I said.

"Well, something has to be done to stop it," she said. "In the meantime, I made these." She handed me a flyer: MISSING: MULTIPLE DOGS. "Check out item three."

I scanned the flyer until my eyes settled at the appointed spot. "People who steal dogs often operate in rings and target a house with chalk marks."

"There's a 'C' written in pink chalk on the curb in front of your house. Don't worry, I rubbed it off."

"A pink 'C'?"

"According to an article I read on the Internet, a 'C' probably means 'chien,' which is French for dog."

"What do the cops say?" I asked.

"They don't know anything; they don't speak French. Besides, it's not always a C. The thieves use different letters and numbers. Probably their own perverted code."

"No, I mean about the dognapping? Can't they do anything?"

"Well, you know. The cops always *seem* sympathetic, don't they? But they say there's nothing to be done. Just 'keep our eyes open,' and 'report suspicious behavior.' They tell you to 'keep your dogs with you.' Hell of a lot of good that does. I've heard of dognappers coming up and yanking leashes right out of owners' hands, dog attached, thank you very much."

"Sheesh, that's disturbing."

"And what's the point of having chips put in your dog if they don't get scanned when somebody who doesn't own them tries to bring them on an airplane? If they scanned every dog, I bet they'd find a lot of dogs are owned by somebody else!"

"Maybe they're being smuggled out on little airplanes or trucks and not commercial jetliners?"

"Chips, schmips," Ellen said. "It's a scam if they don't get scanned or if they can be taken out so easily."

"I've heard chips can be pretty effective, actually."

Now I had her full attention. "Really? What have you heard?"

The chip I was referring to was Udi's, Madelyn's Israeli heartthrob, the one Jelicka thought was still alive.

"Never mind," I said, "that was a Mossad agent with a chip, not a dog."

"Mossad agents are chipped?" she asked, incredulous.

"Apparently, and in his case the chip even worked. His people tracked him to my friend's house where he lay dead."

Ellen's jaw dropped open. "A Mossad agent with a chip was dead in your friend's house? Who *are* you?"

"My friends are ex-screenwriters with active imaginations," I said. "I have no proof of any of it."

Though Ellen was more intrigued than concerned, I didn't want to be the subject of any new rumors.

"I'd believe it," she said. "It's another example of people thinking they're superior, putting higher quality chips in people than animals. Makes me sick." She thrust a bunch of flyers into my hands. "Here—post them anywhere you can in a hundred-block radius."

She turned to go. "By the way, something sure smells good in here."

"Oh God, my cookies!"

I rushed Ellen out and bolted for the kitchen.

CHAPTER 12

GIRLS *&* *Sex: Navigating the Complicated New Landscape* is probably an important book that should be read by women everywhere. But Jelicka's pick for the next meeting of *The Muffia* had yet to inspire me. It didn't help that Jelicka picked it because she said it would piss us off. Did she think that was a motivator? She even went so far as to say we'd be comforted by seeing, in print, all the stuff we're always talking about, which is to say all the stuff muffs—read: women—have to put up with on a daily basis. I'm sorry, but I don't need a book to tell me things I already know about the pressures of being female. Yay, Peggy O. for putting it in writing for those who somehow missed it, but the challenging aspects of living the female life are in stark relief, thank you. If they became any more stark it would only make me want to shoot something.

And shooting is exactly what Jelicka had in mind. As part of hosting her next book club, she was proposing the muffs wrest power back from the universe and what she called "the very real possibility of *The Handmaid's Tale* becoming reality" and take a group field trip to her favorite shooting range in Oxnard, about an hour west up the coast.

Jelicka's point was that *Girls & Sex* was a wake-up call, which meant we all needed to become better prepared for anything that might happen. Several muffs had already spent an afternoon at Shooter's Paradise and claimed to find the shooting of paper pedophiles empowering. Madelyn, Quinn, and Rachel went there just before they took down the porn house next to Kiki's—without guns, I might add.

Madelyn told me that Rachel, the healthy, yoga-practicing vegan, had really gotten into it at Shooter's Paradise, her bullets ripping through the target of a full-body paper rapist, tearing it to smithereens. I told Madelyn not to worry, because Rachel was just fired up over her latest series of paintings. She'd been trying to finish Men Missing—and here I couldn't remember which body part—for a while, so shooting the body parts off a target was just what Rachel needed to fire her up enough to finish the series. As I recall, she completed it in two weeks.

I would not be joining the next muff posse to Paradise, even if I had my own share of things to get fired up about.

First, it turns out Colin Blackpool was back at Science Camp. Apparently Colin's father was an executive at Disney, and he made a ridiculously large donation to the umbrella corporation under which the camp operated. They "couldn't say no," even if it did come with one major string attached; that string being Colin had to be welcomed back to Science Camp with open arms. That was bad enough. But worse, or so it seemed to a few of us, while he was away, Colin had devised several new ways of bullying Natey and the other kids. Sure, we could have pulled our kids out of camp, but it's the principle of the thing, right? We, ordinary non-deep-pockets parents had to fight back.

Second, and of far greater concern, was that Nate Sr. had still not delivered on his promise to pay the rest of the mortgage. Where did he think I'd get the money?

I couldn't charge Apryl any more money for the guest room, and the thought of going through another round of job board searching and applications that never got responded to filled me with gloom. Thus far, my job-seeking efforts revealed that I'd been off the market for too long and would need retooling to get back to where I was when I stopped working. Why would a new job board be any different? And if I took the kind of job I might get as a barista or waitress, I'd have to pay a nanny more than I was making to watch Natey.

While I still had dreams that my baked goods empire would ultimately be bigger than Tate's and Mrs. Fields, my flagship flan cookies weren't there yet. The recipe was almost there, one could taste it. But I still needed a business plan and a huge cash infusion if there was any hope of scaling up.

It all felt like something that might never happen. And I needed money *now*. So, when I found myself sitting in another therapy session with Nate, going over the same ground, I was ready to blow.

Nate pulled off his glasses and ran his hand down his face, resting two fingers between his eyes in a display of weariness. "Sarah only wants money from me."

"Hold on," I said. "You said you'd give me the money for the mortgage and you haven't. How am I the bad person? Didn't you also sign the loan papers? We have a mortgage!"

Nate had no answers. I was sick of it.

Lloyd, seated across from us in his familiar office, did not offer me his box of Kleenex. I got the impression he was sick of us, too.

"What sort of progress have each of you made since last session?" Lloyd asked, calmly sipping from his porcelain teacup.

"Yes," I said. "I would be very interested to find out what, if anything, Nate, you have done this week toward making a positive change from your, excuse me, *our* current state."

"Nate, can you do that?" said Lloyd. "Tell Sarah what she wants to know?"

There was a silence that no one filled during which Lloyd, sipping his tea, looked from me to Nate and back again.

"I'll go first," I said, launching into the void, recounting everything I'd done for the last month, not just week, from my meeting with Tobias, to bringing Apryl in as a paying boarder, to sending out resumes and my baking progress.

There was another silence.

"Nate?" Lloyd finally asked. "It seems like Sarah is doing her best to turn things around. What kind of steps have you taken this week?"

Nate ran his hand down his face again and put his glasses back on. He seemed so tired and I did feel for him, but in the way a person often feels for something helpless. I wanted to feel more than that for the man who was still my husband and my son's father. I wondered how other women handle it when they watch their husbands implode.

I did promise to love him and care for him until death do us part. Why does that promise become an idle one for so many, myself included? Why is that promise included in marital vows when so many couples part long before death?

We'd been in love once, Nate and me. All our available time we'd spend together, taking day trips to favorite hikes, checking out wineries in the Santa Ynez Valley. For years and years, I felt passion for him. When our careers were at their most promising, we'd often meet up for a quick rendezvous at a hotel, not caring what it cost, because we just had to feel each other. That feeling carried us through the early years of our marriage. We found our house together, and together we made Natey. But then I stopped working, Nate's career faltered, and everything changed.

Now I felt he regarded me with a combination of tolerance and loathing, like I was his mother telling him to get his life together. It wasn't the way any woman wants her partner to feel about her. If he could give me a little something, a little hope that he'd change for real and make me believe him, maybe I could be pulled back from the point of no return. But with every meeting, the line between us only threatened to become a wall. I didn't want to be single, but that's where I was headed—alone, like so many other women. But the alternative of staying with someone who didn't love me, and who, with his behavior, was demonstrating daily that he had given up on us was worse.

"Never mind," I said.

Nate looked up. "What?"

"I can't do this anymore." I glanced at Lloyd, then back to Nate. "I know we're not supposed to do anything rash or act too quickly, but it's been over a year since Maddie saw you in the Tapas bar. We can't keep doing this. We need to take a break."

Lloyd put down his teacup and started cleaning his glasses. "If I might suggest . . ."

"What does that mean?" Nate said, ignoring him. "'Take a break'? Aren't we already taking a break? How long *is* this break? Am I supposed to put everything on hold?"

I stared at Nate, realizing he was once again making our situation all about him. No—that wasn't right. What I'd come to understand was that with Nate, it had always been about him—what he was going through, what he needed and wasn't getting. Some part of me had probably always known it. It was just something I hadn't wanted to admit. I realized now that he'd never even thanked me for giving up my job—my *career*. Because it had been a career, something that I could grow with. But Nate assumed I'd want to give it up—for him. After the fact, he said he'd thought I'd want to quit once Natey was born. In one way, for Natey, I *had* wanted to quit. But not for Nate. And now we were busted and broke.

Silly me. All this time I'd been thinking about where *we* were, and all he could think about was himself.

CHAPTER 13

"MAMA, MAMA—!"

My eyes scanned the giant room for the child, but he was nowhere in sight. Not that he should have been, because he didn't belong here. Kathleen King, empress of Tate's Bake Shop, and Debbie Fields, cookie maven of cookie mavens, were battling it out for which of them would be crowned Bestest-Best Cookie Maker of all Time. Chocolate chips, blocks of butter, and bags of brown sugar flew across my field of vision, all landing on or near the combatants who were too busy to notice me quietly baking nearby. Both were slowly being buried in piles of cookie ingredients and the man holding the crown appeared worried indeed.

"Mama!"

Damn that child. Did Kathleen or Debbie have a kid? Why hadn't she left him at home!

The combatants were covered now, with only their heads and hands above the mountains of wasted ingredients. The man with the crown was unsure sure what to do. And with Kathleen and Debbie now gasping for air, he saw me, looked down at the crown, and began walking my way.

"Mama!"

The man lifted the crown over my head, but then someone pushed me. Was there another baker aspiring to the crown? "Get back! This crown is mine!"

"Mama, wake up!"

The crown—so close—eluded me. If I could just—but

the pushing continued.

My eyes fluttered open.

I flipped over to see Natey. He was shaking me.

So close. I'd been so close.

"I'm awake!" I said, running a hand over my face.

"Mama, can I have a horse? I want a horse."

"Give me a minute, Natey. I was having a really good dream."

Horse? Natey had never mentioned wanting to ride, let alone have a horse. It appeared that Apryl was working some sort of magic on him.

"I thought boys don't ride horses."

"Inigo Montoya rides horses in *Princess Bride*," he said, dead serious.

"Really? I only remember, 'I am Inigo Montoya. You killed my father. Prepare to die.' Then there'd be a sword fight." I didn't bother pointing out that this occurred in a movie—a fairy tale, at that.

"He awso rides a horse, a white horse!"

Clearly I hadn't been paying attention. Natey knows his *Princess Bride.*

"When they escaped Prince Humperdink's castle! You don't remember?"

A vague image of the scene came to mind. "Oh, yeah, when they rescued Buttercup. You're right—the three of them were on matching white horses."

"Aprw says riding horses buiwds character."

"Well, she's a little biased, don't you think?"

"What's biased?"

I wondered if this was a direction I wanted to go this morning. "Is Apryl going to buy you this horse?"

"Huh?" Natey thus far had remained blissfully ignorant of the family's financial straits, but even if we were flush, it was difficult to imagine owning a horse.

"She says she can bring me to the barn one day and give me a yesson 'cause I'm not too wittew anymore. There's a dog there named Rotten. He's a Wottwiewer."

"Let's not be lazy with our letters, just because you're excited, Natey—"

"My name is Nathaniew."

"All right . . . Nathaniel. You know you can say 'R' so, come on—'Rottweiler.'"

"Rottweiwer."

"Good." I repeated the word again, getting the same result. Then, because he'd been doing so much better when the "Ls" came at the end of the word, I repeated just the first two syllables. "Say 'Rott-weil.'"

"Rott-weil," Natey said perfectly.

"Great! Now say 'Rott-weil-er."

"Rottweiwer."

It wasn't going to happen this morning. "You can go to Apryl's barn," I said. "But I'm coming, too. I want to see this Rotten dog myself."

"He isn't rotten. His name is Rotten."

It was a rotten name. But Apryl had said it was appropriate for the dog in question.

"Can we bring Fwan?"

"We'll need to ask Apryl, but it'll probably be okay if we keep him on a leash."

Natey stood up on the bed and began bouncing.

"Hey—watch my legs," I said trying to protect myself. "I'm still recovering from the last attack of the dreaded bouncing Nathaniel."

He giggled as the bouncing only went higher. "My name is Inigo Montoya, prepare to die!"

"Shhhh, Apryl's sleeping," I said, before he collapsed onto the bed next to me and put his hand on my face.

"You didn't kill daddy. He just lives somewhere else now."

My heart hurt.

"There was a study done in New Zealand? Or maybe it was England," Apryl was saying later, the sun still moving toward midline. "The researchers found that people who ride horses are more determined, enthusiastic, structured, and balanced than non-riders. They also showed greater leadership, were more assertive, and demonstrated greater resilience."

"Seems to me researchers say that about pretty much everything they're paid to do research on," I said. "I think I've heard the same thing about aquatarians."

"Who?" She leaned toward me, pushing her tea aside, then whispered, "It's that last part I thought might be helpful, you know, resilience. Because of the kid that's bullying Nathaniel."

I looked at her. "Doesn't it take years to develop these skills?"

She shrugged. "Depends."

"On what?" I asked. "The horse?"

It seemed equally plausible that if a nasty nag threw its young rider off repeatedly, his confidence and assertiveness could be destroyed.

Across the room, Natey was watching—what else?—*The Princess Bride*; only this time he was probably hoping to pick up riding tips.

"Not necessarily," Apryl said. "Though a good horse can speed things up. Nathaniel has already demonstrated animal empathy. You can see how he is with Flan. I have a feeling horses will take to him, and he'll pick things up really quickly."

Oh God, what if he really started asking for a horse? That would be out of the question. Maybe we shouldn't even start down that road.

"We can't buy a horse, Apryl," I said, making it very clear.

She shook her head. "You wouldn't have taken me in as a boarder if money wasn't an issue, I know that. But if people want to ride, they find a way." She gestured at the screen. "Inigo Montoya didn't have his own horse."

"He apparently stole horses from rich princes. That's not a lesson I want Natey to learn."

She let out a laugh. "Seriously, a lot of professional riders don't own their own horses. We're paid to ride other peoples' horses."

"Who insures you if you fall?"

Apryl shrugged. "Usually, if the owners are nice. Anyway, I love the horse world, but I've also realized it'll take a miracle for me to make it rich."

"Join the club," I said, having reached a similar conclusion about my own prospects.

"Takes money to make money, right? So I'm considering other options, including going back to school."

"Always good to have more skills," I said. It struck me that Apryl was a person quite capable of anything she set her mind to.

On screen, Westley, played by Cary Elwes, was swinging on a rope, while Mandy Patinkin as Inigo Montoya was nowhere to be seen.

"I don't want to be presumptuous," she said. "*Buuuttt* . . . I have a solution if Natey wants to ride. One of my clients owns a horse. He's what we'd call bomb-proof. Literally, a horse that can have a bomb go off next to him and he won't move."

"Is he deaf?" I asked, which was a perfectly legitimate question.

Apryl laughed. "No. He's just very gentle and trusting. They said I could teach lessons off him. He's older, but likes to have a job."

"I can't pay you," I said. "I can't even deduct it from rent.

We need the cash."

"No, I get it," she said. "Absolutely. The only thing it will cost you is time and gas. Just come up to the barn and let Nathaniel take one lesson. He may hate the whole experience and that'll be the end of it."

Hmmmm . . . I took in the screen again, and this time saw Inigo Montoya wielding his sword.

"*Thwack, clack, crack*!" Natey said, giving Flan the blow by blow.

It was probably better to let him try riding than to resist. Otherwise it could become one of those moments of parental denial he'd remember forever.

"Deal," I said, turning back to Apryl. "I guess I should be happy he doesn't want to be a swashbuckler.

CHAPTER 14

WITH EVERY new batch of flan cookies, I was baking my way closer to my dream.

Natey and Apryl, my regular tasters, always reacted enthusiastically even when they weren't able to give precise reasons for their enthusiasm. I'd get words like "chewier" or "crunchier" from one batch to the next. Both were positive, if somewhat contradictory descriptors. Still, I knew the cookies were getting better.

The trouble was Natey and Apryl devoured the cookies so quickly I hadn't been able to figure out just how long they'd stay fresh—let alone crunchy or chewy—and under what conditions. I needed to find the answer to both questions if I was going to create a consistent, winning cookie recipe.

So I'd resorted to hiding cookies under my bed, and in the refrigerator and freezer using a labeling system designed to make any who discovered them believe the contents were frozen chicken, edamame, chili—anything other than cookies. It was the only way I'd get them out of the house for outside tasters. Recent tastings with a couple of muffs, and some of the moms from Science Camp, confirmed to me that I was ready to go to the next step.

I had just put a new batch of cookies in the oven when the doorbell rang. Natey was at camp and Apryl was at the Equestrian Center in Topanga—the barn, as she called it, where Natey and I would soon be going for his first lesson. Though he had yet to sit on a horse, it seemed like he was already demonstrating some of the traits Apryl said so many horse people display—leadership, assertiveness, confidence, even kindness—and it was the last of these that he'd used on Colin Blackpool, with surprising results.

The new head counselor, Sandra—promoted after Emily departed in shame over the Lucinda hair-pulling episode—had called a few days earlier to tell me that Natey had Colin in tears. But in a good way.

According to Sandra, Colin had been sitting on Chloe Moritmer's hair, and she was screaming and couldn't get up. Natey went over and "told Colin he understood why he got so mad and acted mean to people, but that it wouldn't do any good to sit on Chloe's hair." Then Natey told Colin about how his father "wasn't around lately and that he was sad about it, and that maybe Colin was upset because his father wasn't around much, either, but that sitting on people and pulling their hair wouldn't make their dads do anything different." This, according to Sandra, had made Colin sad, and he got off Chloe's hair and got more choked up. So Natey led him away and proceeded to tell him the story of Westley, Inigo Montoya, Buttercup, and the entire story of *The Princess Bride* and now "Colin was acting very nice to the other kids."

"You have a young diplomat on your hands," Sandra said, impressed.

"Who would have thought?" I said. "He's an interesting kid, all right."

It was hard to imagine Colin changing so quickly. But perhaps Natey caught him at a vulnerable moment when he was ready to stop playing the bully. He also could have been warned that, despite his father's wealth, he couldn't bully indefinitely. When Natey started talking to him, he was reminded of the warning.

Regardless of the reason, the effect was that Colin was no longer bullying Natey, which was all I really cared about.

The doorbell rang again, and I hurried to the bay window to do my neck craning routine. At this hour, it was probably someone asking for money, preying on lonely housewives who'll talk to almost anybody. But I, despite outward appearances, was not a lonely housewife. I told myself I was too busy with Natey, the muffs, and my cookie dreams to be lonely. Apryl was usually around, too, and she'd proven to be a good tenant—self-sufficient and sociable without being needy. She was often in the house on those rare evenings Natey was with Nate Sr. and, though we kept mostly to ourselves, it was nice having her around. So lonely I was not; if this solicitor was bent on luring me into conversation, he or she would not get it from me. And depending on what they looked like, I might not even open the door.

I found, to my surprise, that it was Tobias. How had he gotten my address? But then Natey's baby shower flashed through my mind, and I remembered thinking he'd been so out of place that day eight years ago amid all the strollers, bouncers, Baby Bjorns, and female energy.

It had been kind of him to come to the shower and, as snarky as he is capable of being, he was on his best behavior. Dapper dressed, as always, he'd worn a dove-gray suit with a lavender tie, and I remember him looking like Easter, not that I'd know. Easter wasn't a holiday I celebrated growing up. Neither had Nate. Was it significant that we hadn't experienced egg dying, rolling eggs along a grassy knoll in pastel-colored outfits? The closest either of us ever came to an Easter ritual was eating the heads off chocolate bunnies. Too bad that hadn't been enough for a successful marriage.

Now Tobias was on the stoop in dark gray sweats, his complexion gray, as well.

"Hi," I said pulling the door open. "What a surprise!"

He held a small, black tote bag in one hand and his

demeanor suggested he hadn't been sleeping. "I was in the neighborhood," he said. "I was concerned you might have moved, so I thought I'd stop by."

"Not yet," I said. "The mortgage was tough this month, but I paid it."

He moved his tote bag from one hand to the other.

"My girlfriend tells me I could drag the whole thing out for a year if I had to," I said, backing away from the doorway. "Come in. What's up?"

He shuffled a little on the stoop before stepping inside.

"Remember what we were talking about at that horrible bakery?"

"Huckleberry is a very good bakery, Tobias."

"Any place where I have an unpleasant memory goes on my shit list. Funnily enough, it's mostly bakeries."

"Lucky you live in a city where there's a good bakery every mile of paved paradise."

He let out an exaggerated exhale. "Joni is so underappreciated by today's youth."

What? It took me a couple of seconds to catch his Joni Mitchell–paved paradise connection.

"A lot of things are underappreciated by today's youth," I said, closing the door. "Of course we don't always appreciate their music, either."

"I love Joni, particularly her Thelonius Monk period."

Now he was going dreamy-eyed, and I had things to do. "Yes, I remember what we were talking about. I was asking you to help me find a job at the company we started at together, when you announced you'd just been fired and thus could be of little assistance."

From where he stood in the foyer, he scanned the living room. "I still like shabby chic. I don't care what anyone says."

"No snark, Toby."

"You are not to call me that in front of anyone. And who's

snarking? Decors are cyclical. It'll come back around. Ugh, I'm a mess," he said, deflating. "My real name is Kevin."

"You're a mess because your real name is Kevin?"

"I was named after my father—homophobe that he revealed himself to be. When I was old enough to call myself what I wanted, Kevin had to go. Funny that my first boyfriend out of college was named Kevin. What does that say, I wonder?"

"I could ask Lloyd."

Tobias narrowed his eyes.

"Our marriage counselor. Attractive, single. No idea about his sexual orientation though," I said. "So what's this about?"

"I don't know my own orientation at this point, but it's all headed south."

He dropped his bag and moved into the living room. "I have always been employed. I've always done the right thing, always done what my parents wanted. I mean, I'm gay, and they weren't too thrilled about that, but I'm talking about being a contributing member of society. If I'd been gay *and* a drain on taxpayers, I'd have been written out of the will. So Kevin Sr. cannot find out about the unemployment!"

"Can I get you some tea or something? Here, sit down," I said, leading him to a chair.

He remained standing, but Flan took the opportunity to sit and assess the new person. "Toby, meet Flan."

"Charmed, I'm sure. A Frenchie was just stolen from a woman in my building."

"Are you serious?"

He looked at me blankly. "What?"

"That makes four dogs that have been stolen. There has to be some sort of organized ring of dog thieves."

He sighed, nonplussed into a chair.

"Desperate times call for desperate measures."

"That's no defense," I said. "They're living creatures and

peoples' loving pets."

"All right, then let's round up the bad guys and watch 'em fry."

I decided I didn't want to know if he meant it.

"Anyway," I said returning to a safer subject, "you're very employable. It's just going to take a while to find the right position."

Flan was now on Tobias' lap, wriggling with the joy of having a human's undivided attention. Tobias was charmed.

"You are a delightful little package aren't you?"

"He can be," I said.

"And he is a lovely custard color. I could eat you up, you're so cute."

Suddenly he stopped rubbing and faced me, all business. "Okay, enough small talk. Have you thought any more about renting me a room? I can pay you $1500 a month, possibly more if I had my own bathroom."

I hadn't given the idea any thought but I managed to keep my jaw from dropping. I'd only been charging Apryl $800.

"And if you haven't thought about it, think about it now. I'm a tidy, grown up man who won't make a mess—when have you had one of those?—and as I pointed out before, it's a win-win. You get to pay your mortgage and you help me save money and my condo while I find a job."

What flashed into my mind was, if I could have both Apryl and Tobias as tenants, my mortgage would be covered and then some. The issue was, where would I put him?

"My stars, something smells good," he said, prompting me to look at my watch. "Better than Hucklefuck by a longshot."

"Would you stop."

"With the country divided on everything else, why not bakeries?

Fine, I'll shut up about Fuckleberry." He went back to stroking Flan but it was obvious he wanted an answer.

If I could somehow make him a second tenant, I'd be set. But how? Could we do a quick garage conversion? No. There was no money for it, and garage conversions are never "quick." Could Natey and I share a room? No, that would be inappropriate, and both tenants would rightfully look askance. Could I move into Nate's former study? That might work with a little rearranging of furniture. I'd use the half bath downstairs and shower upstairs after Apryl left the house. And that would give Tobias his en suite bathroom.

"What *are* you cooking in there?" said Tobias, disrupting my calculus. "Smells amazing."

"Cookies. If you're good, I'll give you a couple."

"Tell me what I need to do," he said, smiling. "I can be very good."

"Here's the thing," I said, getting to the point, "I already took on that tenant, the young horsewoman I told you about. She's renting the guestroom, and it's working out pretty well. She's quiet and really good with Natey."

His despondence was palpable. "That's how I would have been."

"There might still be a way. How long do you think you'll be out of work?"

He let out a sigh. "I have no idea. It's a tough market, as you've discovered."

I hesitated, but only for a second. "I'd consider giving up the master suite for a little more—say $1650? We could try it for a month and see."

I could see him weighing his options as the idea grew on me.

"That's a little more than I wanted to spend. But it is a nice neighborhood and I suppose we could, as you say, try it for a month. Will you be making cookies regularly?"

"My cookies!" I was in the kitchen, puling them from the oven as the alarm went off.

"What kind of cookies are they?" said Tobias, watching over my shoulder, as I put the trays of carmelized cookies on the counter. "They smell outrageous, but they're so . . ."

"Plain?" I suggested. "They may look plain, but they're a taste explosion. I've been trying to develop a consistent recipe that can scale so I can sell them somehow."

Tobias grabbed the spatula hanging on the rack and lifted a cookie from the pan.

"Tobias, they need to cool."

"And you need to cool it," he said, blowing on the cookie then cocking his head. "If I go for the $1650, do I get a closet? I need a closet."

"Yes," I said. "I'll clear out a closet so you have a place for your vast wardrobe. I know how important it is for you to be perfectly dressed for every occasion."

"You mean like today?" He gestured, self-deprecatingly, to his sweats. But he was being disingenuous. Dick's Sporting Goods they were not.

He blew on his chosen cookie once more, then lifted it off the spatula and popped it into his mouth. He chewed, assessed, and chewed some more. Then swallowed.

"If you keep these available at all times, you have a deal. Bakery-schmakery, who needs a bakery when you have Sarah Pizzo?"

CHAPTER 15

GIRLS & Sex remained unopened at my bedside. I felt I deserved credit just for having checked it out of the library, but now its cover reprimanded me whenever I was in the room. "Read me," it said. "Read me now!"

I covered it with the latest circular from Trader Joe's.

Why had I bothered taking it out of the library if I wasn't going to read it? I felt no pressure from the muffs; not one of them expected me to read *Girls & Sex*—or any other book, for that matter. And now there was a new reason not to read it, a generous and selfless reason—I'd be disrupting an established pattern.

According to a recent episode of *Hidden Brain* on NPR, if I were to suddenly start reading the books, it might disrupt the rhythm of the group, which could then lead to an imbalance within *The Muffia.*

Shankar Vedantam, the host of *Hidden Brain,* interviewed social scientists, anthropologists, and psychologists, all of whom agreed that changing the way things are done within a group can undermine group dynamics, which can then lead to the disintegration of the group, and ultimately, civilization.

All right, that's a little extreme, but the podcast delved into things like how eBooks have altered the publishing industry in how people read; or how cars and planes altered how we travel. I know we're just talking about my book club, but the analogy still holds. If I started reading all of a sudden,

I could be a "disruptor." My non-reader status is so firmly cemented in who I am and what the muffs think of me, that if I were to become a reader, it could have devastating consequences. Or so went my rationale for not reading on this particular evening.

Still, I would have risked it all if the book promised to be a romp of a story involving girls having fun sex. Since I was having no sex myself, why not get my kicks from reading about others enjoying sensual pleasures? And in so doing, I might even get myself worked up enough to pull out my purple rabbit and go at it.

Where had I put that purple rabbit? Had I tossed it after I saw Natey playing with it in the bathroom that day? Note to self: Find the vibrator.

The thing is, *Girls & Sex* wasn't a "fun" book. Neither a bodice ripper nor erotic thriller, it was three hundred pages of tragic anecdotes and case histories with statistics about the crap girls put up with from the time they reach sexual viability. It was probably more about bad sex than good sex. So, no—I'd rather read the Trader Joe's circular and find out about sales on locally sourced cheeses.

Maybe I'd crack it open right before book club and read about child prostitutes, but for now I left the book covered on my bedside table, which was formerly Nate's desk, in what was formerly Nate's study, and now my bedroom since Tobias's arrival.

I was alone in the house. Natey was with his father, Apryl was away at a horse show in a place called Portuguese Bend, which sounded more like a Pilates move than anything equestrian, and Tobias had an interview. Funny that just a short while ago I relished the quiet and having the house to myself. But I'd already grown used to, and now even missed, having everyone around.

When I heard a commotion in the backyard, I knew it could only be Flan. It sounded like one of those televised wildlife programs in which a large animal chases a smaller one into the African underbrush with the usual result. With Flan, in the wilds of our Santa Monica backyard, the only smaller animal he could logically be chasing would be a rat or mouse. Both made me squeamish, but either was better than thinking Flan was the creature being pursued. And if a larger animal *was* back there, it could only would mean there was access to the backyard, which also meant that Flan might escape again.

I left the room and moved quickly across the obstructed distance—shoes, cleaning supplies, dog toys—through the kitchen and laundry, to the back door. As I was about to put my hand on the door knob and call out, the scurrying and scratching stopped, replaced with another sound.

It was a voice, a human voice. Could it be the meter reader? No, I thought. The meter wasn't in the backyard.

Multiple thoughts traveled over my synapses at once, and I backed away from the door.

From where I stood, I could not see Flan but could make out the walkway on the side of the house through the kitchen window.

Someone in a hoody was standing at the open gate. He, or she—I couldn't tell—had opened the gate and was talking to Flan in a cooing, coaxing voice.

A vision of Ellen Pirosh and her missing dog flyer hit me like a box o' rocks as I watched the hoodied person—a man, I was sure now—reach into his pocket and pull out a Pupperoni stick. Yikes, Flan loved those.

There was no time to waste. Flan was about to be dog-napped, and I needed a weapon. A quick assessment of my surroundings revealed little, so I tucked a frying pan under my arm, grabbed the Swiffer, and yanked open the back door.

"Hey," I said. Then with as firm a voice as I could muster:

"Get out of here, or I'm calling the police."

The hoody bolted, and yes, it had to be a guy. At least I'd never seen a woman run like that, not even on the US Women's Soccer team where the women are beasts in the best sense of the word. The trouble was, Flan liked the chase-me game and took off after the guy.

"Flan," I shouted. Then with greater force, "Flan!"

The dog paid me no mind. There was nothing to do other than start running, too, which is difficult in Birkenstocks while carrying a frying pan and a Swiffer. Down the back steps I ran, noticing ahead of me that Hoody had dropped the Pupperoni. I let the pan go, picked up the Pupperoni, and shouted with even greater conviction, "Flan! Cookie!"

Flan stopped. Then I stopped. The little guy turned to face me, and I held up the Pupperoni. "Treat?"

I could feel myself starting to tear up, my voice cracking. "Flan, here—cookie?"

Flan and I stared at each other in this pivotal moment. I had to admit we hadn't bonded as much as we should have, Flan and me. He was obstinate and had a chip on his shoulder from his previous owner, and I'd been going through what Lloyd called my "Dark Period." It seemed that circumstances had kept us from a perfect pairing.

Finally, he trotted toward me with everything wagging: Tail wagging his body, which in turn wagged his head.

I dropped to my knees and began to cry. "Here you go, Flanny," I said, wiping my eyes while he munched and snorted, wriggling his compact caramel body against me. "What a good boy you are. That bad man was going to steal you, but you told me about it. Good dog. If I'd come outside just a few minutes later—I don't want to think about it."

Flan went on snorting and carrying on, oblivious to the averted tragedy.

In retrospect, I probably should have expected this might

happen. Ellen Pirosh warned me about the brazen actions of the dog thieves. It was by sheer luck Flan hadn't joined the ranks of the stolen.

If you wait long enough, one emotion will become something else. Now my fear of what could have happened to us had turned to rage over how it was being successfully perpetrated on others. Too many dogs were getting stolen.

Something needed to be done and something *would* be done.

It could even be a matter for *The Muffia.*

CHAPTER 16

THE NEXT morning, Lauren called. She and her family had just come back from a month in St. Tropez—poor things—but she was kind enough not to rub it in. There was a reason the rest of us called Lauren "Rich Muff," and that's because she *was* rich. She jetted around the world on the millions and billions of dollars her husband, George, had inherited through his iconic American dynastic forbears—the Buschs of the Anheuser-Busch beer empire. It seemed to me that Lauren and George or their friends had houses in every exotic and expensive location. Through knowing Lauren, I'd discovered that the rich really do have a club, and unless you have money, they don't let you in.

But Lauren was also kind. She and George had two adorable children, Amanda and Gavin, in whom Lauren was attempting to instill a sense of responsibility, rather than privilege, about the way they lived. She emphasized the importance of giving to the less fortunate and included the kids in philanthropic causes ranging from Ronald McDonald House to Save the Ocean. Most recently, Lauren and her sister started an organization to combat Alzheimer's disease, and hosted its first benefit gala a few months ago. Throughout the lead up to the event, Lauren included the kids whenever possible, and let them know they were raising money so others could live better lives.

"I just heard what happened to you yesterday," she said.

"I'd still be shaking. Rachel said you chased the guy down the street. What if he had a gun?"

"Well, I chased him away. But yeah, if the guy had aimed a gun at me, my Swiffer wasn't going to help me."

"What's a Swiffer?" asked Lauren, revealing her lack of cleaning expertise.

"Sometimes you just react," I said. "I didn't want him to get Flan and that was the only signal my brain registered: 'Don't let him get Flan, Don't let him get Flan.' So I ran after them. I couldn't stop thinking about how awful it would have been if the guy got Flan."

"So, what's their M.O.? Do they take the dogs and sell them to other people?"

"That and a lot worse."

"Don't tell me." Lauren had two very cute, very fancy, overbred Boston terriers.

"I just wish I'd seen the guy's face," I said. "He was wearing a hoody."

"The costume of America's youth."

"And sloppy housewives. Just around the house of course."

"Of course," said Lauren.

Lie. I wore hoodies all the time.

"Anyway," I said. "There's been a spate of dog thefts in this neighborhood. And not just this one. Rachel may have told you her neighbor's Spaniel was taken. Apparently this is happening all over so keep your eyes on Molly and Mack."

"Don't worry. We put security cameras up everywhere so no dognapper's getting onto the property undetected."

"I wouldn't be complacent about this, Lauren. These people are brazen. They've been known to snatch a leash right out of a person's hands."

"Well then it's lucky we don't walk them."

Was she kidding?

"I know what you're thinking right now and yes, I'm

kidding. Thanks for the tip. We'll keep our eyes open. I'm just glad you're okay and they didn't get Flan."

"We missed you at Kiki's," I said, moving on.

"Me too; without the hashtag, I mean."

She'd lost me.

"Hashtag me too. I can't say 'me too' anymore without thinking I'm joining a movement. I mean I'm all for the movement but . . ."

"I know what you mean. It's been appropriated."

"Exactly. But I loved *Bernadette* and missed seeing everyone and hearing the news. Jelicka didn't do much of a sum-up."

"She never does," I said. "It's not her thing."

The day after book club the next muff to host sends out an email distilling everyone's roundy-round from the night before into an amusing story for those who weren't there. Then everyone else piles on with what she forgot. It's always entertaining to see what people remember of the evening. Jelicka, for some reason, doesn't put in a lot of effort, while Paige and Quinn, on the other hand, have a flair for detail and comedic spin.

"Like no one mentioned Natey," said Lauren. "He's not still getting bullied, is he?" Her kids were younger than Natey, so she often asked these progress-related questions.

"Fortunately not," I said, before launching into the story, minus the part about Colin's father buying off the people running Science Camp. Rich people fix things with money, or try to, and less-principled people often take the payoff. It isn't right, but it's a waste of breath to say life isn't fair and the rich play by different rules. I didn't tell her about the payoff because I didn't want to know whether Lauren and George would have done the same thing.

"It's actually turned out to be a good thing," I said. "Natey's sort of, I don't know, changed this summer. The counselors tell me Colin isn't bugging him anymore. And Natey says they've even become friends. He's getting a lot better with his Ls, too."

"What do you think happened?"

"It seems to be some combination of our new tenant, Apryl, who trains horses, and *The Princess Bride*."

"That's an interesting formula."

"And, I hate to say it, but it might have something to do with spending less time with his dad. Nate was hard on him. I know it's because he cares, but Natey's seven."

"Sorry you're going through this, Sarah," she said with compassion. "Are you okay—really? You'd tell me if you needed something, wouldn't you?"

I did a quick assessment. I *was* okay. I had never confessed to Lauren just how desperate my financial situation was before taking on tenants. She could have bailed me out at any point and never felt it. My mortgage payment was probably less than one half of a percent of a dividend George got from a few shares of inherited stock. I wondered if it was awkward for her having poor friends because it was occasionally difficult for me having a rich one. But that was my problem. She had taken the time and trouble to call me and ask how I was. I had nothing to offer *except* myself, and that's what she seemed to want.

"Thank you for caring," I said finally. "Could some things be better? Yes. But I'm counting on being able to look back at this time and being proud I got through it."

"It will happen," she said solemnly, letting it hang in the air before launching into a new subject. "So the reason I called, other than to say 'Hi' and catch up, is that I want to introduce you to someone."

"You mean a guy? Oh, Lauren, I don't know . . ."

"What?"

"It's too soon, I think. Isn't it?"

"Up to you, I won't push," she said backing off. "I just thought . . ."

"No, you're right. I mean, it's over with Nate, it is. And it has been for a while. But it's just, well, you know. Or, maybe you don't, married to George. You're like the perfect couple."

"We have our issues, I promise you."

Of course they did. Perfect is not an adjective one applies to a marriage, but the way Lauren and George appeared on the surface *was* perfect.

"To the rest of us, you're pretty close," I said, already making a list in my head of why I shouldn't meet the guy she wanted to set me up with. "It's really sweet of you to think about fixing me up, but it's too soon, so it wouldn't be right. Plus, I'm working on a business plan for the cookies, and I have tenants, and Natey, and the dog. I don't have time for a boyfriend."

"Who's talking about a boyfriend? I was thinking we'd have a playdate at our house and you bring Natey, Paige can come with her kids, and I'll have Denny come with his daughter. I don't think he's ready for a commitment, either."

"His name is Denny?"

"Dennis, why?"

A pile of pancakes flashed in front of my eyes. "Nothing."

"He's an old friend from home, but he lives here now, and he lost his wife last year. You two might be friends, if nothing else."

"There'll be a whole group of people and kids, then," I confirmed.

"That's the plan. Then we'll segue into an impromptu barbecue."

A *planned* impromptu barbecue, I thought. "What are you telling him?"

"Same thing. Playdate, barbecue, but nothing about you."

The set-up didn't *sound* awkward. "I'll think about it," I said.

"Good."

"But I don't have any dating clothes."

"First of all," she said, "remember it's not a date."

"Right."

"Come on, you always put yourself together so imaginatively. And besides, he's not the type to recognize the latest fashion."

This was good, but I wasn't sure if putting myself together *imaginatively* was a compliment. It sounded like she was talking about her children's artwork.

"I'm thinking Labor Day weekend," she went on. "Last hurrah for summer kind of thing. So keep it open."

My social calendar was nothing but open, though I had hopes of taking my cookies to the farmer's market that weekend. "The only thing is," I said, "I might have to be baking."

"Keep it open," she said again, firmly. "And bring some of those cookies. Goodbye."

"Bye, and thanks for thinking of—"

But she'd already hung up.

Upstairs a door opened. A few seconds later, Tobias appeared wearing an impeccably tailored dark gray suit with his hair swooped into a style last seen on Adam Levine in the fourth season of *The Voice.*

"Wish me luck," he said. "I gotta get to the car and turn on the air before I melt."

"It's not *that* hot," I said, taking note of a sort-of unnatural glow to his face. "Are you wearing makeup?"

He let out a gasp, his face a mixture of concern and defensiveness. "Can you tell? It's just a little concealer. I haven't been sleeping—no fault of yours or your bed, doll. It's just I have to look my best now that I'm competing against youngsters."

"Who are you meeting?" I asked.

He put down his briefcase and opened the refrigerator. "Sur la Table. Screw Williams Sonoma. They let me go, so I am going to sell the shit out of the competition. Besides, Sur la Table's better, and they have cooking classes like WS used to do, back in the glory days." He pulled a yogurt from the refrigerator and began scooping spoonfuls, without missing a beat. "So if it works out with Sur la Table—let's stay positive: *When* it works out—I should be able to help you get a job. Not right away but within a couple of months. You'd teach, wouldn't you? I mean, you could teach baking if you wanted. Got any cookies I can bring for them to sample? Skip it. That might be awkward. I'll wait until I'm further along in the interview process. Don't want to appear too eager."

He was like a little kid, with a little kid's enthusiasm. Far be it from me to dash his hopes.

He rinsed the yogurt container and dropped it into recycling. Then he picked up his briefcase and headed for the door. "Wish me luck."

"Good luck."

He opened the door. "You're a good person, Sarah." Then he turned on his heel and was gone.

I smiled, feeling appreciated, and glanced at my watch.

Damn, I was late and Natey was scheduled for his first riding lesson.

CHAPTER 17

"READY?" SAID Apryl, smiling at Natey and pulling on a piece of the bridle around the pony's face.

"Ready," said a beaming Natey.

There we were, the three of us smiling away, while inside I was terrified. What if the little white beast Natey was sitting on ran off with my precious boy? I supposed there was some comfort in the fact that the pony's size was that of a large St. Bernard. And whereas in the past, people on horseback were always above me, this pony was so small I found myself looking down into Natey's smiling face.

I had been on top of one of these beautiful animals exactly three times that I could remember. The first was as a little girl at summer camp, and the experience had not been life changing. Nor do I remember falling madly in love with horses as many of my fellow campers had, who had gone on to spend every free moment brushing and fussing over their assigned horses, braiding every bit of hair that could be braided.

My second horse experience had been less benign—a drunken spring break in Cozumel from the University of Washington that found a group of us galloping on a beach one evening. The facts are blurry, but I remember not being able to stop my horse, who, after racing one direction on the beach for what seemed like miles, decided he'd had enough and wheeled on his heels for home, dumping me in the process. Lucky for me I emerged from the incident unscathed, save for being shaken and possessed of a headache probably caused more by the tequila than the fall.

The third time on a horse took place on a visit to Portland, Oregon, when a cop I dated briefly let me sit on his horse. (I will point out to any law-abiding citizen who might report the incident that neither the officer nor the horse were on official duty at the time). He said I should sit on his horse in order to establish that "horses are perfectly safe." What I'll say about the experience, other than to say, wow, those police horses really know how to stand still, is that the cop was a narcissistic, passive-aggressive power tripper, and we broke up soon after. But that wasn't the horse's fault.

To get to the Equestrian Center where Apryl trained and taught, you need to drive up Topanga Canyon Boulevard from the Pacific Ocean, at the point where Santa Monica turns into Malibu. If you get to the Reel Inn, you've gone too far.

Topanga Canyon "Boulevard" is a complete misnomer. All over the world, boulevards are broad avenues flanked by large multi-story buildings with a center divider featuring flowering plants. There are parking meters and trendy restaurants and people strolling with dogs on leashes.

Topanga Canyon Boulevard couldn't be further from that. From the Pacific to the San Fernando Valley, most of it's a dangerous two-lane road that cuts through the mountains rising on either side of it, which in the winter is closed for days at a time due to rock- and mudslides, leaving residents with limited routes of egress.

Upon reaching the top of Topanga, near the intersection of Topanga Canyon Boulevard and the turn-off for Old Topanga Road and Apryl's barn, one encounters a collection of quirky shops, real estate offices, and restaurants that will make you feel like you've travelled back to the 1960s, the era of hippy chic with a thousand twirling rainbow decorations. At one end of town is a collection of life-sized wooden animals, presumably for purchase, arranged as a wildlife park, where predator and prey co-exist peaceably. This time through, I caught a glimpse of a giraffe nestled next to a lion. At the other end of town is a shop displaying hundreds of wind chimes, tie-dyed clothing, and stone Buddhas.

On high traffic days (read: most), if you're moving slowly with your windows down, you can smell the incense, like it's been burning so long it's permanent.

I'd seen pictures of Topanga from "back in the day," and it hadn't changed much, though what "back in the day" meant, I wasn't sure. People who use the phrase don't often specify. It's like we're all supposed to accept that their "back in the day" was a day, some time ago, a day better than the current day, where we now were. But because it's never clear which time period we're talking about, there always remains the possibility that we're not talking about the same "back in the day" at all. Chances are we weren't. In the case of Topanga, though, it seemed pretty clear that "back in the day" meant late 1960s.

The little white pony was standing very still. He might have been a statue if I didn't see him flick his tail. I told myself to relax. He seemed harmless enough, though there was the pony's name to consider.

"Didn't you say this pony's name is 'Diablo'?" I said, hoping to sound as though I had no judgment about the pony's devilish tendencies. Apryl guffawed.

"He's white like Inigo Montoya's horse," said Natey.

"There was a change in plans," said Apryl, leaning toward me. "Diablo isn't the best first horse. This pony's name is 'Windy,'" she said.

"Because she runs like the wind!" Natey said, enthusiastically.

"These days, Windy doesn't run, Natey, which makes her

the perfect first horse. She's very happy to walk and maybe trot. We're going to have to make a lot of noise if we want her to go faster than that. She'd much rather keep cool in the shade and eat hay."

Natey made a face. "Eww, hay."

"Better than eating you, right?" Apryl said, which made Natey giggle.

"It *is* hot up here," I said, gazing around at the empty parking lot and arena. "We're the only ones out in this heat."

"Most of the boarders ride either very early or very late," said Apryl. "But this is good for Natey's first time; no distractions for him or the pony."

I took her word for it. It was too hot to protest.

She made an adjustment to Windy's girth. "Here we go, then. Hold on right here." She held out a strap attached to the saddle.

"What's that?" I said.

She hesitated. "It's called a bucking strap. But don't worry, Windy doesn't buck."

"Don't worry, Mama," Natey said, anxious to get going.

"Yeah, Mama," Apryl teased. "Stop worrying."

I relented and backed up a couple of steps, determined to keep my mouth shut for the rest of the lesson.

Apryl showed Natey how to grasp the bucking strap. "Good. Now sit up tall."

He didn't move, and Apryl gave more of a direction. "Try to make your helmet reach the clouds."

That challenge worked. Natey seemed to grow taller on Windy's back.

"Excellent," Apryl said, giving Windy a few pats on the neck. "Here we go."

She attached a long lead to Windy's bridle and slowly let it out. Soon Windy, with Natey on top, began circling around

Apryl at the walk. Apryl had to cluck a couple of times to keep the pony from stopping.

"Told you she was lazy," Apryl said. "Stay tall and give her a little kick with your legs. Just open and close, not too hard."

It seemed like Natey did what she asked, and the pony went from a slow walk to a slightly faster slow walk. I could see Natey's confidence growing, and I felt myself relax a little.

"Can we go faster?" he asked, after about the sixth time around.

Apryl looked at me.

"How much faster?" I asked.

"Not much." Apryl focused her attention on Nate. "So, let's try a t-r-o-t. I don't want to say the word, because Windy knows what it means and you are the one who's boss, not her. Keep holding onto the strap and keep your body tall in the middle of the saddle. Helmet touching the clouds. Do you know what I mean when I say stay in the middle?"

"Don't do this," Natey said leaning severely to the inside.

"Watch out!" I shouted, startling everyone except the pony. "Sorry, I thought he was going to fall off."

"Somebody's a wise guy," Apryl said. "Okay, here we go. Ready? Windy, *trot*!"

"Trot," Natey said with glee. And with a few nudges from his legs, the pony finally trotted.

It was a very slow trot, but it was clear Natey didn't care. He was riding.

"It's a sissy sport," said Nate, when he called that evening.

"Men dominate at the highest levels," I said. "And what about the fact that most racehorse trainers and other people who make their livings off horses are men."

"You should have asked me."

Hadn't I? No, I had not.

Nate and I were on the phone, coordinating the upcoming weekend. I had just told him about Natey's next riding lesson, and, I now realized, hadn't mentioned the first. He was right. I should have asked him, or told him, or something before now. It made no difference that Natey was the one who pushed to ride, not me pushing him. Clearly we hadn't been sharing much.

"I'm sorry," I said. "You're right. If you'd taken him bungee jumping without asking, I would have been furious."

"We don't have the money for riding lessons," he said, ignoring my apology.

"Well, we didn't have to pay for the lessons."

I realized I hadn't told Nate much about Apryl, only that there was a paying tenant in the house, who was young and female, which seemed to eliminate any concern he had for his son's welfare. Hmmm, I wonder what he's going to say when I tell him Tobias is living in the master suite.

"Oh, why not?" he asked.

"Apryl offered. And as far as more lessons, if there are any, we'll work a trade." He didn't need to know what we were trading yet, which was good because *I* didn't know.

"Who's Apryl again?"

"My tenant? I know I told you. Young woman? Pretty? She's paying rent for the guest room, but she's also a riding instructor. You can blame *The Princess Bride*. Natey wouldn't shut up about riding, so I thought it was better to let him do it, under entirely safe conditions, of course. Apryl gave him the first lesson for free."

There was a pause, an inhalation of breath and a slow release that felt like it lasted a full minute.

"This riding teacher is your tenant? In *our* house?" He was displaying his selective memory again.

"We need money, Nate. You don't seem to get that. We are going to lose this house. One of us had to do something, and taking in a tenant seemed like the easiest way to do that. It may be forestalling the inevitable, but it's better than doing nothing." I prepared myself and forged on. "I've actually taken on a second tenant."

"You've taken in two tenants? Who's the other one?"

"My old boss, Tobias. He's in the master suite."

"I thought he was supposed to be making a fortune!"

"Not anymore. He was downsized just like you." "Where are you sleeping?"

"Your study. It's a little cramped, but way more comfortable than sleeping on the street."

He let out a hrumph. "Figures this tenant would try to get her rent reduced by getting Natey hooked on riding lessons."

"What is the matter with you? She's not paying less rent. Our son wants to learn to ride, so I came up with a way to make it happen for free. The only change is I now do her laundry and vacuum her room, which is stuff I do anyway. Do you really think everyone's out to get you? Maybe it's not everyone else that has problems, it's you. Have you thought of going to your own psychologist or going on a retreat or something? Maybe Sophia would help."

"Why would I do that?"

Letting out a sigh, I tried again. "Listen, I'm sorry I didn't tell you about the riding lessons. But I don't want to argue anymore. I'm really tired of it. But Nate—I'm also worried about you. You just seem really disconnected. Even if we're not going to marriage counseling, I hope you'll, you know, keep trying to figure things out. For yourself, mostly. I mean each of us is all we really have at the end of the day, you know? I do care about you, even if you think I don't."

"Gee, thanks," he said. "Well you can quit worrying; I'm fine. I hope you and your tenants enjoy *our* house."

"You think I'm doing this because it's enjoyable?"

"Goodbye, Sarah."

Then he hung up and was gone.

CHAPTER 18

SUMMER STILL controlled the narrative with camp, riding lessons, and mastering the recipe for flan cookies by Labor Day dominating my thoughts. But moms of young children ignore the period known as "back to school" at their peril. I wanted to be ahead of the game this year, to make sure Natey was equipped with school supplies and new clothes before the end of August.

Money wasn't as tight as it had been pre-tenants, but that didn't mean there was anything extra in the kitty. And so, operating under the eighty-twenty rule—that most of us use twenty percent of our stuff eighty percent of the time—I moved through the closets, cupboards, garage, and crawlspace above the master bedroom one morning, gathering together every whatsit we weren't using in order to sell it.

A giant assortment of stuff formed in the garage, which I separated into two piles, one—those items that were saleable and, two—those items no person in their right mind would buy. A single golf ball? No, this second pile would be sent to landfill or driven to Goodwill.

This morning, I had my laptop open and began posting items from the first pile to eBay, Craigslist, and, when warranted, more specialized websites. A large collection of Lladro figurines had been willed to me by my paternal grandmother. Fortunately, I didn't inherit her Lladro gene, so I had no internal dilemma over selling the stuff. Other people would pay lots of money for the porcelain angels, clowns, bunnies, and other miscellaneous pastel tchotchkes that made up my grandmother's collection. And I stood to make more than back-to-school money if lladrosales.com came up with a buyer.

The key to selling stuff online is in writing achingly personal or catchy copy, neither of which was my forte. We've already established I'm not much of a reader, so it would tend to follow that I'm not much of a writer. The achingly personal essay I sought to write about how my Lladro collection had been in our family for generations, and how I was regretfully selling due to the death of a beloved—no, I didn't have the chops. The catchy angle came easier, but I'd still need help.

Tobias. Yes, I'd ask Tobias for help. Catchy copy was not only in his wheelhouse, it was the wheelhouse itself. And at the moment he was upstairs in "my" room; I could just go up and ask him. No, that would violate the house rules we'd established that ensured we all had our privacy. In the end, I sent him a text and turned my attention to easier items, like Natey's old highchair.

Twenty minutes later, Tobias made his grand entrance to the garage attired in a brown velour sweat suit and Gucci flip-flops. Flan snorted.

"Good morning, *Chiquita y chiquos*, or whatever. *Me espanol es muy malo*," he said, striking a pose in the doorway.

"You're awfully chipper this morning."

"*Si*, I got an email that I'm still in the mix for the Sur la Table job."

"Good news."

"I suppose," he said, equivocating. "But they're still meeting people—never a good sign." He waved his hand and sat down on a tufted ottoman, one of the many things I hoped to sell. "Enough of that; nothing I can do. So, what's the game? I want to stock up on good karma."

"We are selling almost everything you can see, including what you're sitting on."

"Oooooh," said Tobias. "A shopping opportunity. I want to be ready for shabby chic when it comes back."

"Stop it, you. I'm raising money for Natey's upcoming school year."

He stood and flip-flopped his way to one of my piles of stuff. "Ooooooo, what's all this?" he said, lifting two pieces of Nate's mother's fake Louis Vuitton luggage set.

I pointed. "That's a makeup case, and that's a pet carrier."

"I know what they *are*, but why do you have an entire set of Vuitton luggage? It doesn't exactly scream Sarah Pizzo, if you know what I mean."

"Just more of Nate's mother's cast offs; just like Flan."

"Your gain, girl."

"Tobias, it's fake."

"No!" he said, truly shocked and eyeing an inside seam. "They'd fool anyone. The inside label is completely authentic. What do you want for the set?"

"You want to buy it?"

"I don't know. Do I?"

"Are you asking me? Because I don't know."

"Maybe because I've been out of a job, fake stuff is starting to look real."

"That doesn't make a whole lot of sense, Tobias, but the Vuitton pattern goes very well with your track suit." On cue, Flan snorted again. A fashion critic.

Tobias's eyes shifted from the luggage to Flan to me, wary that he was being made fun of.

"Let's do this—" I said. "I won't sell it to you now, but I won't sell it to anyone else without going by you first. How's that? But I think you're just suffering from shopping withdrawal, and that if you were in your right mind, making $200K, you wouldn't want fake Vuitton."

"On the other hand, I've always been a smart shopper,

and why would I pay full price for the real stuff when I can get a deal on such convincing fakes?"

"Because you're a snob?" I said it gently.

"Good point," he said, putting down the suitcase he'd been examining. "All right, let's get started."

Tobias's wit made short order of every item that could use a clever turn, and he seemed to enjoy the creative exercise. I took the photos, uploaded everything, and an hour and a half later we were done.

"I think that's it," I said, giving everything one more pass, just to be sure. "That would have taken me three days without you, so thank you."

"You underestimate your abilities, missy," he said, standing and making for the door. "But it was fun; happy to help."

I woke up the computer and prepared to face over a hundred unopened emails from worthy organizations and their never-ending pleas for money. I wanted to give them all enough money to fix their problems, but could they be fixed with any amount of money? And why were there so many with the exact same mission statement? Surely they'd be more powerful and successfully reduce the Great Pacific Gyre, for example, if they bonded together. I got as far as the Marine Mammal Center's latest when I felt a presence. Sure enough, Tobias was still there, lost in thought.

"Tobias," I said, jolting him a little. "Something on your mind?"

"Actually . . ." He hesitated. "I wanted to talk to you about a couple of things."

Unlike the sales copy he came up with so quickly, he was now agonizing over his phrasing.

"Go for it."

"I have been thinking about this for a few days now, and I think—well, it could turn out to be . . ." He trailed off.

"Turn out to be . . . what? Toby?"

"It's about your cookies."

I knew he liked the cookies, but I had no idea what he meant. I smiled, recalling our deal for his tenancy. "Am I not keeping the cookie jar stocked or something?"

"No, no. I'm curious if you might like some help."

"With the cookies?"

He nodded. "I think I can help you sell them, make you and them become something," he said. "Marketing, finding sales channels, packaging, scaling . . . The farmer's market is a good first step, but what's the step after that?"

I had no idea, but I also had no doubt that Tobias could help. I just wouldn't want it to get messy; the old adage of not mixing business with pleasure came to mind. On the other hand, he was my friend and also a paying tenant, and that was business.

"Think about it," he said. "Just wanted to put it out there. While I'm still unemployed, why not, you know? We'd write up some sort of contract, so you felt comfortable. The cookies are not only delicious, they're unique. And you're an excellent baker. You deserve to have them succeed."

"Thanks, I'll think about it. What's the second thing?"

"Hmm?"

"You said you wanted to talk about a *couple* of things.'"

"Oh, yes. How well do you know Apryl?"

I wasn't expecting that question. Or maybe I wasn't expecting the tone. It was suspicious.

"Not very. I mean I didn't know her before she moved in, but I checked her references. And she's been here a few weeks now and seems like a good person. Why?"

"Does she come from money?"

Another surprising question. "I have no idea," I said. "What makes you ask? She doesn't seem to have much. I mean, judging by her car. And she doesn't have a horse. You'd think if she came from money, she'd have a really nice horse, probably several really nice horses, like Georgianne Bloomberg."

"Okay, maybe it wasn't her," he said, turning to go.

But he'd piqued my interest, and I could tell there was more. "Tobias, just say it."

He took a few steps toward me. "Hand to God, I saw her decked out in Alexander Wang, wearing a pair of leopard print Louboutins, coming into Providence a few nights ago."

Providence was just about the most exclusive, expensive restaurant in Los Angeles. It was certainly in the top three. I'd never been, not even when I was making money. I gazed at Tobias, trying to remove the judgment from my face.

"Don't look at me like that," he said. "I was having a cocktail and only spent fourteen dollars."

"Did I say anything?"

I couldn't recall seeing Apryl in anything other than riding clothes and the occasional gym outfit, nor eating anything more extravagant than take-out from the Brentwood Country Mart. It seemed unlikely she would dine at Providence. Still, Tobias had been around her long enough to be able to recognize her if she changed her clothes.

"Are you sure it was Apryl?" I said.

He pursed his lips. "I mean, everyone has a doppelganger, but she's pretty distinctive, that whole little package she has going on, don't you think?"

That was true, she was a package. But even if it *had* been Apryl he'd seen, his assessment of her as a moneyed rich girl was flawed for other reasons. "If it was Apryl, what makes you think she was paying her own way? Or that wearing a pair of expensive shoes equals rich? They could be fake. And even if they were real Louboutins, how do you know someone didn't give them to her?"

"Fine," he said. "It's possible I have too much time on my hands, so I'm making stuff up. It's also possible the girl is *not* as she appears."

He sounded like Jelicka when convinced she's uncovered a secret plot. "You could have been a muff," I said.

An expression of shock came over his face. "I hope you don't mean that overly injected friend of yours."

"Stop. She's not doing that anymore," I lied. "It's just Jelicka always thinking there's a conspiracy—everyone's leading a double life, and it's *The Muffia*'s job to figure out what's really going on. Listening to you talk about Apryl feels very familiar, that's all."

He was pouting.

"Tobias, it's a good thing to be vigilant. So, thanks. Maybe I'll have a look in her closet."

"Up to you, doll. Just sayin'." He took a couple of steps toward the door. "Do think about my cookie offer?"

He opened the door and Flan raced in, making circles around Tobias before bounding over to me, begging to be cuddled.

"I will absolutely consider your cookie offer."

As the door closed behind him, I stroked Flan's belly and assessed the garage and its contents, imagining everything gone with the slate, or cement, wiped clean.

The computer dinged, and, with Flan on my lap, I started to see responses to the ads already arriving in my inbox. In all things, a sense of possibility filled me. I even had a sort-of date soon. So what if one of my tenants was living a double life? I got the feeling that good things were about to happen.

CHAPTER 19

THE HAZE hung heavy outside the paned windows of Nate's former study as I pulled open the drapes. My back hurt but that's what you get sleeping on a twenty-year old sleeper sofa. Being stressed didn't help.

It was Labor Day, the weekend I'd hoped to have my cookies at the Santa Monica Farmer's Market, but I'd chickened out. Or something. Stress point number one. I was still trying to figure out why, other than being late sending in the money and registering to become a vendor, I'd stalled so long. Probably fear. Great. What do I do with that?

Stress point number two—today was the day of Lauren's romantic playdate/barbecue between me and her widower friend, Denny. I'd been looking forward to it, but then I went and had an extra glass of red wine last night, worrying about what to wear. Why was I doing this to myself—especially if Denny didn't even know he was being set up? Which he didn't. All he knew, if Lauren was telling me the truth, was that he was bringing his kid over for a playdate and hanging around for a barbecue. So why was I stressing? It wasn't a date, even if I did harbor a fantasy of falling madly in love with him and he with me.

Was it that Denny was a widower? Vicki dated one and her take on widowers was, "Don't—you can't compete with a ghost." Even if a guy and his wife were having issues, once she gets sick she becomes a martyr, the epitome of kindness and grace, with imagined golden halos framing her pretty head in every photo of her for evermore. How do you compete with that? More to the point, I didn't want to. I had to protect myself. My self-esteem hadn't yet recovered after what Nate put me through, thank you very much. The wounds were still too fresh.

The rationalizing got me nowhere. Despite all the good reasons I had for not putting pressure on myself, I wanted Denny to like me. I wanted him to like me so much, I'd make him forget about his deceased wife and fall for me. It was ridiculous, like being back in middle school, except now I longed for the attention of a grown-up man. Ugh—why hadn't Lauren just invited us and not mentioned the set up?

No one was awake except me, so I quietly padded my way to the kitchen to make myself a cup of coffee before returning to my room to shop for Natey's school supplies. So far, I'd collected over $1500 selling unwanted stuff. Nate's mother's fake Vuitton luggage alone fetched $800. Was it bad of me not to tell the woman who bought the whole set that it was fake? I hadn't lied, exactly; I just said it was a gift and I couldn't vouch for its authenticity, which was true. But fake or not, $800 is a good deal for a five-piece set of never-used, well-made luggage. She seemed to agree and happily handed over the cash. At the end of the day, Tobias's comfort level for fake Vuitton topped out at $400, and he gave me the thumbs up when he saw the woman loading her Lexus.

As I scanned websites searching for slightly used books on Natey's second grade reading list, I laughed, thinking about his last riding lesson. With just three lessons on Windy under his belt, Apryl declared him a natural, and ever since, he'd been telling people—people at Science Camp, people in grocery stores, people we didn't know.

"I'm a natural rider," he says, apropos of nothing.

"According to his instructor," I'll say, to the mystified person. Natey was acting almost cocky, a little too Inigo

Montoya for my liking. But it was also sort of adorable seeing him become more confident and assertive. And it had an unexpected upside: His Ls. Yesterday, he'd said a perfect "lullaby for Lionel" five times in a row. And as the weeks ticked down to the beginning of school, I felt optimistic that Natey would show up on that first day, brave and confident instead of picked on. And that's despite the fact that this year he'd be going to public school for the first time. There was obviously no more money for private school, and Nate's mother, once willing to help, had once again changed her mind.

My own mother wanted to contribute, but since she was subsisting on my father's pension, the idea was ludicrous, if not impossible. So public school it was, while I worked on getting Natey into a charter or magnet. At least we were lucky to have a good public elementary school in our neighborhood. And, perhaps, if he put in a stellar second grade year, he could even matriculate to a private school on scholarship. As I confirmed my purchase of "Captain Underpants" and "A Dragon in the Sock Drawer," I could hear Natey getting out of bed above me. I listened as his little feet pattered to the bathroom where I heard him pee, flush, and patter back to the hall where the pattering stopped. Would he come down the stairs to find me? Or would this be the day he decided he was too old to jump on my bed?

I heard Flan join Natey in the hall, making his usual snuffling noises.

"Shhhhhhh," I heard Natey say to no avail.

Then with joy I leapt up from the desk and onto the sofa bed as the two of them started down the stairs. Back under the covers, I pretended to be asleep and readied myself for the pounce.

CHAPTER 20

WITH TOBIAS rewriting his resume yet again, this time in hopes of landing a job with a food conglomerate, and Apryl at the barn, Natey and I set out for Lauren's house bearing two tins of the latest batch of flan cookies. One tin was a housewarming gift and the other, one more test of unsuspecting cookie eaters. Like the film director watching her film with an audience that doesn't know she's there, I wanted to watch peoples' expressions as they ate my cookies and see how quickly they disappeared.

Lauren, George, and their two young kids, Amanda and Gavin, had only recently moved back into their house after extensive renovations and a new wing, built out as the offices of Lauren's Sweet-Busch Alzheimer's charity, and I was excited to see it. Supposedly the colonial-style house had once belonged to actor Glenn Ford and stood on a very large lot with sprawling grounds. It was more the type of house one might see on the other side of the country, in Greenwich, Connecticut, instead of a mere half a mile away from O.J. Simpson's former property on Rockingham Drive, where he shed his bloody gloves.

In this Brentwood neighborhood, all the houses were big and the lawns expansive, which posed a problem given the years of drought. Homeowners either let their lawns die or incurred massive fines for going beyond their water allotment. There *was* a third, very expensive option: Fake grass. And this is what Lauren and George had opted for.

"Kids and dogs need to play," George had said to Lauren, who'd agreed. "We really don't have a choice."

Well, of course they had a choice. No one was forcing them to live in a giant house with problematic grounds. They could have lived near a park or a school with places to play. I mean, one doesn't have to show off one's fake grass.

But, as I've said, I didn't want to make Lauren feel bad about being rich. She's a generous person and gives back to the world, so I really can't fault her. Some people are rich and help no one but themselves and other rich people. Lauren wasn't one of them.

"Look at *that* house," Natey said for what seemed the fiftieth time, pointing at yet another giant manse as we wound our way along the heavily tree-lined streets. It was a hot day, but as we drove, a light breeze blew through our open windows, bringing the fragrant scents of jasmine, lavender, sage, and heliotrope to waft into the car. This was a neighborhood where you could even smell the wealth.

"Wow, look at *that* one," Natey said as we pulled past Lauren's gate.

"Yup," I told him. "That's Lauren's house."

"She lives there? That house is giant!"

"It certainly is." Now that I was seeing the house again, it was more Southern Gothic than Colonial. I take back what I said about Greenwich. This house was a shingled Tara from *Gone with the Wind*, with gables and front columns obscured only slightly by the largest balloon display I'd ever seen.

From the few cars that were parked outside the gate, I thought we must be early. No, not early, the party was just small. This meant it would be harder to get lost in the crowd and avoid Denny, should we take an immediate dislike to each other. Ugh. I really needed to stop thinking so negatively.

When Lauren pulled the front door open, her two Boston Terriers, Molly and Mack, were jumping up and down barking next to her and Natey immediately dropped down to pet them. I could see behind Lauren that there were far more people in attendance than the number of cars suggested.

"Quiet, you two," Lauren said to the dogs before noting my expression. "Most people took Lyft," she explained. "Guess they want to drink."

She closed the door and leaned down to Natey. "Hi, Nathaniel. The kids are out by the pool, if you want to head out there. You can take the dogs with you."

Natey, still petting Molly and Mack, gazed up at me.

"Go ahead, honey, just—"

And he was gone, the dogs in hot pursuit.

"No running by the pool!" I yelled uselessly.

Lauren smiled. "He's adorable."

"He's grown up two years this summer," I said.

"I've grown two years older, too. It does go by fast. Yesterday Amanda was crawling; this morning, she walked."

"Wow, that's a reason for a party right there." I handed her the cookie tins. "One's for you and the family. The other's for the guests."

"Oooo, did you make something? If you made something I know it's going to be delicious."

"You weren't at book club, but I think I'm close on these cookies. So if we could put some out, you know, to see if people like them?"

"Mmmmm," said Lauren, pulling open a tin, and scarfing down a cookie. "Oh my God. So good, I don't know if I want to share."

"I sort of need to know what people think, Lauren."

She smiled. "I'm kidding. We'll put them out and watch how fast they disappear."

"Hope so."

She closed the lid. "Come on, the bar's out back."

As we moved through the house, I became aware of all

the expensive art on the walls. Lauren was "rich muff" all right.

"I think I'll stick to Pellegrino today," I said, catching up to her. "I did my drinking last night."

"What was going on last night?" she said as though she'd missed a party.

"Oh, nothing. Just preparing for this."

She rolled her eyes and leaned into me. "He's just a guy. There's absolutely no pressure."

Easy for her to say.

We'd reached the kitchen, and I tried not to let my jaw go slack. It had to be two thousand square feet of carpentry, with all new, top-brand appliances, even if most were hidden under custom wooden cabinets. There was a giant center island that could seat twenty.

"Lauren your house is . . . !"

"Staggering, I know. It seems a little much." She put one of the tins in a cabinet that otherwise was entirely empty.

Ya think? "Maybe," I said. "But it's gorgeous. And if you can afford it, why not?"

"I guess. It's just—I feel a guilty spending so much money, you know? If I didn't do charitable work, I'd feel like an entitled bitch."

I smiled. "You *are* entitled, but you're not a bitch. Seems to me you've done nothing but be generous. Like loaning out that investigator so Quinn could find a boyfriend? Was that in the back of your mind when Frank got sent to help her find out who was sabotaging her?"

She smiled. "I can't take credit for that. It was an unintended consequence. I just didn't want her to get fired. You, on the other hand—" She took in the environs, making sure we wouldn't be overheard. "Stop worrying. Frankly, there are enough people here, you could successfully avoid him altogether if you want."

I didn't want. "No, I want to meet him."

"Great." She started walking again. "Just pretend you're meeting one of Natey's teachers or something. You know? A low-pressure person."

"What about him?" I asked.

"What do you mean, 'what about him'?"

"I mean, what did you tell him about me?"

"Nothing, I told you. I didn't want there to be any pressure."

"Oh, I see. You only wanted to put pressure on *me*!"

She gave me a gentle push, and together we headed for the back patio, stopping to put the second tin of cookies on the dessert table.

As I followed her through one of four sets of French doors onto the enormous slate patio, the doorbell rang. Lauren turned, hesitating, as I took one more step, bumping her slightly, just as Molly and Mack bolted between my legs and I found myself falling.

"Molly!" Lauren, also off balance, shrieked, just a full second too late.

I became aware of the unforgiving gray slate rising to meet me and the realization that the teetering wedge sandals I was wearing had probably not been the right choice for this event. I braced for the splat upon slate, but instead of the pain and abraded flesh, I felt strong arms break my fall.

I was caught and lifted upright, gazing into the eyes of a man who reminded me of—there was no other way to say it—Inigo Montoya. Or to be clear, Mandy Patinkin, the actor who played Inigo Montoya. Or, more accurately perhaps, like Mandy Patinkin if he'd aged better. Or differently.

This man, whoever he was, had caught me and saved me from injuring myself—if not embarrassment—a few feet from where George was tending to a mass of burgers cooking on the grill. He collected my purse and handed it to me with a smile.

My face flushed.

"It's not your fault," he said. "Those dogs are holy terrors."

"Sorry, Sarah," said Lauren, before calling to those inside. "Can somebody get the door? And don't let the dogs out the front."

She directed her attention back to those on the patio, specifically me and my rescuer. "Sarah, Denny; Denny, Sarah."

The guy Lauren is setting me up with caught me—how romantic is that? Or was it embarrassing? In any event, it only made me blush more.

"Sorry, Sarah," said George, flipping a burger. "I think we need a new dog obedience person. Cesar Millan is too busy helping Julia Roberts and Gwyneth Paltrow with their dogs."

"What if they'd knocked her off her feet and she really got hurt?" Denny said, turning back to me. Not flirting exactly, but his attempts to make the dogs the villains, rather than clumsy me, earned him several points.

"They weren't the only ones at fault," I said. "But thanks for blaming them and not me."

Was he really a widower? He was pretty hot. Somehow I couldn't imagine him sitting next to the bedside of his dying wife for a year, like Lauren said he had.

"How old *are* Molly and Mack now?" I asked; a question with a clear answer.

"Four," said Lauren's son, Gavin, as he ran by with a soccer ball.

"Walk when you go by the pool!" George called after him. "Gavin!"

Gavin stopped.

"What did I say?" said George.

"You said walk when I go by the pool."

"Right."

"But I'm not by the pool," Gavin said, taking off again.

George sighed. "I might as well be talking to these burgers, the way my son and dogs listen to me."

Lauren gave him a kiss. "You're a good dad."

"Trained or not, keep an eye on them. And tell your friends with dogs," I said. "There have been a number of dognappings lately."

"I think I heard about that," said Denny.

"Molly and Mack would be prime candidates," I said. "According to my neighbor, who had her dog stolen, there are a lot of people who'll pay big bucks for dogs, and they don't care if they're stolen. So far in my neighborhood alone they've made off with an albino Pug, a Standard Poodle, a Bichon Frise, a Boxer, and those are just the ones I know about. Someone even tried to steal Flan!"

"I might steal some flan if I saw it lying around," George said.

"Flan is their French Bulldog," Lauren explained, before gently poking at George's midsection. "You're on a diet, my love."

"But Lauren, he has to taste my cookies for market research."

"Yeah," said George. "For market research. I almost *have* to taste them."

Lauren gazed at George lovingly. "Maybe. If you're on your best behavior."

George pouted, throwing a look at Denny and me. "Meany."

They loved each other a lot.

"Mack, *no*!" yelled Lauren, spotting the dogs causing some new sort of issue near the bar, where we could see them darting between guests, causing one to lose her mimosa.

"I'll be right back."

"How did you keep your dog from being stolen?" Denny asked, and I realized I'd sort of left them hanging.

"I was alone in the house," I began. "And I thought I heard something in the backyard, so I went to investigate. And as I got closer, the sound stopped, and I saw this guy in a hoodie. I thought I heard him saying, 'Here, sweetie,' 'Come, baby' 'Want a treat?' Things like that."

"Sure he wasn't talking to you?" said George, winking at Denny.

I felt myself blushing again. "He was holding a Pupperoni, so I certainly hope not. So I saw this and I realized I needed to do something or my dog was going to be stolen."

"So disturbing," said Lauren, who had returned with one of the dogs in her arms. "Tell them what you did."

"I grabbed a frying pan, opened the door, and started waving my Swiffer, telling the guy to scram in my harshest, firmest voice, and he did."

"You have a harsh voice?" said Denny, flirting again.

"Don't believe me?" It was a dare. "Get out of here, or I'm calling the cops," I snarled.

Denny smiled. "Yeah, I'd run away if I heard that."

George laughed. "Scared me."

"Way to take charge," said Lauren.

"I did call the cops, but so far they haven't exactly been proactive, according to this woman in my neighborhood who had her Pug stolen. So we need them to know it's an epidemic."

"It's really horrible," said Lauren. "I'm so glad they didn't get your boy." She gave Mack— or was it Molly?—a pat and put him down on the patio. "You chill out."

"Yeah, good luck with that," said George.

"Where do you live?" A preppy-looking woman who'd been eavesdropping assumed a proprietary spot next to Denny. "Certainly these thefts didn't happen around *here*!" she said.

She asked the question like she thought I might live in East LA."Santa Monica," I said, to her surprise. Then to drive it home: "On a good street."

She eyed me curiously, even disbelievingly.

"It's happening everywhere," I said. "And the guy was white, if it matters, so . . ."

I didn't think this woman was a friend of Lauren's.

"Melissa, this is one of my good friends, Sarah. I don't know if I told you about *The Muffia*, but Sarah's a muff."

Melissa looked puzzled. "A muff?"

"I guess I didn't tell you," said Lauren. "Muff?" She began moving her hand in the general vicinity of her lower half while Melissa appeared to be mildly insulted.

"Sounds interesting," said Denny.

"Can we refrain from all the muff stuff today please?" George said, lifting a burger onto a waiting bun.

"Excuse me," said Melissa suddenly. "I just remembered I need to meet an old friend from elementary school."

"One doesn't have control of ones' neighbors," said George, as we watched Melissa retreat through the French doors. "Melissa lives there." He pointed to a McMansion next door. "Used to be an adorable ranch house, the love nest of Clark Gable and Carole Lombard. Now it's—"

"Shhhh," Lauren said, taking the platter of completed burgers. "She's not the only one with a McMansion."

"So what's a 'muff'?" said Denny. "I mean, other than . . ."

"You heard him," Lauren said with a nod to George. "We can't talk about *The Muffia* right now under threat of reduced burger production. It's distracting."

"Sorry." I shrugged.

Denny seemed mildly crushed. "Maybe some other time, then."

"Sure. Right now, these two muffs are going to bring

burgers to the kids," said Lauren, giving me a nudge as she started off.

"Nice to meet you, Denny," I waved. "Thanks for saving me from falling."

"That was rather abrupt," I said, once we'd moved out of earshot. "Hold on a sec," she said, calling out: "Kids, the burgers are ready—chicken, beef, veggie, we got 'em all!"

Seconds later, children swarmed the kiddy table, and, once they all had what they wanted, she faced me. "You're out of practice, Sarah. If I hadn't pulled you away, you would have given away the store. You have to keep guys guessing, especially in the beginning."

"Aren't I too old for that? Why does it matter?" I said with a sigh. "I don't want to play games. It's too much work, especially when I'm trying to start a business, end a marriage, keep my house, and raise a kid. I don't have the energy to create a mysterious aura."

"Fine," she said. "But you need to let there be a tiny little pursuit, or the guy won't think he scored dinner."

"Wait—*what*?"

"Men need the hunt. They want to pursue and score. If a woman's too easy, it's like capturing a wounded rabbit, and where's the fun in that?"

"The metaphor isn't working. Besides, I sort of *am* a wounded rabbit," I said. "Anyway, I don't think *all* guys need the hunt. Especially these days. It's not cool to be talking about taking down big game unless you live in the wilderness and use every bit of what you shoot—you know, eat the meat, make cream from the fat, skin the hide to keep warm, make a house with the bones. Or maybe just a bird house." I turned to face her. "You've been off the market just as long as I have; how would you know how we're supposed to act?"

"Some things don't change, Sarah. This is stuff my mother told me when I was sixteen, not that I absorbed it at the time. There were a lot of women who wanted George, and I really did love him, but I thought, He won't choose me. I was more or less protecting myself by being a little aloof, but in some weird way, I think that's what kept him interested."

"Maybe," I said. "But he may also have known you were the one from the get-go."

"Guess there's no sure way to know," she said.

One thing was sure—if anything happened between Denny and me, it would need to be because I wasn't trying.

The rest of the afternoon went by quickly. The kids, all of whom were under ten, got along. Natey was in and out of the pool, the bounce house, the real house, and having a fantastic time, not needing me at all. Only one child was ever seen crying, through no fault of the dogs, when he bounced out of the bounce house onto the lawn. But in that wonderful way that happens with kids, his tears departed soon after they'd arrived, replaced by smiles and laughter. If only adult hurts, so often concealed behind masks of fortitude, vacated so speedily.

Once the Earth spun round toward evening, the party wound down and people began leaving. But Denny and I hardly noticed. He'd come in search of me after tasting a cookie, wanting to give me his rave review, and when I saw him coming toward me my breath caught. Then, once we started talking, we didn't stop. The conversation flowed easily between us, though we stuck to safe topics—cookies, kids, school—and avoided things like divorce and dead spouses. Lauren went by a couple of times, and, I noticed, got close enough to eavesdrop, but she did nothing to break us up. I was sure she'd call me later to tell me I overshared and once again ruined Denny's "hunt".

We were having such a good time mildly flirting with each other, that when Natey appeared saying he was ready to go home, I realized I wasn't. I wasn't quite ready to say goodbye. That's when Denny's daughter, Kayley, appeared, took his hand, and began pulling him toward the patio. "Come on, Daddy, we have to go outside."

"See you," Denny said, smiling and waving as he was led away, without suggesting how that might happen.

"Mom, look." Natey was pointing to the people gathering on the patio, where Kayley was pulling Denny. Soon the rest of us had joined them, with misinformation spreading regarding what we were all doing out there.

Looking in the direction everyone else was, I could see Lauren along the back fence line. She was yelling. "Molly—Mack, come!"

I made my way over to George, who was still beside the grill.

"We can't find the dogs," he said with a frown.

"Don't say that."

"But I'm afraid it's true. Lauren's been trying to find them for twenty minutes."

"Mack!" Lauren yelled again, before I saw her pivot toward the house.

Several kids had formed a circle of worried faces, while some of the adults began fanning out across the yard.

"Oh my God. They've been stolen, I know it," Lauren said as she got closer.

"Not in this neighborhood," Melissa said. "This is a good neighborhood."

Ugh—I thought she'd left.

Lauren ignored her. "You warned me, Sarah. I didn't listen." She was near tears.

"We don't know that for sure. Have you called your neighbors?" I said, going to her.

"Most of the them won't even talk to us because of the construction." Lauren gestured toward Melissa. "She's only here because she stopped me when I was getting the mail one day."

"Then let's go," I said, hoping to sound optimistic. "We'll knock on doors. Come on."

I was rallying the remaining troops when I remembered the chalk marks—that the dognappers often made a mark on the street outside a home where there was a valuable dog to steal.

I headed to the street. "Come with me."

"Where are we going?" said Lauren, joining me and matching my gait.

"I need to check something in front of your house."

"What are we checking?" George said, abandoning his grill and following us, with Denny right next to him.

"Just something that might be on the street," I said. "If it's there, it might explain what happened." I sounded like Jelicka.

"But what is it?" Lauren said.

"It *might* be on the street; it's not a sure thing. That's why I want to check."

"But what is it we're checking *for*?" Lauren was insistent, even panicking a little. "Why are we going to the street, Sarah?" She stopped. This was a demand.

I wasn't trying to hide anything, but I didn't want her to get more upset than she already was. Calmly, Denny turned to Lauren and George, and everyone else who'd followed us, including most of the kids. "Sarah and I will go to the street, and Sarah will check. Then she'll come back and tell everyone, okay?"

"That's a good idea," I said. "You all wait here."

"Hell no, we're going to the street," said Lauren, heading off again. "I just want to know what we're looking for."

"A sign," I said. "That's all I'm going to say."

"A sign?" George said, his eyes narrowed. "What kind of sign? There's a limit to how many street signs they can put up around here."

"Absolutely true," said Melissa. "Signs of all types are strictly monitored in this area of Brentwood."

"Fine!" I said, stopping again. "I'll tell you."

They stopped and faced me, waiting for answers.

"Sometimes, but not always, the dognappers make a mark on the street outside a house—a number or letter—usually in chalk, to tell others that there's a dog inside worth stealing. Then a different team goes back later and takes the dog. That's it. I wanted to see if there's a chalk mark."

Lauren's jaw dropped, and she took off at a run, racing ahead down the long driveway, away from us to the street.

When she reached it, we all watched as one hand flew to her mouth, and the other, wavering slightly, pointed to the ground.

I jogged over to where she stood and followed her gaze.

There, just outside the gates, scrawled in blue chalk, was the number "2".

CHAPTER 21

"YAUREN AND Gavin were crying a yot," said Natey, as we drove through the gates, turning toward home.

"They love their doggies," I said, glancing at his pensive expression in the rearview mirror. "I bet we'd be crying, too, if something happened to Flan."

That was a dumb thing to say—just get the kid more upset.

I quickly covered. "Tobias has been home with him all day so there's nothing to worry about. Flan will be waiting for us when we get there."

After seeing the chalk mark, several of us formed search parties, even going so far as to drive around the neighborhood in the dwindling hope we might still find Molly and Mack. But the writing was literally on the road. All signs pointed to the dogs being stolen, and the mood became one of despondent gloom. People who'd been laughing and enjoying themselves an hour earlier were as deflated as the bounce house currently having the air sucked out of it on the lower lawn.

Natey and I had stayed and waited until George called in the disappearance, but when Natey started regressing on his Ls, consumed with fears that someone might "Steaw Fwan," it was time to go. The speech expert warned us that emotional events could trigger a relapse, and this event certainly qualified. Not just the kids were crying, several adults had tears in their eyes, as well.

"How do we know he's there?" Natey was brooding, his face against the window.

"Because we called home and talked to Tobias. Flan is there with him."

He wouldn't be satisfied until he saw his dog. Relief moved through me again at having foiled the hooded dognapper. If Natey was this upset over other peoples' dogs, I could only imagine what he'd be like if his own had been stolen.

"Bad people might want to steal Flan," I said. "But we are going to watch him very, very closely, so that nobody can."

"What if Tobias had to go the store?" he said, the panic escalating.

"They'll be there," I said. "Besides, the dognappers have been busy this afternoon. They didn't have time to steal other dogs."

This was ridiculous, of course, just as it was ridiculous that I kept telling myself the dognappers wouldn't return to a house where they'd been chased away, an event I'd spared Natey any knowledge of.

"We have to bring him with us everywhere we go." It was a rational thought, if impractical.

"It would be great if he could come with us everywhere," I said. "But sometimes dogs aren't allowed. And sometimes it's too hot to leave him in the car."

"We could open aw the windows," Natey suggested.

I smiled, catching his eye in the rearview mirror. "That's good thinking, honey, but if we left Flan in the car with all the windows open, somebody could reach in and steal him for sure."

I watched as he processed this information.

"Mom?" he said after a minute.

"Yes, honey?"

"How many dogs have the bad peopew stowen?"

"I don't know. Do you mean in our neighborhood or in the whole wide world?"

"Both."

"Mmm, four or five in the neighborhood, I think." I bet Ellen Pirosh knew exactly how many dogs had been stolen.

"Were there marks on the road, same as Mahwee and Mack?" Natey asked.

"I think so. It seems to be their M.O."

"What's M.O.?"

Given all his video games, I thought for sure Nate Sr. would have told Natey what an M.O. was. He'd consider it his fatherly duty.

"M.O. stands for 'modus operandi,' which is like 'the way somebody does things.' It's kind of like a pattern. You know how Flan is in the backyard and hears a dog walk by, then he runs like mad through the house and jumps on the couch to look out the window and bark?"

This brought a tiny smile to Natey's face.

"That would be Flan's M.O.," I said.

"M.O. is the bad dognappers putting chawk marks too."

"That's right."

"Those stowen dogs have fwamiwies yike us," Natey said.

"They do, yes. It's very sad they lost their doggies."

"The yady with red hair. Her dog was stowen too."

I looked up at the rearview mirror and our eyes met.

"I knew you were listening, you little eavesdropper. I have to watch you."

"Mama, she was youd," he said defensively.

"You're right. The lady's name is Ellen. She had an albino pig, I mean Pug."

"What's owbino?"

"Albino is, well some people—actually it's not just people. It's all mammals, I think. See, there's something called genes . . ."

"Pants?"

Why were there "jeans" and "genes"? Had the word creators run out of sounds such that we had to take existing words and give them completely different meanings? All that did was cause confusion for children and immigrants from foreign lands trying to learn the native tongue. No wonder the driver's test is in twenty-five languages.

"Not pants, no. Genes are something we all have in us, but basically it means her dog was white with red eyes," I said.

"There was a girl in school with red eyes. Is she owbino?"

"Could be. What was her name?"

"Jennifer. She was nice."

"No reason an albino person wouldn't be nice," I said. "Except if someone like Colin Blackpool bullies them. Then they might get mad. But that would have nothing to do with eye color. albino anythings are rare."

"Cowin thought she was spooky."

"You've realized something very important," I said, pulling up in front of our house. "When people are unusual, like albinos, other people are afraid of them. But when a dog is unusual, like an albino Pug, people want them."

But I'd lost his attention. Flan was on the couch looking out the window at us, and Natey was halfway out of the car, racing for the house.

The next muff book club and cocktail gathering was days away, and I found myself doing more than skimming *Girls & Sex.* I was reading it, and no one was more surprised than I was. What finally made me give it a try was a combination of *Muffia* spirit and fear that I could be missing vital information should I start dating again, and meeting Denny showed me that was a real possibility.

Four days after the party, he called. But the conversation hadn't flowed as smoothly as it had at Lauren's. Nor had it been as flirty and fun I felt like both of us were hesitating. For my part, I couldn't figure out how to fit a love life into my life and I put on the brakes. If he was feeling the same, it explains why we made no plans to see each other. Now a week had gone by since the party and we'd been reduced to exchanging animal videos on Instagram. The whole thing was disappointing, but the experience had a positive upside: the possibility of sex in my future. Hence making the attempt to tackle the muffs latest read.It had also been a week since Molly and Mack's disappearance, with no clues about who took them, despite George throwing a lot of money into the search.

According to Lauren, no other dogs in her neighborhood had been stolen, or none anyone would admit to, which only increased the family's grieving. Lauren blamed herself for not listening to me and letting the dogs have the run of the place during the party.

Meanwhile, the 'nappers in my neighborhood had made off with a Goldendoodle and a one-year-old yellow Labrador Retriever, the latest leash-snatch victim.

Apparently, the Retriever had been out for a walk with his owner, a middle-aged woman with muscles who regularly attended Reformer Pilates, when the dog's leash was snatched out of her hand by a napper, who then ran down the street with the dog into a waiting van, pursued by the owner. There was something about that story resonated. I recalled somebody chasing a van in front of the house a couple of months ago. Or had I been watching a TV show in which somebody was chasing a van? Things were blurring together.

By this point, any reasonable person would think that after the theft of seven dogs in the immediate neighborhood, the nappers would move on to another city, or at least a different neighborhood. The reality was, they only seemed to get bolder. But, as Ellen Pirosh told me, the police maintained there was nothing they could do. Still, the situation seemed unsustainable. At our house, everyone grew more protective of Flan. Tobias and Apryl were sworn to vigilance, and Natey set up elaborate systems involving nails and falling crockery to scare would-be dog nappers and to alert us if anyone tried to tamper with the gate, fence, and doors. If anyone took Flan for a walk, he or she was to carry a knife. It was a dull knife, for threat purposes, mostly. But fueled by adrenaline and a good angle of entry, even a dull knife can do some damage.

It may have been illogical, given the dognappers' boldness in stealing a leashed dog out of the hands of his walker, to think Tobias and Apryl could foil a plot to steal Flan, but they'd both grown to love the little beast so much I think they'd protect him at their own peril. Apryl was an animal person by nature, and Tobias, despite calling Flan "the fantastic farter," didn't want to take a nap without him. So I was sure if anyone tried to lay a hand on our dog, that person better watch out.

We were also in and out of the house all day long and at different hours, so a prospective thief of any kind was, in theory, less likely to choose our house to break into. Burglars tend to target homes where the occupants maintain a consistent and predictable schedule, nine-to-five, say. In the absence of an alarm, such a person leaves a thief eight hours of unhampered thieving time. But that was house was not our house. Our house and our dog were rarely left alone and if they were, it was never on any sort of predictable schedule.

Having Tobias and Apryl around had proven to be not only good for theft prevention, but for a lot of other reasons too. They hadn't created more work, as I'd feared; instead they had lessened the load.

And whereas the mood in the house might have been one of morose sadness, given what was happening between Nate and me, with engaged housemates, the house was one of hope and optimism. Apryl talked to Natey tirelessly about horses and riding, and though Tobias was hardly father material, he seemed to enjoy being a mentor. The fact that I felt he focused too much time on developing Natey's innate color sense and appreciation of fine colognes was nothing in the scheme of things.

Yes, I thought, taking Natey's hand. On the home front things were looking up—other than a pending divorce, lack of a job, half-baked business plan, and fear of dating, of course.

CHAPTER 22

JELICKA SAT in the middle of her velvet sofa, holding court and a cocktail I'd mixed for her. She was dressed in a pretty flowery sheath and glowed from within, completely in her element as hostess of this evening's gathering of the *Muffia* book club.

"So, the reason I wanted us to read this book is because—well, it should be obvious—we're all girls, we are the mothers and sisters and aunts and daughters of girls, and sex—capital S-E-X—is, like our muffs, front and center. There's no getting around it, sex is huge in all our lives, and we are living in insane times."

"Nothing's changed," said Rachel. "HashtagMeToo may have made a tiny divot, but I seriously doubt the patriarchy is going to change its behavior. Committing unwanted groping is like a rite of passage as far as these guys are concerned. As for the act itself, it's never changed. You put the peg in the hole. Some do it nicely, while some are serial abusers and Supreme Court justices."

Jelicka rolled her eyes, but Rachel was just being her contrary self, and this was touchy subject matter.

"There's nothing different about the *act* and yes, there will always be those men who don't think they need to adjust," said Jelicka. "But I was hoping the book might get your creative juices flowing. There are certainly a lot of big themes you could put into your paintings."

"Possibly," Rachel said, unconvinced.

"I'm talking about the whole gestalt of it—how women negotiate the landscape, you know?" Jelicka was speaking to all of us now. "What are the games girls play in the twenty-first century—pre and postcoital? What are the societal norms? How do we negotiate the new landscape?"

I had no idea, and I found no answers as I scanned my friends' faces. Some were scowling, and some looked relieved to be in committed relationships, not having to deal with it. A couple of muffs, I noted, weren't even there to express their opinions.

"I read it," I said. "Don't be shocked."

"How could we not be shocked?" said Paige. "Sarah reading disrupts the status quo."

Just what I was worried about.

"I know I am quite alarmed," Kiki said, winking at me.

"So little faith," I said, taking a sip of my Manhattan. "I'd even lead the discussion but I think we should wait until everyone gets here. Sex is a topic people don't like to miss. Lauren's never gotten over missing the vibrator discussion."

"Well, people need to be on time," said Madelyn. "Sorry, but why is that so difficult? Quinn won't even be here. She's in Australia with Taraji P. Henson doing an Ugg commercial."

"Fun," said Vicki. "I need new slippers. Can she get us a deal?"

"It does get to be too late when we start late," said Paige. "We don't have time to talk about everything there is to talk about. Besides, Lauren has a manny and she's still late, so we should start."

"Great—I'll start," said Vicki. "To me the book was about everything surrounding sex and less about the act itself. I found it fascinating, and I'm glad I'm not twenty years old. Things are bleak."

"Yeah," said Rachel, eyeing a tray of samosas on Jelicka's

glass and steel coffee table. "I admit I didn't get that far into it. Chapter Two was called 'Are We Having Fun Yet?' But since I wasn't, I stopped." She popped a samosa into her mouth.

"It wasn't meant to be fun," wailed Jelicka. "I thought we all could learn something."

Vicki snorted. "But book *club* is supposed to be fun."

"I found it fun," said Kiki. "In a sort of 'let's observe the wildebeests' sort of way. But I'm with Vicki, and I'm just glad I'm not dating."

"Me too," said Paige, then realizing. "I mean just 'me too.' You know, no hashtag."

"This got me," Rachel said, cracking open her copy. "Page forty-eight, subchapter entitled, 'Why do they call it a blow *job*?' Here's your answer: because it *is* a job. There's about fifteen thousand words here on whether to spit or swallow." She snapped the book closed. "So no, I don't need to read that. I'm not sure I'll ever give a blow *job* again."

"It isn't a 'hopeful' book," said Madelyn, a muff with an adolescent daughter. "I'm just relieved Lila isn't asking to get her muff waxed anymore. I tried to find out if she'd gone to one of those 'rainbow parties.' She swore she hadn't, but I still went snooping for lipstick and could only find gloss. They don't do it with gloss do they?"

"Wait, what?" I said. "I read the book, I swear. How did I miss the rainbow parties?"

"It was on 'Ellen,'" said Kiki. "Packs of little girls wearing different shades of lipstick go down on lots of little boys, one after another, and whichever girl gets her color lipstick farthest up a cock, wins."

"Oh yeah," said Rachel. "She wins real big. Giving head is the path to popularity!"

At that moment, I was very happy not to have a beautiful daughter. Then again, the image of a lipstick ring on Natey's penis wasn't a pleasant thought, either.

Rachel continued. "I think women must be taking drugs if they say they like giving blow jobs. I mean, think about it."

There was some general mumbling, but no one wanted that argument. Depending on your prevailing viewpoint, going down a guy could be laborious, joyous—I remembered it being so a couple of times—or just mildly amusing."

Paige sighed. "So sad. Carlotta's only six, and I was hyper-vigilant about her playdates *before* reading the damned book."

"Who'd think *you'd* be a prude?" Jelicka said, eyeing Rachel. "Ms. 'I-paint-men-without-dicks' getting all righteous . . ."

"I'm not a prude," said Rachel. "I just refuse to be like-able—or give blow jobs—in order to get a guy."

"If it makes you feel better, they say reports of rainbow parties are exaggerated," Paige said. "It made me feel better."

"The fact that they happen at all is appalling." Rachel sure was up on that high horse. "And I don't even have kids."

Madelyn, ever the diplomat, got us back on track. "The thing is, there is this instinctual imperative to mate, like it or hate it. So what the book was about for me was the whole dance of deception we do to get laid."

"Or avoid getting laid," Rachel said, snatching another samosa. "And I also want to make the point that the English language has fallen on hard times. Someone has to speak up for what things mean. Sex is the act. The rest is the dance."

Paige sighed again. "The Internet's made everything so accessible now. Boys watch porn and think that's what sex is, and girls see it and say, 'Yikes, I'm supposed to do *that*?'"

"Not to mention feeling like they have to send twat pictures," said Rachel. "The pressure put on them to have pussy surgery is huge."

Jelicka shifted in her seat. It was a surgery that most of us thought she'd had.

Madelyn got up and returned with a bottle of dry rosé and poured a glass for Jelicka and me before topping off her own. She only ever brought wine to book club, and no one minded because she always brought really good wine. We also didn't mind that when she hosted us, she took care of everything. Some of us had decided this was because Madelyn lived farther away than the rest of us and feared if she were to call a potluck, people would be less likely to make the drive. I admit, we did complain (but only to each other) about the hour and a half it took to get to Agoura Hills and Madelyn's McMansion, but once we'd arrived and saw the spread, it was always worth the trip. Although there had been that one awkward evening, just after Udi died, when the food kept coming, only it was multiple deliveries from multiple take-out places. But when your hostess's lover dies on top of her hours before book club, such things are understandable.

"Vicki, is it my imagination, or have you stopped videotaping us?" asked Madelyn, changing topics. "It's making me think we're not interesting anymore."

"Oh no, we're plenty interesting. I just had so much footage, I decided to go back through everything I'd already shot. This would have been a good meeting to shoot, but there's still plenty of muffia movie to mine, trust me."

"I better not be in it," said Rachel.

"Wow, Rachel, what's with you today?" said Paige. "Anything you want to tell us?"

"Nope." Rachel stood, heading for the bathroom.

Kiki shrugged. "Guess she'll tell us when she's ready."

Madelyn glanced at Vicki. "I'm sure Vicki will show us what she's working on before she shows it to outsiders, right Vicki?"

"Absolutely," she said, getting the message. "Everyone gets to approve the cut before I show it to any non-muff. I also might need to do reshoots."

"Better hurry up," said Paige, "I'm getting older by the second. Pretty soon people will think I was played by two different actresses."

"It's documentary," said Vicki. "People age in documentaries all the time."

"Ugh, could we not talk about aging," Jelicka said. "I just spent too much on Botox and injectibles." She deposited a large platter next to the tabbouleh and kale salad. "Seared Portobello mushrooms for all of you food-phobic types."

"What are you talking about?" Kiki said. "Mushrooms are like the number-one thing people are afraid of eating. Mushrooms, insects and romaine lettuce."

"We aren't food *phobic*," said Paige. "There are foods some of us are *allergic* to."

Jelicka sighed. "I get it, but you have to admit, as a group we are running out of things all of us can eat. Mushrooms weren't on the banned substances list put out by the allergic muff subcommittee."

"Ha-ha," said Kiki.

"And hey—they're seared! How unusual," Vicki said, with no hint of irony.

I threw her a look.

Jelicka's fixation with searing had begun when her now ex-husband commissioned a custom set of searing implements bearing their intertwined initials. Together they branded their initials into steaks, vegetables, even ice cream. When he left her for an older woman, Jelicka threw the locked initials off Mulholland Drive and commissioned her own custom searing tool—a giant "J" with a knife running through it which she used to sear most of his belongings before returning them via Uber. She knew it was more than a little vindictive and was in therapy, but judging from the mushroom tops, she wasn't done working out whatever it was she was dealing with.

"It's not like we're pretending to be allergic just to make it difficult," said Paige.

"I'm only saying that being allergic to foods is 'in' right now. It's trendy to have a food allergy." Jelicka wasn't one for political correctness.

"So what are you saying, Jel?" said Kiki. "You think people want to have food allergies?"

"I just eat what I want," Rachel said, reappearing. "Screw it."

She was really working that "brand is bitch" thing.

"Maybe doctors have finally started connecting our symptoms with actual allergies?" I suggested.

"Here's what's coming up for me right now," said Madelyn, diplomatically inserting herself once more. "We are lucky enough to be in Jelicka's beautiful home, with all these yummy Portobellos to eat, hand-seared by Jelicka, and talking about one of our favorite topics. Let's enjoy the food and each other's company, knowing none of us is at risk of being stoned to death or forced to give blow jobs."

There were murmurs of agreement, but I know I saw Rachel wince.

"And we're going to keep it that way," Madelyn said, lifting her glass.

That was something else we could all drink to.

CHAPTER 23

"YOU'RE WAY ahead of me but I'm determined to catch up," Lauren said, coming through the door an hour later. "I need wine. It's been an awful week but I just had to see everyone." With minor fanfare, she collapsed onto Jelicka's sofa. Madelyn had her glass of rosé ready.

"To paraphrase Betty Davis," she said, clasping the wine glass, "'Running a charity when you have a husband and two kids is not for sissies.' It probably goes without saying: I didn't read the book." She raised the glass to her lips and took a giant gulp.

Running a charity was a big job to be sure, but Molly and Mack disappearing was the real reason her week had been awful. Her face appeared drawn, and I got the impression she'd lost weight since the dogs had gone missing. Though Lauren was always trying to lose ten pounds, having your family's beloved animals stolen was no way to do it. But no one was talking about the dogs. Did they not know?

"Then you won't be annoyed we already started talking about it," Paige was saying.

"Not at all," said Lauren. "I'm relieved. What's the verdict?"

"Depends on who you ask," Jelicka said with a trace of annoyance, before setting a plate of food on the table in front of Lauren. "Here—to go with your wine."

"Your entrance was perfectly timed," said Kiki. "We're ready for the roundy."

"Do you want to go first?" Jelicka said.

Lauren choked out a "yes" as tears formed then she launched. Starting with the party—explaining first that it was mostly for neighbors and people from the kids' school—she told them I was there to be set up with her friend Denny.

"Nothing happened," I told them.

Lauren looked at me. "But he really liked you. It was obvious."

"Well, it didn't carry over to the phone," I said. "Keep going."

Lauren continued, from the moment she realized the family's Boston Terriers weren't running around anymore, to the search, the chalk marks, calling the police, how sad everyone was, and how no progress had been made in the investigation. The only "break" in the case, which was no break at all, was the discovery that Lauren's home was one of many in her Brentwood neighborhood tagged with chalk marks, indicating there were stealable dogs living inside. This had led the authorities to become more vigilant, or so they claimed. It was small comfort for those whose dogs continued to go missing or were already gone.

Jelicka was riveted. Given her penchant for the exposure of malfeasance of any kind, we all knew what she was thinking.

"You're getting ideas, Jel," said Vicki. "Chill."

"What ideas am I getting?"

"Dognappers should be shot," declared Rachel.

Jelicka nodded. "I did think that."

"If each of us shot the people we don't think deserve to live, there'd be no one left alive," said Kiki.

"Just because we *want* to shoot them doesn't mean we're *going* to," Jelicka retorted.

"No matter how much we might want to," agreed Rachel.

"How are the kids?" I asked. "Any better?"

"Gavin's really upset, but I don't think Amanda fully understands, which is probably for the best. George is the one I'm worried about. I had no idea he was so attached."

As far as I knew, George had never known hardship. He was born into privilege, and this might well be his first brush with adversity.

"Dog theft is on the rise," Paige said. "I heard it on NPR. It's like a fad."

"A fad?" said Vicki, derisively. "Kombucha is a fad. This is more like an epidemic. Another example of societal decline."

"Let's stick with epidemic," said Paige, "If it's happening all over, it must mean there's more than one group doing the stealing."

"Maybe one main ring with lots of members?" I suggested.

"The question is," said Jelicka. "How are they still getting away with it when so many people know it's happening? Are the cops in on it?"

I didn't roll my eyes, but the thought crossed my mind. "In my neighborhood, seven dogs have been stolen. And there was that day when I foiled an attempt to steal Flan."

"Did I know that?" said Jelicka. "Did you tell us this?"

"It was in an email," Paige said.

"I mean, I'm pretty sure that's what I foiled," I said. "The guy was wearing a hoody."

"I take back my take back. Dognappers really should be shot," Rachel said.

"The cops say short of catching the bad guys in the act, there's nothing they can do," Lauren sighed. "They claim they don't have the officers and the city's too spread out to just post patrol cars."

Jelicka had that look in her eye—the one she got whenever

something was amiss that she believed she could fix. She wore the same expression when she decided Udi wasn't dead but involved in a nefarious international plot in which he was only pretending to be dead. As far as I knew, she was still trying to "decode" the note Quinn found in her suitcase when she returned from Tokyo—where Quinn swears she saw Udi walking around the airport. How Quinn could have recognized the guy when she'd only seen him once, naked and dead on Madelyn's day bed, was a question nobody but Madelyn and I seemed concerned about.

"Speaking of conspiracies," said Paige, making the same mental connection about Jelicka that I had, "what did you find out about that note in Quinn's bag?"

Madelyn stood. She hated this topic. "Going to get some air."

Paige forged on. "Did you take it to Peet's Coffee where those Israeli guys hang out?"

"I did," said Jelicka. "I mean, it's just down the hill from here."

"Well, what did it say?" Kiki asked.

"Still hard to tell at this point," said Jelicka. "There are conflicting translations. One guy thought it said, 'Ask for Rivka and sit on the patio.' Another said, 'Two pounds of potatoes, lambs to slaughter' or possibly 'roast lamb.' My friend Schmool says it's difficult to make out the letters. But the truth is, I don't think any of them have kept up with their Hebrew except to speak it."

"Can we please not talk about this anymore?" Madelyn said, coming back into the room. "Udi was *my* lover and I am asking—No, I am *demanding* that you all let him and the subject go. Okay—? Enough."

"Maddie, how can we not pursue it?" Jelicka said. "It could be important. 'See something, say something' right?"

Madelyn picked up the wine bottle and poured herself

another glass. "Go catch some dognappers instead. But don't shoot them."

Jelicka, presumably in deference to Madelyn, turned her attention back to me. "Are you sure you didn't notice anything about the person who tried to steal your dog—what's his name again?"

"Flan," I said. "Like the dessert."

"Like her amazing cookies," Lauren said. "She really needs to start selling them. They are *so* good."

"Can we stay on topic please?" said Jelicka. "Was he white? Black? Latino?"

"White."

"So, did you perfect the recipe since the batch you brought to Kiki's?" asked Paige.

"I'm still testing safe organic preservatives," I said.

"She needs to stop testing and sell them. They're so good!" Lauren continued. "I'm telling you, everyone at the party wanted to know where they could buy those cookies."

"I'll buy some freakin' cookies," said Jelicka, exasperated. "I'll buy ten bags of cookies. But after we talk about the dognapping."

"That hoody was to throw suspicion on our people, I bet," said Kiki.

"Your people?" said Vicki, smiling. "Rich people from Encino?"

"Ha—" said Kiki, who *was* a rich person living in Encino, but the fact that she identified as black was also true.

I didn't think any of us should lose track of our origins, nor the roads we've traveled. But it seems to me we also have to consider where we *are* at any given point and to acknowledge we are all part of many groups—parents, residents, yoga practitioners—even Italian-Jewish single mothers who live in Santa Monica and bake is a defined group with interests to protect. The dividing lines between us can be drawn in different places, depending on what serves us at the time. I've always felt we are more alike than different and that the tribal, competitive "my" people and "your" people only serves to divide. Then again, I'm a privileged white woman. So, even though I'll likely never be in Kiki's financially superior league, I'll never feel the full extent of what she's endured by being born Black.

The roundy went on, and the muffs made me realize I was dragging my feet on the cookies. At the last book club, I still hadn't worked out the recipe. Now that I had the recipe, the holdup was getting from the test kitchen to market, and that would require solving the issue of needing gobs of money and hiring people. These were more formidable obstacles. But unless I tried, nothing was going to happen.

Vicki's big news was planning a Kickstarter campaign for her political documentary that she'd announced at Kiki's. She was still tight-lipped about the subject matter, but she promised to tell us at the next book club. All systems were go with Paige. She was teaching tennis and loved being married. Kiki told us an extended family had bought the porn house next door and so far they'd been good neighbors. Madelyn was going slow with Cullen, the guy she'd met vibrator shopping and didn't want to jinx it by saying more. Jelicka passed her real estate exam on the second try, and was seeking referrals so she could begin her new life as a realtor. But she reverted to form as we gathered up our things announcing, "Now that I'm a realtor, I am uniquely positioned to do all sorts of things. One of those things is using my new-found access to end dog theft. The dognappers better watch out because *The Muffia* is on the case now."

I didn't want to ask Jelicka what she had in mind or why she'd volunteered all of us to the cause, but Madelyn was visibly relieved she had a new wrong to right, and offered to help. So did the rest of us. Paige already went to neighborhood meetings and said she'd organize a new pet-vigilance council. Kiki and Vicki knew whom to call in their own neighborhoods. I offered to get in touch with Ellen Pirosh and Lauren said she'd get George to ask the company for another investigator.

And as Jelicka opened the door to send us into the mild fall night, she turned to Rachel. "We may not shoot them. But we're going to string 'em up by the balls."

CHAPTER 24

WHEN I came through the front door from book club, Flan was in one of his favorite spots, on Tobias's lap, while the latter sat enthralled with *The Man in the High Castle*, a TV show that imagines an America if the Nazis had won.

"What is it about that show that people like?" I said. "Could it be the producers are trying to tell us, 'See—things could be even worse!'"

"I can't take my eyes off Rufus Sewell's Nazi Commandant," said Tobias, gazing at the screen. "I wonder if it means something."

I assessed Mr. Sewell. "Well, he's terrifying. I hope he's not your type."

"Don't wreck it for me," said Tobias, pausing Rufus mid-scowl.

Flan showed his indifference by hopping off the sofa to snortle around my legs.

"How was book club? Get enough Muff Stuff 'til the next time?"

I shrugged. "What would you expect when you read a book called *Girls & Sex*?"

"You do realize that for a gay man, listening to that would be a mild form of torture."

"Well then, you can alert your hetero brethren about how not to treat women."

"I don't usually socialize with macho types but if

something changes, I'll be sure to tell him about that enticing title."

He switched off the TV and opened his laptop. "As for your son and I, we did a PG-13 marathon starting with the remake of *Incredible Journey* followed by *Finding Dory*, where the only thing sexual is the opening and closing of clam shells; though it was a welcome break from *Princess Bride*. And just so you know, Mr. Sewell called me back to him only an hour ago. I have been *working*."

He said the word up a full register.

"Well, good. Any progress on the job front?"

"The big news is," Tobias glanced up from his laptop, "I have decided to retool."

"As in learn a new skill?" I let out an inadvertent yawn. "Sorry. I thought you said it looked good for Sur la Table."

"That *is* what I said, but it's taking forever and not only will I go insane waiting with nothing to do, if something happens at the end of their search and they 'go a different way,' I will have been six months out of the labor force. That's like being permanently unemployable."

It sounded like an exaggeration, but I'd been seven *years* out of the labor force.

"So," he was saying, "I've been thinking I should learn computer systems design, but I loathe computers. I'd rather be beaten with a rolling pin. So I'm going to . . ."

As soon as the words "rolling pin" left his mouth, I felt as though I'd been hit with one. The memory the hit had shaken loose? His offer to help me get my cookie empire off the ground a few weeks earlier. Paige quizzed me about my cookies the whole way home from book club. She reminded me of what Lauren said about how good they were and asked what was taking so long if I'd perfected the recipe. The answer to the question, "Where was my business plan?" was I had no plan, only dreams of a cookie empire with no clear way to get there. And now that I was ready to move forward, I was afraid to, which was only sensible, or so I told myself, since I lacked know-how and start-up funds.

So was I now ready to take Tobias up on his offer? I figured it was worth a conversation.

"Would you like a flan cookie?" I asked him.

"Would I like Chris Hemsworth to give me a scalp massage? Don't be daft. Where have you been hiding them? Because you know I went looking."

I let out a laugh. "They're well hidden, believe me. I have to come up with some pretty ingenious ways to make sure they don't get eaten with all you cookie monsters around. I'm still vaguely testing preservatives, but I'm pretty sure they're ready for the Farmer's Market."

"Give me your oldest cookie," he said, moving the computer off his lap. "Let me taste."

I opened a drawer containing our DVDs and long-unplayed CDs and extracted a small tub. "These have been in here for ten days."

"You sneaky, sneaky woman. You mean to tell me if I had gone searching for R-rated fare, I would have found them?"

He devoured the first cookie, which was a golden color with buttery reddish brown edges, and took another while still chewing. "Delicious. Never would have known they aren't fresh."

I produced another sealed, tamper-proof tub from under the couch. "This one is ten days with a little diatomaceous earth mixed into the recipe."

He snatched it up and took a bite. "Crispier," he said, still chewing. "Also delicious."

I nodded. "Now taste this."

"Wait, I need a palate cleanser." He took a sip of bottled water.

I offered him the next cookie, to which I'd added the

smallest amounts of honey and garlic—yes, garlic—both supposedly healthy preservatives.

"Tastes different," he said. "Hold on." He cleansed his palate again, took a bite of the first cookie, thought a bit, took another sip of water, took a bite of the second cookie, chewed that, then took a second bite of the third cookie."

"Well?" I said.

"Not that one," he said, putting down the garlic-honey cookie. "Something . . ."

"What?"

". . .store-bought about it."

"Not garlicy?"

"What? No!" he said. "The other two are both delicious, but one's crispier and the other chewier. Hard to know which I like better."

"I could make two versions: a crispy *and* a chewy."

"What have you done with them since the last time we talked—I mean beyond trying different recipes and ways of keeping them fresh?"

"Just getting people to taste them, you know."

"And what do they say, these people?"

"They like them. I feel pretty good about that. They say they'd buy them if they were in a store."

He took another cookie from the first batch. "Well, what are you waiting for? Get them out there."

This time, he didn't offer to help, which was probably my own fault for shooting him down the first time. He picked up his laptop and put it back on his lap. "What do you think about a 'Social Network Marketing' class? I'd try it but I know whatever I learn will be obsolete three months later."

"Tobias," I said. "Taking a class is a good idea. But you know how you offered to help with my cookies?"

He stopped chewing and looked at me. *Did he remember?* I forged on.

"Because, well—if the offer still holds, I'd like to take you up on it."

He finished chewing the cookie in his mouth and swallowed.

"I mean, you need something to do and I need help with my cookies. If your job does come through, I'm sure we can work things out. But in the meantime, you can say you are an executive of a start-up in the snack industry. Sounds better than saying 'unemployed,' don't you think?"

He closed the laptop. "Have you been drinking?"

"No! I mean yes, I had some wine, but that was hours ago."

"Why'd you change your mind?"

"I didn't change my mind. But when you originally offered, I didn't know how I'd pay you. I still don't. But flan cookies will only be successful if I get them out in the world. Until then, they're only a possibility. So maybe you take a piece of the company in return for getting it off the ground?"

"That's generally the way it's done," he said examining the remaining cookies.

Collecting the last cookie from each batch, he scrutinized them before again tasting and comparing flavors. He chewed more carefully this time, not giving anything away, and I felt uncomfortable, like I was waiting for a verdict in my misdemeanor fraud trial for selling fake Vuitton luggage.

"No pressure," I said finally, picking up the empty containers. "I just thought since you brought it up, you might still be interested. That's all." I headed for the kitchen.

"By the way," he said, calling me back. "Remember how you didn't believe I'd seen Apryl all dolled up?" He popped the last bit of the last cookie in his mouth, then started swiping at his phone. "She went out not long after you did. I took a picture."

I'd never seen Apryl in the glamorous altered state Tobias claimed to have seen her, but I also knew he was not her biggest fan. It almost seemed like he was waiting to expose her—for what, I don't think he knew.

"Sometimes I think you just like to create drama," I said. "She's a simple girl."

"Simply slutty is more like it, but this time I caught her. It's through the window, but you can still tell."

"You don't like Apryl, that's what this is about," I said. "Have you seen how good she is with Natey? Which reminds me, I need to schedule another riding lesson."

"We don't always know what's lurking in the hearts of humans," he said. "Take your ex. Ah—here we are." He'd found the picture and held his phone out for me to look.

It might have been Apryl in the picture, except for the four-inch heels and tight minidress. Whoever it was looked hot, but I would never have said it was Apryl except for the fact she was getting into her own car.

"It does look like her," I agreed.

"It's her," he said emphatically. "Got any more cookies hidden away?"

"If you gain weight, you'll be even more miserable than you are now. Only fatter."

"You're right—there's plenty of time to get fat and happy after we make twenty million bucks in the cookie business."

"Does that mean you'll help? Really?"

He smiled. "I don't want to get ahead of ourselves, but these cookies could be just the start of something huge, Sarah. There are so many ways to go—capturing flavors in new baked forms. The possibilities are endless."

"You really think so?"

"I really do. And another thing—it's going to be fun."

"Yes," I said, in full agreement. "If it's not a little bit fun, why do it?"

Flan, on his bed nearby, let out a couple of grunts, causing both of us to laugh.

"We're naming our debut cookies after you. How about a little gratitude?" I told the dog before facing Tobias. "You'd think we were asking him to do all the work."

Suddenly Tobias and I looked at Flan, then back at each other, two bulbs blinking on at the same time.

"He's the perfect mascot for the company," I said.

Tobias nodded. "Perfect."

And with that we'd made our first business decision. We were in business.

CHAPTER 25

THE FOLLOWING morning, my arms were full of dirty laundry when I collided with Apryl in the upstairs hall as she came out of the bathroom, eliciting a frightened yelp from both of us.

"Sorry," I said, even though she was the one who had stepped into the hall like she was the only person in the house. One might think, after all the noise I'd been making picking up Natey's room, that she might have checked the hallway before proceeding.

She gasped then shook her head, grabbing hold of the doorframe for support, and I noticed she hadn't removed her eye makeup from the night before.

"Where'd you go last night? Looks like a wild one."

She was doing some sort of recovery breathing. "I just shouldn't have had that second cocktail."

She offered nothing else, and, with the laundry growing heavy in my arms, now wasn't the time for a pop quiz. And despite her caked makeup and Tobias's concerns, I still couldn't believe Apryl was living some sort of double life. She was just behaving like most young American women. It was hardly newsworthy.

I squatted to pick up a pair of fallen underwear, and as I came back up, she was facing away from me, moving off down the hall.

"Hey," I said. "When's good for Natey's next riding lesson? With the cookies and everything else, I have to get something on the calendar."

She stopped but didn't turn back.

"Is this a bad time?" I asked. Maybe something *had* happened last night.

"Apryl, are you all right? You can talk to me; I'm a pretty good listener."

I could see her hands fidgeting with what seemed like too many rings. "I'm fine. Really."

No, she was not fine. I waited, wondering whether, if we were to swap places, I would appreciate advice from someone like me, or if I'd tell her it was none of her business. I decided I'd appreciate the offer, if not the advice, so I forged ahead, dropping the laundry onto the carpeted hall to give Apryl my full attention.

"We just read *Girls & Sex* for book club," I began. "Well, *some* of us did. But after listening to everyone talk last night, let's just say I know what you're dealing with—hook-up apps, having sex with people you don't like, not having sex with people you *do* like. I mean, women have always had to deal with dating bullshit but—just don't let anyone disrespect you, that's the main thing. Don't do anything you don't want to do."

Apryl's discomfort now seemed more like embarrassment, her arms covering her chest.

"Maybe it's not my place to say anything. I just wanted you to know I'm here and can lend an ear if you need. I can also keep a secret."

Her wan smile told me that any secrets she might have would remain her secrets.

"Well, now that that's out of the way," I said, "check your schedule and let me know if you have time to give Natey a lesson this weekend."

"Sure," she said vaguely peering out the tiny hall window onto the street. "I, um, might need to go out of town."

"Another horse show?" I asked.

For the first time since the conversation began, her eyes focused on me. "Yeah, it's, ah, upstate."

I would have thought if one was going to a horse show one would know ahead of time. Then again, I had a lot to learn about horses, horse shows, and, so it seemed, my equestrian tenant.

"Hey, don't you go to Pilates on Wednesdays?" Apryl said suddenly, dropping her arms.

Had I told her I had a regular Pilates class? Why was that even interesting?

"Sometimes," I said. "But today Tobias and I have a cookie meeting."

"You're going to eat cookies?"

"Why do you ask?"

She focused on something non-existent near my feet, her expression unreadable. "Mmmm. . . I just thought Flan looked a little uncomfortable yesterday."

What did that have to do with Pilates? "He seemed fine last night," I said.

Seeing Tobias and Flan happily watching TV when I returned from book club, it was hard to imagine he could be any more comfortable.

"No, really, he was scratching a lot," said Apryl. "There's some nasty thing going around with the dogs at the barn—some kind of dermatitis. I thought maybe he should go to the vet this morning."

"I'll keep an eye on him," I said. "We can't have his coat falling out if he's going to be the mascot for Flan Cookies."

"He's going to be your mascot?" This seemed to cause greater distress. She went to the window and gazed out. "I didn't check to see if he'd rubbed himself raw anywhere, but if you're going to take pictures, you might want to do that right away."

The whole discussion was bizarre. Something was definitely off. "Apryl, you don't seem like yourself this morning. What happened last night?"

"Nothing. It's like I said, too many Moscow Mules. But seriously, Flan might need to go to the vet. Soon. Like today. So it doesn't get worse."

She pulled her cell phone from a hidden pocket and began texting. Then she looked out the window again, and I felt compelled to do the same. "Is something happening out there?"

"Just checking the weather," she said, as if glancing out the window was all it took.

On the street, I saw nothing out of the ordinary. A van emblazoned with the words "Big Mac's HVAC" was parked across the street in front of the McMansion. A couple of teenagers on motorized scooters went by.

There was the sound of a text hitting her phone. She looked at it and seemed immediately relieved.

"Sorry, I don't mean to worry you," she said. "The vet will probably give you some ointment for him and it will clear up in a few days."

"As I said, I'm not worried, but I'll have a look just the same."

She moved off down the hall toward her room. "I'll text you about the weekend," she said over her shoulder. "Right now, I'm going back to sleep." And with that, she disappeared inside, closing the door.

I stepped to the window and could see that on the street, Big Mac's HVAC van had gone, leaving the usual morning view from this window. The street sign at the corner was still crooked and most of the parked vehicles were those I saw every morning. The ones I didn't recognize hardly appeared suspicious.

I let out a sigh. There was something Apryl wasn't telling me, and it had nothing to do with Flan's skin condition.

Natey's laundry started up in the washing machine, and I went looking for Flan. Though I doubted he had any issues requiring the attention of a veterinarian, I'd also doubted Nate would fool around on me with another woman. That belief had been proved wrong multiple times.

I found our new mascot on the arm of the couch in his usual position, staring out the front window and whining as a fancy-clipped Standard Poodle strolled by with his equally fancy-panted owner. I wondered if anyone had tried to steal him or her as they'd tried to steal Flan? Perhaps poodles were not on the list of most stealable pooches.

"Flan, that's enough whining," I said, sitting down next to him as he collapsed into a writhing, wriggling puddle, part in and part out of my lap, asking to be belly-rubbed.

I happily complied while searching for evidence of his alleged skin condition. But after turning him this way and that, I found only two small patches of dry skin—one on each of his front elbows. Neither seemed raw or remotely new. So what *was* Apryl talking about? I gazed out for the third time that day and saw nothing unusual on Sixteenth Street. It was a day like any other.

On my way back upstairs to clean the bathroom, Flan let out a bark even before the doorbell rang.

Whoever was at the door had snuck up on us but Flan was no slouch in the guard dog department, even if he fell down on the job as soon as he smelled a treat. Peeking out the front window, I saw it was Ellen Pirosh on the stoop. She had a sour expression on her face, making it unlikely her Pug had been returned. But as *The Muffia* was now committed to ending dog theft, I owed it to the cause to pursue all avenues. Ellen Pirosh had her finger on the pulse.

"Hi, Ellen," I said, opening the door.

"I stopped by to tell you even more dogs have been stolen,"

she said wearily. "And not just your friend's dogs in Brentwood." She thrust some flyers in my direction. "Here—I printed up new ones showing five more dogs that have gone missing in the last week. And they're just the ones we know about. We need to get the word out that dogs in all neighborhoods are at risk so they'll put pressure on the police."

"Thanks," "I'll post and pass on. And what about starting a Google group so we can share more widely?"

"Ugh, the Internet and I don't get along," said Ellen. "But if you start it, I'll share it."

I'm not on intimate terms with Tech either, but I figured it wouldn't take too long to create a Facebook page or a free website.

"We should probably do everything we can, don't you think?" I said. "Even if it seems like a waste of time. One of these days, someone will see something, say something, and these horrible people will be caught."

"That's why I'm doing this." She said this but she also seemed not to believe it.

I felt sort of sorry for her. Ellen's Pug had been her life; now it seemed like her life was about tracking down the thieves who'd taken her. She was on a mission. Jelicka was like that too, I thought. Give her a wrong to right and she's a dog on a bone, won't quit until she's exhausted all . . .

Of course! I have to put them together. Between the two of them, Ellen and Jelicka could come up with a plan to foil the dognappers. "Is your email address on here?" I glanced at the flyer and verified it was. "I'm going to put you in touch with a friend, not the one whose dogs were stolen. Another friend named Jelicka Gelman, and I am positive you will hit it off. She wants to set up a sting operation to catch the dog thieves."

"Really? Like the movie with Paul Newman?"

"Exactly, but the people won't be as well-dressed."

"Oh my God, if only we could have Paul Newman be in our sting."

"I know. Those eyes," I said.

"I was so sad when he died."

For a few seconds, I saw Ellen Pirosh mourn something other than her dog.

"He was a little before my time," I said, "but as actors go, he was a hero of mine, too. The good news about our dog sting is it won't require a Hollywood budget, because we've got Westside women on a mission."

She smiled. "I might have to watch *The Sting* again—you know, just to get in the mood." She grabbed a flyer. "This is my home number," she said, writing it down. "Tell her to call."

"I will," I said. "Meanwhile, if you have contact info for everyone you know who's had a dog stolen, or has been affected by dog theft, let's pull all that together and I'll create the Google group and Facebook page. But whatever you do, don't say anything about the sting operation. That part stays secret."

Ellen stepped onto the stoop, then turned back, a wistful expression on her face. "Even if I never see Pearly Girl again, it feels good to do something."

"Better than quitting, right?" I said. "We live at a time when our information gets stolen by Azerbaijani hackers and we have to fix it, our health insurance changes and we have nothing to say about it, our elected officials spend taxpayer funds to do things we don't want them to do and they can't be bothered protecting the rights of ordinary people." I paused, realizing how depressing all that sounded. "And on that cheery note . . ."

"No, it's true. You're right," said Ellen, who'd heard a call to action in my rant. "You gotta keep fighting."

"Yes," I said. "Giving up is not an option."

She smiled a slightly diabolical smile and I saw I'd ignited a rage inside her. "We'll show them."

"Yes, we will," I said. Then we shook on it.

CHAPTER 26

PEOPLE SURPRISE you every day. Sometimes it's the awful things they do that you just want to block out of your mind, like extremist religious groups killing each other over a difference in belief over an unprovable god, or a crazed mass shooter whose friends describe him as "the nicest guy," or the Women's Gymnastics team doctor and too many other perverts to mention.

Even though a lot of bad things happen, there's still more good than bad, it's just you don't hear about them. They aren't newsworthy in the same way mass death and destruction are. Just as people are capable of atrocities, they can also surprise you with their humanity. The key was learning how to focus on the good stuff.

Lloyd, the therapist Nate and I were seeing, suggested at one point that the two of us go out to a museum or sit in a park, to do something that would get us out of our negative rut and maybe rekindle the good feelings. So when Nate asked if he could take me for coffee and a walk on the beach one day, I said, "Sure."

He showed up in his old Volkswagen Jetta, returned to service after he surrendered his leased BMW, and we drove to the southern end of Santa Monica via Main Street, at the north end of Venice.

Coffee at Urth Cafe was civil. Both of us were on our best behavior, keeping the conversation to topics not likely to cause controversy—the causes of climate change, for example. Unlike our warring politicians, Nate and I agreed we were probably responsible—not just us, of course, but all of Western Civilization. I also filled him in on plans for marketing the cookies, as well as the latest on the dognappers. Nate didn't offer much about what was happening in his life, and I didn't probe for fear of ruining the first decent conversation we'd had in months.

When we were finished with coffee, we headed west on foot toward Venice Beach. The day was unseasonably warm and getting hotter. After the two-block stroll, we found a bench under a tree on the greenway outside Perry's Beach Cafe. From here, we could watch the rollerbladers, cyclists, dog walkers, volleyball players, surfers, kite flyers, yoga practitioners, and others performing activities I had no name for but were apparently legal.

"I want to apologize," Nate said after we'd sat there in silence for several minutes. "Sorry it's taken so long."

I shrugged. "It's okay."

It wasn't really, but I just wanted to keep him talking, wherever it might lead.

"Since I moved out," he went on, "I've been watching Natey become more sure of himself. Seems like he's almost rid of his 'L' problem."

"It's getting better," I said.

He seemed to be focusing his attention on a cruise ship on the horizon.

"I've also watched you dig in and keep going. Like scraping the money together for the mortgage every month. I couldn't have done it. I don't know what I expected, but it wasn't that."

It was a backassward compliment, but I didn't call him on it. Doing so would only shut him down. "Necessity is the mother of invention?" I suggested, making it sound like finding a way to make the mortgage every month was the result of luck, rather than any intelligence on my part.

With Nate being more vulnerable than usual, I did the dance and toned down my initial reaction.

It would be nice if one day women won't need to adjust what they say and how they say it in order to protect the fragile male ego. But for today, I wanted to keep Nate talking.

"I just got lucky with these tenants," I said. "It could have gone the other way."

A scantily-clad rollerblader rolled by slowly. Nate pretended not to see her.

"Well, it seems like you're doing really great without me," he said.

"Not *great*," I said as encouragingly as I could. "But things could be a lot worse I guess."

"The point is . . ."

I waited. He was gazing at the horizon again.

"You are moving on with your life and I'm spinning my wheels."

"Well, I don't know what else I can do," I said. "I mean—"

He held up his hand, presumably to keep me from talking. I closed my mouth.

I'm just trying to survive, I thought. But as a couple of muffs had pointed out, some women in my position might not have handled it so resiliently. They might have become alcoholics or began taking anti-depressants. Some might've lain down and quit.

Spiritual types, far more spiritual than I'll ever be, say things like, "Ten percent of life is what happens to you, and the other ninety is how you react to it." Watching the people around me and people I'd known, I was starting to see how true that was. Stevie Walls from high school blamed his cheating, ex-wife for everything that went wrong in his life, started taking pain meds, and was now in a rehab place for the third time, while my college roommate, Petra, has a violent ex-husband who hurt her. But instead of leading with that, her attitude has been: "Yup, that happened. But it's not who I am—next!"

Likewise, when something good happens, some people read too much into their success, while others see such an event as a blip on the continuum, not to be rated higher or lower than any other. They just keep going, good or bad.

"I've made a decision," he said, lowering his hand. "Let me just say it and get to the end."

I nodded for him to continue.

"It's no secret I've been having a rough time. I did some things I don't feel good about, and I hurt you. And I'm sorry for that."

This apology had been so long in coming, I thought there would be no tears left. But my blurred vision told me otherwise.

"I didn't ever not love you," he said. "You have been my rock. When things started going bad at work, I don't know, I didn't feel good about myself. And there you were, just carrying on, being you, being nice, trying to be a good mother and wife and make it all work. I didn't want to give you my weight, you know?"

Nate looked away, but I saw he might cry as well.

Just then, another rollerblader, this one male with more clothes on, went by. Both Nate and I watched as he ran over a bump in the pavement, lost his balance, tried to regain it, moving from foot to rolling foot and, at an ever-increasing backward angle to the earth, made his descent to the ground. He was now lying flat on his back. Despite his helmet and pads, he wasn't moving.

Nate stood, moving to assist, when a young woman skated

to a stop next to him. She kneeled down, a worried expression on her face, then they both started laughing. Soon the blader was back on his feet and they were off again down the path.

"I was afraid," Nate said, sitting back down. "That's all."

I still didn't, and perhaps I'd never, understand why he had felt he couldn't come to me with what was bothering him.

Why *is* it that a lot of men believe they are supposed to act like they have the answers? That they've always got it together, even to the point of lying about it? Who thought that was a good idea?

"When we got married," he went on, "I know we said no secrets—not about things that mattered. Sure, we might have fantasies, and we don't need to share those. But when I lost my job, instead of telling you and figuring it out together, I lied and treated you like crap."

"Pretty much." I wondered, if he could admit to this, what other surprises might come.

"I'm giving you the house."

I must have misheard him.He nodded. "It's only right. If our situations were reversed and I was the one in the house, it would already have been foreclosed on. I am who I am, Sarah."

"Everyone can change," I said, knowing how idealistic that sounded.

"Possibly. I guess my sitting here and being honest with you is a move in the right direction."

I smiled. "What I want to say is I won't argue anymore if you want a divorce."

"What do *you* want, Nate? What is it you really want?"

He gazed out to sea. "I want what I can't have. To go back a few years, before I lost my job, when you still looked at me like you adored me. Then when the shit started I would tell you so we could deal with it together."

I burst into tears and he reached out to take my hand. I

was crying because I *had* loved him just like he said I had. I had adored him. I was *capable* of adoring. Was I still? It felt like I was mourning a part of me that died.

"I'm sorry for all of it," he said. "I don't expect you to ever look at me that way again. It's gotten to the point I can't even look at myself. So I'm going away for a while."

I opened my purse and took out a pack of tissues. "What are you going to do?"

"I'm going to South America, I think. To work for an NGO building houses and put my architecture degree to use for people who really need it. I need to figure out what's important to me before I can be a real partner to someone else."

It was my turn to gaze out to sea. "It's so sad when love dies."

"Even sadder when you're the one who killed it."

"It wasn't all your fault, Nate. You could have been dropping clues and I wasn't paying attention."

"You're not supposed to read my mind, Sarah. I should have said something."

He stood, offered me his hand and lifted me to my feet. Our hug was filled with emotion and forgiveness but it wasn't enough to close the distance between us. It was, sadly, a bridge too far.

I watched him walk away, up the paved path away from the beach, then sat back down on the bench for several very long moments.

Half an hour later, a young Boxer dog bounded toward me, followed at a short distance by a middle-aged woman, waving a collar and leash. She was desperately trying, and failing, to keep up. "Oliver!" she cried. "Oliver, come!"

The dog was oblivious to any real concern on the part of his owner, but considered himself in the midst of a joyous game.

I stood up and whipped out a piece of leftover Urth vanilla-blueberry muffin and held it out to the exuberant pup. "Want a treat?"

Oliver stopped in front of me and cocked his head, tempted but wary. His tongue, which had been lolling to the side, had fallen in line between his teeth and his nostrils zeroed in on the muffin.

"Good boy," I said, handing it over, while gently slipping the strap of my purse over the dog's head. "You are a very handsome but naughty boy, running away from your mama."

Oliver sniffed the bag, hoping for more.

"No, that's for my doggie," I said in the voice reserved for animals and six-month-old children.

"Thank you," the woman said, catching her breath as she reached us. "He gets away from me. I should have gotten a Chihuahua." She put the collar on Oliver, fastening it tightly.

"He's a pretty boy," I said.

"He is that. Also incorrigible and very strong."

She had the situation summed up perfectly.

"Well," I said, getting to my feet. "The good news is he'll grow up and slow down. But until then, keep an eye on him. There's a dognapping ring in LA stealing dogs, mostly on the Westside."

"How horrible." The woman gave her dog several strokes to his head. "I live in Silver Lake."

Silver Lake was a hipster part of LA, adjacent to Hollywood to the north and east.

"We just came over for a change of scene. Oliver, sit."

Oliver sat.

"Do you think he's in danger of being taken in Silver Lake?"

"Unfortunately, it's happening all over the city." I reached into my bag and pulled out one of Ellen Pirosh's newest flyers. "These are just the dogs we know about. And at least one Boxer went missing on this side of town so we know they like the breed," I said, handing her the flyer. "There's a phone number and email address on this. If you hear anything or see anything, let us know. You just reminded me I was supposed to set up a Facebook page."

"Yes, I'll let you know," she said looking at the flyer. "I'm Frances, by the way. Your dog didn't get napped, did he?"

"Almost. I scared the guy away before he was able to."

"How scary," said Frances, taking a firm hold of the leash. "Well, thanks again for nabbing—I mean, grabbing, Oliver for me."

"My pleasure," I said, smiling at the dog. "Good sit."

"Yes, he can be good when he wants to be."

"Can't we all," I said.

She gave me a rueful smile as she pulled the Boxer to his feet. "Heel," said Frances. And with that, they headed off down the greenway.

That was when I realized Nate had picked me up and I had no ride home.

CHAPTER 27

"WHAT WE want for Flan Cookies is to walk the line between evoking the feel of being homemade with the perceived safety of store bought." Tobias was measuring and examining the surface of each cookie as it went into and came out of the oven. "It requires a formula and process that will produce near identical results."

"It's hard when you're using spoons," I said. "But does it really matter if one cookie is one-sixteenth of an inch bigger than the next one?"

"From past launches, I've learned that people like predictability. But keeping the subtle variations within the uniformity is also vital. People *say* they like variety, but imagine a Hershey's kiss with an inverted nipple."

"Yeah, no inverted nipples," I agreed. "I just wish it didn't take so long to get the deliberate-yet-subtle variations customers expect from a store-bought-slash-homemade cookie."

I slumped into the nearest chair, and Tobias came over to give me a mini-massage. He worked my shoulders and my neck, which was particularly stiff and sore.

"I know you've been working your butt off, baby. Just remember, if it was easy, everybody'd be doing it. No one has made—marketed, anyway—a flan cookie before, and you and I both want it to be very hard to imitate."

I had lost track of how many cookies I'd made, and that's just since Tobias and I decided to go into business together.

I hadn't even bothered to count the ones I'd made before that.

The timer on Tobias's phone rang out for the umpteenth time.

"I know, but I'm exhausted," I said, rising to pull the latest batch from the oven. I placed the sheet of cookies on the tiled counter and Tobias started measuring. I thought they were perfect, but that's what I said about the previous twenty batches.

"Assuming these taste as good as the others," he said, retracting the tape, "which of course they will, I think we're good to go. As nice to gaze upon at as they are delicious. And we have insured we can replicate for shape, size and that subtle, inimitable variety."

"Now for the fun part." He smiled and headed out of the room. "Don't get too excited, but I want to show you something. It's a preliminary design, but I want your input, partner."

So far, the division of labor had been pretty equal, and we hadn't argued about anything. There had been a slight disagreement when I'd requested help in the kitchen but had been denied in order to save money. He was nonetheless paying for most of the start-up costs in return for a fair, but minority, percentage stake in the company, which we had named "The Superior Baking Company."

Tobias came back into the kitchen carrying his laptop. After a minute or two and more than a few key clicks, he brought up a screen and flipped it around for me to see.

The first thing I saw was a picture of Flan looking golden and adorable.

When did you take that picture?"

"The other day when you took Nathaniel to the dentist. And it's only five percent photoshopped!"

Above Flan, at the top of the page, was printed: Superior Baking Company, and under that, printed in a simple but elegant font: Flan Cookies. In small print, under the picture of Flan, it read, "My name is Flan, and these are my cookies for humans." Then there was some other text, necessary FDA info.

"We're actually doing this."

"Silly Sarah, what did you think we were doing?" Tobias pointed at the screen. "Scroll down for the back of the bag."

I moved my fingers on the track pad, scrolling down, and at the top was "The Story of Flan's Cookies."

"Personal stories capture hearts," said Tobias. "It's cold and calculating of me to come up with such a heartwarming story, but we want to win."

I began reading, and it was like Tobias had stored every bit of information he'd collected about us: How we adopted Flan (without saying anything about Sophia), how Natey asked me to make flan cookies, and how I'd foiled Flan's abduction. The story closed with a commitment to donate a portion of Flan Cookie proceeds to animal adoption efforts all over the United States.

"Oh, Tobias, I'd buy these cookies from the story alone."

"And once they taste the damned things, we'll have a hit on our hands!" He closed the computer.

"So what's next?" I said.

He lifted a cookie off the sheet and held it up, examining its visual and olfactory appeal. "Oh, 'cookie of Flan,' release me from this mortal coil." Then he put the whole thing in his mouth and chewed, his face revealing nothing.

"Well?"

"We are in one-hundred-percent-go mode, girlie."

I glanced up at the clock. "I'm not sure what you mean by that, but I have to pick Natey up in fifteen minutes."

"I can pick him up," said Apryl, bounding into the kitchen. This was a completely different person than the twitchy unkempt young woman from the day before. She found her way to the sheet of fresh cookies. “Can I?”

Tobias, having gone silent upon her appearance in the kitchen, sat down on one of the high-backed stools at the counter, and I gestured for her to take one. “Tell us what you think.”

She lifted a cookie from the sheet and placed it on her palm and examined it. She was, after all, well-aware of all the testing going on, and her opinion had been requested more than a few times.

“I’ve been thinking a lot about these cookies. You know one of the things I love most? I mean other than the taste?” She flipped the cookie over in her hands. “They don’t jiggle. Flan jiggles, which always sort-of creeped me out. So flan that doesn’t jiggle is cool.”

“Yes, I think that’s a key selling point. Flan that doesn’t jiggle.”

“Glad you’re feeling better,” I said. “What was going on with you yesterday?”

“Yeah, I’m sorry if I was acting weird,” she said. “I think somebody might have spiked my drink the night before.”

“You looked smokin’ when you left,” said Tobias, opening the fridge for a bottle of kombucha. “Doesn’t surprise me somebody might slip you something.”

Apryl blushed. “Nothing happened.”

“Do you know who it was?” I asked.

“I mean, I have an idea. But I don’t have any proof.”

“I was date raped once,” said Tobias, with little expression.

Both Apryl and I stared at him, slow to respond. Though Tobias had never struck me as the type to be taken advantage of, this might not always have been the case. If the pedophile priest scandal had taught us anything, it was that victims, like perpetrators, could come in all forms.

I put my hand on his arm. “Tobias, that’s horrible.”

"I'm so sorry," said Apryl.

He shrugged. "That which does not kill me . . ."

"Fortunately for me," said Apryl, "my friends saw that something was wrong and pulled me out of there before anything happened." She continued flipping the cookie from one hand to the other. "To tell you the truth, I still feel drugged."

"Are you going to eat the cookie or just play with it?" said Tobias.

"Oh right," she said, putting the cookie in her mouth.

We watched her chew. Tobias drank kombucha. I assessed my cuticles.

"Oh my God. It's amazing!"

"Remember, she always says that," I said, turning to Tobias. "When you're Apryl's age almost everything is amazing! The best this, the best that, oh my God!"

"I'm serious," said Apryl. "And look at them all lined up so even and organized." She gestured to the cookie sheet. "They're perfect."

Tobias was beaming at me. "Choosy eaters agree. Flan Cookies are a taste sensation!"

"So are we finally ready for the Farmer's Market?"

He picked up his computer. "I'll do some recon about mass production, the FDA, and fun stuff like that, then we'll talk strategy. But yes. Farmers Market, here we come."

I managed a "Yay!" before Tobias vanished. It was a tempered "yay" filled with all the work we hadn't done yet.

I looked at my watch, then went to the sink to wash my hands. "Okay, I'm off to get Natey. Thanks for the offer, but he has a doctor's appointment."

As I toweled my hands dry, I watched her take and eat another cookie.

"Apryl," I said, "What was all that yesterday about Flan having a skin condition? He doesn't have a skin condition. He has chafed elbows."

She chewed, giving me a blank expression. "Wow, I really was out of it. Did I say he had a skin condition? I must have been thinking about one of the dogs at the barn."

I didn't know what to make of her. I picked up my bag and pulled out my keys. "Any word on the horse show this weekend? Are you going?"

"Horse show?" she said. "Did I say I was going to a horse show?"

"I asked you if Natey could have a lesson and you made it sound like there was a horse show. Upstate, I think it was."

Again, she seemed baffled.

"Doesn't matter," I said. "I'll see you later. Wrap up the cookies when they cool?"

And as I headed out, I began to think that perhaps Tobias was right about Apryl. She was both more and less than she appeared.

CHAPTER 28

LEAVES CHANGE color, the sun gets lower in the sky, and temperatures drop. That's how people all over the world know that winter is coming. It's not that dramatic in Southern California, where ninety-degree days can extend deep into fall and there are few physical signs that summer is ending. Sometimes the only way is to watch the changing merchandise in store windows as clothing goes from tank tops to bomber jackets; as the muffs like to joke, you know it's September when the Christmas displays appear.

Now that the recipe was finalized for Flan Cookies, we were proceeding apace with planning their debut, which would also be The Superior Baking Company's introduction to the world—or at least to the world west of the 405 Freeway.

Tobias was in charge of all the business details—licensing, pricing, and packaging—while I made the cookies and took them around to local shops that might agree to stock them. Most said "they'd think about it." Fortunately, we agreed that subletting space at the Santa Monica Farmer's Market would be the best way to debut the cookies and build fans by word-of-mouth. That strategy had worked for several brands, like Neal Gottlieb's Ice Cream and Jennifer Carlsen's Baby Food.

I still needed help in the kitchen, but Tobias wanted us to have one successful market outing before we hired someone. Anyone who's started a small business knows it's hard work, long hours, and you have to save money where you can—even if it means you don't sleep.

Life pressed forward in other respects, as well. And considering that I was now, officially, a single mom, I thought I was doing pretty well keeping all the balls in the air. I still wasn't reading the book club book, nor had I started dating Denny or anyone else. Both pursuits still eluded me. But generally, I was handling my life and Natey's life pretty well, meeting events head on. Even if there were those days when I'd sit down in a panic, immobilized by fear and uncertainty, which I guess are the same thing.

Natey had taken to horseback riding like a natural. He recently graduated to Diablo, the bigger, more athletic pony he was going to ride before Apryl swapped him out for the calmer, quieter Windy. When I asked her what had changed, she just said, "Nathaniel is ready for more horse," assuring me that Diablo had left his devilish days behind him.

And thanks to Apryl's and Tobias's rent payments, there was money to safely equip Natey for this sport he'd taken to with such a passion. I found some hand-me-down boots on a local horsey Facebook page and an almost-new, name-brand helmet on Craigslist, which Apryl confirmed was "a steal."

Thankfully, there'd been no more episodes causing me to question the girl's grip on reality, because when considering a horseback riding teacher for your child, sanity would seem to me absolutely vital.

Nate Sr. was out of the country. And for now, no longer part of our lives. He'd come over one morning, not long after our walk along Venice Beach, to tell Natey and me that he'd narrowed his South American possibilities to Guatemala and Costa Rica. Both, he said, would let him use his skills to help lift people from poverty. Two weeks later he was gone.

I suppose we were prepared as well as we could have been. He'd told me he wanted to offer himself to people who needed him, instead of the snooty clients of the architectural firm that had fired him.

At the time I'd said, "Your son needs you." But despite the fissure I saw open as soon as I said it, I could also see he'd factored Natey into his analysis and found him not enough reason to stay.

In the days before he left, he'd signed over the house and brought over everything he owned, telling me to sell or toss whatever we didn't want. I found this alarming because Nate had always been a borderline hoarder. Should I worry about his mental health? Was it a cry for help? Or was getting rid of things another signal of his effort to change?

Surely he didn't mean for me to throw away his college yearbooks or favorite Steely Dan T-shirt.

I told him I'd take care of it, knowing I would hold on to everything until he came back. So much for my recently emptied garage.

The final goodbye had gone as well as it could, considering Natey wouldn't have his father around. Watching my son, I couldn't tell what he was feeling. His underwhelmed response might have been masking huge upset, which might not show up until days, weeks or months afterward. But, to Nate's credit, he said all the right things—he'd be back, he'd call, he'd send postcards—and Natey handled it all bravely. I wished it wasn't happening, but now that it was, I still couldn't hate the man. He was hurting, too.

Tobias was more practical and had been pushing me to file for divorce before Nate left. His concern was that if Superior Baking Company became truly superior in Nate's absence, enough to be a takeover target for the likes of the giant snack conglomerate, Mondeleze, Nate would be entitled to half the proceeds of the sale. He kept asking me, "Do you want to give your philandering husband half your company?"

I probably should have cared, but I didn't and still don't. I figured if the company ever became *that* big, there'd be enough to go around. So I told Nate I was fine with doing nothing about dissolving our marriage in the short term. I guess I was worried about him and wanted him to know he had people and things to come back to.

And then he was gone. Life after Nate went on much like it had before he left, except that now instead of being half an hour away, he was living in a little town in Guatemala, separated by a couple of time zones. He'd sent a postcard explaining that the village of Flores was on an island in the middle of a lake, many miles from what Angelenos would call civilization. However, it bordered the former civilization of the ancients, with its Mayan ruins featured on the card he sent. Flores was also home to the "Center for Bio-Diversity and Self-Sustaining Architecture," the group Nate had signed on with. I looked it up and discovered the village cathedral was called *Nuestra Senora de los Remedios*, which roughly translates to "Our Mother of Remedies." It struck me as significant that I hoped that's what Nate's journeys would bring him: a remedy for what ailed him, inside and out.

Catching up on morning emails, I was reminded that Paige was the next hostess of *The Muffia* book club. And she'd started early with the first in what was bound to be another epic thread:

> From:vonhooter@gmail.com
> To: The Muffia
> Subject: The Next One
> Hola Chicas! Given that the last two books were contemporary and non-fiction, we're going to change it up and go back in time. Our next read is Flannery O'Connor's ***A Good Man is Hard to***

> ***Find***. Not only is it an American classic, a truer statement was never made. Plus, it's a short story collection, so if you only have time for one, please read the titular one. That will guarantee we can all talk about it. I'm thinking first week of November for our next gathering? Weigh in on dates. xP

Titular? *Show off.* Now I have to look up what it means. It had nothing to do with tits but you could never be sure with *The Muffia.*

Well, no sense misremembering things I should have learned in school. I did what everyone does in this age of Attention Deficit Disorder—I Googled it.

Titular, I learned seconds later, was synonymous with eponymous—another word I didn't remember learning. Both words seemed to mean "a thing named after another thing of the same name"—not that that makes it clear. Now all I had to do was remember both of them and use them in a sentence, along with every other word I'd handwritten on Post-It notes over the years, hoping to use one day: disabuse, sesquipedalian, crepuscular, inhere . . .

The computer dinged.

> From: cunningquinn@Talentpool.com
> To: The Muffia
> Subject: The Next One
> Great call, Paige. A good man is rarer than a ripe piece of fruit at the grocery store. I thank you every day, Lauren, for sending Frank to save my job and here he is saving my life. Alright, that's extreme but he IS making it better. Will read and think about what it was like before I found him. X Q
> PS Sarah—I hope things have resolved. Let us know.

Since hooking up with Frank, Quinn seemed like a different person. She no longer behaved like the snarky, jaded, irritable, contrary woman she once did. She'd also started dressing differently, wearing longer skirts and lower heels. I didn't like to think that Frank was the only reason for the changes, because that would go counter to *The Muffia* manifesto of never changing for a guy. But there did seem to be a direct correlation between Frank and Quinn's increased kindness toward others. Before Frank, I don't know if she would have been the one to initiate concern for my wellbeing. That would more likely be the purview (another good word) of Kiki, Vicki, or Madelyn; Lauren, too, if she weren't still in crisis with her dogs missing.

From: sapizz11@connect.net
To: The Muffia
Subject: The Next One
Well, with Nate gone to Guatemala, I am officially single, though dating is premature. You'll remember Lauren tried to set me up and watched as I missed every cue the very cute guy was sending. Can't do Tuesday the 4th due to parent-teacher meeting but all other days good. Cookies are going to be at farmer's market starting this Saturday! Please, anyone who can, stop by the booth and act like you love them. It would be greatly appreciated! And thanks for the short read, Paige. I'm pretty sure I can manage twenty pages ☺

From: MissJelickaG@aol.com
To: The Muffia
Subject: The Next One
Hi, everyone. It's official. Got the business cards with Jelicka Gelman Real Estate on them. So I get

> to eat lots of those cookies. And I don't even care if a good man ***is*** hard to find. I am going to make a fortune in real estate! Sorry about Nate, Sarah. I know you thought this might happen, but it's still a shock when it does. Better things are out there for you, I'm sure of it. And now you can become the next cookie queen and not have to share with a would-be king. xxJ

I still wanted a king, I couldn't help myself. But Jelicka wasn't done.

> From: MissJelickaG@aol.com
> To: The Muffia
> Subject: The Next One
> PS—Sarah's neighbor (whose albino Pug was stolen) and I are working on a plan to foil the dog thieves. Anyone who wants in, send me an email. My soon-to-be real estate empire is the key to the whole thing.

Key to the whole thing? Real estate empire? That was a little premature; she just got her business cards. Leave it to Jelicka to be both cocky and vague. I think she cultivated a certain knowing mystery because it went along with her ideas about espionage, like the time she dragged Madelyn around in a quest to find out what happened to Udi, Maddie's dead Mossad agent lover, and they hadn't told anybody where they were going. So much for secrets; they could have ended up in a freezer. This time, the muffs needed to make sure any plan to foil the dognappers was thoroughly vetted before launch.

Within a couple of hours, the rest of the muffs had weighed in, each giving their condolences about Nate leaving. Rachel said, "Good riddance." Vicki and Kiki both said they knew some attractive available men they could introduce me to when I was ready, and Jelicka thought it would be good for me to have recovery sex, prompting me to consider calling Denny. He seemed too nice to use in that way, but maybe he could use a little recovery sex himself. Madelyn, having been the muff who first observed Nate's bad behavior with the tart—maybe not tart; Nate probably lied to her—in the tapas bar, was more circumspect, saying only that she hoped I could see his departure as a door opening.

The truth was that since Nate left, life was so full of cookies and cookie plans and riding lessons and school that I wasn't aware of doors opening or closing. Doors contained metaphors, sure, but they're also pieces of wood you place between yourself and others when you go to bed at night. And most nights I fell into bed exhausted and didn't wake until I heard Apryl and Natey, usually one after the other, get up to use the bathroom.

I did miss Nate Sr. once in a while, often in moments that surprised me. Like when I brushed my teeth and he snuggled up behind me and started kissing my neck when my mouth was filled with toothpaste, or when I was feeling sick and he'd mix up his delicious "tea," which was mostly honey and rum.

But now when any feelings of loss or loneliness struck, emotions that a few months ago might have derailed me for an entire afternoon, they were balanced by recalling moments from our miserable last year together. Lying in the same bed, each of us in our own worlds, staring at the ceiling night after night, had made me feel lonelier than anything I'd felt since he'd left.

Natey missed him. He acted out and could be sad when those feelings erupted, and I let him. I helped him write postcards to his dad, and said he could keep the ones Nate sent back from Guatemala under his pillow. I worried about my son growing up without his dad. But the reality was half of his friends were also growing up in non-traditional, blended families—even former bully, Colin Blackpool, who lived with his dad and step-mother. His real mother had apparently left to be with another woman. According to Natey, Colin thought it was weird at first, seeing his mom kiss her girlfriend, but now he says they're cool. The reality was, no kid growing up in America, especially now, should be made to feel bad because his parents are separated or because he has two moms or two dads. No kid should be made to feel like a misfit. It was a lesson most adults needed to remind themselves of, too: We can't be made to feel a certain way. We have to choose to.

CHAPTER 29

IT'S TRUE what they say about friends—they're there when you need them to ease the pain of life's hard knocks. But what's also handy is they make for an instant fan base when you need one—like when you rent a stall at the Santa Monica Farmer's Market to sell your cookies. That's when you need your friends to make your stall seem like the place to be, and walk around the market, shilling for you.

The Santa Monica market wasn't the first of its kind in Los Angeles. That honor goes to the Original LA Farmer's Market, which dates from the 1930s and is still in existence at the corner of Third Avenue and Fairfax, down the street from Canter's Deli. Rather than a weekly or biweekly event, the LA Farmer's Market is more like a permanent installation, with not just farmers purveying produce, but all sorts of vendors offering handmaid crockery, chocolates, cheese, and most anything else one associates with farmers, short of livestock. There are also restaurants of seemingly every ethnic variety.

The Santa Monica market opened on July 11, 1981, in the downtown retail district. Its aim was to provide high-quality produce to the population of the seaside area at a reasonable price and to draw visitors to the downtown Santa Monica shopping district. The market is held twice weekly, on Wednesdays and Saturdays, and draws visitors from all over Los Angeles and beyond. It stretches along Arizona Avenue between Second and Fourth Streets, in the middle of the Third

Street Promenade, and has the reputation of being one of the most diverse grower-only certified farmer's markets in the nation, featuring growers and food artisans from all over California. Some even come from Oregon and Nevada. The markets draw more than ten thousand shoppers a week, and many of them are chefs from the Southland's best-known restaurants. KCRW, the NPR affiliate based in Culver City a few miles away, even has a weekly program called "Good Food," which airs Saturday mornings and focuses on the tastiest, ripest produce at the market that week. Jonathan Gold, the Southland's former pre-eminent food critic, used to make a regular appearance on the show and give the market even more props, commenting on dishes currently being prepared at local restaurants using the market's produce.

The market is also a destination for families and is often clogged with strollers pushed by harried new parents. In its history, I've only heard of one bad thing that's happened at the market, when an elderly man plowed his Chevy through a crowd, mistaking his gas pedal for the brakes.

Saturday at this particular market, Flan Cookies would make their first public appearance, and most of the Muffs promised to be there to represent. They volunteered to hand out samples and walk around singing the cookies' praises. I was a little worried about Jelicka being her brash self and possibly putting people off, but because she'd also be trying to drum up clients for her new realty business, I hoped she'd tone things down a few notches. Natey said his friends would be at the market, too. Most of the kids at Science Camp, and now at school, had tasted, and fortunately liked, the cookies and wanted more.

Tobias, Natey, and I roused ourselves early to pack up the SUV, while Apryl made an effort before retreating to her room, claiming too many glasses of wine the night before.

Natey grumbled about getting up so early, but I promised him new riding boots if we sold all the cookies, which woke him instantly. That settled, the three of us, along with the mascot of the titular Flan Cookies (learn a word, use it in a sentence), headed off to the market with two hundred bags of cookies. They weren't the official bags, which weren't ready yet, but we had a huge poster made up featuring a giant picture of Flan, which was so cute it was guaranteed to draw attention. Tobias said when people saw the poster, then saw the real Flan, they'd buy the cookies just for the cute factor.

We'd be sharing our market stall with an almond grower from Fresno who knit pink pussy hats between almond sales. I thought pink pussy hats went out of style after the Women's March, but apparently there was still a market for them. When I talked to her earlier in the week to ask if she minded Flan being there, she said absolutely not and she'd knit him a hat. I pointed out that this would technically make her a knitter of pussy and *puppy* hats, but she said if people saw Flan wearing a hat, it might increase sales for both of us.

"No," said Tobias, when he heard about the hat. "That's brand adulteration. Flan's head must remain bare." I didn't argue, because he'd done such a good job getting us to this point and he'd lately evolved into Mr. Positive. Sur la Table wanted him to start in a month, and his attitude about the cookies was nothing short of glowing.

On the other hand, where he was building a home in Mallorca with his cookie profits, I maintained a cautious optimism. Realistically, even if were to do really well with Flan Cookies, unless the Superior Baking Company had more sure-win products in the pipeline, they weren't going to bankroll a house in Mallorca.

Vendors at the market usually begin showing up by 5:30 a.m. If you're getting there at 6:30, you're late. Even though you know where you'll be selling whatever it is you've got to sell, getting close enough to easily move through all the cars, palettes of stacked fruit, dollies, and carts is difficult, especially if you've never done it before. As a shopper, I'd never been here this early. Usually I waited until the end of the market when prices came down, so this was a new experience for all of us.

We had the cookies packed in two giant rolling suitcases, so decided to park the SUV at the mall. Then we walked through the mall to the Promenade, past the Arclight cinema and the revamped Nordstrom, where I used to spend too much money. Tobias and I each rolled a bag, and Natey had Flan on the leash. So far so good.

Our stall was located in front of Lululemon, the brand once known for selling see-through yoga pants. It wasn't the best spot, according to Tobias, because Lululemon meant exercise and seeing our cookies next to skinny mannequins in workout wear might guilt people away from buying them.

I argued the opposite—they'd buy the cookies and look up to see Lululemon and say to themselves, "Eat a cookie, do ten sit ups." It was win-win, as Madelyn would say. She said mediators like her used the term to settle cases. The hardest thing is to convince two warring parties that they probably won't get everything they want, Madelyn says, so if they both get off their positions a little, they both win and save money not going to court. The logic was there, but having gone through counseling with Nate, logic isn't really the point. I know first-hand just how difficult it is, especially in a breakup, to get much of anything one wants.

When we got to our stall, the almond and pussy hat lady—whose name was Kitty—was already set up. Bags of different flavored almonds were displayed in neat rows on the table in front of her, and a proliferation of pussy hats hung from a portable stand. She cooed over Flan and placed the custom-made pink puppy hat she'd made squarely on his head.

"Adorable," she announced, though I got the distinct impression Flan felt diminished wearing it.

I handed her a bag of cookies. "Thank you. He loves it," I said.

When Kitty turned to put the cookies away, Tobias caught my eye and pulled me under the table where he was tying Flan to the leg. "No bartering. We're here to make money."

"I know, but . . ."

"And lose the hat. We want unadulterated Flan."

"I agree, but we need to be nice, so . . ."

"Whoops!" said Tobias, flicking the hat from Flan's head and sending it into foot traffic while Kitty was pulling a hit off her vape pen.

"Opportunist."

Vendors continued to set up as customers began to trickle by, and both groups proved to be fascinating people-watching. The shoppers arriving as the market opened seemed to be of two varieties: The professionals—I saw Nancy Silverton, chef at Mozza, and "the Suzannes," Goin and Tracht, whose restaurants were legendary—who focused on two or three specialty produce stands. This type of shopper made her purchases and left within twenty minutes.

The other early birds may also be focused on securing the ripest berries and the greenest greens. But this type, unlike the professionals, also swoops in and swipes samples from any vendor offering them, often making two and three passes. Like most Costco shoppers, this type believes if you can't put together a free meal from tasting samples, then it's not a successful shopping trip.

"I should have told you not to put samples out until later," said Dan, the chocolate man at the stand next door to ours. "This time frame is mostly what we call the grazers. They sample, but they rarely buy."

I watched as a grazer snagged a cookie sample and popped it into his mouth. When he'd taken about ten steps he pivoted. "I'll take two bags," he said, walking back.

From Dan's expression, it was clear he was not amused.

"Probably just beginner's luck," I said.

By nine, we'd sold ten bags of cookies and were down twelve, considering the one we'd given Kitty and the one we'd opened for samples.

The couples and singletons yielded to families, and that's when we started seeing just how powerful a draw Flan was. For some, he even proved a salvation. Moms and/or dads with babies would get their upset child's attention, point to Flan, and say, "Look, Dashielle (or Hyacinth, etc.), see the dog?"

The baby would then stop crying, and the parents would thank us and buy a bag of cookies.

We must have sold fifteen bags that way, and, whether it was the vaping or almond selling, Kitty had yet to comment on the missing hat.

Then came the families with toddlers and slightly older children. Any kid in this group who spotted Flan was drawn to him like a vacuum sucks lint, and Flan basked in the attention, never once getting snippy. Unlike his behavior at home, where he took issue with dogs passing by on the sidewalk, he ignored the few therapy dogs that went by.

The parents of these kids were polite, but they didn't care about Flan or Flan Cookies. They'd been on their way to the breakfast burrito stands for a cheap and delicious breakfast and were hungry. It seemed like many of these parents bought bags of cookies so they could pull their kids away from Flan with a little more force than was perhaps necessary.

"Where's his hat?" Kitty asked at one point when there was a lull. Tobias and I made a mad effort to "find" the hat, but it was long gone. Kitty, rightfully, did not give the cookies back.

Tobias pulled me aside at ten. "We'll be sold out by noon," he said. "We've already sold half the bags and things are just getting started."

I couldn't believe it. "Really?"

"I'm going to start taking orders for next week. I should have thought of that before." He pulled his tablet from his messenger bag and right there created a spreadsheet on which to capture names and email addresses.

Whether people were intrigued by the idea of getting their flan fix in the form of a cookie or they were entranced by the novelty factor of the Frenchie named Flan, it didn't matter. The cookies kept moving and, some people came back for a second or third bag after consuming the first on their stroll around the market.

By eleven, most of the muffs had come to support me and were thrilled to see the cookies selling very well without their help. In fact, Tobias had to keep the muffs from buying them so he could sell them to new fans.

Lauren took over sales for a while, pulling in people who wanted "on" the pre-sale list, while I went in search of Natey who'd gone off with Colin Blackpool and his father. I made a quick loop, but didn't see them, and returned to find Amanda and Gavin crying over Flan.

"They're still missing the dogs," Lauren said quietly. "We better go. But I want to buy stock in the company."

"It may remain privately held," said Tobias, overhearing, with a too-superior tone. "But we'll keep you in mind."

"Don't mind him," I said, stepping a short distance away.

She leaned in to me. "Denny called about you. What should I tell him?"

"Do you need to tell him anything?" I asked. "We've been talking but it's just—I'll call you. Get the kids home."

The truth was, I was avoiding Denny even though I was attracted to him. I was avoiding dating. I was avoiding even the thought of dating. I knew all this and yet did nothing to change it. Maybe I needed a podcast on, "How to Date in Your Forties."

I waved goodbye to Lauren and the kids and headed back to the stall, colliding with a man standing directly in front of it, holding his own French Bulldog.

"Oh—I'm sorry," I said. "Who's this cutie pie?"

"This is Atticus," said the man, unperturbed. The dog was adorable, but the guy was gorgeous and the spitting image of Gregory Peck as Atticus Finch.

"And this is Flan," I said, scooping him up. "Atticus, Flan; Flan, Atticus."

The two Frenchies gave each other a perfunctory sniff then proceeded to ignore each other. French Bulldogs are people-oriented and often merely tolerate other dogs, even those of their own breed.

"I adore the whole idea of your cookies," he said as we put the dogs on the ground. "How did you come up with it?"

Tobias, who'd been observing our exchange, came around the table. "It was all his fault," he said, with a nod to Flan. "Sarah's the baker extraordinaire, but that one sealed the deal."

Tobias extended his hand. "Tobias Miserocchi. And this is Sarah Pizzo. Sarah I are in business together in this little enterprise."

Why introduce us now? He hadn't been introducing himself to the other prospective customers. Did Tobias sense a professional interest from this man, or was he just flirting his ass off? Gregory Peck was definitely Tobias's type.

"John Fritz," said Gregory Peck. "Visiting from Chicago."

"Well, it's very nice to meet you, John, and Atticus," I said before excusing myself. I wanted to listen, but a woman was pulling cash out of her wallet.

"I'll take three bags," she said. "They're so good."

If John Fritz turned out to be some important person in the food business, Tobias would be the person to get him excited about investing. If Tobias was flirting, well, I didn't need to hear that.

Natey, who'd gone off with Colin Blackpool and his father an hour earlier, finally came back with each boy sporting a hat featuring some new Disney-themed movie.

"We went to the mall. Hope you don't mind," Colin's father said, handing me a bunch of flowers as he assessed the few remaining bags of cookies. "Congratulations. Looks like your cookie launch was a massive success."

"Thank you," I said, taking the flowers. "It's a little too soon to say 'massive success,' but I'll take what I can get."

He leaned closer. "I also wanted to tell you how much I appreciate what you and Nathaniel did for Colin this summer. At Science Camp, I mean. I was a dick. Colin was bullying everyone, and I didn't want to deal with it."

"Nah," I said, thinking he was sort of a dick, both for his behavior and for using the word dick. "I didn't really do anything,"

"No-no," he said firmly. "You stepped up and wouldn't stand for the school's solution, which was to take my money and do nothing." He shrugged. "But you can't blame me for trying, can you? I mean, if you can pay people off, it's what you do. But it doesn't make it right. Sorry I was an ass."

I accepted his apology, and the word ass over the word dick. But—and this had to be my imagination or the exhaustion of the last few days hitting me—it felt like Colin's father was flirting. Just as Tobias had flirted with John Fritz. No, it couldn't be flirting. Colin's father was a slick Hollywood producer. That type smooth-talked everybody.

And I realized at that moment that in the years between marrying Nate and raising Natey, I knew less about dating and men than I'd ever known. The landscape had altered completely and permanently. I no longer knew how to feel, how to flirt, how to date, even how to be with a man when the relationship was not simply platonic. Now that I'm older, my pool of eligible men had also aged, going from young single men to widowers, divorcees, the previously jilted, and men hoping to land a sugar mama to take care of them. What was worse was, if I wanted a man, I probably had to find him online, because so many of the nice ones were too scared to approach a woman in real life for fear it will be misinterpreted as an unwanted sexual advance. If we are, all of us, damaged goods *before* our first failed relationship, what hope was there after we had a couple under our belts? If such a human were a car, an insurance company would probably consider him totaled.

"Hey—" It was Tobias giving me a gentle nudge. "You okay?"

I didn't know how I'd gone off on such a personal and emotional tangent but was grateful he pulled me back.

"Yeah," I said. "I think I'm in shock."

He smiled. "Get used to it. I think we have a hit on our hands."

I surveyed the stall, but there wasn't much to see. The cookies sold out an hour ago; all the flyers we'd printed up were gone. The suitcases stood, closed but empty, and I could barely zip my money pouch closed for all the cash inside. In another half hour, all market activity would supposedly be cleared away, and the streets reopened as if nothing had happened. Meanwhile, I was feeling a seismic shift.

Not only had we sold everything we'd brought, we'd taken lots of orders—so many I worried about being able to accommodate them all. Someone wanted to know if we could produce forty mini-bags for a birthday party. Or how about fifty bags for the International Cocktail Guild Conference in San Diego?

While I took down an order for two hundred individually wrapped cookies with a sticker of Flan for an awards dinner gift bag, Tobias had leaned in and whispered, "Always say yes. We'll make it happen."

"We?" I said pointedly. "I'm getting that assistant now, right?"

"We'll talk about it," he said, rolling up the poster.

Natey untied Flan from the table, and we said our goodbyes to Kitty and anyone else who hadn't finished packing up. And as we rolled the suitcases back to the parking structure, Tobias said,

"We have a lot to talk about, but let's get some rest and regroup tomorrow."

"Tomorrow can we get new riding boots because we sold all the cookies?" Natey was too full of energy.

I took his hand. "A promise is a promise." I'd keep that promise, too.

"Be careful what you wish for" is one of those overused sayings that's become a cliché, but it had its origin in some real-life event. I wondered what that original wish had been, and what happened when the person who'd wished it got what she'd wished for.

I said I wanted a baked goods empire, and now that dream might really happen. Was it still what I wished for? Was I ready?

CHAPTER 30

IT WAS Sunday, the morning after the market, and my eyes squinted their way open with a wary exhaustion. The days leading up to the market had been long and stressful, and I now lay in bed not having to move for the first time in a week.

The market was a Flan Cookie success. It had gone far better than expected. Tobias agreed. But how, I worried, was I going to make all the cookies I needed for the following Saturday? For yesterday's market, I'd had to deprive myself of sleep to produce two hundred bags of cookies. Next Saturday, we'd committed to four hundred! And that's not including the presales.

I covered my head with a pillow and made a futile effort to fall back asleep. What I needed was to take my mind off cookies for a few hours. Natey's riding lesson later would help, though that always provided a different type of worry. Still, I was grateful Apryl had decided to stay in town and teach.

I stretched and tried one of Madelyn's mantras while attempting to breathe without thinking: Inhale with Yes, yes, yes; then exhale with Thank you, thank you, thank you. I made it a couple-three rounds but was ultimately unsuccessful. Fortunately, I was spared from trying again when Natey leapt onto my bed with a mantra of his own: "Boots, boots, boots."

"Shhhhh, people are sleeping," I said, lifting Flan up on the bed with us. "We'll get your boots. But right now, we need to tell Flanny what a superstar he was yesterday. Thanks to our adorable doggy, we sold even more cookies than we brought to the market."

Flan wiggled and snorted with delight as both Natey and I made him feel loved and appreciated as quietly as possible.

Then Natey suddenly stopped and frowned. "Mom, how can we sell cookies we don't have?"

This question made perfect sense.

"Well, Mr. Smartypants," I began. "Let me tell you a little something about credit."

Thus began a rudimentary explanation of the concept of debt. Maybe his seven-year-old brain wasn't quite ready, but given how many people—his father and the Federal Government included—abuse their good credit, I figured it was never too early to introduce the harsh realities of debt. Whether one owes money or cookies, the danger of failing to deliver was essentially the same.

"I get it," he said. "You make a promise with the plastic card at the grocery store and pay the money later."

"Exactly," I said, leaving out the bank that issued the card. "And when I take money from people for cookies I don't have, I am promising to give them cookies later."

"You have to make even more cookies than last time." This caused another frown.

"Right again."

"What if you can't pay the cookies? Will you get in trouble?"

"I don't think we need to worry," I said. "But sometimes when you owe money and don't pay it back, you can get into trouble."

We had to hire a baking assistant. It was the only way.

"Will you buy my boots with a plastic card or the cash money from the cookies?"

"Card."

He considered the process again. "We try on the boots,

then you put the credit card in the machine. But mom, then you'll be in debt! What if you can't pay it back? You'll get in trouble."

I cupped his worried face in my hand. "I already have the money to pay it back. We made a lot of money at the farmer's market yesterday, more than enough to pay the credit card people for letting me use the plastic card to buy your boots. I just need to put the money in the bank tomorrow to pay the credit card company."

"So you put the money in the bank and then you take it out to buy the riding boots after the plastic card goes in the machine? Does that mean we have to wait until tomorrow?"

His frown had turned to disappointment.

"No, honey," I said. "We don't have to wait. The beauty of the credit system—or flaw, depending on how you look at it—is you can use your plastic card whenever you want, even in the middle of the night on the Internet."

His face perked up on this news. "Really?"

I probably should have left that part out.

"Mmm," I went on. "And you can wait a few days before you pay the money back. Like I don't owe the cookies until next week. If we use the plastic card today to buy boots, I have time before I need to pay the money back. So—" I popped off the bed. "You ready?"

Flan seemed ready for anything.

"Mom, *shhhhh.*"

"You're right. That's too loud." I leaned closer. "Let's go for breakfast!"

Natey's lesson wasn't until mid-afternoon, which gave us enough time to head over the hill for breakfast at the old Sagebrush Cantina in Calabasas, then on to Calabasas Saddlery for the promised boots. The "hill" is not just a hill, but the entire Santa Monica Mountains, which stretch from Camarillo to the northwest, southeast toward Hollywood, finally dwindling into the manmade mountains of downtown LA. The Santa Monica mountains are in large part protected from further development, though exceptions abound. And the area is nevertheless riddled with roads, trails, passes, and canyon boulevards that, in several places, connect the ocean to the San Fernando Valley.

We took Topanga Canyon Boulevard to get from one side to the other, passing the barn where Natey rode and continuing down the northern slope into the community of Calabasas.

The town is situated in an area originally settled by Chumash Indians who supposedly gave the town its name. The word "Calabasas" means, depending on who you talk to, either "where the wild geese fly" or "pumpkins." It could be either since there's no shortage of Canada Geese or pumpkins. But I'm going with the geese theory. The Spaniards didn't show up until the late 1700s, which means the Spanish word for pumpkin wasn't heard in the area until long after the Chumash arrived. The Canada Geese, on the other hand, probably predated the Chumash.

When the Spaniards decamped in the area, staking their unwarranted claims, it didn't sit too well with the Chumash, as one might imagine, and violence erupted. There was so much violence between the Chumash and the Spanish that, at the turn of the 20th century, Horace Bell, a soldier, lawyer, journalist, historian, wrote of the time and place: "Inhabitants killed each other off so steadily that a human face was a rarity."

But the settlers kept coming, and the Chumash moved on. Soon the area began to thrive. The settlers built taverns, lodging houses, a blacksmith's shop, and the Leonis Adobe, which still stands on the main street through town. In fact, several period buildings have been preserved, giving "old town Calabasas" a character and charm that's been lost in so many early California settlements. Most fell victim to sprawl; some even fell to the pornographic film industry.

It's a relief of sorts that in spite of the violence of the early days, the Chumash tribe survived and has even prospered. In the Santa Ynez Valley, for example, the Chumash casino draws not only for its gaming and hotel spa amenities, but nearby site-seeing and wine tasting for which the Santa Ynez valley is renown.

Leonis Adobe sits next to the Sagebrush Cantina, another vintage structure, this one dating to the 1920s. The Sagebrush was once a collection of shops and farm stands, but for the past forty-five years has been a restaurant and watering hole for families and motorcyclists alike.

Natey and I were finishing up our breakfast in the shade of the Sagebrush's big oak tree when my phone chirped. Jelicka.

"Don't answer it," Natey said, jumping to his feet, though the waitress had yet to bring the check.

"Easy there, pardner, it won't take long." I patted his seat and said, "Sit."

Flan, tied to the table leg and already sitting, snorted with indignance.

I hit Accept. "Hi, Jel, what's up?"

"Ellen and I have a plan." She sounded pumped.

"Great," I said. "But I can't really talk now. Natey and I are out for breakfast."

"Fun," she said unconvincingly.

Breakfast was one of several reasons I didn't want to talk about the dognapper sting operation right now. I didn't like it when people were on cellphones in restaurants was another reason. There was also that Natey was ready to get to the new boots portion of the day. Lastly, I avoided talking about dog theft in front of him. Though he was well-aware that dogs had been stolen and had even been present when Mack and Molly went missing, I still hadn't told him we might have lost Flan to the dog thieves. I *would* tell him, maybe even soon. It was just that, despite his father being out of the country, Natey was doing so well with school, his Ls, riding, and friends, I didn't want to risk jeopardizing his new confidence. I know parents can't protect their kids from fear, disappointment, and grief but is it such a horrible thing to want to?

"I'll talk. You listen," she said.

As the check came and we paid and headed for the car, Jelicka outlined the plot while I listened, letting out the occasional monosyllabic response to avoid the consternation of other breakfasters.

"Can we meet at your place to talk about it?" Jelicka asked.

"Mmm," I mumbled.

"Ellen said we could go to her place, but it might blow her cover."

"What?"

As was often the case with Jelicka, the plan sounded ridiculous. As did Ellen blowing her cover. *Cover?*

"Not really a 'cover,' but she wanted one, so now she has one to blow. We can meet at my place if you want, but you're all on the Westside and I'm the one in the Valley, so I'm offering to come to you. Lauren wants to come, too."

"When?"

"Tonight," said Jelicka.

"Tonight-tonight?"

"No time like the present," she said. "Shouldn't take long."

I opened the car doors and Natey and I climbed in.

"How did I get involved in this again?"

"You almost had a dog stolen."

"Right. Can we meet at a coffee shop?"

"People might be listening."

"Really?" Seemed hard to believe the dognapping ring would be hanging out at Starbucks.

"It could happen," said Jelicka. "Why take the risk?"

"All right, fine," I said. "You guys figure it out and let me know. If it's at my house, it needs to be after eight."

I hung up wondering if I'd just agreed to help bust up a dognapping ring. No. I'd only agreed to be part of a meeting to *discuss* a plan to bust a dognapping ring.

"Mom—" said Natey. "What's after eight?

"Just a bunch of ladies talking about stuff," I said, strapping him in, and gazing at his sweet little face. "Okay, my little cowboy, let's get you those boots."

We drove away from old town and took the overpass over the 101 Freeway to Calabasas Saddlery, which occupies a former ranch house on what had once been a working ranch. Now the saddlery sits amid several low-slung warehouses, office buildings, and self-storage places, along with the Los Angeles Pet Cemetery, arguably the nation's largest and most interesting. It might have been sort of morbidly interesting to see the crypt of Rudolf Valentino's Doberman or the grave of Steven Spielberg's Jack Russel Terrier. But with all the missing (and possibly dead) dogs, it didn't feel like the right time to visit.

The last, and maybe only, time I'd been to a saddlery, or tack shop as they're more commonly called, I was overwhelmed by the smell of leather. Calabasas Saddlery is no different. It's a horse lover's one stop shop for most things horsey, whether she rides English or Western. They have bridles, halters, saddles, britches, boots, helmets, and all sorts of training "aids"—whips, spurs, lunge lines, side reins, long reins—as well as substances to make coats gleam, keep flies away, ensure proper hoof moisture, and maintain quality gut flora. It was boggling to behold. It might even be necessary if one owned a horse, but most of it just left me with questions. I became fixated on some rubber, bell-shaped objects, some with Velcro, some with little buckles, available in multiple colors, but in every case, designed to go over a horse's foot.

"Are they for decoration?" I asked someone. "Like horse jewelry for their feet? Certainly the hot pink ones."

The young saleswoman shook her head. "They keep a horse from grabbing his front heels with his back toes."

"Grabbing how? Why would they want to do that?"

"It's not that they want to," she said. "It's just some horses take too big a step with their back feet and touch the heel of the front ones, sometimes pulling off their shoes, or even gouging their heels. It can get pretty ugly." She clasped her arms over her chest and rolled her eyes knowingly. Clearly she had firsthand experience.

"Surely if they're clumsy enough to step on their own feet, you wouldn't want to ride them, would you?"

She shook her head again smiling, though it seemed to me common sense.

"It means they have an overreach, which is highly desirable for competition."

It was still baffling why anyone would want a horse that would step on its own feet—particularly in competition. I put the bell boots down, happy none of this was my problem.

All we needed was one pair of riding boots, which seemed a relatively simple, not-too-expensive proposition; especially compared to the two-thousand-dollar saddle I pulled Natey off of while our salesperson went in search of boots. Two thousand dollars for a saddle—it didn't even have stirrups!

After trying on three pairs, Natey was equipped with his shiny new boots that zipped up the front, and we were out of there without much collateral damage, just some horse cookies and a riding crop Natey said he'd use if Diablo was "bad." If Jelicka saw him suited up with that crop in his hand, I'm sure she'd make some sort of S&M joke.

Now, new boots on and looking polished astride Diablo, Natey was having his second group lesson and learning to jump. This was more than a little terrifying, even if the jumps were only three inches off the ground.

The kids in the group were the same four from last week's lesson, and all of them girls.

This could go one of two ways, I thought as I watched them trot around the arena: Natey would either determine, as his father had, that riding was a sissy sport and quit; or he'd realize that being the only guy meant he didn't have to share these four adorable girls with bigger, attention-demanding boys. He had them all to himself.

There was a third way, which was that Natey was gay and didn't care about girls. I didn't care, one way or another, but people say most parents can tell early on, and so far I'd only seen him flirt with girls, these four included. Poor little Chloe, Natey's girlfriend from the summer who he'd planned to marry. She had been all but forgotten after riding horses with Amanda, Athena, Amy, and Alison.

There was only one other boy-man I'd seen riding at Apryl's barn. And to watch him ride his big chestnut mare with the chrome—that's horse-speak for white on the face and legs—was to see synchronicity in motion. When Tony jumped Sky Pilot, Natey and I would find a spot along the rail and gape, unable to believe how high they'd jump and how easy they made it look. They'd come around one corner of the arena and Sky would focus on a jump. Her ears would prick forward, and she'd canter down to it and snap her knees up, clearing it by several inches.

"I want to do that," Natey said every time.

Diablo was no Sky Pilot, but he had proven to be an ideal mount: Not a horse, exactly, but what they call a large pony. As Apryl explained, horses and ponies are measured in increments called "hands." One hand equals four inches, and the measurement extends from the ground to the highest point along the spine above the horse's shoulder, called the withers. Only the horse's head and neck are higher. A large pony at the withers can be no taller than 14.2 hands. Another two inches, at 15 hands, makes that pony a horse. Diablo measured 14.3 hands with shoes on.

The "hand" is an archaic form of measurement, supposedly reflecting the width of a long-ago male monarch's appendage. For the monarch's sake, I hoped hand was indeed the appendage they were referring to, and not a euphemism for something else.

Though I'd determined that riding had so far been good for Natey, boosting his confidence and social skills, watching him jump a creature that would crush him if things went the wrong way was not good *for me.* It might even be shortening my life. I caught myself holding my breath whenever Natey pointed Diablo at a jump.

"How are you doing?" she said after the lesson was over. "I was watching and you seem a little shell-shocked."

She helped one of the girls—Alison?—dismount and loosen her pony's girth. "Good job, today, Amy."

Nope, not Alison.

"Thanks," said Amy, who then bounded over to another girl—Amanda?

I tried to smile brightly. "Just a little. I'm hoping it gets easier."

"It's normal. Most parents go through this. My own parents even got used to me falling off."

"Good for them." I said this with just a hint of sarcasm.

She caught it and let out a guffaw before leaning in. "He *will* fall off one of these days. But little kids are resilient, and they usually bounce. They cry a little bit but then they want to get back on. Like my own trainer, used to say, 'It's a long way from your heart.'"

"It might be a long way from *your* heart," I said. "But my heart is in my neck and I can't breathe."

She smiled, squirting something that smelled like tea tree oil on Amy's pony, and rubbed it with a towel. "I still think of that saying every time one of my students falls off. Actually, I still think of it when *I* fall off, which fortunately hasn't happened lately." She quickly formed a fist and gave the wooden fence a quick knock.

"Where do your parents live, by the way? I've been meaning to ask you."

"Seattle area," said Apryl, taking off Diablo's saddle and draping it over the fence alongside the others.

"Nathaniel, Alison—go ahead and lead your ponies into the pasture right there," Apryl pointed at a patch of dirt with a fence around it. "Hold the reins tight under the chin with your right hand and the end of the reins in your left. That's it. The guys will help you when you get there."

"Can you take him, Apryl?"

We both turned to see a girl I could only describe as elegant standing nearby, holding an elegant brown pony with a wrapped leg. The girl's bearing was serious, making her seem older somehow, though I'd say she was no older than Natey.

"Sure, Suzannah. If they're waiting."

Suzannah nodded. "Thank you."

In the small parking area, a navy blue Bentley stood idling, its windows sealed tight.

"Did he seem a little better today?" Apryl asked.

“I don’t know,” said Suzannah wistfully. “He’s still lame.”

“Well,” said Apryl, trying to get a smile out of the girl. “You’re doing everything you can for him to make the tendon heal. It’s just going to take time.”

“I guess.” Then the poor little rich girl began walking toward the Bentley.

“She’s a nice girl,” said Apryl, stroking the pony’s neck. “I’m almost sorry her parents have all that money. They buy her this fancy pony, who was probably lame when they got him, and they send her up here with the chauffeur. I think I’ve seen her mother once.”

“Maybe they’re as scared to watch their child ride as I am, and that’s why they stay away.”

She shook her head, her focus still on Suzannah. “There are kids with parents like you, and then there are kids with parents like Suzannah’s who just don’t seem to care.”

CHAPTER 31

"ARE YOU sure we're alone?" Jelicka said as she peered around the corner into the kitchen and did a quick scan of the first floor before joining Ellen Pirosh and me in the living room. "We know how *roommates* can be. How many do you have, again?"

"I'm not running a youth hostel for international exchange students, Jel. I just have the same two I started with. And besides, they're not here. I thought we'd established that."

Apryl hadn't returned from her day, and Tobias was on a date with John Fritz, the well-dressed French Bulldog owner so taken with Flan Cookies at the market on Saturday. Tobias worked quickly when it came to romance. At least someone did, I thought. I sure didn't.

"Well—can't be too careful," Jelicka said, closing the drapes. "Somebody could have snuck back in. We need to keep this on the down low to maintain a tight inner circle. This is 'need to know' material only."

I went to the kitchen and came back with a plate of cookies.

"Absolutely," I said, tongue in cheek. "I wouldn't want to blow anyone's cover."

"Absolutely not," said Ellen, oblivious to the irony.

Despite my wanting to meet elsewhere, with both Apryl and Tobias out of the house, I was left without a babysitter. So instead of going over the plan to nab the dognappers at Ellen's place, we were here on my couch. We'd only had to wait for Natey to fall asleep before Jelicka laid out her plan.

"Let's get started," I said, pouring out three waters. "Unless someone we don't know about has installed a listening device, you can speak freely."

"Is that possible?" Jelicka asked.

"The Mossad could have," I teased. "They want to find out my cookie recipe."

"Stop it," said Jelicka going to her bag. "Wait, I brought wine."

She held up a bottle of Malbec.

"Congratulations on the cookies, by the way," said Ellen, while I went to get wine glasses. "Sorry I couldn't make it, but I'll buy a couple of bags tonight if you have them. Do you have a gluten-free version?"

"Working on the recipe." I put down the glasses.

"Doesn't matter. I'll still buy them," said Ellen. "I can eat gluten; it's my husband who can't. But he's about thirty pounds overweight and shouldn't be eating cookies to begin with."

Jelicka poured out the wine and I indicated I only wanted a splash.

"I'll let you know when I have them," I said. "I'm making a lot more cookies this week. Making cookies has become my life. That and driving Natey around."

"Don't complain," snarked Jelicka before facing Ellen. "She's the next Mrs. Tates, or whoever, and she's complaining about commanding an empire."

"We're a long way from empire," I said.

Flan let out a snort, and Ellen's head spun to see him, asleep on his tuffet. It had been a couple of months since her dog, Pearly Girl, had gone missing, but it might as well have been last week given how quickly Ellen got upset seeing him.

"Sorry," said Ellen. "Brings back memories."

Jelicka took a long pull from her wine glass before putting it down. "Here's the deal—I'm a realtor now, right?

Right. And, with a couple of exceptions, I can put out my shingle in whichever geographic area I want to. So . . . I will be specializing in Westside properties."

She picked up the wine glass and sipped.

"I would have thought you'd choose the Valley, since you live there," I said.

"Ah, but see that's just 'the story,'" Ellen chimed in. "It's so she can be in the neighborhood where most of the dognappings are happening."

"Why is that, though? Why do you need a story?" I asked.

"It's Phase One," Ellen said, equally unclear.

"Because," Jelicka went on. "If I want to dabble in real estate in other areas and later change my mind about the Westside . . . *Oh well*!" She held up her hands in helplessness.

My gaze went from Jelicka to Ellen then back to Jelicka. "I'm still not following," I said. "What does it matter where you declare your real estate specialty?"

"It's the backstory, Sarah. How I came to be knocking on their door in the first place. In case anyone asks."

"Yeah," said Ellen. "It's a really good way to talk to people, you know?"

"I got it, it's a way to get in the houses and talk to people; so what?" Clearly I was missing something, but they were making things unnecessarily complicated.

"Why can't you just knock on peoples' doors?" I said.

Ellen jumped in. "People don't open the doors for religiosos or people running for the school board. They didn't open them for me when I was looking for Pearlie. But everyone wants to know what their house is worth, even if they don't want to sell it."

"Right," said Jelicka, "And *we* get to find out who has a dog, and who doesn't."

"And that tells us what? Which dogs are still available to steal?"

I was thinking this was all a ruse for Jelicka to drum up listings for her new real estate business.

"It gets me in the door, so I can talk to them and enlist their support. The only reason not to is if one of the homeowners is responsible for the thefts. You don't think that, do you?"

"Of course not," I said.

Ellen shook her head. "No."

"Well, there you go. I get in the door, tell them what they want to know about their house, and then casually ask if they are aware of the dog thefts going on in the neighborhood. Then, no matter how they answer that question, I tell them we are arranging a sting."

"We finally have a police officer willing help us, too," said Ellen. "Officer Lauren Eschrich, in the Brentwood division. She's very sympathetic. She worked with bomb-sniffing dogs in the airport before taking it easy in Brentwood."

"I don't think police officers in the field ever 'take it easy,'" I said.

"To be clear," said Jelicka. "Even though Officer Eschrich is willing to acknowledge dogs have been stolen and to be someone whom we could call, she is not willing to expend law enforcement energy or funds to catch the dognappers."

"And she does not know about the sting," added Ellen.

"No 'need to know' on that one" said Jelicka. "She'd only try to stop us."

"Let me get this straight. Your plan is to enlist the help of everyone in the neighborhood and somehow keep it a secret? Why not just drive through the streets with a bullhorn?"

"There are ordinances against that," said Ellen, completely serious.

"Fine," said Jelicka, putting her wine down. "There *are* some details we still need to work out, but the sting depends on getting neighborhoods to be alert and to know where the stealable dogs are, so if they see something, they can say something."

Ellen was nodding her head.

"There are a few definite things we need before we start," Jelicka said. "So let's talk about them."

"Let's," I said. "And can we try to be concise. It's going to be a busy week, and I need to go to bed."

"Okay," Ellen began. "We know the dogs that these scumbags steal are usually expensive and well-bred."

"Seem to be," I agreed.

"So," said Jelicka, picking up the plot, "in order to tempt the thieves, we need to either raise money to buy one of these dogs or entice the thieves with a dog somebody already owns."

Both Ellen and Jelicka let their gaze drift in Flan's direction, abundantly obvious they considered Flan the ideal candidate.

"No," I said flatly. "Our dog is not going to be dognapper bait. Just *no.* He's the mascot for The Superior Baking Company now. We can't risk it. And don't forget somebody already tried to steal him and I scared the guy away. They wouldn't strike twice."

"Maybe they would," said Jelicka. "Maybe they know you think they wouldn't strike twice and that's the very reason they *will.*"

It wasn't an unreasonable observation.

"Either way," I said. "You are asking me to risk a member of our family and the mascot of our promising new baking company."

"It *is* promising." Jelicka said, probably trying to score points.

"Very promising," Ellen agreed, taking the last cookie off the plate and depositing it in her mouth.

"Here's the thing—" I said, aiming to appeal to whatever maternal instincts either might have. "Natey doesn't need to lose both his dad *and* his dog, so I'm sorry, but no on the Flan plan. We need to find a different doggie."

Jelicka and Ellen glanced at each other. It seemed clear that Flan had been Plan A, and, suspecting I wouldn't go for Plan A, they would now launch Plan B.

"Let's table the question of which dog we're going to use," Jelicka said, beginning again. "We can work that out. Here's the rest of the plan . . ."

Jelicka and Ellen took turns explaining how, once acquired, the "bait" dog would take up residence at the home of a volunteer. Ellen was willing, but she thought it better to find some cold, heartless person who generally hates animals but hates criminals even more. Her theory was such a person wouldn't have her heart broken if the plan failed and the dog was stolen, whereas hers could be broken a second time.

My job, since I'd put the kibosh on Flan's involvement, was to help check out animal shelters to find a well-bred rescue to be our dognapper bait. I didn't necessarily approve of this plan, nor did I think the shelters would go for it, even if they all agreed that dognapping was a crime and shelter volunteers thought it punishable by death.

In the end, I went along with the broad strokes of the plan, telling myself that the dog chosen to bait the thieves would be vigilantly monitored and protected. After all, it wasn't like we were asking a shelter to waive adoption fees. Lauren volunteered to pay all costs.

The three of us agreed that a full-grown, yet still youngish dog would be the best candidate to tempt the thieves, given what we knew about why dogs were stolen when they weren't being resold to unwitting or uncaring purchasers—namely to produce offspring in puppy mills or rip each other to shreds at dog fights.

It pissed us all off to learn that people dump dogs in shelters all over the country when they don't behave as their owners think they should. It's often their own fault for buying a dog without conducting even a rudimentary background check of their prospective four-legged friend. It's one reason you shouldn't buy a dog from a puppy mill: You can't see the puppy's parents. Trust me, once you see a puppy's insane mother tearing down a fence, there's a good chance her progeny will become a couch ripper or worse.

But when it came to our sting operation, a discarded couch-destroying canine might be our perfect dognapper bait.

The meeting was over an hour after convening, with next steps laid out and another phone meeting scheduled. Jelicka's assignment was to appear at a few different neighborhood meet-and-greets while Ellen and I tried to find the right dog.

With neither roommate having come home yet, I took Flan out for a quick walk, never losing sight of the house where my boy lay sleeping. While we walked, it was cookies that filled my head—the hundreds of cookies I needed to make. It was still cookies I was thinking about as I fell into bed, dreaming of one large cookie that turned into a flying carpet and took me away.

CHAPTER 32

THE NEXT two weeks went by like an Angelina Nasso painting—blurred objects on a bed of blurred colors. It was hard to focus on any one thing long enough to do it well. There were cookies and more cookies, then two more farmer's markets with another doubling in sales, which meant even more cookies. Two more dogs missing from two different Westside neighborhoods; two more weeks that I should have been reading *A Good Man is Hard to Find*, two more riding lessons for Natey, who was getting the hang of jumping, two more weeks of me watching him and still freaking out. And two weeks during which time, Apryl began acting more and more peculiar. When she was teaching Natey, I didn't notice. But at the house, I saw less and less of her, and when I did, it seemed like she was avoiding me. The door to her room, which she used to keep open, now seemed to be closed whenever she was home. I'd been meaning to ask her if there was anything she wanted to talk about, but that had yet to happen.

Encouraged by the early success of the cookies, Tobias had relented and found me a helper in the kitchen. Deandra was a twenty-three-year-old student at the New School of Cooking and knew enough about baking that she was instantly of assistance, while at the same time respectful and ready to learn. She was also kind to children and animals—two vital qualities for working at the house, and though Superior Baking Company was still a way's out from becoming an empire, I immediately sensed she was a keeper.

I say Tobias relented. He was relenting on a lot of things these days, like no longer hurrying me to come up with another winning cookie recipe. I suspected the new, easier-going Tobias was due to his blossoming love affair with John Fritz. Though the two had only met three weeks earlier at the farmer's market, seeing them together now made me wonder how one had ever existed without the other. Each was tall, thin, patrician, and prone to overdressing, particularly for Southern California, tending to wear three-piece suits, and even overcoats when the temperature dipped below sixty-five degrees. Regardless of activity, the two knew how to put together their outfits. When they set off on a hike through the Santa Monica Mountains, they brought to mind a color-coordinated spread in the Patagonia catalogue.

Despite the nascent love affair, Tobias wasn't slacking on the cookie hustle. He'd begun making inquiries at local specialty food shops, and though there were still industry stamps of approval we needed to proceed, he was confident we'd soon have them. That would open up opportunities for selling our cookies almost anywhere.

"Then," he said, "and only then, can we grow the business."

Scaling up is not something a new business does without careful thought, however. Doing so too soon can cause collapse when accounts receivable don't keep up with accounts payable; doing so too slowly can cause problems when demand outstrips supply and clients lose patience. Another problem that besets food companies specifically is that products have expiration dates, meaning if they misjudge orders, the product owners could be left holding the bag—or in our case bags of cookies—and sell at a loss. Tobias said if this were to happen and our orders came in less than expected, we'd have to destroy rather than risk the horrible optics of discount Flan cookies.

Where I was now getting help in the kitchen from Deandra, Tobias and I were both benefitting from John Fritz's business savvy. Turns out the guy was an angel investor and a hero to start-ups. After meeting all of us, Flan included, he'd gone home with two bags of cookies, and three days later, he approached Tobias about investing in Superior Baking. We came to find out, of course, that the cookies weren't the only thing John wanted to be involved with, but I suppose great business relationships have been forged on less.

"How can I *not* be involved?" John said when we met to talk terms. "I have a French Bulldog myself."

So we drew up the paperwork for John to purchase five percent of the Superior Baking Company, which Tobias said would give us the money we needed to keep "scaling up" at a slow but steady pace and allow us to gain "traction" in the "impulse" food category.

"You sure you want to mix business with pleasure?" I asked Tobias one afternoon, as he helped Deandra and me put cookies in our official bags.

"Absolutely. It's the only way."

"So much for that saying," I said. "When does he go back to Chicago?"

He made a face. "Next week. Insert sad face emoticon."

"Maybe that's good. Take a break," I said. "You guys have been moving pretty quickly."

"When you know, you know. You know? Happy face emoticon."

The front door opened and closed. "It's me," said Apryl, her footsteps going up the stairs.

"That girl has issues," said Tobias, leaning toward me in an attempt to avoid being overheard by Deandra, which was pretty much impossible. "More and more I'm seeing her in her hottie clothes. You must have noticed."

"Mostly what I've noticed is that she has a full life. And at the end of the day, we have to remember she just rents a room here. It's not really our business."

"Maybe not, but if she brings whatever she's got going on out there into this house, it becomes our business."

"She's young," I said, as if that fact alone exonerated her from any bad behavior. "Remember being young? It seems like a hundred years ago when I was in my twenties and had that kind of energy."

"I've had my suspicions about her since the beginning, it's true," he said, pulling off his standard food-worker gloves. "But it's getting worse."

Deandra pretended not to be listening but her body language suggested otherwise. I don't know if I could have done any better.

"What do you think is going on then? Vagueness doesn't become you, Tobias."

"A couple of nights ago, she was wearing those four-inch heels of hers and she hadn't even zipped up her sparkling purple dress when a van pulled up and whisked her away from the curb. Then yesterday morning, she straggled in while you were taking Natey to school and went straight into the bathroom, whispering into her phone."

"She probably has a friend going through a bad break up or something."

"So if there's nothing to hide, why whisper?" said Tobias, crossing his arms. "A—we can't hear you, and B—it's not like we know who you're talking to or about."

"She was her usual self this afternoon for Natey's riding lesson," I said.

"She has your number. That's what I think." He started collecting the completed cookie bags and placing them in boxes for transport.

"What do you have against her?" I said. "She's pretty,

she's smart, and she's a really good riding teacher, even if she's the only one I know."

He sealed up two boxes with packing tape. "*Mmmm* . . . I'll figure it out."

"This may sound ridiculous," I said, "but apparently her husband left her for a man. Maybe she has a thing against gay men?"

"That's ridiculous," he said, shutting me down. "She's duplicitous, but I'd know if she was a homophobe."

"I'm not saying it's something she's aware of," I said. "It's no different from, say, he left her for a blonde so she now has a thing against blondes. It operates under the surface."

He had his hand on his hip. "You'll see. I have a nose for these things."

We then dropped the subject. We made some short-term cookie plans and went about our days, but what Tobias had said about Apryl needled at me, and I had to admit, it was because I had noticed a change in her myself.

CHAPTER 33

To: The Muffia
From: Vonhooter@gmail.com
Subject: Good Men
Two weeks until book club, ladies, and I'm not going to be my hard-ass self. The only story you MUST read (can't help myself) is the one the collection is named for: ***A Good Man is Hard to Find***. For those of you who are single, I can say it does not contain one shred of dating advice, but it's only about twenty pages, so I don't want to hear any excuses about not being able to read (oops, did it again). More later on what you can bring but I'm thinking I'll make ham hocks or fried chicken in honor of Ms. Flannery O'Connor's southern existence.
Xx Paige

To: The Muffia
From: JelickaG@aol.com
Subject: Good Men
Here I was hoping with a title like ***A Good Man***, I was going to get some useable information. I can bring some Southern Comfort or something else Flannery might have drunk as long as it's not sherry. Or was she in a dry county? I'll check. But count me in for the alcohol.
Love y'all, Jel.

To: The Muffia
From: Madelyn MSC@MSCMediate.com
Subject: Good Men
I read it and contrary to what Paige said, the story contains some good advice for the single gal. Mostly stay off dirt roads in southern states when a misfit is on the loose. You misfits I'd hang out with on a country road any day. Will bring wine.
xxx M

It was Monday, and I sipped my morning coffee as I scanned the latest email chain from the muffs, which was already ten emails long. It was started by Paige the day before, Sunday, which I try to make the one day a week without screens. Though I don't always succeed, this week I did, and when I logged on, there were 145 unread emails. Many were from the muffs, but most were requests for money or to sign petitions for every political and charitable organization known to woman and man alike.

Ding—there was another email from Vicki: She'd bring sushi. And ding—one from Rachel: She sold another painting.

I probably should enter the stream, but I was having one of those mornings. I felt neither witty nor sociable, two must-haves when it came to the muffs. Or so I felt. It was my own insecurity, nothing the muffs ever consciously did to make me feel inferior. They were just witty and sociable all the damned time.

Not contributing to a thread, however, was to risk an email from one of them inquiring about my health. So after another cup of coffee and loading in the day's second load of laundry, I jumped in with the latest on flan cookies and a cellphone pic of Natey jumping Diablo.

"Amazing," "Wow," "Good for him," "Good for you!" Were some of the responses that came back. I don't know why I worried about writing clever emails. The muffs didn't care if what I wrote was worthy of a prize. So why did I put myself through the worry of thinking they did? I guess I just add it to the list of everything I need to work on to become a better person. It's a list that just grows longer with every passing day, going from a list of to-dos to a list of observations of self that I'd like to change: Remembering that I need to just write the email and it doesn't need to be smart or funny goes beneath the note to check in with my mother more often, and when she criticizes me, to remember she has her own demons. I closed the laptop and put it on my bedside table.

Regardless of any "sharing" economy, work-from-home, or other twenty-first-century work arrangement, Monday is still the day working people complain about most. It's the one they need to "get up" for, to shake off the weekend and face the fact they need to stop doing what they really want to do and go work for someone else—The Man.

I'd been one of those people before getting married, each Monday reaching for my work outfit of pencil skirt and blouse instead of the jeans and T-shirt I'd spent the weekend in, but it had been almost ten years.

Now I *was* The Man, with only myself and Tobias to answer to. That meant if I didn't get up and get-to, The Man (i.e., me) would need to berate the employee (i.e., also me). I felt another frisson of "Be careful what you wish for."

All I'd wanted was to sell a few baked goods and make enough money to make the mortgage and pay for Natey's schooling. Had that been a lie? Had it been disingenuous of me all along to think that I didn't want more? Maybe I had, and, as would be typical for me, just didn't think it could happen, so I set my sights lower.

It almost didn't matter how I'd gotten to this point. I

now found myself at the start of what could be a baking success story. Flan Cookies were still a long way from the empire Tobias envisioned, but we'd made a very, very good start—the best start for a Southern California Baking Company since La Brea Bakery, according to the hyperbole-prone Tobias. One-tenth of that success would have been fine with me. In any event, I didn't want to blow it. And not blowing it meant not caving in to fatigue and insecurity.

But on this Monday, as with most, I lingered over my coffee, delaying that first step into the kitchen. Monday was the lightest day of the week when it came to the growing cookie empire, but once I started, there would be no break until Saturday afternoon when the farmer's market closed down. Sundays were reserved for Natey and resting.

I zapped my coffee in the microwave. Deandra wouldn't be arriving until eleven o'clock, when we'd go shopping for ingredients, so there was plenty of time to linger over more pressing distractions. Sitting down on the sofa with Flan, I reopened my laptop and scanned the unopened emails. How had I received them all? Suddenly, without thinking, I was signing petitions. The picture of a motherless baby elephant was what got me started, then it was endangered sea tortoises and rhinos. I signed three petitions to label genetically modified food, one to support mosquito netting in the Congo, and maybe six to advance free speech and women's rights.

I signed most petitions, wondering if any I'd signed over the years had ever made a difference. Surely one of them must have. But it troubled me that they always ask for money *after* you sign them. And why were there so many organizations with the same or similar mission statements? Surely if all the organizations wanting to, say, stop illegal sex trafficking joined forces and became one, they'd be a force to be reckoned with rather than a collection of disparate groups, weakened by a false division. I know non-profits need money, but their methods often make me suspicious of their motives. I'd heard so many of them use donations not for their cause, but to send out more email requests for signatures and money.

Still, I oblige as much as I can—five dollars for the wild mustangs in Montana and ten to fight nuclear waste, fifteen dollars to build a school in Vietnam and twenty to end hunger on the streets of LA. The amounts varied depending on what was in my checking account, but it was never over fifty dollars. At the end of the day, one can't do much to cure the ills of the world, but one needs to feel like they're doing something. Perhaps one day, if and when Superior Baking Company became superior, there would be enough money to truly make a difference to one of these causes. There I go wishing again.

The *Muffia* email chain had grown longer while I was away doing good, and it was my turn to make it even longer. I began typing, judiciously avoiding any reference to *A Good Man is Hard to Find*, which I had yet to pick up from the library. Instead, I focused on how I planned to bring a batch of my new pumpkin cookies to book club—Halloween was coming, after all, and I needed their input.

Ding—This time it was Lauren. I couldn't keep up.

To: The Muffia
From: LBSweet@aol.com
Subject: Good news!
Dear Muffs, Mack is home! He was found wandering the streets of Arcadia. Some asshole dumped him in Arcadia. Poor little guy is skinny and pretty beat up, but we have him back. Still no sign of Molly. I hate to think what might have happened to her. But the kids are so happy to have Mack back. We're giving him tons of love and think he'll be fine. Tell me what to bring. Love, L

This was good news, even though every time they look at Mack now, they must miss Molly more. Though there was nothing Lauren or George could do to avoid the feelings of loss, I gave them points for dealing with the feelings head on. Just as they had when Lauren's mother started showing signs of dementia. They didn't pretend it wasn't happening. Lauren and George could have replaced the pair of Boston Terriers as soon as they were stolen. But by not doing so, they allowed their kids the unavoidable life lesson of grieving loss, which left room for the unexpected joy when Mack came home. Had there been new puppies in the house, the kids would have had a sort-of shock-absorber for both sets of feelings.

No one wants their kids hurt if it can be prevented, but a parent isn't doing her child any favors by protecting him from life.

I took the lesson. Natey's dad was gone and might never come back. I needed to give him the opening to talk about it.

Mack's return also made me realize I'd been slacking on my assigned task for the sting operation. I was supposed to be helping to locate a dog that Jelicka referred to as "napper bait."

Ellen was regularly scouring the Westside and parts of the Valley, not finding suitable candidates. It was clear we needed to expand the search beyond LA. But that was going to take time. The only way to get the job done was to ask for help, and Rachel would be the perfect person. She hated abusers of all kinds and would thoroughly enjoy putting a pack of serial animal thieves behind bars. I would just need to make sure no guns were around because she had made it very clear her preference was to shoot them. I poured another cup of coffee while I considered my next move, knowing that what I was really doing was further stalling the workweek. Sitting back down, I reopened my laptop. I typed "Dog Adoption Los Angeles" into the search bar and hit "Return."

CHAPTER 34

A COUPLE OF hours later, Deandra and I were back from shopping. Among other needed ingredients, we'd purchased fifty pounds of unsalted, sweet butter—from organic, anti-biotic-free cows—sixty pounds of unbleached flour, twenty pounds of brown sugar, and real vanilla beans, which were at that moment working their magic on my secret formula on the kitchen counter. There was no place to store all the eggs we'd need to make six hundred bags worth of Flan cookies, about eight thousand of them, accounting for rejects, so those we'd need to pick up more as we went along. And fortunately, through new friends from the farmer's market, we'd found a reasonably priced egg supplier.

Deandra was now organizing the bags, cleaning the ovens, and making sure we had everything we needed to turn the kitchen into an assembly line the following day. I'd just made a pit stop at the Santa Monica Library where I'd snagged their last copy of *A Good Man is Hard to Find*, and I was on my way to pick Natey up at school when my phone rang.

I try, though often fail, to avoid texting while driving, but I believe myself capable talking and driving at the same time, even if I can't tell who's calling. I hit the talk button on my steering wheel and hoped it wasn't a request for money.

"Sarah? Hi, it's Denny."

A pleasant memory formed in my mind as I pictured the cute widower who saved me from an embarrassing faceplant.

After Lauren's party, we'd never quite managed to get together. We were attracted to each other, I knew that. But there had been a distinct lack of follow-through on both our parts. *Why* we hadn't followed through was a question I hadn't spent much time on. I just assumed we weren't as interested as I originally thought. Perhaps we'd realized we hadn't healed enough from our previous relationships, or maybe, as was the case for me, we realized starting a relationship meant taking time away from other things. And I already felt pulled in too many directions.

Denny seemed like a good man, but if good men were as hard to find as the title of Flannery O'Connor's story so blatantly stated, he'd come too easily. "How are you?" I said, belatedly fastening my seatbelt at the first red light.

"Good, thanks," he said. "How's the new baking company?"

"Pretty good," I said. "Except for the need to always be baking."

"Too bad the cookies don't bake themselves," he said.

If only. I watched my indicator blink on and off. On and off.

The blinking seemed to slow, and I felt him hesitate. "I'd like to take you to dinner. Friday night? A person can't live on cookies."

The light went from red to green, but my foot remained on the brake.

"Sarah?"

I was aware I'd stopped traffic and that this had caused particular annoyance to the driver of a souped-up Audi directly behind me. I waved him on, but Audi man only blared his horn, causing more angry drivers and more horns.

"Hold on," I said. "I'm causing road rage."

"Exciting."

"Let me pull over." I managed to get the car to the curb but not before Audi man revved his engine, shooting exhaust skyward as he screeched away.

"I think I know that guy," said Denny.

"There's one every other block," I said, turning off the ignition.

He was asking me on a real date. At night. This we hadn't covered in our texts, which had pretty much focused on meeting for coffee one day, a day that had never come after several weeks of texting. Even if I wanted to go to dinner with Denny—and really, why not? I liked him—Friday nights were impossible because of the Saturday market. So I had to say no, while making my regret in saying no palpable.

Experts, and I include the muffs here, say the key to successful dating is to leave the door open. If you like someone, but their initial proposal doesn't work for some reason, answer with a different one. So what night could I propose? I didn't want to suggest Saturday because the muffs had also made it abundantly clear that when dating someone new, you don't go out on a Saturday night until you're ready for sex.

"Okay, I'm here," I said finally. "I was on my way to pick Natey up from school and my head was elsewhere."

"So what do you think?" "It's nice of you to ask . . ."

"Sounds like there's a 'but' coming."

"No-no," I said quickly. "I'd like to go to dinner with you, but Friday nights are impossible because of the market. There's all that last minute prep and we have to get up at four in the morning."

He sighed. "Right. I should have thought of that."

"Is there another night?" I asked. "How's Sunday?"

He didn't hesitate. "That should work. My sister's visiting, and she can watch Kayley."

"Great." I said, hoping Tobias or Apryl could keep an eye on Natey.

"I can pick you up if you like. How's six thirty?" Denny said. "Or I can text you the name and address of the restaurant and meet you there."

I liked that he was offering to pick me up, but I wasn't quite ready to give him my address. Nor was I ready to deal with having Natey see him and ask questions. I was sure he'd recognize Denny from Lauren's party, and even though that one event might be harmless, it could have unintended consequences. I made a commitment to myself when Nate and I separated never to let our son get attached to anyone I wasn't very, very serious about. I still found it hard to forgive my mother for all those times she brought "boyfriends" home. I'd meet them, they'd bring me gifts—or *bribes*—then after a few weeks or months, they'd be gone.

"This time I'll meet you there, if you don't mind," I said finally.

"That's fine," he said. "I just wanted to be on record as offering to pick you up in my chariot, even if it does have a child seat in the back."

I laughed. "Yes, duly noted. And for that same record, I like that you offered. It's just—"

"No explanation necessary." He paused. "I won't tell Lauren and George we're doing this if you don't."

There were two reasons he might not want them to know we were going on a date—one, that he wanted to abuse me without having to answer to Lauren and George, which was unlikely; the other, more realistic reason was that he didn't want them asking questions about how "we" were doing before we were actually a "we."

"I agree. Besides, nothing to tell them, right?"

"Right. They got one of their dogs back, did you hear?"

"Yes. Such a relief, though of course Molly's still out there somewhere," I said. "And since they were taken, a lot of other dogs have gone missing all over LA."

"Why hasn't anyone been able to find out who's taking these dogs?" he asked.

It was a question everyone was asking, still without any clear answer.

"The police say they don't have the manpower to work on it. They say violence against people takes precedence over violence against animals. So we—*The Muffia,* that is—are doing something about it."

That's right—Rachel and I had a date to visit animal shelters. When *was* that? I made a mental note to call her as soon as Denny and I hung up.

"Ah yes, the *Muffia* women," Denny was saying. "It's all pretty secretive but if Lauren is to be believed, you're a formidable group. Isn't one of you a former FBI agent or something?"

"In her dreams," I said, knowing he must mean Jelicka. "One of the muffs fancies herself a private investigator and another dated a member of Mossad, though I doubt she dated him long enough to pick up any tips. And that's the extent of our espionage capabilities."

"Well, the people stealing these dogs are very good at getting away with it," he said. "They'll probably stop at nothing to protect their interests. So be careful. We have a date."

That made me smile. "See you on Sunday," I said.

We hung up. And as I started the car, I glimpsed in the rearview mirror the same souped-up Audi that had been revving its engine at me earlier idling behind me at the curb.

I watched as the driver, a middle-aged white guy with a baseball jacket on, got out of his car and came around to my front passenger window. What did he want? He didn't look like he wanted to punish me for substandard driving.

As I put the window down, I scrolled through my contacts for Rachel's number, ready to dial. "Can I help you?"

"Sorry if I scared you before," the man said, glancing into

the back seat. “I was just trying to get your attention. See, I recognized you from the Farmer’s Market and I wanted to know if you have any cookies I could buy.”

CHAPTER 35

RACHEL AND I stared at the caged dogs, all heartbreakingly adoptable to someone wanting to find a loving companion. But that wasn't us. We needed a purebred, and sadly none of the canines at the Riverside Animal Shelter, east of Los Angeles, was a candidate for Operation Nab the Nappers, or "ONAN," as Jelicka had dubbed it, saying, "You gotta have the acronym or it's not official."

There had been a purebred Bull Terrier and a Cocker Spaniel on the shelter's website earlier in the day, but apparently pictures of dogs on shelter websites bear little relation to the dogs that are there. The only way to find out what dogs they have is to go; hence this visit. But physically going to shelters in the middle of the day during the work week was time-consuming, particularly when many of them were so far away.

"I needed help," I'd told Jelicka. "So I brought Rachel into the operation and swore her to secrecy. She can do most of the legwork and will be better at it than I am anyway. You know how she likes to make men pay for their crimes."

"Yes, I've seen her paintings. What's she going to do if the dognapping king pin is a woman?"

"She'd probably want to nail her, too," I said.

Jelicka relented, and now here we were. I'd made arrangements for Natey to go home with Colin Blackpool and left Deandra to bake alone. Though I felt a little guilty, isn't that what assistants are for—so you can step away when you need to? I wasn't great at delegating to begin with, but as Tobias pointed out, "It was something I better learn if Superior Baking Company was to be successful."

Our search began earlier in the day in Beverly Hills, where we had made the erroneous assumption that its moneyed residents were most likely to abandon their purebred animals. Turns out, despite the plethora of fancy, expensive canines in Beverly Hills, residents of that tony enclave will drive a long way to dispose of them when they're deemed no longer "suitable"; turns out these callous dog dumpers choose to betray their pets where no one will recognize them. Hence our journey to Riverside County.

But today we were a few hours too late for the prize puppies, and I was ready to call it a day.

"How can there be so many animals without homes?" I said, pushing open the door to the street and the late October day. "It's so sad."

A carved Halloween pumpkin, exposed to the afternoon sun, sat caving in on the front steps.

"Dogs will be dogs, right? But is it so hard to spay or neuter your fucking pet?" Rachel was fuming. "This place even does it for free. Of course the people who don't spay and neuter their animals are the same people who abandon their kids and beat their wives."

"That's kind of a generalization . . ."

"Maybe, but see, I know I'd be a terrible parent so I don't have a pet or a kid. But if I did, I'd neuter him."

"You'd neuter your kid?"

"It takes a special kind of asshole to dump a living thing," she said, backing down only slightly.

"Maybe we shouldn't be so harsh. What if the dog belonged to someone's child or parent and the person died?

What if they had to move to a foreign country for work and couldn't take the dog?"

"I always appreciate you trying to spin things in a positive direction, Sarah, but you don't get to abandon your dog when it's inconvenient," Rachel said. "If you die, I'll cut you some slack."

I sighed. "I agree a lot of it's avoidable."

"Welcome to my world," said Rachel. "Wars, climate change, fracking—the difference between me and the average depressed person is I take all that negative energy and make art out of it. How do you think I came up with the 'Men Without Faces' and the 'Men Missing Something' series?"

"I've always been afraid to ask," I said under my breath.

"I was reflecting reality in a positive way! I could do the same with abused animals." She paused. "That's actually not a bad idea."

Whether Rachel's paintings of men missing parts of their anatomy were "positive" was questionable at best. They certainly weren't positive for the men missing those parts. Her large painting of the eyeless, disembodied head was downright disturbing.

"I'm glad painting them is cathartic," I said. "But I need to cheer myself up. Hey—Disneyland's close. As long as we're already playing hooky, why not take a quick bobsled run on the Matterhorn?"

"That's what my dad would call a long haul for a short slide," said Rachel, with no irony. "Three minutes of screaming and then 'Back to Black.' We miss you, Amy Winehouse."

"Fine. No Matterhorn. Let's find a happy hour. A cocktail is a guaranteed fifteen minutes." I pulled out my phone to search while we continued walking.

"The idea for a new 'something missing something' series is starting to form: 'Dogs missing people.' What do you think?

Dogs walking by famous Beverly Hills store fronts, maybe the Santa Monica pier, places like that. The dogs are on leashes, but the leashes sort of hang in mid-air. The dogs are walking themselves."

I looked up from my phone to find we'd stopped in front of a contemporary art gallery featuring mostly kitsch. Meanwhile, I was zeroing in on the best local cocktail places.

"The dogs are walking themselves. That *would* be a departure for you," I said. "The whole person is missing."

She rolled her eyes. "Tell me again why we can't use Flan? I mean, we'd protect him. Seems like it would save a lot of time."

I rolled my eyes back at her. "Because it would kill Natey, and now that Flan is the mascot for Flan Cookies, he's irreplaceable. Tobias even took out insurance on him to protect the brand."

"Right. Just don't let it go to his head," said Rachel. "Nothing worse than a stuck-up French Bulldog."

She pointed at a large acrylic in the window. "I sort of like that one." The painting featured several brightly colored dogs of different shapes and sizes. It was the kind of art Rachel would usually go out of her way to avoid.

"You need a cocktail more than I do," I said, taking her arm.

"Look, I don't like failing, but it's not our fault we didn't find the right dog. When Jelicka came up with this plan, she didn't think it through."

"I agree," said Rachel. "Let's get that cocktail and contemplate our next move."

Cocktails are big everywhere—Riverside, California, included. We needn't have worried about settling for mediocre house wine at Olive Garden. Any concerns about finding a good mixologist were extinguished immediately upon entering

W. Wolfskill, which from the name alone was the obvious choice. Wolf-dog, get it? Actually, we picked W. Wolfskill based on Yelp reviews and the fact that it was open.

Walking through the open restaurant we marveled at all the people knocking back cocktails at 4:00 p.m. We opted for a shaded table on the outdoor patio, with a view of the Fox Performing Arts Center, its marquee touting the upcoming presentation: *Magic Men Live!*

Seated at a nearby table was a woman of about sixty-five, with short gray hair cut into a chic, spikey style, a hairless Chinese Crested on her lap. One wants to believe all dogs are cute in some way, but Chinese Cresteds, particularly those of the hairless variety, are cute only to their owners. They're also not completely hairless, it's just that the hair is strategically placed only at the tops of their heads and whipping around their feet. If you can imagine skinny, miniaturized Clydesdale horses, you'll have the visual.

"I doubt anybody's going to steal *that* dog," Rachel whispered as she opened the cocktail menu.

"No Chinese Crested has gone missing," I said. "So you could be right. But it's not too late. Some people will steal anything."

"She's a service animal," said the woman on whose lap the Chinese Crested was perched.

"Excuse me?" *Had she heard us speaking ill of her dog?*

"I have a condition," the woman went on. "I need Daphne with me at all times."

Rachel leaned toward me, sotto voce, "Guaranteed she heard us. Now what do you want to bet she tells us what her condition is?"

I gave Rachel's knee a nudge to prevent further comments that would only make me laugh.

"She certainly seems well-behaved," I said.

"Oh yes, she's such a comfort," said the woman. "Like the daughter I never had."

"I'm going to get the 'New Old Fashioned,'" announced Rachel, slapping the menu down before craning her neck around in search of a waiter.

Daphne's mom seemed lonely, but she was well dressed and had an air of having lived a full life, so I was curious what her story was. But it was obvious Rachel was in no mood to engage with her or her dog.

"Do you know about the *Magic Men!*?" asked Daphne's mom, gesturing toward the marquee.

"Only that I don't believe they exist," Rachel said, still trying to flag down a waiter. "Case in point, where's the magical man to take our drinks order?"

"Oh, I suppose that's true," the woman smiled wistfully, petting her dog. "But what if there *were* magic men? Wouldn't that be lovely?"

"It would be nice," I agreed, thinking now that we'd never know this woman's story because she was crazy. "But the only magic men *I'm* familiar with are in fairy tales. Frankly, in real life I've been disappointed."

Daphne's mom stroked the tufts of hair on the dog's head, pulling them up to their full height, three inches from the top of her head. I noted the similarity to the woman's own hairstyle.

"Well," she said. "The show is breathtaking. It's *Magic Mike*, *Fifty Shades of Grey*, and every woman's sexy handyman rolled into one. That's *The Magic Men!*"

Not a great recommendation, I thought, praying that Rachel wouldn't mention *The Muffia*'s hatred of *Fifty Shades of Grey*. Fortunately, or unfortunately, she had another line of inquiry to pursue.

"You mention your dog is a service dog," Rachel began. "I was wondering, is the lack of good men the reason you need a service animal? If so, I think that's a perfectly legitimate reason."

The woman looked first to me, then back at Rachel, unsure if she was being made fun of. Then she said, "Fuck it," and spilled. "That's a very astute observation, young lady. I come here to Riverside from Palm Springs because seeing *The Magic Men!* is a reprieve from reality. The show provides me with an intense state of euphoria for several days before I fall back into the same old patterns. That's when I need Daphne most. I don't know what I'll do if the show closes."

Yes, she was crazy.

"Well—" said Rachel. "We've been observing a lot of dogs and their owners lately, and you two—you're a great pair."

I gave Rachel another jolt with my knee. No one wants to be compared to a Chinese Crested, especially a hairless one.

"Oh?" said the woman.

"You seem devoted to each other," I said.

"We are. Thank you for saying so. I know she's not the most attractive creature in the world, but I needed a dog I could feel beautiful next to."

What do you say to that? Even Rachel was stumped, muttering something about how attractive the woman was.

"Hi, I'm Rita," said Daphne's mom, extending her hand in Rachel's direction.

"Nice to meet you, Rita. I'm Rachel, and this is Sarah."

I gave a tiny wave.

"We're a little tired, Rita," Rachel said. "We were on a mission today, and we failed."

"Oh?" said Rita.

"Yes, we saw a lot of dogs, but none was quite right."

"Don't you know it," said Rita. "It takes time to recognize the right canine companion, the one you can bond with and be your heart of hearts."

"Actually, Rita," I said. "What we were looking for—"

"See, Rita, a lot of purebred dogs are getting stolen in Los Angeles right now," Rachel interrupted. "A friend of ours had her Boston Terriers taken."

"That's horrifying," exclaimed the woman.

"She got one of them back, but the other's probably a breeder now in some puppy mill out in Death Valley."

Rita gasped.

"It's an epidemic, right Sarah? How many dogs have been stolen?"

Both Rachel and the woman were waiting for my answer.

"Thirty?" I said, unsure. "No, I think it's more—fifty."

"It's a lot," said Rachel.

"Oh my God," Rita exclaimed again. "I think I'd die if something happened to Daphne."

It would only hurt her to find out Chinese Cresteds weren't in danger. Why bother telling her?

"Is anything being done about it?" she asked.

"Well, we have no magic men working the case, that's for sure," said Rachel, moving closer to Rita. "But we came out here on a mission to find a dog to help us nab the nappers."

"Rachel, I'm sure the woman wants some peace before seeing her show," I said. "She doesn't need to hear about the operation. It might actually be better for her not to know."

"Oh no—" said Rita. "I *need* to hear it. I am an animal lover, and I donate a good portion of my dead husband's hard-earned money to animal charities. If he were alive, he'd probably kill me."

The faraway expression on her face I noticed earlier was completely gone, replaced with a steely resolve. "Now—how can I help?"

CHAPTER 36

"TODAY WE are going to talk about impulsion and rhythm," Apryl said. "Any idea what I mean by those things?"

Natey, astride Diablo, had no idea. Nor did I. Impulsion? Rhythm? It might as well have been a lesson in drumming, which thankfully he had no interest in.

"You know how I tell you sometimes to give him a kick when he's not going fast enough?"

Natey nodded.

"That's one way to get impulsion, but it's not the only way. This is sort of advanced, but I want to start talking about it because it's one of the most important things in riding. A horse needs to be going at a speed and in a rhythm where he can get the job done. It's not too fast and it's not too slow."

"It's just right, like the three bears," said Natey.

Apryl smiled. "Right. If the horse is too slow and you want him to go over big jumps, he probably won't make it. And if he's going too fast, you can't steer him very well and he could knock the jump down, because he doesn't have time to balance himself before taking off, right?"

Natey was nodding, listening intently to the young woman who seemed in good form today. Whatever Tobias thought was happening in her off hours was not in evidence.

"Do you ever play kickball?" she asked.

"I like kickball, but I'm not good," Natey said. Diablo flicked his tail and stomped.

"Well you know how when you run to kick a ball you can kick it farther? It's kind of like that. You can kick a ball from a standstill, but it won't go as far, and you can run at the ball to kick it, but you need to slow down when you get close so you have enough time to bring your leg back to kick it. If you don't collect yourself, you're probably going to run past the ball."

There was a life lesson here, but I'd have to mull it over before I figured out just what it was.

"So," Apryl went on. "That's what we're aiming for. Take Diablo out on the rail, and, before we jump, we're going to work on getting Diablo to change his speed in the trot and canter so you can feel what too slow and too fast are, so you get to 'just right.' Now show me. Pick up a left rein trot."

"You're a good teacher," I said, moving behind her at the rail of the arena.

"I love kids. so it's easy, so blissfully free of complications."

I wanted to ask about those complications, but it wasn't the right time to quiz her. Besides, all I had on her were a few comments from Tobias, who seemed to have it in for her. She was occasionally moody, but had I been any less so in my twenties? Even thirties? On the other hand, I had the opportunity and an idea about how I could get closer to her.

"I hope everything else is going all right. I've sort of noticed a change in you at the house."

Apryl was watching Natey. "Come on, make him go forward. He's just testing you to see if you're going to make him. So make him."

Natey kept trying. Without taking her eyes off him, she said, "What do you mean?"

"Just that you have this life with horses, and then there's this other, glamorous Apryl."

"What?" She seemed shocked at the idea, her focus

shifting between Natey and me. "Who told you that? I have another job in the evenings, sometimes. Is that it?"

I couldn't remember her saying anything about having another job. "Is that something new?"

"No one ever asked," she said before shouting out,

"Better, good. Now keep the same trot and reverse across the diagonal."

Natey did as he was told and seemed in total control of his pony.

"So what is it?" I asked. "The job. Not that it's any of my business."

"It's fine. I'm a hostess at a club a few nights a week."

Well that explains it, then; Tobias seeing her in fancy clothes and shoes. She had a good reason for being all dolled up. Though it did seem a little odd that Tobias noticed her leaving only after I'd gone to bed. One would think a hostessing job would start earlier. But no matter, it meant the girl had clothes.

"There you go then," I said as casually as I could before changing subjects. "I wanted to ask if you could help me figure out to wear on this date I have. Maybe even borrow something?"

A suggestive smile appeared on her face. "A date? Good for you. I was wondering about that, when you'd start dating."

"It's not dating really," I said. "It's just one. Date."

Her smile disappeared as she called out to Natey: "Make a circle around the water jump. And when you're ready, ask him for a canter."

"I haven't been on a date in ten years so I need help from a younger person who's done it more recently."

"Dating probably hasn't changed much," she said, not taking her eyes off Natey. "How you *get* to the date has changed, but not the date itself. But sure, dressing you would be fun."

She took a few steps into the arena. "Right now, however, I need to get back to this lesson."

"Right," I said, realizing I'd been selfishly monopolizing my son's riding instructor.

"You look great, Natey," I called, a little too loudly perhaps, as he and Diablo went by, smoothly negotiating the canter. With nothing better to do and time to kill, I sat down, opened my bag, and pulled out *A Good Man is Hard to Find.* With book club mere days away, I'd better get cracking.

"I told you I had nothing to wear! All my clothes are old and out of fashion."

It was date night with Denny, and Apryl, saying very little, was rifling through my paltry selection of my date-worthy attire, laid out on the sleeper couch.

"Mama, no swearing," said Natey, appearing at the door.

"You're absolutely right," I said. "Bad Mama."

His gaze drifted to my clothes. "What are you doing?" He took a curious step.

"I'm going out tonight, and Apryl is helping me pick out what to wear."

"Boring," said Natey, summarily, before stomping off down the hall. "I'm going to find Flan."

Was he missing? No, I'd just seen him on the living room couch. But the ongoing dognappings were triggered alarm whenever we couldn't locate him immediately.

"Find Flan, but don't let him out," I called to Natey as he padded away down the hall.

I jotted down a note to call Rachel about our sting operation. After our lunch in Riverside, she'd volunteered to get Rita hooked up with Jelicka and Ellen, but I needed to find out what the status was. It felt kind of stupid not making conversation with Apryl about the operation but Jelicka had been adamant about keeping the information to a very tight group.

"Well, I'm happy to loan you something of mine to wear," said Apryl, giving up on my wardrobe options.

I did a once-over of her slim frame. "Will anything fit me?"

She gave my less-than-slim frame a once-over in return. "The tops will for sure; bottoms, maybe."

"I don't want it to seem like I'm trying to be twenty," I said. "You know? I'm a decent-looking forty and that's what I want to maximize."

"Mmm-hmm . . ."

"I also don't want anything fancy. What I really want is something nice but casual that makes me look like I'm not trying at all."

"So ideally like a haggard, single mom running a start-up?"

I got her point. "A little better than that. But that's the general idea. Like I changed into a clean shirt and put on mascara."

"Then just wear something like this," Apryl said, pulling out my denim shirt circa 1990.

"Won't that make me seem stuck in the past?"

"Huh, I thought it was new," she said, putting the shirt back on the bed. "I saw something like it at Madewell last week."

"It's one thing when clothes are designed to look old," I said. "It's something else entirely when everything in your closet is just old."

"Didn't you go on dates with your husband?" she asked. "I just find your wardrobe to be . . ."

"Uninspired?" I suggested. "Completely. We haven't had money for years. So not only did we not have date night, we had no need for clothes to wear on date night."

She shook her head, clearly amazed that I'd put up with this sorry state of affairs. "I'll be right back," she said, heading out of the room. "It's really not as hard as you're making it."

"Well, it's not easy, either," I called after her. Maybe I should cancel the date. I'd already invested too much mental energy. I had an empire to build and dognappers to catch. I liked Denny, but this was feeling forced and planned.

Apryl reappeared carrying some blouses and a couple of pullovers. She held up a peach colored stretchy number with three-quarter sleeves.

"I like the color, but I know it'll make my boobs look huge."

"What's wrong with that?"

"Too suggestive," I said. "If my boobs are the first thing he notices, he'll think that's the reason I chose the shirt. Dress tarty, and guys think you're asking for it. I'm not saying they *should*, but that's what I believe."

"You're not exactly flat-chested," said Apryl. "He's going to notice your boobs no matter what you wear."

"Maybe so, but I just want to be pretty and non-threatening."

She held up a dark blue top next. It had white buttons, pockets over both breasts, and it was longer in front than back. "My mom gave me this one. I don't think I've ever worn it." I took the shirt from her and examined it. The fabric was nice, and there was a lot of it, possibly too much.

"It's a possibility," I said, handing it back.

"How about this one? If you like it, you can have it." She held up a blouse of white eyelet, which might have been on the cusp of being too young for me. It had a collar and simple buttons, with sleeves that ended at the elbow. I liked that, other than the eyelet fabric and styling, it was a simple button down. I also took note of its sexy, virginal qualities. And the fact that the bottom of the blouse would cover the top of my mom jeans and tiny muffin-top made it extra appealing.

"The Forty-Year-Old Virgin?"

"Why not?" said Apryl, handing me the shirt. "Go pop your cherry, baby."

I held the shirt against my chest and considered the possibilities.

"Like riding a bicycle, right?"

"Am I that obvious? Ugh, I'm just trying not to be nervous."

"You like the guy, right? I mean, you must if you're going out with him."

I put the chosen blouse down gently. "I do like him. He's a handsome, single dad, whom I met through someone I trust, and he ticks all the right boxes. But his wife died, and when a marriage ends like that there can be a halo around the dead spouse no mortal can live up to. I just feel like I should get back out there, you know?"

"No matter what age you are, there's always something to worry about."

"You got that right," I said.

"So where I was going with that question was: Sleep with him if you want. My mom died in a car accident when she was forty-two. You have to grab your fun, you know?"

I found myself nodding at this piece of advice from my twenty-seven-year-old tenant, realizing she was the only person, other than Denny, who knew I was going on a date. Why hadn't I told any of the muffs—not even Lauren, who'd introduced Denny and me? If asked, my excuse would be thinking I'd already told them. But the real reason was fear of failing. I reasoned, probably selfishly and even speciously, that it would be better to tell them I was seeing someone if we made it to date number two.

"Just make sure you use a condom!" She said, waggling her finger.

"Yes, Mom."

"And like you told me, 'Don't let anyone disrespect you,

and don't do anything you don't want to do.'"

"Did I tell you that?" I said.

She smiled. "Yes you did. I'll watch Natey until nine Monday morning. If you aren't home by then, I'm calling the cops."

"Glad to know you care," I said, picking up the blouse again.

She gave me a sly grin, then was off down the hallway. "Have fun!"

Apryl was a blend of intelligence, generosity, and warmth. But there was something else I couldn't quite name. For Tobias, it was that she was a party girl with a dark secret.

A secret, maybe; we all have secrets, but a *dark* secret? I didn't think so, though I had to admit that now that Apryl had become a big part of my life, it might be harder for me to believe anything negative about her.

CHAPTER 37

THE RESTAURANT was virtually empty, and I spotted Denny sitting alone against a bank of windows overlooking the Santa Monica pier. He'd chosen The Lobster for our date, the iconic, hipsterized, and pricey seafood joint that dates from the early 1920s. I'd been there only once before, back when I was making money and had an expense account.

"You look pretty," Denny said, standing to greet me.

"Thank you, so do you." *Idiot.* "I mean you look good, too."

He was smiling, and I saw his gorgeous dimples. *How had I missed those before?*

Actually, he didn't just look good, he looked really good—better than I remembered—and I felt that bolt of whatever it was shoot through me. Desire? Wanton lust? I'd felt it so sporadically in the past few years, I couldn't be sure.

"I'm sorry that I—well, not *sorry* really. I don't know what the word is," I said. "I just feel awkward."

"Me too." He reached down to pull out my chair and I could smell his clean, masculine scent.

"Really," he said. "I haven't dated anyone in twelve years."

"Well it's only been ten for me," I said. "It only feels like twenty."

We sat down opposite each other, nodding our heads at our shared discomfort wondering—at least I was—what the other was thinking. For me, I was curious if he wanted to be naked with me as much as I wanted to be naked with him. I picked up the menu, glad for somewhere else to focus my attention.

What I knew at the time was that I wanted him more than I wanted a glass of wine and a sumptuous meal. But I was determined not to appear that I was. I focused harder on the menu, trying to remember how to read.

This is ridiculous. How could I be so attracted to this guy? Had he gone through a makeover since Lauren's barbecue? Why had it taken so long to get together?

"What would you like to drink?" he asked. "I was a little nervous, so I got started without you. Hope you don't think I've got a problem."

On the table was a glass of wine, his hands resting next to it. What nice hands he had."Sarah?" He'd startled me.

"Oh, sorry. Yeah, no, I didn't. Think that. I was just . . ."

We were staring at each other again.

"Thinking about your drink?" he said. "This is the house white. It's pretty good."

"Actually . . ." I said, letting it hang there. *What was the matter with me?*

Needing a little fortification, I picked up his wine glass, still half full, and guzzled it down in its entirety, placing it down in front of me before meeting his gaze again.

"At the risk of having you think less of me, how hungry are you?"

"How hungry?"

"Yeah. Because neither of us has a lot of time."

"For . . .?"

I could see in his eyes that he didn't dare dream I was saying what I was saying.

"I'm not doing this well," I said.

"Wait, are you saying we should . . .?" The color of his eyes deepened, and I knew he knew exactly what I meant.

"Yes, that's exactly what I'm saying."

"Really? You're—No. That's—"

He shook his head and I nodded mine.

He glanced over his shoulder and caught the waiter's eye before turning back to me. "I just—I didn't expect this."

"Neither did I."

"No matter what, I owe you a meal."

He pulled out cash for the tab and counted out several bills.

"I just promised you dinner, and I don't want you to think I'm reneging."

"Never, this was my idea."

"Believe me, I had the *idea*," he said taking my arm and assisting me to my feet. "I just didn't dare dream we'd have the same idea at the same time."

Then we were driving. His hand reached over and found mine and I felt his warmth course through me. "Where can we go?"

"My sister's with the kids at my place."

"And my tenant is babysitting Natey at mine."

I looked over at him, his brows furrowed, as he negotiated the turn onto Ocean Avenue.

"I thought situations like this were supposed to get easier when we got older."

"Yeah," I said. "What a bunch of crap our parents told us."

He smiled. "Was this a bad idea? Should we go back to the restaurant and imagine what might have been?"

I didn't feel the car slow but suddenly there we were, lips locked in the loading zone in front of the Santa Monica Women's Club, groping each other like twenty-year-olds. I would have said teenagers, but the groping was fractionally more experienced. Oh, how I'd been depriving myself!

"This is fantastic," I managed to say between kisses.

"You're fantastic," Denny murmured before clamping his

lips down on mine once more.

"Wow," I said, pushing him away, perhaps half an hour later. It was so good I may have even come. "I did not expect this."

"And I *really* did not expect this. It's been months since we met, and I'd almost given up on ever getting together." The eagerness hadn't left his face. It was almost feral.

"I'm sorry," I said. "I wasn't *trying* to be difficult."

"I know. Our lives are insane. But do you know—? I thought it might be like this. You and me. If we had the time, I'd call the Ritz Carlton or The Bacara up in Santa Barbara, or anywhere else you wanted to go, and book us into a suite for a week starting as soon as we could get there. Room service, massages, cocktails on the beach . . ."

"That is the most romantic, generous thing a man has said to me in over nine years."

He smiled and leaned in to kiss me again. "It's not like I wouldn't be getting something out of it."

My hand was pressed to his chest, refusing to decamp. Why was I behaving reasonably all of a sudden? I didn't want to be reasonable.

"As tough as this is going to be for me," I began.

"And me, I can tell."

"Both of us. As tough as it's going to be, I think we should go back to The Lobster and eat something."

He smiled, touching my cheek. "You're right. Given neither of our places is available and the only option is a quickie motel, I think we should wait. This doesn't feel like a one and done."

"Not that either of us has experience with such a thing."

"Of course not," he said.

I squeezed his hand. "Let's go back to The Lobster and be the couple people point at, the ones who make them say, 'Get a room.'"

CHAPTER 38

"SO—I HEARD you were out with Denny last night." It was Lauren calling, catching me loading bags of raw sugar on my Monday morning shopping run.

"Did he tell you?" I couldn't think who else, though we'd agreed neither of us would say anything. There hadn't been anyone we knew at the restaurant, not that we were paying attention.

"A little birdie told me," said Lauren.

"'A little birdie.'"

"I'll get the salt," Deandra said, wandering off to collect more ingredients.

"George saw you coming out of The Lobster. He said you were arm-in-arm, looking very cozy."

I wondered if George had seen us leaving the first or second time, because the visuals would have been very different. The second time, we were no less interested in each other, just a lot less handsy. As we dipped and sucked on our lobster as we might have done to each other, we decided to hold off on "the deed." We would instead savor the anticipation, a side-effect of which was the frequent jolts of desire coursing through me since we'd parted company, including the ones I'd been enjoying this morning, while shopping at Bakers' Supply.

Lauren cleared her throat. "So? Nothing to offer?"

Clearly it was difficult to concentrate. My phone vibrated with an incoming text. I ignored it.

"We had a really good time," I said.

"A good time? Could you be a little more vague?"

"I don't want to get ahead of ourselves. What if it doesn't work out?" In truth, I couldn't wait to see him again.

"Well, what happened?" she said, sounding slightly annoyed.

The phone vibrated again. And again, I ignored it.

"Nothing. We like each other. And maybe let's not tell the muffs about it until, and *if*, it becomes more?"

"Such a secret-keeper, Sarah. You're probably not going to say anything about it at book club, either. Why does it matter if people know?"

"What does Buddha say?" *Did I have that right?* "I think it's Buddha. Something about giving away energy."

"I have no idea what Buddha says," Lauren sighed. "I don't do yoga or any of that stuff—meditation—the things people do to commune with Buddha."

"If Madelyn was on the call, she'd know," I said. "I'm just more private than the rest of you."

The phone vibrated with another text. Someone was not taking my lack of response for an answer. I found a quiet aisle, put Lauren on speaker, and pulled the phone from my ear to find out if it was important.

"Okay, fine," Lauren was saying. "Anyway, that's not why I called. Jelicka left me a message saying she and the woman with the albino Pug are getting antsy to find a dog for the sting operation. She wanted to know if I should buy one for the cause, because apparently you're taking too long."

"No-no, I have news on that!" I said, reading the texts, just in from Rachel, who'd finally responded."I could tell them," Lauren continued, "that you've been too busy starting a love affair. That would give you a legitimate excuse."

"Ha-ha. Rachel says, well, long story short—" Now was not the time to tell her about Rita, the Chinese Crested nor the Magic Men of Riverside. It would take too long and people would likely gather to listen, causing a fire hazard in the flour aisle—"we have a dog!"

"Where'd you find him, or her? LSS version please," said Lauren.

"LSS—it's a them: Three Bichon Frises or Frise. When Rachel and I were searching shelters, we met a woman named Rita who has a dying friend with three dogs she was trying to find homes for. So Rita talked to the friend, told her about our plan, and the friend said 'yes.' Her dying wish is to put the dog thieves in jail. At least, that's what Rita told Rachel."

"So that's it?" Lauren said. "We're ready to go?"

"Pretty much. We just have to wait until the friend dies, then we can get the dogs here—but it sounds like that's imminent."

"Jelicka's not arranging to kill the dying woman, is she? I wouldn't put it past her."

"Of course not. She could die at any moment, apparently. Then Rita says she'll drive the dogs to LA."

What Rachel actually texted was that Rita wouldn't just drive the three Bichon Frises to us from Palm Springs, she wanted to play a principal part in Operation Nab the Nappers and was prepared to rent a suite at a hotel for the duration. Rachel said finding out about ONAN had kindled in Rita a commitment to save animals from horrible people everywhere. At Rachel's instigation, she donated two thousand dollars to a covert operation to stop Rhino poachers in Africa, another two thousand to save endangered sea birds, and a third two thousand to a group risking life and limb to release dolphins from tuna nets. All this made me wonder just how much money Rita's husband had left her.

"Aren't Bichon Frises the little white dogs that look like stuffed animals?" Lauren asked.

"Exactly—like giant cotton puffs. They're also on the most stolen dogs list. But wait—I think there might be a catch. Hold on—" I pulled the phone away again to make sure I'd read Rachel's text correctly. "Yes, Rachel says after the sting is over, one of us keeps the dogs or we find forever homes for them."

"I'll take them," said Lauren after the tiniest of pauses. "Not only are those dogs adorable, they're hypoallergenic."

"Perfect. I'll tell Rachel to tell Rita and Jelicka we're on."

She let out a little groan. "I wish there was another way to get these bastards."

"We all feel that way. We just have to take precautions and hope we can nab the nappers before they nab the cotton puffs."

"So, just confirming, once the dogs are here, we're ready to launch."

"I think so," I said. "And remember—we're all sworn to secrecy. Jelicka has some realtor algorithm and said she's figuring out the neighborhood where the dogs should be placed. Then Ellen Pirosh is supposed to go around, signing up families. Jelicka said she'll explain at book club."

"I doubt we'll be talking much about the book at book club," said Lauren.

"No," I agreed. "Fortunately *A Good Man is Hard to Find* is very short."

CHAPTER 39

"DID EVERYONE read it?" Paige scrutinized each of us for the answer, as we piled our plates high with the comfort food she was famous for. Most of us had plates heaped with her amazing vegetarian Shepherd's Pie, the four-cheese mac and cheese with crusty crouton topping we always craved when Paige was hostess, and green salad with green goddess dressing.

"I read it." "I did." "Yes." Everyone appeared to have complied with Paige's edict.

"Awesome. Fan-*tas*tic," she said, adjusting the volume on her Sonos as we sat down at her long table to eat. "Irony aside, do you realize this will be the first time that all the members of *The Muffia* book club read the book and can speak intelligently about it?"

"That *is* a shocker," said Madelyn. "Almost as shocking as the story itself."

Vicki smirked. "Reading it doesn't mean we can speak *intelligently* about it."

"There sure were a bunch of dummies *in* the story," said Lauren.

"Right? I thought it was going to be a story about dating." Kiki was incredulous. "But mass murder?"

"Total rip-off, if you ask me," said Jelicka. "Flannery O'Connor should have called it: 'Beware the Misfits.'"

"It's an elliptical title," Paige corrected. "You know she never married."

"With men like the ones in the story, no wonder," said Rachel.

A Good Man is Hard to Find probably only served to intensify Rachel's wariness of men.

"She kept warning her idiot son about the Misfit being 'a-loose' in Florida," said Lauren. "No one listened."

"She should have just said 'escaped convict,'" said Madelyn. "Who says 'a-loose'?"

"I appreciated how the old lady was all dressed up just in case there was an accident. She'd be dead, but she'd look like a lady."

Madelyn threw Quinn a wry smile. "Fashion plate. Too bad for granny her 'accident' happened down an old dirt road with nobody there to appreciate her outfit."

"The story was so racist," said Vicki. "Seriously—pickaninnies? Sorry you had to read that, Kiki."

"About the only positive thing I can say is the writer sure did capture a bunch of ignorant Georgia white folks! If she'd written them all post-racial awareness—not that we're there yet—it would have been dishonest. Felt sorry for the kids, though," Kiki added. "They didn't deserve to die."

"Why did we read this book again?" Lauren said.

"Because it was short and, quote-unquote, 'well-written,'" said Rachel. "Gotta separate the art from the artist."

I wasn't sure if she was serious, but given her own art, I suppose this was accurate. She didn't dismember men. She just painted them that way.

"I'm sorry, Kiki," Paige said. "I broke my own rule. It's supposed to be a classic, so I did what you're not supposed to do—I assumed it was good before reading it."

"We'll forgive you because the food is so damned good," said Jelicka, pushing her empty plate away. "But now, if we've all had enough of bad men and insensitive white people, let's get to the important business at hand."

With some of my newest baking experiments laid out for dessert, we started in on the roundy-round: Kiki's son, Troy, won a photography prize; Paige's daughter, Carlotta, just got a spot in a magnet school, which was great even though it meant a disruptive transfer; I gave my update, which was that Natey's "Ls" were perfect, I hadn't heard from Nate and Superior Baking Company was getting a warehouse! Tobias had secured us a low-interest loan based on our Farmer's Market success, John Fritz' involvement and a women-owned business grant. I paused and glanced at Lauren. Then, told the muffs I'd gone on a promising date with her friend, Denny, but I didn't want to jinx it by saying more; Quinn was still in love, and Madelyn was mediating an estate case between squabbling adult children over a painting of a giant turtle. The roundy was cooking along with everyone oohing and ahhing about various exploits. That is, until it was Jelicka's turn. She skipped her roundy and launched directly into Operation Nab the Nappers.

"All right, ladies," she said. "We are in agreement that too many dogs have been taken from their families. The police say they can't do anything, so it's time for us to nab the nappers."

It wasn't really up to us, but it was futile to argue. She was on a mission.

"To that end—" she said, whipping out her laptop and facing the screen toward us. "I got the IT guys at work to repurpose the algorithm we use in real estate to project home sales, and made one for dogs."

"To show where they might be stolen based on where they already have been?" asked Paige.

"Exactly," said Jelicka, working the computer keyboard. "And I remind you, this is not to be discussed with anyone, or in earshot of anyone."

"Seems pretty hard to predict," I said. "What about when dogs have been snatched right off their leashes? That's happened in a lot of different places."

"True," said Jelicka. "But we didn't include those random events in the algorithm."

The screen filled with a map of Los Angeles from the coast to downtown and Orange County out to the San Fernando Valley.

"One of the perks of being a realtor is having fun with the IT guys, and I do mean fun."

She winked, hit a couple of keys, and flashing green dots filled the screen.

"The green dots represent dogs taken last month. You can see they're scattered mostly on the eastern edge of the Westside." Her fingers moved again, and the green dots vanished, replaced with pink dots. "The pink dots show the dogs stolen the month before. And see how they're mostly on the northwest edge of the Westside."

"That's me, I think," said Lauren, pointing to one pink dot.

"Could be," Jelicka said.

"Clustered where the money is," Rachel said.

"Surprise, surprise: Rich people usually have fancier, more desireable dogs. No offense, Lauren." Jelicka pulled the laptop back toward her and changed the page view. "I'll cut to the chase."

Suddenly on screen, the pink and green dots were accompanied by more dots—these of blue, orange, and black.

"This screen shows all the dogs that have been nabbed since May, a month and a half before Ellen Pirosh's dog was stolen in Sarah's neighborhood."

"Wait, I have a dumb question," said Kiki.

"There are no dumb questions," said Jelicka.

"If dognappers 'nab' dogs, why isn't it dognabber instead of napper?"

A second or two went by.

"You know what, Keek," said Jelicka, "that's a really *good* question, but not critical to plot right now. Maybe do some investigating and let us know. So, back to ONAN. The same month Ellen's albino Pug was stolen and Flan almost got stolen, the thieves got a Rottweiler and a Saluki here and here, a few blocks away in opposite directions." She indicated two red dots.

"What's a Saluki?" asked Quinn.

"Ancient Egyptian. Like a hairy Borzoi."

"A hairy what?"

Lauren turned to Quinn. "Just think exotic, expensive, overbred, and prone to health problems. Go on," she said to Jelicka, who gestured to the screen again, zooming in then out. "Notice anything?"

I looked closer at the screen. "My house seems to be the epicenter of the thefts."

"Exactly," said Jelicka. "That's absolutely one of the things I noticed. But Rachel also noticed there's a cyclical thing happening. The thieves hit an area, then move on, but these dots show that they come back to an area and hit it again. It's like they know when to move on and when it's safe to come back. Your neighborhood is cycling back now, Sarah. Four days ago, an English Bull Terrier was snatched off a sun porch right here." She pointed at the screen, at a dot on a street about five blocks from me.

"So let's cut to the chase," said Paige. "I'm guessing you propose to put the Bichon Frises with a family in Sarah's neighborhood, right? Who's the family?"

Jelicka closed the laptop. "Me," she said. "I'm the family."

"But you don't even live in the neighborhood," said Paige.

"Ah, but that is where you would be wrong," said Jelicka. "As a realtor, I really live all over the city, and I have access to housing information that ordinary people do not. Like when a house is empty because its previous occupants are getting a divorce and they're about to list it, so you buy it before it hits the market."

"Are you saying we're going to be neighbors?" I said.

"You and your drama," said Rachel, rolling her eyes. "Tell them the truth." "All right, fine," said Jelicka. "Rita, the woman who found us the dogs, thanks to Rachel and Sarah, just purchased a fully furnished home in Santa Monica, dab smack in the strike zone."

CHAPTER 40

THE KEY was to make it all look normal in case the thieves were watching, which is what we were hoping. Rita and Jelicka were just two ordinary people moving into an ordinary house. Granted, they did have three extraordinary dogs—four, if you count Daphne, Rita's Chinese Crested—but the dogs should be the most unusual thing about them. Nothing else should draw unwanted attention or cause the thieves to think they were being set up.

The two women would play mother and daughter, and they did bear more than a passing resemblance. Both were tall, thin, blonde, and coiffed. Both had had plastic surgery and wore a lot of mascara. If anyone asked, the story was that Jelicka, a recent divorcee and owner of three Bichon Frises, purchased the house and moved her widowed mother in with her. Only the muffs knew the house really belonged to Rita.

Once again, I wondered what kind of business Rita's husband had been in that allowed her to drop three million on a house for a sting operation that she probably wouldn't want afterword. Then again, there'd been ample evidence that afternoon in Riverside that Rita needed to change her life. Perhaps meeting us had finally given her a sense of purpose.

Now that they were moved in, the plan, such as it was, was put in motion and a schedule established. Rita and Jelicka would walk the dogs in the morning and evenings, lingering as people do when meeting neighbors on the street. During the day, Jelicka and Rita would be out of the house, Jelicka to her real estate job and Rita to her new volunteer position with Save Animals Facing Extinction, the group trying to shut down the rhino poachers.

At precisely noon, three days a week, Rachel would arrive at the house to take the dogs for a walk. She made an obvious display of letting herself in via an unlocked side gate and pulling the dogs out of an air-cooled dog run, which had been installed in the back yard. Anyone watching would see that the dogs were left unattended for most of the morning and might choose that window to attempt a theft.

What anyone watching would not have known, was that Jelicka had, all by herself—a technical wizard, that Jelicka—installed cameras that were aimed at the dog run and hooked into the house's WiFi network. So now she or Rita—not a technical wizard, that Rita—or anyone else with the WiFi passcode could see, in real time, exactly what the cameras saw. The system also sent an alarm whenever something larger than a Labrador Retriever crossed a lens. That meant that as long as one of us in the sting's inner circle was within three minutes of getting to the house to foil any would-be napper, we could leave the dogs alone. And just in case we couldn't get there fast enough or the thieves looked too dangerous, Jelicka had another idea. She planned, under cover of darkness, to install a lock on the gate that also hooked into WiFi, which we could engage or disengage directly from our phones. We wouldn't use it to lock would-be thieves out, but we might need to use it to lock them in.

Other than the muffs, we weren't supposed to talk to anyone about the sting, and if we were talking about it on the phone, we had to make sure no one was listening. I hadn't even told Apryl or Tobias. All they knew about the dognappers was that someone tried to steal Flan, so they needed to keep an eye on him and never leave the house without locking him inside. I could talk to Denny about the plan, because he'd been there the night Lauren's dogs were stolen and we knew he had nothing to do with it.

Since our date, talking on the phone, with a little panting thrown in, was about as much as we'd been able to do. We hadn't found a time to go out again. Between trying to find a warehouse, baking cookies, coming up with new recipes for Superior Baking, Natey and Operation Nab the Nappers, too much was going on. But he had come over to walk Flan with me a couple of times. And we always walked by Rita's new house.

The only other two people who knew what we were up to was Officer Lauren Eschrich of the Brentwood Division and Frank, Quinn's ex-Seal Team boyfriend, who presumably knew how to keep a secret. Frank wasn't a fan of ONAN, and thought we should leave the whole thing alone, but Quinn convinced him that "leaving it alone" was never an option for *The Muffia*, especially not Jelicka. He should have learned that from the last time we took matters into our own hands and shut down Kiki's next-door neighbor's porn operation. Officer Eschrich told us she couldn't go on record as supporting our plan but would stay alert for updates.

CHAPTER 41

DAYS WENT by. On the seventh day after Jelicka, Rita, and the Bichon Frises took up residency in the new house, no day of rest would be had. I had just let Deandra in and the two of us were starting in on a day of cookie-making when my phone buzzed. I'd learned to recognize the various types of low-grade vibratory stimuli that came with my notifications—two pulses for email, a longer buzz for text, three short pulses for an Amber Alert. This, however, was a new vibration.

I took the phone from my pocket and assessed the screen, which read, "C4."

What the hell was that—was somebody hacking my phone?

Then I remembered. C4 was Control 4, the app we'd installed on our phones to monitor the cameras at Rita's house. I clicked the link and started for the door. "I'll be right back."

I headed down the sidewalk toward Rita's house, waiting for the images to appear, because whatever had triggered the cameras and sent the notification would soon be visible on my phone—or so the app claimed. While it might not be smart to go over there by myself, theoretically—again, according to what the app claimed—there was no reason to worry, because Jelicka, Rita, Denny, and Ellen Pirosh would have received the C4 notification, too. They'd be on their way to Rita's at that very moment to join me. So there was nothing to worry about—I stopped walking.

There, on the screen in front of the dog run in Rita's back yard, was a person in a hoody, his face shrouded from view, and I felt the same chilly frisson I'd felt all those months ago watching a hooded person luring Flan with a dog treat.

Cameras captured the person from four different angles as he moved around the dog run where the three Bichon Frises ran back and forth, excited to see him.

Wait—did they know the person? Was he a gardener? He did have a plant in his hand.

No, if he was the gardener, he'd have no reason to be wearing a hoody—especially on such a warm day. The reason he's wearing a hoody is so no one can tell who he is.

I watched as, onscreen, the person lifted his hand to open the latch on the dog run. Then suddenly, as if hearing something, he turned and looked straight into the lens of one of the cameras. I knew that face.

Picking up the pace, I headed toward Rita's, tucking my phone into my back pocket. Now that I knew who was attempting to steal the dogs, I wasn't afraid of being alone with her. And this time, the hoody was a her, no question. Pennies dropped, puzzle pieces aligned. The hushed phone calls. A double life. Mysterious vans. Odd behavior, Tobias had said. *Odd behavior, indeed.*

The question was, how had Apryl gotten herself hooked up with a group of dog thieves?

Rounding the corner onto Rita's block, I stopped short.

A van was parked at the curb across from Rita's house with "Norma's Floral" printed on the side above a multi-colored bouquet. Other than the logo, it was exactly like the van parked across from my house several weeks ago with the name of an HVAC company on it, and yet another van I'd noticed recently that read: "Painting by Carlos."

I remembered thinking how all these companies must get their vans at the same place and wondering where that place was because pretty soon, we'd need a van for the Superior Baking Company.

Now I wondered if was the same exact van, just repainted, and if the person sitting behind the wheel was Apryl's partner. He looked big, whoever he was. And where I might have been able to handle Apryl, this guy was another matter. He was not only large of body, he had a big, mean-looking head. If only I could see the license plate number. But there was a car parked in front of the van, blocking my view. I'd needed to get closer.

I ducked out of sight behind a wall and pulled my phone out again. I snapped a couple of pictures and withdrew. I should call someone, I thought—Denny? Jelicka? They were probably on their way; Ellen, too.

Officer Lauren Eschrich of the Brentwood Division answered on the second ring.

"This is Sarah Pizzo with *The Muffia*," I said.

"Yes, Mrs. Pizzo. How are you today?"

"It's 'Ms.' now, but fine, thank you. Listen—I know you're aware of this sting operation we were planning, and that you thought it was stupid and wouldn't work . . ."

"I don't know where you got that idea," she said, like I hadn't been there when we told her the plan.

"Doesn't matter," I continued. "There's a dognapper in the backyard of the home right now with a suspicious van parked across the street and I'm going to casually walk down the sidewalk and get you the license—"

"Ms. Pizzo, I don't advise approaching—"

"I'm not going to do anything stupid. I'm phoning it in, aren't I? But this is the closest we've been to catching these scumbags and we might not get this chance again."

"Ms. Pizzo, I'm going to send a car, so please stay out of sight."

"I will in a minute, but just in case they get in the van and take off, I'm going to casually walk by and get the license plate."

The officer continued her warnings as I slowly came out from behind the wall and headed down the block with the perfect blend of unhurried purposefulness, like a jogger who decides to stop and smell the roses.

The driver seemed to be looking at the dashboard, unconcerned, which seemed strange. Could he be a real delivery guy—delivering real floral arrangements?

By this point, if Apryl thought something was wrong, she would have called or signaled him somehow and he'd be reacting. So maybe she hadn't signaled. Maybe, as far as she was concerned, nothing had made her want to abort the mission.

It's true she'd swung her startled face to the camera, but I didn't know why. I'd assumed she'd heard the sound of Jelicka remotely triggering the lock on the gate, but for all I knew, Apryl was reacting to the AC going on.

I swiped back to the C4 screen and saw that Apryl was now in the dog run, readying a syringe!

I gasped. "Oh no! She's going to give them shots!"

"Shots fired?" said Officer Eschrich. "I'm on my way."

Shit. "No, Officer, what I said was, 'She's giving the dogs a shot.'"

"Do not engage," said Officer Eschrich, amidst a bunch of car sounds.

"I have no intention of engaging, I just want to give you the license plate number so you can track them down in case they get away."

"I repeat—seek safety and do not engage."

Then she was radioing something unintelligible in to dispatch: "045 possible 309 at 247 18th, SM. ETA 11:24. RBU."

"Easy for you to say."

Fifteen feet away now, and I still couldn't see the plate, though I had a very good view of the side of the van. "Yes, they've been changing the logos but it's the same van," I said.

More interior car noises and the rumble of driving came through the line. "What's that?"

"The dog thieves. I'm sure it's the same van. It said HVAC before, and now it says 'Norma's Floral,' but you can see it was painted over, and ugh—they did a terrible job on the flowers. Up close, they're just blobs of paint. Hey—are we being recorded? Because if I give you the license plate, I know you can't write and drive."

This was likely not a rule police officers worried about.

I was now close enough to peer around the car in front of the van and get a glimpse of the license plate. "Okay," I said, "the first three characters are 'TF5,' but I need to make another pass, so bear with me while I examine this lilac bush. Wow, these are beautiful, lilacs don't usually survive in SoCal . . ."

"Lilacs! Where are you at this moment, Ms. Pizzo?" said Officer Eschrich. "We are en route and need you to seek cover."

Ignoring her while committing the crime of lilac theft, I stood and smelled the delicious scent as I read off the last part of the license plate. "Now you can find out who the van is registered to and hopefully get a warrant and all that."

Just then, Jelicka's car came screeching around the corner onto the street.

Sensing something amiss, the driver at the wheel of Norma's Floral started his engine.

I waved my arms frantically to get Jelicka's attention and she quickly swerved her car next to the van, boxing him in.

Jelicka knew, like most anyone who's watched a police

procedural on TV knows, you don't mess with a crime scene. And even though this was still a crime scene in progress, that van could not leave.

"Ms. Pizzo, what is happening there?" Officer Eschrich demanded over the phone.

"The driver started his van, but Jelicka—Ms. Gelman—just parked her car next to it and now he can't get out."

"Do not engage," said the officer.

"Yeah, tell that to Jelicka," I said. "She likes to engage."

"No you don't; no, no; bad, bad, very bad; we'll show you, you bad, bad—"

My head swung around to find the source of the enraged muttering, and there was Ellen Pirosh, loaded for bear and barreling toward me with her hair wild and Eileen Fisher flapping. In her hand, she had something that looked like a gun.

"Ellen put that away," I said. "The police are coming, and they might shoot first and ask questions later!"

"Who is shooting, Ms. Pizzo?" the officer demanded.

"No one is shooting," I said again. "There are some justifiably angry people here, but they do not have weapons so when you get here do not shoot them!"

I watched Ellen tuck whatever it was out of sight into one of her voluminous Eileen Fisher pockets as she continued with her manic mantra. "Bad, bad, people; we'll show you how it feels, you very, very bad . . ."

Meanwhile, the guy behind the wheel of Norma's Floral couldn't get out through the driver's side with Jelicka's car next to him. So he started climbing over to the passenger side, which, given his heft, didn't look easy.

In the distance, I became aware of a siren.

"Uh oh," I said, as Ellen breezed by me.

"What's happening now?" said Officer Eschrich. "We're a few blocks away."

Jelicka was out of her car now and moving toward the house.

On my phone screen I saw Apryl—bags presumably filled with drugged Bichon Frises—at the gate, trying to open it. Jelicka *had* locked it. *Go Jelicka.* Apryl was trapped.

But she was also resourceful. She might drop the dogs and climb over the fence, especially now that the sirens were approaching.

"I hope that siren I hear coming is yours," I said into the phone. "Because things are getting very interesting here."

The van driver pushed the passenger door open and started getting out. He didn't see Ellen approach, pulling out the thing that looked like a gun again. She aimed it at the driver who, with a yelp, went down in a clump.

Oh shit, it *was* a gun.

I stuck my phone in my pocket and ran to Ellen, intending to take whatever it was away from her. "Ellen, no—what did you do?"

"Tazed him good," she said, facing me and holding up a small, black cylinder. "Wasn't sure if it would work. I ordered it from Amazon."

I let out a relieved sigh. "I thought you shot the guy," I said, looking at the guy on the ground, who was beginning move.

"I did shoot him, just with electric current. But don't worry, it's not police grade. They said it's designed to immobilize an attacker long enough to let you escape."

"Well, he's moving so you better immobilize him again," I said. "We don't want him going anywhere before the police get here."

"That's for Pearlie Girl, you scumbag," said Ellen, inflicting another shock.

Denny turned onto the block next and, seeing us standing over the crumpled driver, quickly got out of his car and started toward us.

"We're fine," I said, pointing to the house. "Help Jelicka keep her from escaping."

With the sirens very close now, Denny raced toward the house as a squad car whipped around the corner onto Rita's street.

"Hide that thing," I said quickly. "We might not legally be allowed to have it."

"Jelicka said we could, but still—" she dropped the taser back in her pocket. "Why draw attention to it? At least he won't get away."

Officer Eschrich got out and approached Ellen and me as a second squad car arrived from the other direction.

"No thanks to the police." I gazed across the street, where we could see Denny and Jelicka emerging from the shadows next to the house with Apryl between them. "Looks like they have that one well in hand, too. She's not going anywhere."

"Unless it's to prison," said Ellen, focusing on Apryl. "Hey—isn't that your tenant?"

I nodded my head, feeling stupid. "And all this time, she was right under my nose."

EPILOGUE

"YOU'RE SUPPOSED to be an animal lover," I said. "I just don't understand. And what am I supposed to tell Natey—that his riding teacher is a dog thief? That the young woman he shared a bathroom with stole his friends' dogs, almost stole his, and is going to jail?"

I glanced around the small holding chamber at the Santa Monica jail where I'd been led. Apryl sat in a chair on the other side of a table wearing her dark blue prison outfit, and she either couldn't or wouldn't meet my gaze.

"Yup, that's what I'll have to tell him, because I don't believe in lying to your kid."

"I'm sorry," she said, starting to tear up. "I didn't mean to hurt him. I didn't want to hurt anybody. I regretted it from the very first day, but it was already too late. They had me."

"Just curious," I said, "but did they have you before or after you moved into our house?"

"Before." She sniffled.

"So did you really need a place to live? Or were you just looking for a place where you could scope out rich peoples' dogs?"

"No, no—" she said, cutting herself off. Her hair was in a high ponytail and I watched her hands move over her head as she formulated what to say next. "Both, I guess. I really did just get a divorce, and I was broke. I owed ten thousand dollars on credit cards, and teaching riding wasn't going to get me out of debt."

Her logic wasn't complete. "All right, but once you were in my house, you were making enough money from riding to pay rent and start working on your debt, no? Just not enough to cover the fancy clothes and shoes."

She winced. "I didn't have anything to do with the attempt on Flan, in case you're wondering. That happened before I moved in, before I even met you."

"*Mmm* . . ."

"And after I moved in, he was off-limits. I made sure of it."

Well, that seemed believable.

"And they went along with it, because if he'd gone missing, suspicion might have fallen on you?" I asked. I wasn't sure I could trust anything she said.

"So you were really just using my house to target other dogs, like Ellen Pirosh's albino Pug. No wonder so many dogs went missing in a ten-block radius. You broke that poor woman's heart, you know."

Apryl picked at her thumb nail. "I'm sorry."

"You should have thought of that before. But I want to believe you regret it now, so I'm glad you're cooperating and ratting out the—"

"Don't say it like that."

"—the other gang members, or whatever you call yourselves. Maybe cooperating will reduce your sentence. And from what the cops told me, it could be a long one. Anyone who steals a dog worth more than $950 is guilty of felony theft and can go to jail for up to twelve months. Based on the number of pricey dogs you stole, you could go away for fifteen years."

She put her head in her hands and moaned. "These people aren't just into dognapping; there's a lot worse stuff. I'll have to move and change my name when I get out; that is, if I don't get killed first."

"I suppose you didn't know how bad they were when they asked you to join them?"

She shook her head. "They told me we'd take this one dog, and I'd net a quick thousand bucks. But they taped me doing it. After that, I was stuck. They threatened to show the tape."

"Will Lauren get her other Boston Terrier back?"

Apryl finally met my eye, and it was clear Molly was gone.

I saw another tear before she dissolved into sobs. "I didn't know!"

"Apryl, I want to believe you, but what you did is unforgiveable. Peoples' dogs are part of their families. And now they're gone, because you took them. There has to be accountability."

"I'm sorry," she sobbed again. "I didn't think it would get this bad."

Though I found this hard to believe, I didn't hate the girl. I was disappointed. I put my hands on top of hers. "It's hard to know, when you begin anything, how it will turn out. But it seems to me once you start living a lie, it's really hard to stop. So the key is not to start."

"Once Apryl and the driver were apprehended, they caved, and turned over the names and addresses of everyone involved," I said, as I led Jelicka, Rachel, Lauren, and Kiki through the warehouse and new home of Superior Baking Company. "It won't be as exciting as the 'El Chapo' trial, with the protected witnesses and jurors and everything, but apparently there's enough evidence to put the whole lot of them away for years."

"Good job," Lauren said.

"I still don't think Apryl's sentence should be reduced,"

said Rachel. "She was complicit. We have to stop letting people off the hook with loopholes."

"I hear you," said Jelicka. "But she was a little fish. Without the big fish, the crime continues, so I'll cut her some slack to get the whales."

"Yeah, she's smart. She won't go down that road again," I said.

Rachel exhaled hard. "If it was humans getting kidnapped, you know they'd put these creeps away for a lot longer than fifteen years. But because it's dogs, they don't count. I just think that it's a messed-up system that does that."

Kiki nodded. "I'm still amazed she was living in your house, Sarah, and able to get away with it for so long."

"I'm not proud of that," I said. "Believe me, there were signs. I think I wanted her to be a model tenant. I needed her rent money. Then she sort of became part of the family. Natey loved her, Flan loved her. Then the riding lessons and all that. In my defense, all her references checked out."

"It wasn't your fault, Sarah," said Lauren. "She could have done what she did living anywhere. And like the authorities said, there were other scouts. It could have been somebody else who staked out Molly and Mack."

I had to believe that Apryl found out about the Boston Terriers from me, but it was nice of Lauren to let me off the hook.

I pulled open the door of the main room of the warehouse, where Deandra and Kate, formerly of Huckleberry—or Huck 'n' fuck, as Tobias insisted on calling it—were busy baking. "This is it."

"Good for you, Sarah," said Jelicka. "We're proud of you."

Even Rachel dropped her grim and grisly routine and said, "What an incredible space. I want to paint in here."

"Thanks you guys. A warehouse and now, with Apryl gone and Tobias back in his condo, I have my house back. It feels like a new beginning."

"We love our three new Bichon Frises," Lauren said. "Mack just tolerates them but he's coming around."

"What did you name them?" asked Rachel. "I'm sure Rita will want to know."

"We haven't settled on names yet," Lauren said. "But we want to name one of the females Muffy."

"Cute," said Kiki.

"*Nooooo*," said Jelicka. "If one of us is going to have a dog named Muff, she has to be a big dog, a dog with a sense of purpose."

"Oh, yeah," I said. "Maybe a dog that can read *Girls & Sex*, and who will speak out for less fortunate dogs."

"You know what I mean. Not a toy dog."

"We could have multiple dogs named Muff," Rachel said. "Just like *The Muffia* has multiple muffs."

Somebody else had an opinion, and even Kate and Deandra had an opinion.

"Oh, and I have a suggestion," Deandra said. "Not about dog names. But you know those muffin-scone things you've been working on? How 'bout calling them 'muffians'?"

The muffs stopped to consider this.

"I like it," said Lauren.

"Me too," Jelicka said, trying it out. "I'll have a berry muffian, please."

"The topping possibilities are endless."

"*Great* name," said Kiki. "I'll order a dozen right now."

So that's what we went out that day, sampling baked goods and congratulating ourselves on another *Muffia* case solved. Stories were swapped, books debated, and I even told them about my upcoming second date with Denny, a weekend in Cayucos up the coast, which had been too long in coming.

And though it was out of character for me to say much more, this time I told them I was sure it would go very, very well.

The End

ACKNOWLEDGMENTS

I would never have completed one *Muffia* book, let alone three, without the members of my real life book club: Michelle Joyner, Lisa Mohan, Carolyn Calvert, Sonya Walger, Lysa Hayland Heslov, Denise Gruska, Susan Hoffman Hyman, Betsy Salkind, Clare Foster, Janine Eser and Jann Turner. These women continue to inspire and entertain and, though the truth of our stories rarely comports with the fictional, I owe them a huge thanks.

Many others contributed to the successful completion of this book. Flo Selfman offered invaluable support, guidance and wisdom, Elizabeth Nunes shared her significant analytical and editorial skills and Ben Scuglia provided pet wisdom like nobody's business. I also want to thank the following people who contributed financially to *The Muffia*'s success, thereby earning the privilege (or misfortune) of having characters named after them: Ellen Pirosh, Kevin (Tobias) Miserocchi and Lauren Eschrich.

And thank *you* for your purchase. Ten percent of all sales from *The Muffia* books are donated to charitable organizations benefitting girls and women in the United States. But given the subject matter of this particular book, we might need to isolate sales and send proceeds to dog rescue organizations.

Please follow *The Muffia* on our Facebook page, Facebook.com/annroyalnicholas and at www.themuffia.us.

INDEX

The members of *THE MUFFIA*:

Madelyn Scott-Crane MSC@MSCMediate.com

The narrator of *The Muffia* (Book I). An attractive, blonde, irreligious, *divorced mom* with a daughter (Lila). She's a lawyer turned mediator and lives in Agoura Hills, outside Los Angeles. She's the oldest of the muffs, yet probably in the best physical shape due to hours relieving angst (usually self-imposed) practicing yoga. She's had a few lovers since her divorce, most notably Udi, an Israeli heartthrob Mossad agent. Udi died of a coronary when he and Maddie were having sex but a couple of muffs think he's alive somewhere and his "death" part of an elaborate international plot.

Quinn Cunningham cunningquinn@Talentpool.com

The narrator of *More Muffia* (Book II). *Single, never married, no children.* Quinn is tall, with thick shoulder-length auburn hair that she often wears in an up-do. She has a job as a talent agent with a top agency placing celebrities in overseas commercials. After a relationship with a married man and a lot of bad dates with actors who only wanted her to get them roles on TV shows, she's finally in a good relationship with Frank (Seal Team Six Sexton) who saved her from getting fired.

Jelicka Gelman MissJelickaG@aol.com

Married, no children. Jelicka's too smart for her own good. An ex-screenwriter, she's also a horny, botoxed housewife with an incredible wardrobe who sort of looks like a double-blonded Angelina Jolie (those times when A.J. isn't traipsing around Vietnam or Africa)—same eyes and puffy lips. Her marriage to Roscoe fell apart in Book I forcing her to go back to work, this time to get her real estate license. She's a news hound, gossip and conspiracy theorist, always looking to right the things she sees as wrongs in the world.

Lauren Busch LBSweet@aol.com

Married, two children (Amanda and Gavin). Lauren's the richest, party-loving muff—that would be keg party— but perhaps the least sexually adventurous; or else she's just so happy married to George (of the Anheuser-Busch beer dynasty) she doesn't care. She's slightly overweight, in a healthy mid-western way, with green eyes and a great big toothy smile. She runs a charity for Alzheimer's research with her sister, and she, like Jelicka, also enjoys dishy gossip.

Sarah Pizzo sapizz11@connect.net

On her way to divorce, one child (Nate Jr.) A brown-haired, brown-eyed, Jewish-Catholic. Cute in an Audrey Hepburn/ Tatou way, only with more hair. She and her husband, Nate Sr., have had marital trouble since the beginning of Book I, because after Nate lost his job, he screwed around a lot and wanted to have an open marriage which Sarah wasn't thrilled about. She rarely reads the books but is such a good cook the muffs let it slide. Before she got married she was working her way up at Williams Sonoma but now she needs to make money and wants to start a baking business.

Rachel Baker rachelbakerart@mac.com

Single, never married, no children. Rachel has a wild pile of blonde wavy hair and a very funky, trendy way of dressing. She's Protestant by birth but practices Kabbalah—at the moment anyway. She's an artist whose passion is painting male nudes in acrylic, usually missing a body part or two. And she makes a good living at it. Has a chip on her shoulder about a lot of things that the rest of us are waiting for her to explain. She rarely dates but says she dates both sexes, though the muffs haven't met anybody she's been serious about.

Kiki Glazer (41) kookykiki@hotmail.com

Married, one child (Troy). Kiki's a gorgeous, Black ex-Catholic woman who's married to Saul, a White Jewish hedge fund manager who makes lots of money. She's an actress — or was—who's taking the long road to becoming a nurse practitioner. She has a great ass and a fantastic shoe collection envied by all and in Book II, the muffs helped her bust up the porn business that was operating out of her neighbor's house in Encino.

Paige Von Hoote (38) vonhooter@gmail.com

Married (Richard), *two children from previous marriage,* (Carlotta, 6, and Dashielle, 4). Paige teaches tennis and struggles with finances. She's a great entertainer who has an ongoing rivalry with Sarah when it comes to cooking. In the course of the series, she got married to Richard and says it's the best thing that could have happened to the relationship, except she wishes money weren't an issue. She's on the tall side, very fit with a brown bob that always looks chic and professionally blown out. She's one of the founders of the book club and is usually annoyed when other muffs don't read the assigned books.

Vicki Butler Mendoza (39) victoriamendoza@mac.com

Divorced, one grown son (Enrique). Vicki's a filmmaker, and sometime script supervisor, who's been working on a documentary about The Muffia. She used to shoot all our muff gatherings but now she says she's editing the footage and we're all a little concerned. She's also raising money for a larger film, now that her son is grown. After winning a bout with breast cancer, she's been in remission, and now keeps her hair short and spiky, sometimes dying it purple or pink. She considers herself an expert in Spanish culture, having lived there during her marriage. She usually reads the books.

The Muffia Book Club Reads:

THE MUFFIA
Lay of the Land by Richard Ford
Deliciously Disturbed and Distracted
(fictional erotic novel)
We Need to Talk About Kevin by Lionel Shriver

MORE MUFFIA
The Glass Castle by Jeannette Walls
When Will There Be Good News? By Kate Atkinson

MUFF STUFF
Where'd You Go Bernadette? by Maria Semple
Girls & Sex by Peggy Orenstein
A Good Man is Hard to Find by Flannery O'Connor.

Praise for Ann Royal Nicholas'
THE MUFFIA Series

"Who can resist a book about a book club where the members refer to themselves as "Muffs"? Meet Madeleine Scott-Crane, a savvy 42-year old single mom and mediator as she and her six friends take their monthly meetings to an unconventional—and often shocking level. Nicholas's romp through suburban Los Angeles is sexy, edgy and laugh-out loud funny. With a few of life's lessons thrown in along the way, *The Muffia* is smart, sassy and simply irresistible—just like her heroine. A must-read.

—Hannah Dennison of The Honeychurch Hall Mysteries & The Vicky Hill Mysteries

"I just loved this book. Such a great read. It really speaks to women of all ages but especially those in their 30's and beyond. What a great surprise from a new author!"

—Ely Pouget, actor & producer. CSI, The Mentalist, The 3Tails Movie: A Mermaid Adventure

"5 Stars. Nicholas deftly walks the tightrope of the sexual landscape unfolding around her—of the young, the older and the in between."

—David Glynn – Artist

"LOVED this book. It's good, not so clean, fun. And 50 Shades of Great Writing. An empowered woman who knows not only what she wants, but who she wants, and how many times a day... I recommend it highly."

—Becca Petersen, Amazon Verified Purchaser

"A great read, couldn't put it down. *The Muffia* should be required reading for every book club in America. It's fun, sexy and smart. Hope this is the beginning of a series. Loved it."

—*Susan Hito Shapiro, artist, filmmaker and attorney*

"I didn't know what to expect when I bought my wife this book on the basis of the *Godfather* style font on the cover. The blurb on the back sounded sort of fun--a story about a bunch of wacky women in a book club (my wife's in a book club). I started reading it on my flight home and I have to say it held my attention (I'm usually reading Malcolm Gladwell or the Wall Street Journal). *The Muffia* is well written and that vibrator shopping chapter cracked me up. Now I'm wondering what else my wife's book club gets up to beyond reading books."

—*Jeffrey Malibu, An Amazon Verified Purchaser*

"The Muffia Book Club babes may talk like sailors when they meet, but they are sensible, condom-packing ladies. Soon enough, you're reading about vibrators and female sex aids, as discussed by a group of "cliterati" (the author's term, not the reviewer's), as if it were a gardening club comparing the virtues of daisies and sunflowers. The literary proposal is that of a "whodunit?" and both in flavor and presentation, *The Muffia* is urbane, erudite, and ironic."

—*Stephen Siciliano of Sidewalk Smokers Club, Highway Scribery, Vine Voice*

"Best serious love/thriller/comfort read ever! Wish I could go back in time and be those women! Their lives are serious and dark and fun!"

—*Linda Mohan, Amazon Verified Purchaser*

"I live in LA, where *The Muffia* takes place, and these women are spot on. They're so realistically drawn, that I could swear I even know a few of them personally! Very enjoyable."

—*Amazon Kindle Verified Purchaser*

"Ann Royal Nicholas writes in a breezy style making this the perfect beach or airplane read when you don't want anything too demanding or heavy. *The Muffia* is the first in a series and I can't wait to read what the smart and wacky Muff women will get up to next. I also really liked that the author and her book club are giving 10% of sales to women's causes. That's cool!"

—*Amazon Kindle Verified Purchaser*

ABOUT THE AUTHOR

Ann Royal Nicholas is an author (*The Muffia, Homegrown: The Terror Within*, published under the pseudonym Cialan Haasnic), *Royal Mack's Teeny Tiny Wine Guide*; a journalist (*LA Times, Vine Times Magazine*), an essayist ("Of Wine and Men," printed in Penguin's *In My Mother's Kitchen*) an award-winning filmmaker (*Univers'l*), screenwriter (*Big Bang Theory*), playwright (*Villa Thrilla, Petting Zoo Story*) and actor. She's a graduate of the UCLA Writers Program, former Managing Director of the Ojai Playwrights Conference, a mediator and single mom.

Find out more at annroyalnicholas.com and annanicholas.com

CPSIA information can be obtained
at www.ICGtesting.com
Printed in the USA
FFHW022158220319
51170544-56644FF

9 780990 708032